Revenge of the Soccer Moms

a largely fictional novel

M. E. Levine

Copyright © Myra E. Levine, 2017

ISBN-13: 978-1542813907
ISBN-10: 1542813905

Library of Congress Control Number: 2017902358
CreateSpace Independent Publishing Platform, North Charleston, SC

THIS BOOK IS DEDICATED TO:

My father, Mike Steinberg, who taught me to appreciate the ridiculous.

My mother, Celia Steinberg, who taught me to be a mom.

My husband, David, who gives me the freedom to write.

Sami and Mikey, who fill me with pride and give me many stories I promise never to put into print.

The Setters Run Playgroup Moms, many of whom still speak to me.

Critique group members: Peter Welling, Lee Snare, Dale Thomas, Elaine Cassidy, and Michael Welling, and the students and instructors at the Iowa Summer Writing Festival, especially the great Sands Hall. *I didn't know how much I didn't know.*

Finally, to the agents and editors who rejected earlier drafts of this book. *You were right.*

ACKNOWLEDGEMENTS

Copy editing by Sara J. Steinberg (any typos you find are my fault, not hers.) ssteinbergediting@yahoo.com

Cover art and design by Peter Welling (friend, teacher, author, and my favorite illustrator) www.peterwelling.com

AUTHOR'S NOTE

This novel was begun when my youngest child began preschool, which gave me a few hours a week to write, take naps, and pee in private. The final draft was finished during his junior year in high school.

After decades writing video scripts, radio and television ads, I figured I'd be a natural to write a novel, especially about something I knew a lot about—living in the suburbs and hanging out with smart, funny stay-at-home moms. As it turned out, I had no clue how to write a novel. I learned most of what I know during nine summers at the Iowa Summer Writing Festival. I highly recommend it if you're serious about the craft.

If you enjoy this book, please do me the honor of telling your friends. But don't let them read *your* copy. We have a mortgage, a kid in college, another kid with expensive taste in shoes, and hungry pets.

Please find my book's Facebook page, share it, and say nice things if you enjoyed it. If you didn't enjoy it, please keep it to yourself. I'm also on Twitter and stuff like that, but I rarely remember to check that stuff. If I could have fun with 140 characters, I'd write short stories.

Much of this book was inspired by actual people and events which happened in my Westfield, Indiana neighborhood. Most of those people and events have been twisted and exaggerated, though a few remain closer to the truth. I'll never tell which ones, so don't ask. Anyway, thanks for reading my book. Writers need readers, and if you're reading my book, I truly love you.

Come over. I'll fix lunch.

www.myralevine.com

To Pam,
Who taught me
other arts!

Myra Levine

PROLOGUE

KARMA, THE FORMATIVE YEARS

Karma froze. She had been hugged, kissed, and patted like a dog by her Grandma Minnie, but never grabbed by the face like this. She held her breath against the choking combination of lilac face powder, peppermint candy, hair spray, and prehistoric dust. Her eyes began to water. Mom said that Dad was fibbing about Grandma Minnie smoking Cuban cigars, but now Karma wasn't so sure. Every inch of her chubby little body screamed to be released, to escape to the backyard where the other cousins were climbing trees and playing cowboys and Indians. *Why did I come in here? Why didn't I pee in the bushes like the boys?*

Grandma Minnie pulled her oldest granddaughter, her darling sweet Karmella, in closer. With her thick new eyeglasses, she could still see pretty good, knock on wood, and Karmella's fat little cheeks were so pink, so healthy, it was a blessing from G-d Himself. She kneaded them like bread dough with trembling fingers, and smiled as they grew even pinker.

"Kahrmellah, sweet child, now you remember vat I'm telling you. I vant you should marry a nice Jewish boy."

Karma let out a strangled squeak. A tiny bit of grandma spit had just hit her chin, and she *really* needed to get away. There was only one way to end this. So underage, overweight, and living in a small Indiana town with no Jewish boys except her own cousins, she said, "Okay, Grandma, I will."

1

It wasn't exactly a lie, it was more like promising to become an astronaut. Not impossible, but you wouldn't bet your allowance on it. Cheeks still smooshed in her grandmother's iron grip, Karma's eyes shifted to her mother, who was watching the whole thing from the kitchen, a damp dish towel in her hands. Charlotte gave her daughter a tiny nod of permission, and Karma twisted out of her grandmother's icy fingers and escaped out the back screen door.

KARMA, THE FRUSTRATING YEARS

Karma, twenty-two, was seated at the long formal dining table next to her Cousin Lisa's brand-new fiancé. As was the tradition, Passover Seder was being held at Grandma Minnie's house, though she could no longer cook the meal without assistance. Lisa's fiancé was lean, handsome, well-dressed, and Jewish, an ideal match for Lisa, with her perfect figure, glossy dark hair, and unerring sense of style. Karma, two years older than Lisa, was no closer to becoming the blushing bride of a Nice Jewish Boy than she was to planting the Israeli flag on the moon. During the customary break in the Passover ceremony, while the younger kids searched for the hidden matzo that would allow the Seder to be concluded, Grandma Minnie led Karma into the formal parlor of her musty old house and onto the yellowed plastic slip-covered sofa. To Karma's knowledge, no human bottom had touched the actual fabric on that sofa. Karma helped her grandmother down onto the plastic, and took a seat beside her. She had a feeling she knew what was coming.

"Kahrmellah," said Grandma Minnie, "I vant you should marry a nice boy."

Karma noted the edit. In an obvious gesture of pity, Grandma Minnie was lowering the bar. Karma fought back the need to defend herself, to explain to her grandmother that not every girl got married these days, and that it was perfectly acceptable to choose a career instead of marriage. If she did meet somebody, she might even decide just to live with him. Or she might become a lesbian and join a commune in Vermont and grow vegetables. Men weren't everything, she wanted to say.

But just in time, a loud cheer from the dining room signaled that the hidden matzo had been found, and the Passover dinner was about to conclude. That meant dessert, and Grandma Minnie practically bounded off the sofa to get back to the table. Frail as she was, she could move fast when she was motivated.

Karma composed herself, peeled her thighs off the sofa and detoured through the kitchen to pour herself another glass of Manischevitz before taking her seat at the dinner table. But she barely heard the final prayers. There was no point feeling insulted or upset; Minnie couldn't help being a relic of a bygone era when woman needed men. Karma, thank God, was a liberated woman with a college degree, a cool new job, and her own efficiency apartment. She was still plump and still single, but she had her whole life ahead of her, and women without men were like fish without bicycles. Anyway, that's what Gloria Steinem said, and that's what Karma told herself on date-less Saturday nights. Maybe she'd get a cat.

KARMA, THE DESPERATE YEARS

Hurricane Andrew hit Florida, Bill Clinton hit on Monica, and Karmella Moskowitz, thirty-one, attended yet another family wedding without a date, much less a husband. At the reception, only her father asked her to dance. Grandma Minnie was now confined to a motorized scooter that she insisted on steering, in spite of near-blindness. When you heard the whine of her motor, you got the hell out of the way. Fortunately, Grandma Minnie spent most of the evening parked at the lavish dessert table.

Remarkably, Minnie's radar for her oldest and only unmarried, granddaughter was sharp as ever. As Karma tried to slip past her grandmother to make another trip to the cash bar, Minnie reached out and grabbed her arm with a grip that was still like iron.

Karma leaned down in front of her grandmother. "Hey, Grandma, how's the sponge cake?"

"Dry. Is a pity. The chocholaht ees better." The old woman gazed sightlessly and silently into Karma's eyes for a long moment. Finally, she spoke. "Ah, my Kahrmellah, you are such a lovely girl." The old lady paused. "You know, I just vant you should be heppy."

Karma tried to smile. The bar, previously lowered, had just been crushed and sold for scrap. With a sigh, Karma pulled a chair over next to Grandma Minnie and helped herself to a piece of chocolate cake. It *was* better than the sponge cake.

Sadly, the following spring, Grandma Minnie fell and broke her hip while sweeping up a Metamucil spill in her kitchen. She died in a nursing home a few months later. The funeral was well-attended, and everyone agreed that the indomitable old woman would be missed. She had been the matriarch, the glue that held the Moskowitz clan together. The stories about her life in the Old Country were legend. She had been a tough young girl, then a tough young woman, and she died a tough old lady.

If only Minya Moskowitz had lived a little longer, she would have seen her beloved granddaughter join Weight Watchers, lose forty pounds, meet a nice Jewish boy named Sam Kranski, marry him under the *chuppah*, and give birth to a baby girl who was named in her honor.

Everyone agreed that it was a shame she wasn't there to enjoy it. On the other hand, it was surely a blessing that Grandma Minnie missed what happened a few years later. At least in Karma's opinion.

During so many sleepless nights, she imagined the old lady, hands on hips, clucking her tongue and tapping her black orthopedic shoes as she looked down from the Great Dessert Table in the Sky.

"Oy gevalt, it shouldn't happen to a dog vat happened to you, Kahrmellah. But knock on vood you hev still got yer health."

CHAPTER 1:   A PERSONAL CHINA SYNDROME

"Mommy, WATCH."

Molly Minya Kranski would make an excellent mother someday; at four years old she already had eyes in the back of her head. She was at the far end of the driveway, facing away from her mother, yet somehow she could detect Karma's straying attention. Molly was making a valiant attempt to jump rope, but she hadn't managed two consecutive jumps in twenty minutes.

It was painful for a mother to watch. Rope jumping was obviously located on some bit of DNA that she, and now her poor daughter, had missed. If she was somehow able to get pregnant again, maybe medical science would be able to do gene splicing with the chromosomes of Olympic athletes, and the next little Kranski would be able to skip, or even do cartwheels. Molly tripped on the jump rope again, toppling over and rolling into the grass.

"God help you," said Karma. Watching this was torture enough, and the sympathetic smiles from the neighbors made it worse, but after twenty minutes of sitting on the itchy lawn, Karma's leg was starting to cramp. It hurt like hell. She kneaded her left calf and swore under her breath.

"What did you said, Mommy?"

"I said to try jumping a little sooner, honey."

Karma loved her daughter more than her own life, but it was depressing to watch Molly struggle with the same things that had stumped Karma as a child. The other girls in the neighborhood were *born* jumping rope and doing cartwheels, but not Karmella

Moskowitz. She had practiced the former in the basement where nobody could see her, but the plastic jump rope alternately banged against the low ceiling and stung her shins. By the time Karma felt confident enough to jump rope in front of her friends, they had moved on to double Dutch and left her in the dust once again. As for handstands and cartwheels, well, some things just weren't meant to be.

Kudos to Molly, who was not embarrassed to demonstrate her dubious skills in public. Maybe there was a rope jumping class she could sign Molly up for. Between Soccer Tots, Little Gymnasts, and Happy Duckies swimming class, Karma would try to find room in the day to stop the cruel cycle of childhood clumsiness that threatened another generation of Moskowitz women.

Karma slapped at an ant crawling up her ankle. The outdoors would be so much more pleasant without grass and bugs. If the cramp in her leg would just go away, she'd hobble to the garage and get a lawn chair. Damn, it really hurt, and no matter how Karma turned or twisted, it just got worse. Now her ankle was also cramping. Karma was so preoccupied with her discomfort that the odd sound from down the block didn't register in her head until it had already alarmed most of her neighbors. It was a sound as foreign to suburbanites as gunfire, thumping hip-hop from a blasting car stereo, vying with the death rattle of a broken muffler. The source of the racket came squealing around the corner, at least twenty miles over the speed limit, and when Karma finally looked up, it was heading for a group of boys playing street hockey. The boys dove onto the grass as the car swerved to avoid them. Now it was heading straight at Molly, who had just tripped over her jump rope again and was stumbling toward the street.

Karma tried to get to Molly, but her calf muscle seized up like a fist and she fell back to her knees.

7

The car swerved again, but too late. In the spray of loose gravel, the rusty, half-detached back bumper caught Molly's small body, spinning her like a top. Molly's scream died as she landed in the street.

Shouts and curses rang out from horrified neighbors as the car sped away. As it rounded the corner, a thin bare arm shot out from the driver's side window with its polished middle finger raised in defiance.

"MOLLY!"

Dragging her useless, cramping leg, Karma reached her daughter only after faster neighbors got to her. Molly lay motionless in the street. Her eyes were closed and there was blood on her forehead. One end of the jump rope was still clutched in her hand. The other arm was twisted at a sickening angle. Karma's impulse was to grab her child up and run to the nearest hospital, but strong arms stopped her.

"You can't move her. You could make it worse."

"Somebody call 911."

"Oh my God, is she breathing? Is she breathing?"

Karma wrenched away from the hands that restrained her, and bent over her injured child, careful not to jostle her. "Baby, I'm right here. Mommy's right here."

She held her breath. Waiting. Waiting for Molly to open her eyes. Waiting for her chest to rise. Waiting for a sign that her own life wasn't about to end along with her daughter's. Nothing was happening.

"MOLLY MINYA KRANSKI," yelled Karma. "You breathe right this second. Breathe, damn it! I said BREATHE."

Gasps of shock from the neighbors were followed by silence. They held their collective breath, and a few hands reached out toward Karma, prepared to pull her away from the poor child if her crazy mom flipped out completely.

Karma opened her mouth to shout again, but Molly's chest heaved and her eyes fluttered open. She began to cry.

"She's alive," someone shouted, and the crowd was suddenly hooting and cheering and laughing with relief, which made Molly cry even louder.

Karma sat down in the street, crying and trying to catch her breath. She gently touched Molly's hair. Strong, reassuring arms folded around her, and Karma looked up to see her best friends, Bianca and Kim, who had pushed their way through the onlookers and were kneeling on either side of her. She stared at them, dazed and leaking tears.

"Sweetie, the ambulance is on its way," said Bianca.

"I think her arm is broken," whispered Kim.

"She coulda been killed," said Bianca. "*Dio vieta.*"

Karma barely heard them. *Molly is breathing. She is alive. She is breathing. She is alive.*

Kim and Bianca lifted Karma to a standing position and held onto her, not trusting that she wouldn't fall if they let go. Voices penetrated Karma's foggy brain.

"Did you see that? I mean did you? Jesus Christ. It was a Fiat or a Volvo."

"It sounded like a Mustang."

"No, I had a Mustang. That was a Charger."

"Did anybody get the license number?"

Karma looked around stupidly. *Where had all these people come from?*

Hands grabbed Karma's face and turned her around, and she found herself looking up into Bianca's intense Italian eyes. "Karma, listen to me. The ambulance is coming. You tell 'em to take you to St. V's because it's the only place your insurance will cover. Andy broke his arm three times, and it's the best. They got plasma TVs in every room and gelato in the cafeteria 24/7. It's better than the freakin' Holiday Inn. Shit, never mind, I'll tell 'em myself."

An ambulance and a fire truck pulled up, and EMTs poured out into the street, swarming over Molly. Bianca pulled Karma out of their way, and Kim grabbed a young man with a clipboard and pointed to Karma. "This is the mother."

Karma answered his questions about drug allergies (none she knew of) and reactions to anesthesia (none she knew of) and what Molly had eaten in the past six hours (Cocoa Puffs, peanut butter crackers, and chocolate milk).

"I wish you were my mom," said the young man.

Karma watched as paramedics secured Molly's neck with a padded brace, slipped a backboard under her little body, and lifted her onto a gurney. They were gentle, and so quick that Molly barely had time to shriek.

Everything seemed to be happening in speeded-up time. Bianca was giving instructions to the ambulance driver, neighbors were talking to the police, and Bianca was talking to the EMTs. Kim appeared and pushed Karma's purse into her hands, but then thought better of it and took it back. She extracted Karma's wallet, found her insurance card and driver's license, and slid them into Karma's back jeans pocket. Then she stuffed Karma's cell phone into her front pocket.

"You've got what you need," said Kim. "I'll keep your purse so you don't lose it."

"If you need anything else from the house, we'll come back and get it," said Bianca.

The EMT with the clipboard helped Karma into the ambulance so she could sit with Molly. "We'll follow you," yelled Kim, as the doors closed.

Suddenly, time slowed down to a maddening crawl. Karma buckled herself into a seat near Molly, and held her breath for the sirens, flashing lights, and record-breaking speeds. But the ambulance didn't even move. An eternity passed. The EMTs checked Molly's blood pressure, which elicited more screaming, checked her oxygen level (still more screaming), and chatted by cell phone to the hospital. Now Karma felt like screaming; why didn't they hurry the hell UP? Finally, the ambulance pulled away from the curb and proceeded down the street. *Very slowly.*

Karma forced herself to stay silent for Molly's sake. She understood that her daughter wasn't dying, but did they have to drive like they had all day? And why were they talking about cartoon characters? What if Molly had a concussion or a brain bleed? What was the point of being in a vehicle that didn't have to obey speed limits if you didn't even drive fast?

She tried to remind herself that these just-barely-out-of-high-schoolers knew what they were doing, but it wasn't easy. She had to admit, though, that their steady stream of chatter about Disney princesses and Nick Junior TV shows was distracting Molly. Her shrieking was down to whimpers and hiccups.

Karma was formulating something nice to say about this when she felt the silent vibration of her cell phone. How had it come to be in her front pants pocket? She read a text from Kim.

u call sam?

It gave Karma a jolt to realize that she hadn't even thought of her husband, the father of her only child. With shaking hands, she dialed, but her call went straight to voice mail, which meant Sam was either on his phone or in a meeting. Karma would have liked to scream an urgent message about the accident, but with Molly six inches away, all she could do was calmly ask Sam to call as soon as he could.

When the ambulance finally pulled into the cool, dark bay of the hospital ER, Molly was gently unloaded and wheeled into the trauma center. Karma was directed to the front desk, where she was soon flanked by Kim and Bianca, and then told to sit in the

11

waiting room until they were ready for her. Karma tugged at her sweaty polo shirt; the neck felt too tight, as did the waistband of her capri pants. There was a spot of blood on the left knee. Was it Molly's blood or her own?

Kim and Bianca barely left her side, except to sneak into far corners to answer their cell phones and tell the callers what had happened. Karma didn't mind; she was glad their mutual friends weren't calling her. Kim and Bianca were her closest friends in the neighborhood, in part because their kids got along so well. Physically, Barbara Kim Wallace was as different from Bianca Antonia Maria Teresa Catalano as it was possible to be. Kim was Asian, short, and a teeny bit thick around the middle. Her tiny feet were nearly always housed in comfortable Keds, whereas Bianca, tall and slender and gorgeous, could have run a marathon in her high-heeled strappy sandals. Bianca was one of those women who look good all the time. Kim was more like Karma, who, except for weddings and funerals, dressed only for comfort. But even Kim knew what colors brought out the best in her winter complexion and what styles suited her short stature. Karma was, admittedly, a fashion victim.

A few minutes later, the ER doctor found Karma and reported that Molly's shoulder was dislocated, and her arm was broken in two places. She would need surgery, but she'd be home in a day or two unless there were unforeseen difficulties. Children heal fast, he said. He gave the mother of the patient his most reassuring smile, and promised that her daughter would be jumping rope in no time.

"That's good," said Karma. "She couldn't do that before."

More hours went by that seemed like days. Adrenaline flowed out and fatigue flowed in. Karma wanted to close her eyes and sleep, but she kept seeing the car hit Molly, over and over. She saw Molly hit the pavement and then lie still as death.

She saw the car speed away with that slim arm and its raised middle finger sticking through the open window. *Who runs over a child and then drives off? What kind of woman flips the bird and doesn't stop to see what she's done? Molly could have died or been brain damaged or in a wheelchair for the rest of her life.*

A police officer came to the hospital to take Karma's statement. He shook his head. He said he'd file his report, but there were no guarantees, since nobody got a license plate number, and they had descriptions of the car that barely agreed on the color, much less the make and model. *Sorry, Ma'am, we'll do our best.*

He asked Karma if she had, by some chance, caught anything on her cell phone camera. None of the other witnesses had been quick enough to do so. Karma said no. She'd had her phone, of course, but immortalizing Molly's attempts at jumping rope had seemed too cruel to contemplate.

Karma thanked the officer, though for *what* she wasn't sure. She wanted to hear that they had caught the driver and beaten a confession out of her. Instead, Karma was the one who felt kicked in the gut. How could this have happened in her neighborhood?

Bedford Commons was a planned community, built over a soybean field in a moderately upscale suburb in the middle of Indiana. The neighborhood covenants prevented Homer Simpson from keeping his bass boat in the backyard or putting up a tacky chain link fence. There were five models to choose from, six siding colors (all beige), two trim colors (off-white and a little more off-white), and three fake shutter colors which coordinated with the brick selections (fronts only, to keep costs down). Bedford Commons was the land of Good First Impressions. Or it had been, until today.

Bianca brought Karma a cafeteria gelato, and she took a shaky spoonful, then slumped in the padded waiting room chair.

She had never even broken a bone, barely had a stitch, and now her only child was going into surgery because of a maniac bitch who didn't even have the decency to stop after she practically killed a child. *Somebody has to do something.*

Somebody has to do something.

Years earlier, coed Karma had joined a college anti-nuke group. Nukes were bad, of course, but Karma was mainly looking to meet cute, smart guys. All the chanting and marching and sign-waving had resulted in only one date, with a skinny modern poetry major who talked all evening about how his anti-fascist, anti-military-industrial-complex, anti-establishment poetry would change the world. Karma had her doubts; his poems didn't even rhyme.

Far more memorable was a guy who hadn't asked her out, the guest speaker at her first Stop the Nukes rally. He was the kind of guy she had longed to meet: tall, Nehru-jacketed, and super handsome, with really nice hair. Karma had worked her way to the front of the crowd so that he might also see her, and in the process had even absorbed a bit of his speech, about the *China Syndrome* scenario of a nuclear plant meltdown. Years later, Karma had rushed to see the Jane Fonda movie of the same name, though mostly to enjoy Michael Douglas, who also had really nice hair.

Now, all these years later, sitting in a hospital waiting room chair, Karma felt the beginnings of a personal nuclear meltdown, as a tiny nugget of rage worked its way down to her core. Her only child had a badly broken arm and abrasions and lacerations to her face. *Lacerations.* What an awful, bloody word. All because of some stupid woman who didn't even stop to see what she'd done.

That was the part that Karma couldn't shake. *You can't hit somebody with your car in the middle of the afternoon and not hear or see what you've done. It's not possible. Somebody should do something. Somebody should DO SOMETHING.*

Karma's appetite was gone, and she stalked over to a trash can to throw away the Styrofoam cup of melting gelato. If only she held a rock instead of a stupid bowl. She would have thrown it through the plate glass window of the waiting room, which looked out onto a picturesque garden with life-size statues of nuns in flowing robes. She could practically feel the cold stone in her fist, hear the chaotic, crashing sound it would make, and see the resulting mess. Very satisfying.

But as the scene continued to play out in Karma's head, it didn't go well. She saw herself being arrested and made to pay for the damages, plus court fees, then being sued by somebody in the courtyard who had been cut by flying glass. The victim would be an aging nun or some sick person, and everybody would know Karma was horrible and crazy, and social services would question her fitness as a mother.

The prosecuting attorney at her trial (no plea bargain for her) would say that it was her fault that Molly was hit by the red car because Karma had let her jump rope practically in the middle of the street, even though she knew that Molly sucked at jumping rope. She would have to admit that she hadn't even been watching because her leg was cramping, which demonstrated to the jury that she thought only of herself because she was such a terrible mother. She would go to prison, Sam would divorce her and marry a gorgeous woman who Molly would call *Mommy*. This woman would teach Molly how to jump rope *and* do cartwheels. Karma's parents and former in-laws would never forgive her, and her friends would refuse her collect calls from the penitentiary.

After she got out of prison, she'd have to check the box on every job application that said I HAVE BEEN CONVICTED OF A FELONY, so she would never find a decent job, and she'd live alone in a nasty subsidized apartment, and maybe not even *that* because convicted felons probably couldn't get subsidized apartments. She'd move to a homeless shelter and spend her days trying to convince drunks and meth heads that she used to live in a lovely two-story, brick-fronted, four-bedroom house in the suburbs. *They'd laugh in her wrinkled, haggard face.*

"Whatcha doin'?"

Startled, Karma looked up to see Kim.

"I take it you're done with the ice cream?" Kim reached up and took the gelato cup.

Karma was startled to realize that she had been standing in front of the plate glass window that overlooked the hospital courtyard with her arm cocked back like a baseball player. She nodded, cleared her throat and stretched her would-be pitching arm to scratch her shoulder blade, as though this was what she had intended to do all along. "I was just throwing it away."

Kim nodded as she ate the rest of Karma's gelato, then tossed out the empty container. "I figured that, you crazy bitch."

Karma followed Kim back to the waiting room chairs, and quietly took a seat between her and Bianca. She pretended not to see the looks they were giving each other; she had bigger things to think about. *Somebody should do something.*

Somebody should do something.

It's just a thing people say when things go wrong. It usually means somebody *else* should do something. But not always.

CHAPTER 2:   FIREWORKS

Days passed, Molly came home with her arm in a cast, and Karma's life began to resume its normal pace. If it weren't for having to keep the cast dry and answer annoying questions (What happened? Did you call the cops? Why can't they find the driver? Aren't you going crazy?), Karma might have almost forgotten about Molly's arm. Even before the accident, Molly couldn't tie her own shoes, button her pants, or cut up her own food, so having her daughter's arm in a cast didn't change much in Karma's life.

She had already forgiven Sam for taking so long to get to the hospital on that horrible day. She hadn't had any rational reason for being mad at him, but it hadn't been a day for rationality. Sam had come running into the waiting room after Molly went into surgery, white-faced and cursing his monthly status meetings. He had hugged his weary, bedraggled wife, asked for details about what had happened, hugged her again, and then hugged Kim and Bianca and thanked them for being there. After the two women left, Sam had redeemed himself further by bringing Karma another chocolate gelato, which she had eaten this time. He had settled himself in the chair next to Karma and put a protective arm around her shoulder.

As they waited for word that Molly's surgery was over and his heart rate returned to normal, Sam had told himself that Molly was going to be fine, and that he couldn't have prevented what happened. He had stared up at the giant flat-screen TV and tried to relax.

The Food Network had been on, and a perky young woman was making healthy crepes with vegetables and a low-calorie, skim milk sauce. Sam had glanced around the waiting room, wondering if he could stand on a chair to reach the controls without getting yelled at. He wanted to watch ESPN. Maybe the lady behind the information desk had a remote control? Unfortunately, there were a few people watching the cooking show, so he gave up the idea. Actually, the crepes looked pretty good, and the perky young blond was nice to watch.

Perky blonds had never showed much interest in Sam Kranski. They went for jocks, and Sam wasn't a jock, although he had played intramural basketball in high school and college. There was no such thing as an intramural jock. In truth, Sam was a nerd. An accounting nerd. *Never mind*, he had told himself back in college. The jocks would end up overweight car salesmen, and their perky wives wouldn't stay perky forever. Time, the great equalizer, had a way of evening that score.

He had met Karma at a party in her dorm. She wasn't the perky blond type, but she was *his* type: smart, funny, and definitely pretty enough, especially when she smiled. He liked her unruly hair, which she called mousy, but which he thought of as brown. What was wrong with brown? He also liked her soft, curvy body, although he knew she didn't. She sometimes talked about getting blue contact lenses and liposuction, but like him, she was too practical for such things. She was real, and Sam was find with that.

That horrible day of the car accident, the subject of his musings had eaten her chocolate gelato in silence. She'd felt much better now that Sam was there. Molly would be out of surgery soon, and the doctor had said she'd be fine. It was a bad break, yes, but there was no vascular damage, no apparent nerve damage, and very little damage to the growth plate. Molly would probably spend one night in the hospital, but that was all. She had a concussion from hitting the pavement, they said, but no bleeding in her brain.

Sam had been a huge help in the days and weeks that followed. He had listened without comment when Karma endlessly recounted the story of Molly's brush with death to friends, relatives, and near-strangers in grocery stores. He held Molly's arm out of the water when Karma bathed her, rocked her to sleep when her poor little arm was aching, and distracted her with funny faces when the cast had to be checked and changed.

So when Molly finally began sleeping through the night again, Karma knew it was the least she could do to agree with Sam's request that they resume their nightly exercise.

Walking, that is.

Karma had never quite managed to lose the entire thirty (okay, thirty-eight) pounds she'd gained while pregnant with Molly. She had joined a ladies-only gym, but it was boring and the women were gossipy. Karma appreciated gossip, but gossip about people she didn't know wasn't much fun to listen to. So after the free trial membership ended, she signed up for a free month of Pilates at the Y, but Pilates made her all sweaty, and who had time to take two showers in one day? Karma tended toward dry skin, so all that bathing wouldn't have been good for her.

Unfortunately, no health club or gym offered the program Karma needed: a large, burly fellow who would come to her house and force her flabby ass into the gym, at gunpoint.

Sam never (never ever) commented on Karma's baby weight. But when Molly turned four, and Karma was still wearing her pregnancy pants, he cleverly suggested that she might help motivate *him* to exercise by accompanying him on nightly power walks around the neighborhood. Karma knew bullshit when she heard it, and told Sam that she would cheer him on from *inside* the house, as somebody needed to stay behind in case Molly woke up.

But Sam had been ready for her. He had already tested the range of their baby monitor, and demonstrated that they could carry the receiver and roam almost two blocks away from home before losing the signal completely. It was an old-fashioned audio-only model, re-gifted to Karma by a cousin, and it had a long effective range.

Karma had no choice but to give in. Besides, she knew she needed it. Her bras were becoming painfully tight, and she found herself intrigued by Pajama Jeans. They looked so comfortable, but would they fool anybody? Or would they be a signal to the world that she had completely lost her last bit of self-respect. Would she find herself on a *People of Walmart* website, photographed from behind, bending over to reach the gallon jars of marshmallow fluff? Did she dare risk it?

So Karma had agreed to the nightly power walks, on the condition that they carry the baby monitor, and return immediately if Molly woke up.

But then Molly was hit by the red car, and the power walks stopped. In just two weeks Karma had gained five pounds. She blamed stress, but knew that part of the problem was her new addiction to gelato. She had to do something about it.

And maybe, she reasoned, by some miracle she would spot the red car. Maybe the driver was lying low during the day, and only venturing out at night. Sam wouldn't have approved of this idea; he had said more than once that the police would find the car and its driver eventually, and that Karma should concentrate on being grateful that Molly hadn't been hurt worse.

Karma had vehemently, but silently, disagreed. Sam hadn't seen his child hit by that car. He hadn't seen the driver speed away, middle finger in the air. He didn't see that horrible scene in his head a dozen times a day, and he didn't dream about it at night. Karma stopped talking about retaliation and revenge in front of Sam, but she never stopped thinking about it.

It seemed impossible to her that nobody had spotted the car since the day it hit Molly. The cops said the car probably didn't belong to anybody in the neighborhood, but Karma was convinced that if the woman had had a reason to drive through Bedford Commons that day, she might have the same reason to do so again. Karma wanted to be there when it happened, and if there were justice in the world, she would be.

On their fourth evening's power walk since the accident, and the fifth circuit around the same two blocks, Karma was winded. It was embarrassing to be *this* out of shape, and her effort to avoid making noises like an asthmatic centenarian was making things worse—she couldn't fill her lungs without wheezing. Part of the problem was that Sam's natural stride was at least a foot longer than hers. He said this made it better exercise for her. She said he should kiss her ass and slow the hell down. On this night, she was about to demand a five-minute break when a loud BANG made her jump, and provided a good excuse to stop running.

As Sam jogged in place to keep his heart rate up, he pointed at violet sparks erupting above the rooftops. "Somebody's shooting off fireworks."

Panting, Karma thanked God for fireworks.

Another bang followed, accompanied by red and green spiraling sparks. Sam stared at the fading lights in the sky. With a dramatic sigh he said, "I guess we'll never know where it's coming from, since we have to keep going around the same block over and over." He sighed again, louder. "Oh well."

A shower of pink and purple sparks was followed by a bang and a blue cascade with white twirling after-effects that whistled before they died out. These weren't the cheap fireworks on sale at the grocery store; somebody had spent serious money on these.

21

Sam, still jogging in place, sighed yet again. Louder. Karma tried to stop the corners of her mouth from rising of their own accord. Sam was liable to hyperventilate in an effort to make his point. "Let's hope they don't start a fire on somebody's roof," he said with exaggerated urgency. "It would be a shame if somebody loses their house because we didn't call the fire department because we only walk around our own block and we didn't see the fire. Think of the damage we could have prevented if only--"

"Oh my God," interrupted Karma. "Stop already." She unclipped the receiver from her waistband and held it up against her ear. Not a sound. If Molly woke up and couldn't find her, that would be bad, but if she and Sam only went a *little* farther from home, what were the chances? Karma was also curious to know who was shooting off expensive fireworks so long after the 4th of July.

"Okay," she said. "Let's go see, but just for a second."

"Maybe we shouldn't," said Sam. "You know how I worry about Molly waking up for two seconds before falling back asleep. She could be scarred for life. Psychologically."

"You could be scarred, too," said Karma. "Physically."

They trotted off again in the direction of the fireworks. As they turned onto a street that ended in a cul-de-sac, he stopped and grabbed Karma's arm to stop her as well. Three people were standing in the center of the wide area at the end of the street. They were just outside the circle of light from the streetlamp, but their waving arms threw shadows on the street. Angry shadows. Angry voices, too, though too far away to be clearly understood.

Karma and Sam edged a little closer. There were two men and a fat woman. No, not fat, pregnant, Karma realized, and then she recognized Joan Handley, a nice, somewhat fussy woman she'd run into a few times at home sales parties. Karma was a seat-warmer who attended mainly for the free wine, but Joan was one of those dutiful types who listened intently to the sales pitch and nearly always bought something.

Other residents of the cul-de-sac were drifting out of their houses to see what the commotion was about. Karma tugged on Sam's arm to pull him forward; something was happening, and she wasn't about to miss it. Joan Handley looked big enough to be carrying triplets and angry enough to spontaneously combust.

"You're disturbing the peace," Karma heard her say as they approached.

"You're fulla shit," said a man Karma didn't recognize. He had thinning brown hair, plaid shorts, a tight black tee shirt that barely covered a little pot belly, and brown leather sandals. The only things missing were black socks with holes in the toe. Grandma Minnie would have called him a *meshugener*.

"I'm going to call the police," said the smaller man, who held Joan's arm in a protective gesture. He had to be her husband. He was half-a-head shorter than the guy in the plaid shorts, with round shoulders and skinny arms. He wouldn't last five minutes if things got physical.

Karma and Sam moved a few steps closer, close enough to hear, but far enough to stay relatively uninvolved. The other neighbors were doing likewise, although a few were recording the excitement with their cell phones.

"Call anybody you want," said the guy in the plaid shorts. "I can do what I want in my own fuckin' yard. It's a free country and I can light fireworks any fuckin' night I want."

Karma was disgusted. Plaid Shorts sounded like he'd had a few too many beers. And he had obviously neglected to read the Bedford Commons Neighborhood Covenants and Restrictions, which stood between the high standards of upstanding residents and the bad taste of tacky people like himself. The covenants were clear about loud noises after 9 p.m., which Mr. F Bomb

23

would have known if he'd taken time to read them. What was a jerk like this doing in Karma's neighborhood?

Karma moved a few steps to one side to get a better view of Joan Handley. The Merriam-Webster people could have used her face to illustrate *righteous indignation.*

"You can't disturb people like this," she sputtered. "Children are trying to sleep."

"You're the one making a scene," said the man with mocking smugness. "You're disturbing the neighborhood."

Joan opened her mouth, but no words came out. Unable to express her outrage verbally, she wrenched her arm out of her husband's grip, raised her index finger and shook it in Plaid Shorts' face.

You go, Joan, thought Karma. This wasn't the kind of thing one often saw in the suburbs, but according to Moskowitz family legend, Grandma Minnie had faced down a band of Cossacks with just this sort of fearless bravado. They had threatened to torch her parent's farm, and she had scared them off. Probably with a rifle, but still, it took guts. Karma's hands tightened into fists as she imagined herself rearing back, taking a powerful swing and hitting the big stupid bully right in the jaw. One punch and he'd hit the ground, unconscious. It was exactly what she intended to do to the woman who broke Molly's arm, if she ever got the chance. And she would. She wouldn't rest until she got the chance, no matter how long it took and how much trouble…

Karma was startled by Sam's strong hand on her upper arm. Did he know what she was thinking, and what she wanted to do?

Karma relaxed her fists. Then she wondered, would Sam take the guy on if he attacked Joan or her husband? Surely he'd step in. Karma's primitive reptile brain was rooting for this, hoping to see Sam go all *caveman* on the guy.

But it was not to be. Just as quickly as the tension had swollen to near-violence, it was over. Joan retracted her angry index finger and dropped her hand back down to her huge pregnant belly. Plaid Shorts hadn't even flinched. His cocky expression said that *he* knew that *she* knew that not only was *she* not going to hit him, but her mild-mannered husband wouldn't take him on either.

Poor little Mr. Handley, thought Karma. He could surely feel the subtext, but he wasn't up for a fight. Taking his wife's arm again, he led her back toward their house. He stopped half-way up the driveway, though, turning back to Plaid Shorts and taking one last shot at reclaiming his manhood.

"The police," he called. "Next time, I'm calling the police."

"Sure, you do that," said Plaid Shorts. Still smiling, he shoved his hands in his pockets and swaggered toward his own driveway. An unseen watcher inside his house opened the front door as he approached, and he disappeared into his house.

Karma felt let down. The guy deserved to be socked in the jaw, and nobody had done it. He had won. He was the bad guy, and he had won. Things weren't supposed to end like this, and it filled her with impotent anger.

With the show over, the onlookers slowly returned to their homes. Sam and Karma lingered for a bit, then headed back toward their sleeping daughter. Neither spoke. They didn't power walk; they just walked. The only things moving quickly were Karma's angry thoughts. *What is happening in my upscale suburban neighborhood? Where are these nasty people coming from? Who let them in? Who let them stay?*

She asked herself, what was the difference between this and international terrorism, besides the scale? The world was falling apart, the neighborhood was falling apart, and nobody was doing anything about any of it. There had been at least six guys watching in the cul-de-sac, and they had all just stood there. John Wayne wouldn't have just stood there; he would have hogtied the guy and dragged him out of the neighborhood behind his horse. Clint Eastwood would have pistol-whipped him and made him apologize to the lady. Brad Pitt would have had Angelina kick the guy's ass.

Worst of all, for Karma, one of the six guys had been her own husband. He'd just stood there and watched, too. If a fight *had* broken out, would he have done anything? What if he had just stood there? The image in her head suddenly felt so real, it made her even angrier. At her husband.

Karma flashed back to their honeymoon in Mexico, years earlier. Too full of free empanadas from the bar at the all-inclusive resort, Karma had stayed up late one night, reading an Amy Tan book set in ancient China. All the men in the novel were total assholes who treated women like crap. Karma had been forced to stop reading the book because it made her want to punch Sam in the face while he slept, just for being a man. She had also had a few frozen margaritas at the bar.

Newlywed Sam Kranski had never learned how close he had come to being assaulted in his sleep. And not-so-newlywed Sam Kranski was likewise unaware of his wife's current disappointment as they walked home on this night. He was just damned glad that he hadn't been forced to defend that crazy pregnant woman and her husband. Sam had been punched in the face just once, back in high school. A varsity football player had called out, "Hey, Jew Boy," and when Sam turned to see who was talking, the guy had hit him square on the nose. Hard. Sam had swung at the guy, of course, but he was off balance, and hadn't even connected.

Sam reflexively rubbed the bump on the bridge of his nose, which is what you get when you're too embarrassed to tell your folks what happened and you never get your broken nose set correctly. He could remember every instant of the blinding pain and the sickening sound as the cartilage of his nose had cracked. It wasn't an experience he cared to repeat. Sure, he would have helped the little guy if that big guy had hit him, but he was glad that he hadn't had to.

Unaware that the silence between him and Karma was anything other than plain old silence, Sam said, "I'm glad nobody got hurt." In all honesty, Sam was including himself.

"Me, too," said Karma. "Violence never solves anything." In all honesty, Karma didn't mean a word of it.

CHAPTER 3:   FRIDAY PLAYGROUP AND WHY
DANIEL WEST STILL WON'T EAT SUSHI

"Mommy!" Allie screamed from the bottom of Sue Ellen's basement steps. "Jeffrey hit Baby Jacob on the head with MISS GABBY."

Karma paused in her retelling of last night's almost-fist fight. But of the five women gathered around Sue Ellen's kitchen table for Friday Playgroup, only Jeanette Jorganson reacted to Allie's complaint. Allie, Little Jeffrey, and Baby Jacob all belonged to her, and Miss Gabby was Allie's plastic doll, so this dispute was intramural. According to the unwritten rules of Friday Playgroup, the rest of the women were allowed to ignore screaming if 1) the mother was present, and 2) no actual blood had been spilled.

The group had been Kim's idea—she'd found it in a parenting magazine, and had vowed to start one when Lindsey was old enough. According to the author, it was a chance for moms to chat and eat while the kids became socialized. Playgroups, according to this expert, were ideal for children who missed out on the benefits of full-time daycare because their stay-at-home mothers kept them socially isolated.

Kim and Karma had cursed this stupidity, but had to admit, playgroup was everything a Mom could wish for—a chance to hang out with other moms, eating somebody else's food and enjoying adult conversation. The best part was that most Friday mornings, your kids were tearing up somebody else's basement or toy room, and if they ate enough, they wouldn't need lunch.

"MOMMY," shrieked Allie. Jeanette pushed back from the table and headed down the basement steps.

Bianca watched her disappear, then leaned in so she could keep her voice low. "Every time Tony complains about our kids, I tell him to shut up and thank God he's not Little Jeffrey's father. Did you hear what the little shit did to their siding last weekend? Permanent marker."

Sue Ellen's bright blue eyes were large and round with excitement. She looked left, right, and left again before speaking in an urgent whisper. "I ran into Jeanette at Kroger yesterday, and she actually *told* me about that. She said he's not even in kindergarten, and he spelled all the dirty words right."

The burst of laughter from the other women impelled Sue Ellen to flap her arms and shush them, which made them laugh even harder. It wasn't her fault. Sue Ellen West was new to the neighborhood, and had attended just one Friday playgroup before volunteering to host this one. Back home in Buford, Georgia, you could talk with your girlfriends about anybody who wasn't present, just like here in the suburbs of Indianapolis, but you certainly did not hang your *own* dirty laundry out where the neighbors could gawk at it. She couldn't understand why Jeanette wasn't embarrassed by her awful child. The realtor had assured Sue Ellen that this was one of the nicest neighborhoods in the school district, but this was one of those times when Indiana felt as foreign as another country.

Still, she was grateful and happy that these women, bless their hearts, had welcomed her into their playgroup, and Daniel was making new friends. This move had been a *good* thing, she reminded herself. She just hoped Jeanette's little heathens weren't messing up her newly-finished basement.

But just then, the little Chinese gal whose name Sue Ellen could never remember reached into her blue porcelain centerpiece bowl. She just *reached in* like she didn't know better and took a bunch of grapes out of the bowl! Sue Ellen had to bite her lip to keep the horror off her face. She didn't dare say anything, as that would have been rude. *Maybe the Chinese gal doesn't understand centerpieces?*

The Chinese gal was actually Korean, and she understood centerpieces, but hadn't identified the bowl of grapes as such. Kim Wallace had been adopted as an infant, and raised by an Irish-American couple from Wisconsin, where grapes in a bowl were generally considered *food*. Oblivious to the shadow that had settled over Sue Ellen's otherwise flawless features, Kim handed the grapes to her daughter, Lindsey, who had walked up to the table with an open mouth and outstretched hands. "Don't choke," said Kim, "and don't spit the seeds on the floor. This isn't Miss Karma's house." She gave her best friend a sunny smile to make sure she'd heard the dig. She had. But now it was Kim's turn to look around to make sure Jeanette was still downstairs. "Is Little Jeffrey on medication? If he were mine, he'd be on medication."

"If he were mine," said Karma, "we'd both be on medication. I mean, how many preschools has he been kicked out of? I never got in trouble at school. Well, once, but I just got too close to a fight between two other girls."

Jeanette's footsteps sounded on the basement steps, and the women stopped talking and composed themselves. Jeanette appeared in the doorway, and started to sit down at the table, but then stopped, sniffing the air like a bloodhound. Her cinnamon rolls were ready. "It was nothing," she said, pulling on Sue Ellen's oven mitts. "Just kids being kids. I'll be so glad when Little Jeffrey goes to kindergarten in the fall. He's got so much energy it just wears me out. I think the problem is he's so smart, he doesn't know what to do with himself."

In a single motion, Karma, Kim, and Bianca looked down at their plates, not daring to make eye contact with each other. Every mother has a blind spot where her own children are concerned, but Jeanette was the Helen Keller of Friday Playgroup. She would give you her last egg and share her secret family recipes, but she was oblivious to her failings as a parent. Jeanette was an expert in three areas: cinnamon rolls, criminal behavior and law enforcement. On the last two topics, she was a font of information, having absorbed every morsel that could be gleaned from primetime cop shows. She watched the reruns of the old crime shows as avidly as the new ones. Karma thought that was wise, as Little Jeffrey's adolescence would surely include police intervention. If only there had been a *CSI: Sucky Parenting*, there might have been some hope for Jeanette.

Jeanette opened the oven door, and the hypnotic smell of spice and butter wafted into the room. Karma took the opportunity to steer the conversation back to the original topic. Everybody had wanted to hear about the previous night's near-fight between the guy in the plaid shorts and Joan Handley's mousy husband, and Karma was the only eyewitness at the table. As always, though, Kim had details Karma didn't, thanks to her husband, who was president of the Homeowners Association and a friend to local cops.

"You missed the best part," chided Kim. "The guy came back out around 10:30, and started shooting off more fireworks. Joan Handley opened her patio door to yell at him again, and he aimed one right at her."

Mouths dropped open and Sue Ellen let out a squeak of alarm. "It barely missed her," said Kim, "and it left a burn mark on the patio. She freaked out and her husband called the cops, and they *arrested* him."

Jeanette, who was reaching into the open oven, gasped. "They arrested Greg?"

"They arrested the fireworks guy," said Kim with irritation. "His name is Jack Lawrence."

The women at the table shook their heads in amazement. This was more excitement than the neighborhood had seen since Maggie Shepherd's kid (the bald one, not the one with the nose ring) climbed out his bedroom window onto the roof and had to be rescued by the fire department.

"I'll bet for disorderly conduct," said Jeanette. She set the bubbly cinnamon rolls in the center of the polished walnut table, careful to center it on Sue Ellen's enamel trivet. "Although it could be attempted murder. It depends on how big the firework was and whether he showed intent to do bodily harm." Jeanette loved expressions like *intent to do bodily harm.*

Sue Ellen began to separate the rolls with her silver serving knife. Jeanette held out plates, and Sue Ellen filled each with a cinnamon roll, waiting until everyone was served before cutting a bit for herself. "Jack Lawrence. I feel sorry for his family," she said. "I assume he has a family?"

Karma didn't answer; she was too busy watching Sue Ellen. With the precision of a surgeon, she shaved off a thin sliver of cinnamon roll and placed it on her plate, then carefully scraped off the desperate drops of icing that still clung to it. No wonder she was so skinny—a bulimic wouldn't have bothered throwing up something that small.

"Three kids and a wife," said Kim, wishing she knew Sue Ellen well enough to ask for her icing. "Her name's Luann. I met her at the pool last summer. You were with me, Karm. She was dressed kinda trashy, like she didn't know she *had* three kids and a husband, if you know what I mean. Not that she looked bad, but you know." Her voice trailed off.

Karma knew what Kim meant, all too well. It always took the two of them a few days after the start of pool season to venture out in their bathing suits, and even then, Kim wore her terry cover-up for the first week. It was Kim's belief that women over

32

thirty who could still wear bikinis did so just to make women like her feel inferior.

Karma wouldn't have worn a bikini in public for a million dollars cash, but she considered Kim overly sensitive. Yes, Kim was short and maybe a little stocky, but she was well-proportioned, whereas Karma felt like a pear on her best days, and a watermelon on her worst. "Maybe I remember her," she said. "Very skimpy bathing suit and a belly button ring, right? So her husband's in jail? Holy crap."

"Nah, she bailed him out," said Kim through a mouthful of cinnamon roll. "I'm still trying to find out what *that* cost; I bet it was a lot."

Karma picked at her cinnamon roll; if she ate it too quickly, she'd want another one, and she had sworn to drop ten pounds before summer. Twenty would have been better, but it wasn't likely to happen. Neither was ten. "Three kids," she said. "Why would anybody marry a jackass like that and let him reproduce three times?"

"Maybe she didn't know he was a jackass," said Jeanette.

"I knew my husband was a jackass when I married him," said Kim. "Didn't you?"

"I didn't know your husband back then," said Jeanette.

Karma almost spit out her coffee. Stunned silence fell over the room, followed by giggles, then snorts of laughter. Kim's mouth fell open, but no words came out, just a bit of icing. Jeanette hadn't *accidentally* said something funny; she had deliberately and cleverly fired one off at Kim. It *always* went the other way around. Karma offered a raised hand to Jeanette, who blushed modestly and high-fived Karma's open palm.

Sue Ellen looked around the table. She wanted to make a good impression on these women, who knew each other so well and mocked each other so easily. They were funny, but so quick to snipe that it made her a little nervous. At least they didn't make dumb-blond jokes. Maybe that was because Jeanette was also a blond, and she actually *was* kinda dumb.

But Sue Ellen had to admit, she was also a talented baker. She brought her Grandma Bibi's special cinnamon rolls to every playgroup, no matter whose house was scheduled. As Bianca had explained, this was the result of a deal the group had made when playgroup was held, for the first and only time, at Jeanette's house. Little Jeffrey had found it difficult to share his toys. Jeanette had called him *territorial*. Her friends had called him *homicidal,* though not to her face. So Jeanette was removed from the rotating hosting schedule, and instead, brought cinnamon rolls every week. They were certainly delicious, but so full of fat, and not really in keeping with Sue Ellen's menu for the morning. She was Belinda Beauregard's daughter, after all, and had hoped to take things up a notch.

One thing was sure, though, Sue Ellen wouldn't create an edible centerpiece again. Everybody was eating the grapes now, and her beautiful centerpiece looked like something the cat dragged in from the woods. Oh well, it couldn't be helped, so she put a cheerful look on her face. "I want to hear more about the man getting arrested. All this happened just last night? How did y'all hear about it so fast?"

Karma and Kim shared a quick look; Sue Ellen was too new to the neighborhood to understand how it functioned. Kim's husband, Dave, was president of the Bedford Commons homeowners' association. When you had a problem with a neighbor that you were too lazy or cowardly to confront, you called Dave. But when you had really juicy dish on said neighbors, you called his wife, Kim. Dave had thought about quitting the HOA, but Kim wouldn't let him; all her best news sources would have dried up.

"I know people in the cul-de-sac," said Kim, with a modest flip of her shiny bobbed hair.

Karma grinned; Kim knew everybody, and if she didn't know you, she knew *about* you. Short, Asian, and assertive, Kim became the center of every group she joined. She had a clever, bitchy tongue, too, and she wasn't afraid to use it, which was just plain *fun*.

"Do things like this happen very often?" asked Sue Ellen. A wrinkle had appeared between her perfect brows. "I mean, I've only just moved in, and you've got speeders almost killing kids and crazy men shooting off fireworks."

"Don't exaggerate," said Bianca. "It was only one speeder and one crazy man."

"Speaking of crazy," said Karma, "I saw Sherry Dobbs at Kroger yesterday, and she asked what happened to Molly. When I told her, she said, 'Maybe you shouldn't let her play in the street.' I didn't *let* Molly play in the street—she *fell* into the street."

"When I was a kid we all played in the street," said Kim.

"Sherry Dobbs is a smug piece of shit," said Bianca. "We both go to St. Anne's, and she had the nerve to hand me a brochure about the benefits of a private Catholic education, like I'm not a good Catholic because I send my kid to public school. I coulda flattened her. She actually handed me a financial aid form, the bitch. Like we can't afford private school." Bianca huffed into her coffee cup. Nobody spoke. "Well, okay," she said. "We *can't* afford it, but Sherry Dobbs is still a bitch."

Karma nudged another cinnamon roll onto her plate, her last one, she promised herself. If only she could have had Bianca's height and muscle tone. Bianca was Italian, transplanted from Pennsylvania, with deep-brown hair, dark eyes, flawless pale skin, and a tough East Coast attitude. Bianca didn't talk much about her extended family, but her confidence and style suggested a wealthy background.

The clatter of more footsteps coming up the stairs sounded from the basement. Molly, in her pink plaster cast and matching canvas sling, announced she was hungry again. Karma led her daughter to the kitchen island. She gave Molly one of Sue Ellen's fat-free muffins, then added a slice of watermelon and half a peach to her plate, and led her toward the breakfast nook, where the kids ate.

Away from the grownup conversation, Karma looked around the immaculate kitchen and felt the knot returning to her stomach. Friday playgroup was one of her favorite weekly activities, but today she felt edgy and anxious. Maybe she'd had too much coffee. Or maybe it was something else.

In a matter of days, it seemed that life in her leafy, pleasant suburb had turned from idyllic to precarious. The streets were unsafe, the neighbors were dangerous, and the police were helpless to do anything about it. She used to let Molly play outside in the backyard, checking on her now and again through the kitchen window. Now she pictured strangers grabbing Molly, shoving her into a car, and speeding off before Karma could reach the patio door. She imagined Molly chasing a ball into the street and being crushed by a car. She saw a car lose control, jump the curb, and run into Molly on her backyard play set. The scenarios were endless, and every single one would be Karma's fault for not guarding her child.

Karma set Molly's plate at the small children's table in the breakfast nook and helped her into a chair. When she returned to her own seat at the grownup table, Karma looked around the table. Her heavy sigh stopped the conversation and turned all heads in her direction.

"I agree with Sue Ellen," said Karma. "It's pissing me off that the woman who almost killed my kid is going to get away with it, and now this jackass Jack Lawrence terrorizes a pregnant woman and doesn't even spend a night in jail. We need to go over there, drag him out of his house, and beat the hell out of him."

Kim didn't miss a beat. "I'm in."

"Me, too," said Jeanette. "Jack Lawrence was rude to me just last week. Guess what he did?" When nobody attempted to guess, she continued. "I was driving past his house, and all I did was give him a little honk because he was backing out and I didn't think he saw me, and he had the nerve to give me the middle finger, just like that woman in the red car. Little Jeffrey was with me and he said, 'Look, Mommy, that man flipped you the bird.' I didn't even know he knew what that meant."

Bianca coughed into her napkin to stifle a laugh.

"He's a bad influence on Little Jeffrey," said Kim. "I say we take him down."

"While we're at it," said Karma, "let's do something about that red car."

"Let's find the red car, steal it, and run over Jack Lawrence," said Kim.

A chorus of cheers rang out.

"As long as we're taking care of business, take out Sherry Dobbs too," said Bianca. "Plus I know how to make shit like that look like an accident."

Everybody was laughing now, and Karma felt a rush of gratitude. She loved her friends and the way they could make her feel better, with just a few kind, supportive words about murder and revenge. Even Sue Ellen wasn't so bad if you overlooked the perky boobs, upturned nose, and naturally blond hair. Karma's dark mood was lifting. She was with her friends, her daughter's arm was healing, and who could hang onto a bad mood while eating Grandma Bibi's cinnamon rolls?

"Hey, Sue Ellen," said Karma, "I love your décor. I mean, you actually have a décor. I just have *stuff*. Did you do it yourself?"

Sue Ellen blushed. "Actually, we had a decorator come in. Our realtor found her for me. She's wonderful; you just tell her your budget and she does all the shopping and all the arranging. It's such *fun*. She even brought in a homosexual man who does nothing but hang pictures in the right places. Can you imagine?"

Karma couldn't. She and Kim had practically celebrated over the Target slipcovers that hid Karma's worn kitchen chairs. They were machine washable and on sale.

"I'd love to have a gay decorator," sighed Kim. "I like staying home with my girls, but I do miss having money. When we both worked, we used to go on vacations and go out to dinner any time I didn't feel like cooking. I miss that."

"Do you like Chinese food?" asked Sue Ellen. "I just love Chinese food."

As though a switch had been thrown, the table went so silent that you could hear the ticking of the big wooden clock over the sink. Jeanette sucked in her lower lip.

Oh jeez, thought Karma, *here we go*. She eyed Kim, who was wearing the look she got when people asked if her daughter was gifted in math, or if they spoke Japanese, or ate with chopsticks. Left eyebrow up, head cocked to one side, and an expression you could have called *inscrutable*, if you wanted to die.

"She's Korean," said Jeanette quietly.

"From Wisconsin," added Karma. "She was adopted."

"Oh shit, not this again," breathed Bianca.

Sue Ellen saw she had stepped in something, though she wasn't sure what. Her cheeks pinked up, and her voice got higher and faster with each syllable. "I'm sorry. I didn't mean anything, I just thought... I can't tell... I don't think... No, I've never had Korean food... Maybe I have..."

"Ask her to make her famous cheddar bratwurst kimchi," said Karma. "It's *delish*."

Bianca uncrossed her long, tan legs and threw a nasty look at Karma. "Quit making her feel bad, you buncha bitches. Sue Ellen, they did the same thing to me when I joined playgroup. Kim is Korean, adopted, and a royal pain in the ass." Bianca turned to Karma. "As for this one, don't get me started on the Jewish Princess. I'm telling you, Sue Ellen, don't you dare apologize for anything. They're just fucking with you."

"Whoa," said Kim, "I didn't say anything."

Karma put up her hands in surrender. "My people have been oppressed for six thousand years," she said. "I was just standing up for a sistah."

"Bitches," scowled Bianca. "Both of you."

"It's okay, Sue Ellen," said Karma. "It's not the Korean part that bothers Kim; it's being a Packer fan."

Kim reached across the table and patted Sue Ellen's hand. "Don't worry about my feelings, sweetie, I don't resent you because you're white, I resent you because you're gorgeous and you have more money than me."

"She's also taller," said Karma.

"Everybody's taller than Kim," said Bianca. "Although, you know what they say, '*Botte piccolo fa vino buono*.' A small cask makes good wine."

Sue Ellen's face was now a deep shade of red. "I'm just gonna shut my mouth. I'll try talking again next week."

Her new friends laughed.

"See? You're smarter than Kim, too," said Karma. "Kim never keeps her mouth shut. And you have bigger boobs."

"Everybody has bigger boobs than Kim," said Bianca. She patted Kim on the shoulder. "Sorry, babe, but even the Italians don't have anything good to say about *that*."

Kim looked down at her meager chest. "Well, I'm willing to admit that part," she said. "If I had Sue Ellen's money, those are the first things I'd buy."

Everybody laughed, even Sue Ellen. Keeping up with these women wasn't going to be easy. They must like her though, to include her in their teasing. She resolved to try to get used to it, and jump in if she could think of something to say quickly enough.

Bianca stood up from the table. She stretched out her back and went to the counter to pour herself more coffee. "Money's nice," she said, "but we're not exactly living on skid row here, ladies."

"Yeah," said Karma, "but when I was single and making my own money, I used to have somebody clean my house every week. That's what I miss the most, coming home every Wednesday to a clean house. Housekeeping is not one of my talents."

"Oh, p'shaw," said Kim. "Your stuff-things-into-grocery-bags-and-then-leave-the-bags-so-long-that-you-can-just-throw-them-away technique is a breakthrough. You should write a book."

Karma was about to make a snappy comeback, but was interrupted by an urgent *shush* from Jeanette. "Did it get quiet downstairs? Maybe I'd better check on the kids." She slid from her seat and moved quickly down the basement stairs.

Moments later she was back. "Little Jeffrey's not down there, and none of the kids know where he went. I didn't see him go past. Did anybody see him go past?"

They hadn't. Jeanette sang out, "Little Jeffrey, where are you, sweetie?" There was no answer, and she hurried out of the kitchen to look for her missing child.

"I think somebody needs to teach her the meaning of the word *sweetie*," said Kim. "It's not a word I'd use to describe that little shit." She stretched and yawned and looked at Bianca. "How come you didn't get *me* more coffee? Who else wants more coffee?"

"Me," said Karma.

Sue Ellen looked uncertainly at the other moms. They were just sitting there like nothing was wrong. Was it possible none of them were concerned about a missing child? "Shouldn't we help her?" she asked. "Do you think he could have gone outside or hurt himself?"

Kim gave a snort. "Don't worry about *him* and don't worry about *outside*. Worry about *inside*. And he never hurts *himself.*"

Sue Ellen felt a stab of dread. She had specifically told the kids to play in the basement. If that boy was upstairs in Daniel's room, which the mural artist had just finished, or climbing on her brand-new bedroom set, she didn't know what she'd do. It was an antique. Sue Ellen jumped out of her chair, raced from the kitchen, and took the steps to the second floor two at a time. It had been a few years since Sue Ellen had led the Georgia Tech cheer squad, done the splits, or turned a cartwheel, but she could still *move* when she had to.

Karma held out her coffee cup for Kim to refill. "She's kinda jumpy."

"You know, if he's upstairs messing with her stuff, she's never coming back to playgroup," said Bianca, "which would be a damn shame. She's too fucking gorgeous, but I like her."

Sue Ellen walked back into the kitchen a few minutes later, winded, but smiling. "He wasn't upstairs, thank goodness," she said. "I've got antiques up there."

The sound of the front door opening and closing again turned all heads as Jeanette returned to the kitchen. "I'm really sorry," she said to Sue Ellen, "but Little Jeffrey is in your front yard. He says all you have are girl toys, and all the kids are babies, and he's not coming back in. He's kind of, um, screaming." She looked nervous, like she thought Sue Ellen might start screaming, too.

Sue Ellen tried not to let her emotions spill onto her face. The little so-and-so was throwing a tantrum on her front lawn? What if somebody thought that he was *hers*? And Daniel did *not* have girl toys. He was a sweet, sensitive little boy, just like his daddy.

Karma yawned and ran her fingers through her hair. If only it would stay fluffed up like Sue Ellen's. "Just leave him. It's a nice day; he's getting fresh air."

Sue Ellen frowned. "Leave him outside? Somebody might take him."

"We're not gonna get that lucky," said Kim.

Jeanette looked forlorn. "Jeff wants to take him somewhere to be evaluated," she said softly, her eyes downcast. "Maybe we should. I don't know."

There was a pause as her friends absorbed this interesting bit of news. Jeanette looked so close to tears that Karma did not jump up and say, "Yes, for God's sake get him evaluated, then get a big bottle of Ritalin for him and a Prozac drip for you." Instead she reached across the table and patted Jeanette's arm. In a gentle voice, she said, "I suppose it wouldn't hurt."

"Yeah," agreed Kim, in the same offhand, yet supportive tone. "There's no harm in getting information."

Nobody else spoke. Again, the only sound was the ticking of Sue Ellen's stylishly-oversized kitchen clock.

Then Jeanette reached behind her chair for Baby Jacob's voluminous denim diaper bag. She unzipped a side compartment and pulled out a gigantic Hershey bar—the Mega Two Pounder. She squared her shoulders and set her face in grim determination. "I'll get him inside." Clutching the candy bar like a cudgel, Jeanette headed once again for the front door.

Sue Ellen's eyes were as big and round as her Havilland salad plates. "What's that candy for?"

"Well, she's not gonna hit him with it," said Kim.

"Is that how she gets him to behave?" Sue Ellen was incredulous.

"It works," said Karma. "Usually."

It worked this time. Within minutes, Little Jeffrey was sitting on the dining room floor, stuffing his face with chocolate as the other kids watched from a safe distance. They didn't bother asking him to share his bounty.

By now, it was nearly noon, and the mood in the kitchen had turned somber. Sue Ellen began putting away the uneaten food and drinks. Karma found a broom in the pantry and swept up the fruit and crumbs under the children's table, and Bianca held the dustpan for her.

Suddenly, a shriek erupted from the family room. This time all the moms jumped. They reached the family room just in time to see Little Jeffrey pull his arm out of Sue Ellen's fish tank, and hold up his catch. It was Mr. Splashy, Daniel's sunrise guppy. Little Jeffrey held it by its colorful tail, and waved it in front of Daniel, who shrieked hysterically.

"Hey, loser baby girly, I'm going to eat your fishy."

"Jeffrey, sweetie," began Jeanette.

But Little Jeffrey closed his eyes, dropped Splashy into his Hershey-rimmed mouth, and swallowed. The screams from the children were ear splitting. The shocked silence of their mothers was somehow just as loud.

Karma's stomach turned over, and she put her hand to her mouth, afraid she was about to throw up. Jeanette grabbed Little Jeffrey by the arm and dragged him toward the front door. Bianca ran in the opposite direction, to the kitchen, and returned with Baby Jacob and his diaper bag. Jeanette juggled her sons and the diaper bag and her purse, somehow never loosening her grip on Little Jeffrey, and stepped back as Bianca opened the door. Allie, thumb in mouth, stood mute, as her older brother wriggled and squirmed against his mother's grip.

"Sue Ellen, thanks so much," called Jeanette. "We had such a nice time, but we'd better go. I'll buy Daniel a new fish right away." She paused in the doorway. "Bye now!"

CHAPTER 4:   THE BIRTHDAY PARTY FROM HELL

Ironically, the next day was Little Jeffrey's 5th birthday party. Karma had volunteered to help Jeanette run the party, which was more than a friendly gesture. Not only could Karma not risk sending Molly alone, but this promised to be the mother of all suburban kids' birthday parties. Updates on Jeanette's progress had been provided each week at Friday Playgroup. She had been on her computer for months, getting ideas for games, bidding on eBay for special cake pans, and downloading graphics for the invitations, banners, and thank you notes. Inaugural balls had been staged with less fanfare.

"Oh my God," Jeanette had said weeks earlier, wringing her hands in frustration. "He said he wanted a *WrestleMania* party, so that's what I've been working on, but now he wants Pokémon. And he wants Wild Wally, which doesn't fit the theme at all, I don't know what to do. What do y'all think I should do?"

Karma was tempted to tell Jeanette what *she* would do, but it wouldn't have been a construction suggestion, and was probably illegal. Walter "Wild Wally" Grunwald was a fixture in town, having figured out how to supplement his meager county zoo salary by moonlighting as a kids' entertainer. The county looked the other way; it was cheaper than paying him a living wage. He told jokes and did rope tricks, but the highlight of his parties was the array of small animals he let the kids hold and pet.

It was party time. Holding tightly to Molly's hand, Karma let herself into Jeanette's house, and was immediately overcome by a wall of sound, coming from the finished basement.

The birthday boy had been up since dawn, whipping himself into a frenzy of birthday excitement. He was wearing a plastic jewel-encrusted wrestling belt emblazoned with "I'm Special" in sparkling gold letters, and he had made himself a matching crown out of construction paper. Karma and Molly reached the basement just in time to see him climb onto the roof of his sister Little Tyke playhouse. He had dragged his mini trampoline into position in front of it, apparently intending to jump down onto it and stage dive into the shrieking party guests. Allie was pushing and shoving her way through the mass of bigger kids, and screaming at her brother to get off her playhouse. The boys were chanting "JUMP JUMP JUMP," like spectators at a preschool suicide.

Meanwhile, Jeanette's husband, also named Jeff, oblivious to his son's impending leap, was performing delicate plastic surgery on the birthday cake, which was decorated to look like a wrestling arena, having been ordered weeks ago, but now sported a glop of yellow frosting in the center, Jeanette's attempt at a Pikachu. Someone had taken a bite out of one corner, decapitating a few sugary spectators in the process, and Jeff was trying to smear frosting around the teeth marks before his wife came downstairs and saw her masterpiece ruined.

She appeared at the top of the stairs, teetering a bit, her arms full of balloons. Unable to see her feet, she cautiously descended the basement steps. Thankfully, she couldn't see Big Jeff doctoring the cake, but between balloons, she saw his namesake on top of the playhouse roof.

"Let's not DO that, sweetie," she called.

Little Jeffrey bent into a crouch.

Panicked, Jeanette released the balloons and took the steps two at a time, smacking balloons and a few children out of her way as she tried to get to her son. She flew past Jeff, pushing him into the card table, which tipped on its flimsy legs. Jeff made a desperate grab for the cake and manage to save two handfuls, but the rest slid off and hit the floor with a soft, wet *goosh*.

"NO JUMPING," yelled Jeanette.

To be fair, it was more a plummet than a jump. Arms outstretched like a skinny flightless bird, Little Jeffrey hit the mini tramp, and landed on his little sister, who had shoved through the crowd at precisely the wrong moment.

"Oh, sweetie, are you okay?" cried Jeanette, picking up her grinning, dazed son. "Allie, stop screaming, you're not hurt."

Once the bodies were sorted out and the crying died down, it was time for party games. Kim showed up with Lindsey just in time for blindfold balloon wrestling. The noise level in the basement had risen from thunderous to deafening.

"We actually weren't late," Kim shouted into Karma's ear. "We've been upstairs. Lindsey wouldn't come down."

"She's smart," yelled Karma.

"Hey, guess what?" shouted Kim. "The cops got a call about that red car last night. They called Dave."

"Where was it?" yelled Karma.

"I don't know exactly, but it was here in the neighborhood. We still don't have a license number, but at least we know she either lives here or comes here. When we find the car, we'll either call the cops or just light the damn thing on fire, okay?"

"I'll bring the matches." Karma bent down to talk to Molly. "C'mon, baby, let's go have some more fun."

After the sack race, which Molly had to watch from the sidelines, due to her arm, the kids popped balloons with their bare feet and ate chocolate pudding out of diapers, using only their tongues.

"I've seen riots that were calmer than this," yelled Kim.

"Get me a towel," yelled Karma. Allie was stumbling toward them, crying and rubbing pudding into her streaming eyes.

Ironically, Little Jeffrey was having a worse time than his sister. He insisted on explaining the rules of each game, which would have confounded Rube Goldberg, much less a group of preschoolers who weren't listening to a word he said. Frustrated and yipping like an over-bred poodle, he was dragged away by his father, his flailing arms pinned to his side in the Loving Bear Hug that Jeff and Jeanette learned in Parenting Your High Energy Child class. Half-a-dozen party games, four pounds of chocolate cake (scraped off the floor, but the kids didn't care), two gallons of ice cream, twenty-eight juice boxes and nine temper tantrums later, the party-goers were herded outside to await the Grand Finale: the arrival of Wild Wally.

"Look, Lindsey," said Kim, prying her frightened daughter's arms from around her left thigh. "Here comes the Wally Wagon."

Little Jeffrey's party might have turned out better if Wild Wally hadn't eaten a gas station burrito the day before. His young apprentice, "Amazon Al," assured Jeanette that he had helped Wally many times and was more than equal to the task. He cheerfully unloaded two big red coolers from the brightly painted Wally Wagon. These were filled, not with ice, but with small animals in boxes and wire cages. He left one cooler near the van, and carried the other into the middle of the front yard.

"You can bring the kids now, ma'am," said Al. "The Birthday Boy can take the animals out of the cooler and pass them around while I talk about them."

"He'll love that," squealed Jeanette.

Unfortunately, the Birthday Boy's idea of "passing the animals around" was to stick them in his friends' faces and make them scream. Amazon Al finally made him stop helping and sit down. That was Al's second mistake. His first was telling Little Jeffrey that there was a *Big Surprise* in the cooler near the Wally Wagon. Al was busy handling the lizards, gerbils, and toads, and didn't notice when the scowling kid left the group and wandered over to the cooler.

By this time, the party was almost over, and parents were drifting in to watch the end of the festivities and claim their children. Amazon Al trotted over to the second cooler and called out, "Hey, Birthday Boy, it's time for your Big Surprise. Moms, you'll want your cameras for this."

How right he was. When he opened the cooler, all color drained from Amazon Al's face. The cooler was empty.

Karma and Kim would later disagree over who screamed first and loudest, but it didn't matter. When the Big Surprise slithered through the grass and over her pink patent leather shoes, Allie let out a shriek and wet herself. Molly jumped into Karma's arms so forcefully they both fell over into the grass, and Karma could only watch in mute horror as the 12-foot albino boa constrictor glided silently by, its yellowish scales just inches from her face. Children stampeded in all directions. Jeanette grabbed her dripping daughter and made a break for the house. Amazon Al dove for the snake, but accidentally tackled Little Jeffrey. At least he *said* it was an accident.

In the end, Little Jeffrey's 5th birthday party became legend, with dozens of people who weren't even there telling the tale, claiming to have personally experienced the whole thing, like Woodstock.

Losing the gigantic reptile cost Amazon Al his job, but motivated him to finish college and pursue a successful career in accounting. And the reports of missing neighborhood dogs and cats in the months that followed may have been exaggerated.

CHAPTER 5: MRS. KRANSKI,
IN THE DRIVEWAY, WITH A PIE SERVER

When the red car that hit Molly Kranski was finally located, four men shared the credit. Three were long dead: Earl Tupper and the Gallo Brothers, Ernest and Julio. The fourth, the bank manager who had laid off Cathy McGreevy's husband, was alive, but never learned of his role in the discovery.

Cathy liked to spend money, but with her husband out of a job, there wasn't any to spare, so she was hosting home parties of all descriptions to earn the things she could no longer buy. She had collected hostess gifts of silver jewelry, skin cream, candles, children's books, and lingerie. Now she wanted a Tupperware Microwave Stack Cooker, which would cook three courses in just minutes, almost as much as she wanted her husband to get off the damn couch and get a damn job.

Cathy's friends rolled their eyes with each new party invitation, but they understood her situation. Besides, snacks and wine and an evening away from their husbands and kids held a powerful allure.

So on that fateful night, Karma, Kim, Bianca, and the other guests happily filled out their nametags, ate, drank, and talked about those who hadn't shown up. Cathy's house was the same model as Karma's, though flipped 180 degrees and decorated more tastefully.

Following the snacks, the guests dutifully took their places in borrowed chairs assembled around the kitchen island, and listened to the Tupperware Lady's opening story of how she had come to sell Tupperware, and how it had changed her life, solved her family's financial problems, and made her a better wife and mother. Guests were supposed to have the Home Sales Epiphany: *Oh my God, that's what's missing in my life--extra money, control over my work schedule, and the chance to meet wonderful women and earn FREE PRODUCTS. Sign me up!*

Karma was able to resist the pitch. In her twenties, she'd sold vitamins, hair care, skin care, makeup, and Amway. Several cousins on her father's side still wouldn't take her phone calls.

"Okay, everybody," chirped the Tupperware Lady, "do we all know what these are?" She waved a stack of small green rectangular papers in the air. It was GO time.

Kim's voice rang out. "Are they Tupperbucks? And do I get one for asking? And another one for asking about asking?" Laughter rang out.

"That's right... Kim," said the Tupperware Lady, squinting at Kim's nametag, "and each time you ask a question..."

"Can it be a question about your products?" asked Kim. "And can I ask about your home-based business?" Kim held out her hand. "You owe me five so far."

Karma leaned in close. "Pace yourself, champ." But Kim continued to pepper the Tupperware Lady with questions. The person who had the most Tupperbucks at the end of the evening would win a prize, and Kim liked to win. A few newcomers tried to mix it up with her, but you don't send in schoolgirls to spar with Mohammed Ali.

Just when Kim was hitting her stride *(What's the best use for the giant batter bowl? Can you order extra lids? What colors do they come in?),* a slim, manicured hand shot up in the air, and a new voice sang out, "What's a good way to recruit new sales associates? Is there another good method? Can you think of *one more* method?" Every head in the dining room turned.

51

It was Sherry Dobbs (the bitch) and every question she asked became three, thanks to her *what's another and another approach*. It was diabolical. Flustered, Kim countered with questions about new decorator colors, the children's snack trays, and, in sheer desperation, a question about the burping technique. This drew a loud snort from Sherry Dobbs. Every woman in North America born after 1949 knew that one.

Sherry and Kim exchanged fire, shooting questions at the Tupperware Lady faster than she could answer, but they weren't looking for answers. Cathy handed out the play money and the Tupperware Lady kept a smile plastered on her face and silently reminded herself that she *loved* her Tupperware business and that it would be *wrong* to walk out on this stupid party and find a bar to get drunk in. Within a few minutes she ran out of Tupper Bucks. She silently thanked Jesus, and announced that it was time to count the money and award the evening's big prize.

You could have cut the tension with tonight's gift, a carbon steel pie server with a mauve flowered ceramic handle and a serrated edge. Cathy counted twice, just to be sure, but the results were clear. Sixty-two to fifty-nine in Kim's favor. Sherry Dobbs (the bitch) had jumped in a little too late. There were hoots and cheers from Kim's corner, and polite, if unenthusiastic, applause from Sherry's. Kim happily claimed her prize as the Tupperware Lady recited the description:

> The New and Improved Carbon Steel Pie Server lends style and sophistication to any kitchen décor. A practical, multi-purpose tool for the 21st Century Domestic Engineer, the blade can cut through the toughest shoe leather and ceramic tile, yet is gentle enough to slice the flakiest pie crust without leaving crumbs.

"*Lei è una donna fortunata*," said Bianca, shaking her head, but smiling.

"It ain't luck," said Kim. "It's pure skill."

"It doesn't match your kitchen," said Jeanette.

"Who cares," said Bianca. "She beat Sherry Dobbs."

After more glasses of wine, Karma, Kim, Bianca, and Jeanette placed orders for Tupperware and headed home. They were on foot, and took the long way around the neighborhood to exercise off some calories and sober up in the cool evening air. It was nearly 11 p.m., and the neighborhood was quiet, save for the tapping of their shoes on the sidewalk.

After just half a block, Karma slipped off her suede boots and rubbed her painful toes. It felt good to walk in socks and she didn't care if they got ruined. "Do you think Cathy sold enough to get the Stack Cooker?"

"I hope so," said Jeanette. "Jeff will shoot me when he finds out what I spent. I told him I was just coming to be polite, but poor Cathy, I just had to buy something."

"You can't have enough Tupperware," said Kim, admiring her pie server.

They had just turned onto a side street when Karma stopped short, nearly tripping Kim.

"Look." Karma pointed down the street. Parked in front of a beige house (what else), in the bright pool of a street light, was *the Red Car*.

"Is that it? Are you sure?" whispered Jeanette.

"I'm sure," said Karma. "I'm absolutely sure."

"Hooray," whispered Jeanette.

"*Santa merda*," breathed Bianca. "We got her."

"I'll take a picture of the plate number and then we can call the cops," said Kim. "Karma, hold this." She handed the pie server to Karma and dug her cell phone out of her floppy canvas bag.

Karma looked up and down the street, then at the house. The lights were off. If the occupants were inside, they were asleep. Then she looked down at the pie server in her hand.

"I'll be right back," she said, striding down the sidewalk toward the car. Kim and Bianca looked at each other in wine-soaked confusion. Then they ran to catch up with Karma, followed by Jeanette.

Karma stopped a few feet in front of the red car. She held the pie server by its decorative handle like a dagger.

"Oh my God," breathed Kim. "Karma, what the hell—"

Karma didn't hear. She stabbed the tool into the left front tire. The carbon steel blade didn't penetrate very far, but the tires were old and bald, so it was far enough. Karma had to use both hands to wrench the weapon back out, but the satisfying hiss of escaping air was reward enough for her efforts. She proceeded to walk around the little red car, destroying one tire after another. In short order, the car was resting on its rusty, mismatched rims. The only sounds now were crickets and a faraway barking dog.

Karma stepped back to survey her work. *Perfection.* Practically skipping with excitement, she returned to her friends. "Well, that was fun. That piece of crap car won't be running over anybody for a while." She stopped, noticing the expressions on the faces staring back at her. "You're not mad that I didn't let you help, are you? It was Molly who got hit, so I just figured..."

What was the matter with everybody?

Karma held out the pie server to Kim, but then pulled it back. "Oh, I'm so stupid," she said, understanding dawning on her face. "You want me to wash this first. You're right, it might have rubber on it. I'll get you a new one." She brightened. "That'll be another order for Cathy. Won't that be a win/win?" Karma grinned at Kim, but Kim just stared back, opened-mouthed.

"Oh, I'm being terrible," said Karma. "You keep this one until I replace it." She thrust the pie server at Kim, who jumped back in alarm.

Bianca stepped forward, gently took the deadly weapon from Karma, and slipped it into her own purse, which she zipped, latched, and flung over the shoulder farthest from Karma faster than a street magician hiding a rabbit. "I got shit at home'll take the rubber right off," she said. "Ok, Kimmy? Sure. No problem." Bianca looked at her wristwatch. "Hey, look at the time, we'd better get our asses home before they send out the dogs to find us." She strode forward with long strides, the sheer force of her will making the others follow.

"What a great night," puffed Karma, bringing up the rear. "Can you believe it?"

Bianca, Jeanette, and Kim said nothing. They could not believe it. Not any of it.

CHAPTER 6: GUILT AND COOKIES

Reality set in around 2 a.m. Sam was gently snoring, but Karma was pretty sure she would never sleep again. When the wine buzz wore off, it had taken Karma's giddy elation with it, and the vacuum left behind had quickly filled with fear and dread. *I vandalized a car. What if somebody saw me? What if somebody says something? What if that wasn't the right car? I'm going to get arrested. I'm going to be humiliated. I'm going to lose everything.*

The ceiling fan spun slowly around and around, and she wished she had a sleeping pill. A little television might have cleared her head, but it would wake up Sam, and then he'd ask her what was wrong and she'd have to lie to him and he would know she was lying and make her tell the truth. He wouldn't understand.

What would Sam do if he found out what she'd done? The woman who had hit Molly could claim it was an accident, but Karma had vandalized the red car on purpose. And not just on purpose. Everybody knew she had been searching for the red car. What would they charge her with? Premeditated vandalism? Premeditated criminal mischief?

How could she explain the feeling that had come over her when she saw that car? It was about Molly almost getting killed. But the woman's legal team—of course she'd have a legal team—would say that Karma was a sociopath who sought revenge for a simple broken arm and took the law into her own hands, when she was at fault for letting her kid play so close to the street. She had destroyed property instead of calling the cops. Why hadn't she just called the cops?

Karma's lawyer, assuming she could afford one, would say she was protecting her neighborhood from a maniac speeder, and that she was justified in stopping the woman from hitting anybody else.

But she hadn't even done that, she now realized. Calling the cops would have brought the woman to justice, whereas Karma had only forced her to buy new tires. She'd be driving again in just a day or two, which would demonstrate that Karma had accomplished nothing except a stupid act of vengeful vandalism. Even if she didn't go to jail, it would cost a fortune, which would make Sam angrier than the fact that she'd committed a crime. They'd have to borrow the money from one of their parents, and the humiliation would drive a wedge between them that their marriage would never survive.

There would be no sleep for her tonight. She might as well get up and do something productive. Would finishing off the Double Stuff Oreos in the kitchen be considered productive?

She inched toward the edge of the bed, listening for any telltale changes in Sam's breathing. It took time, but she was able to slide out from under the covers and slip off the bed without disturbing him. Spike the cat watched from his customary spot at Sam's feet, then stood, stretched his feline body, and followed Karma down the hall, hoping for a snack. Karma was happy for the company, and filled his bowl with kibble.

The decision came to her halfway through her fifth Oreo, at the kitchen table. It was a good place to think, with only the dim light over the stove and the quiet hum of the refrigerator to set the mood. And so she made up her mind: she would not tell Sam what she had done. It would be unfair to burden him with knowledge of her crime because there was absolutely nothing he could do about it. Being a guy, he'd want to fix it, maybe buy the woman a new set of tires, and she'd probably call the cops anyway, because she was just that kind of thoughtless, psychotic maniac who could run over a baby and drive away. Confessing the truth to Sam would be worse than lying, because it would upset her abnormally honest husband, thus putting their marriage at even more risk. Karma was a child of divorce, thanks to her self-centered mother and cheating father, and she told herself that she would never put her own kid through that. For Molly's sake, she had an obligation to keep this secret from Sam for the rest of their lives. It was the selfless thing to do. It was also a big steaming pile of rationalization, but that didn't necessarily make it wrong, right?

When the last Oreo was gone, Karma cleaned up the crumbs and stuffed the empty package deep into the trash where no one would notice it, a habit from a childhood spent sneaking treats and covering her tracks.

Karma slept badly all week. The logic of her decision to hide the truth from her husband seemed to unravel every night as she lay in bed, forcing her to knit it back together again as she lay awake. Maybe, she thought on the third sleepless night, she should get legal advice about her messy situation. If she paid a lawyer, her secret would be safe because of attorney-client privilege. But she couldn't figure out how to pay for a lawyer without Sam noticing.

She discussed her misgivings with Kim, Bianca, and Jeanette at least twice a day, each, and they were probably getting tired of telling her the same reassuring things. How many times could they repeat, "Try to relax," and "None of us are going to tell anybody," and "Wow, you are a nutcase." She was certainly tired of hearing the last one.

Karma thought about calling the *Dr. Laura Show* and confessing her sins. She'd listened for years and she knew the phone number. Maybe she'd feel better if she got it off her chest. Yet when she played that scenario in her imagination, it never went well.

> **Karma:** Hi, Dr. Laura, my name is...um... Sharma, and I'm a really good person, a good wife and a stay-at-home mom, but I vandalized a car. Should I tell my husband?
>
> **Dr. Laura:** You did *what*?
>
> **Karma:** Well, it hit my daughter a few weeks ago and broke her arm in two places, and the woman driving it gave me the finger and didn't even stop, so I slashed her tires.
>
> **Dr. Laura:** So she broke the law and then you broke the law? You are no better than she is, *Sharma*, if that's your real name. Good people don't do bad things. You must turn yourself in to the police immediately. Prison will teach you a lesson.
>
> **Karma:** But what about my daughter?
>
> **Dr. Laura:** She deserves a better mother than you. Divorce your husband and let him find someone with better character.
>
> **Karma:** But—
>
> **Dr. Laura:** Do the right thing. And never call me again. You are a disgrace.

Karma wished she had another packages of Oreo. It was too bad you couldn't buy carbon credits for bad behavior. Karma would have replanted the rainforest, or emptied her 401k into the Lindsey Lohan Rehab Endowment if she could have earned a do-over for that crazy stupid night. Why hadn't she considered the consequences? Why hadn't she simply called the police like a normal person?

Every time the phone rang, her heart raced and her palms got sweaty. *Was it the cops?* Jeanette didn't help matters by assuring her that they wouldn't call first. They'd stake out the house and arrest her without warning, since she had a passport and was a flight risk.

But what if the cops *did* call the house? What if she was in the bathroom and Sam answered the phone? What if a certified letter to appear in court came in the mail? What if the cops picked her up at Molly's preschool? What if they tracked her down in the grocery store and handcuffed her right in frozen foods? Every person she knew would be at Kroger that day, including Sherry Dobbs, when they snapped the cuffs on her.

There weren't enough Oreos on the planet to get through this.

CHAPTER 7:   THE GAME IS AFOOT

Yet some aspects of life had to proceed as usual, like cooking meals, running errands, being late to pick up Molly at preschool, doing laundry, and, of course, attending Friday playgroup. This week it was scheduled to take place at Karma's house, though everybody, even Jeanette, had offered to take her spot.

No, Karma decided, it was time to get back to normal. She had made up her mind not to talk about the red car, not to discuss her worries about being arrested, and not to complain about her inability to sleep. She was driving her friends crazy, and it wasn't helping. No, starting today Karma Kranski would be a good friend, and be interested in what everybody *else* was up to. She would be cheerful and positive and uplifting. She would not burden her friends. Not ever again.

With renewed purpose that Friday morning, Karma looked around her kitchen. The counters were clean and tidy, the snacks were arranged neatly, she had put on powder foundation, mascara and blush, and her hair looked good. This would be the first day of the rest of her life.

Bianca and her girls were the first to arrive.

"Hello, ladies," said Karma, greeting her guests with a cheerful smile at the front door. "Molly is dressing herself this morning, so she'll be down in the next couple of hours. The good news is, you girls can play with all her toys and she won't even know it."

Caitlin and Ginny skipped off to dump out Molly's toy box, and Karma and Bianca headed for the kitchen.

Bianca helped herself to coffee and sat down in a kitchen chair. "Hey, did you hear Sherry Dobbs is pregnant again? This will make five. Can you imagine?"

"No, I can't," said Karma. But then she remembered her promise to be nothing but positive today. "It's very nice. I'm happy for them. It's a blessing."

Bianca squinted at Karma. "It's early to be drinking."

Karma sighed. Being positive wasn't going to be easy. Oh, what the hell, there was no point in trying to be positive about Sherry Dobbs.

"Okay," said Karma, "I can't imagine *me* having five kids. I'd forget their names. I'd lose them at the mall. And Sherry Dobbs has spread her bitchy DNA too far already."

Bianca nodded her approval. "Okay, now you deserve a drink."

Karma laughed. "I'll settle for coffee. Can I get you some?"

She could.

Actually, Karma had wished for a big family at one time. She had grown up jealous of kids with brothers and sisters they could play with. She had wanted at least one brother or sister she could actually talk to, and had resolved to marry and raise a house full of children. Her imaginary family had combined the best that wishful thinking and prime-time television had to offer: a warm, nurturing, kosher combination of the Waltons, the Brady Bunch, and the Flintstones.

Then came a relatively late marriage to Sam and the discovery that Karma's old, unrefrigerated eggs were barely functional. It had taken a fair amount of medical trial and error to conceive Molly, including several rounds of painful shots in parts of her body Karen preferred not to think about.

She and Sam had been hoping for another child without all the fuss and co-pays and deductibles, but it hadn't happened.

So before her biological clock ran completely out of juice, Karma and Sam had made an appointment with a new fertility doctor. She hadn't shared this with her girlfriends. Now would be the perfect time to tell Bianca, but she couldn't bring herself to do it.

When friends heard you were trying to get pregnant, they asked what methods you were trying, and they just *had* to share what had worked for them and their sisters, cousins, and hair dressers. When they ran into you at the grocery store they snuck peeks at your belly to see if you were withholding the *Good News*, and when they found out you had no good news, they casually asked whether you'd thought about adoption. The nicer friends didn't say what they really meant, that you were insane at your age to try to get pregnant, and you'd better have a back-up plan. Like maybe a nice kitten.

Karma didn't have a back-up plan, didn't want a back-up plan, and definitely didn't have any desire to talk about shots in the belly, shots in the butt, mood swings, false hopes, dashed hopes, and disappointments. If frustration were the cure for infertility, she'd have already had quadruplets.

Bianca poured coffee creamer into both cups. "Half the women in this f'ing neighborhood are continuously pregnant and the other half are treating infertility," she said. "Me, I make Tony sleep on the couch when I'm fertile. I'm not takin' chances with his goddamn Olympic swimmers."

Karma felt a flush rising into her face, but fortunately, the doorbell rang. She jumped up to open the door, even though she knew it was probably Kim, who only rang the bell for show, and inevitably walked in without waiting for an invitation. She was right. Kim had already dropped her gigantic purse in the corner and was helping Lindsey unzip her jacket by the time Karma got to the entryway. Lindsey, sans jacket, ran through Karma's kitchen, grabbed a juice box and skipped off to join the other girls.

Kim followed Karma back to the kitchen and took her customary spot at the table, one that put her back to the morning sun. She was working on reducing the squint line between her eyes. Dave had pretended not to hear when she suggested that Botox would make a nice Mothers' Day gift. Sue Ellen and Daniel arrived a few minutes after Kim. As always, Sue Ellen and Daniel, well-dressed and immaculately groomed, looked like they'd just stepped out of *Country Living*.

Moments later, Jeanette and her barely-human brood came bursting through the door. Little Jeffrey was muttering to himself, Baby Jacob was whining, and Allie's nose was running like a garden hose. Karma took the pan of ready-to-be-baked cinnamon rolls from Jeanette, who bounded into the kitchen, practically twitching with excitement at what she hoped would be the morning's fresh hot gossip.

"Did you hear about Sherry Dobbs?"

"Baby Number Five?" asked Karma. "Heard it."

"Yesterday," added Kim.

"Darn it all," said Jeanette. She strapped Baby Jacob into his booster seat and pulled him up to the table beside her. "I *knew* I shouldn't have waited for playgroup. Next time I'm tweetin' y'all. Well, did you hear that her husband isn't happy about it?"

"No," said Bianca. "But I'm not surprised. Maybe he should quit boinking his wife. The bitch."

Kim scooped a handful of taco chips onto her plate. "Did you actually say *boinking*?"

"There's more," said Jeanette. "Sherry says she's putting this one in daycare and going back to work because they can't afford to keep the other kids in private school if she doesn't. Her husband says all his kids are gonna have a private Catholic education, no matter what."

Bianca scowled. "I should give Sherry back the financial aid application she gave me. The bitch."

"I heard it a little different," said Kim. "I heard Sherry *wants* to go back to work. She told Jenny who told Tammy who told Donna who told me that she wants to get back to work before nobody wants her anymore."

Bianca rose from her seat and headed for the coffee pot. "Nobody wants her *now*. She's just too dumb to realize it."

"Speaking of bitches, pardon my French," said Jeanette, "Guess what? I saw that red car yesterday, driving around bold as anything. Karma, you need to call the cops and make them arrest that woman."

"That wasn't French and she can't call the cops, remember?" said Kim. "The cops will find out she vandalized the car and they'll end up sharing a cell. The only good part is that the woman can't get Karma for vandalism because then *she'd* get caught for the hit and run. It's a stalemate."

Jeanette looked thoughtfully into her coffee mug. "I've been thinking about that. I think Karma should claim temporary insanity. Or diminished capacity, or maybe she can say she was on her period. At least the woman is driving slower now. She even used her turn signal, which is something my own husband won't do, and he used to teach driver's education."

Karma played with a little pile of salt that had spilled in front of her plate. She pushed it with her fingertip into a square, a triangle, then a circle. *The woman is driving slower. What does that mean?*

The conversation going around the table faded to dull white noise. *Does it mean she knows why I slashed her tires? Did she guess it was someone who saw her hit Molly? Would she tell the police? No, Kim is right. She can't use the legal system any more than I can. But what if she goes outside the legal system? It wouldn't take a genius to figure out that the mother or father of*

65

the kid she hit probably slashed her tires. Everybody knows what had happened, and where we live. She could try to break into the house, maybe burn it down, or vandalize our cars. If it were me, I'd figure it out. She's probably just coming after me, not Sam. He's a guy, and he would have stolen the distributor cap or cut the brake cables or something. I couldn't find brake cables with a map. She could attack me tonight, and I don't even have the pie server to protect myself with.

Karma had to stop the insane train of thought; it was making her heart race. There were positive possibilities, weren't there? Why should she assume the worst? If the woman was driving slower and using her turn signals, maybe she had learned her lesson? Had something good had come from all this? And like the magical moment when you're driving through a blinding rainstorm and suddenly emerge into sunshine, Karma's fear and guilt lifted.

The woman who hit Molly is driving safely because she knows that we know who she is. She knows she's being watched, and that she'll be punished again if she steps out of line. It's like when I let Molly know that there are consequences for bad behavior. That's good parenting. That woman is driving safely because I acted like a good parent. I'm not a vandal; I'm a good parent.

But Karma's optimism faded fast. Like last year's yoga pants, rationalizations can only stretch so far, and this one was bursting at the seams. Too many people knew what she had done. If this were a *Movie of the Week*, she'd have to kill the playgroup moms, one by one, to keep the secret from getting out. Karma looked around the table. *Would I kill Bianca, the tough, fearless one first? Or start with Jeanette, the dumb one who can't keep a secret? Or would the dumb one turn out to be the smart one? I could recruit Kim to make the murders look like accidents, but when it was Kim's turn to die, it would turn out that she was an undercover FBI informant or planned to kill me and collect the reward money. Probably both. I am losing my mind.*

Karma pushed back from the table to get another cookie from the kitchen island, trying to refocus on the conversation, but it was no use.

"Not to change the subject," she said, "but do you think maybe I did the neighborhood some good? Like if the red car has stopped speeding like Jeanette said, that's a good thing, right?"

Kim shrugged. "You may be right, but it doesn't matter, if you get caught. I don't think anybody would buy that you cut up her tires to save lives. I mean, you were mostly pissed off."

"And drunk," said Bianca.

"But see, *maybe* she was drunk enough to claim diminished capacity," said Jeanette. "It might be a good idea to join AA, just in case."

Karma was disappointed to realize how little she actually liked her best friends. She grabbed another cookie. "Okay, I'm not Mother Teresa."

"No shit," said Bianca.

"Don't be worried about us, though," said Jeanette. "We can't tell on you because we're accessories after the fact."

"Jeanette," said Kim. "You watch too much TV."

"Well, we *are*," said Jeanette with an indignant sniff. "Google it, if you don't believe me."

"What should I Google?" asked Kim. "Practicing law without a license?"

Before Jeanette could answer, Sue Ellen's little Daniel ran into the kitchen, and Sue Ellen coughed and widened her eyes cartoonishly. Her meaning was clear to the other moms; Daniel was at that magical age when children repeat everything they heard, especially the bad stuff.

Bianca smoothly changed the subject. "Hey, Kim," she said, "is Dave going to run for the homeowners' board again?"

"I hope so," cried Sue Ellen with excessive enthusiasm. "I love his emails. He's so funny."

Kim looked modestly down at her plate. "You know my husband; he's a funny guy."

Karma was grinning. Dave Wallace was the president of the Bedford Commons Homeowners' Association, but Kim was his secret weapon, the eyes and ears behind that tiny throne. Kim told him whose kids were on the radar of the police department, and who was behind on child support payments and therefore likely not to pay next quarter's HOA dues. Between collecting the gossip that informed his decisions, she also composed the snappy, sarcastic emails he sent out to nag people who let their dogs poop in other people's yards or played music too loud on the weekends.

Sometimes Kim and Karma collaborated on these missives. When that jackass on Magnolia Circle installed cheap plastic fence posts and chicken wire to keep in his dumb dogs, Kim and Karma had coauthored a message with just the right balance of menace and sarcasm, and the fence had come down within the week. They had written the email warning a neighbor near the pool to stop letting her dog take swims when she thought nobody was watching. Dave Walters, HOA president, was one of those easy-going guys that everybody likes, which got him elected, but when it was time to be Dave the Enforcer, he valued Kim's sharp tongue and vengeful style on the computer. She, in turn, let Karma assist, with the understanding that they never talk about it, lest people think less of Dave.

Sue Ellen's son left the kitchen with a bowl of fruit, but just as the conversation was about to resume, Kim's cell ringtone sang out.

For no reason she could discern, an ominous chill run through Karma. She felt like a guilty kid who realizes that the ringing phone is the principal calling to speak to her parents. And then Kim gave her a better reason to be uneasy. Cell phone held to her ear, Kim's brow furrowed and she turned to stare at Karma. Karma's heart leapt into her throat; the call had something to do with *her*. Kim was mostly listening, rather than speaking, but she was definitely making serious faces in Karma's direction. Karma's stomach did a forward handspring and vaulted straight up into her throat, right next to her thumping heart. *They're coming for me.*

Karma wasn't the only one who picked up on the gravity of the call. The kitchen was silent. Bianca put down her coffee, Sue Ellen sucked in her lower lip, and Jeanette froze, a spoonful of Baby Jacob's strained carrots in mid-air, just out of range of his toothless, drooling mouth.

"I can't believe it. I just can't believe it. Well, thanks for letting me know," said Kim. She ended the call and stared down at her cell phone, not speaking, just shaking her head.

Karma sat back in her chair and stared at Kim, waited for the bomb that would end her peaceful existence in Bedford Commons. *Somebody saw, everybody knows, the cops are coming, my life is over. Somebody saw. Somebody saw.*

"Well," said Kim gravely, finally looking up at Karma. "I have news."

Karma closed her eyes and banged her forehead down on the table. "Oh shit," she breathed.

Kim gave a loud snort. "Relax, killer, it has nothing to do with you. I was just messing with your head. You should see your face, by the way. I didn't know skin could actually turn gray. I mean, you read that in books, but I've never seen it before."

Karma raised her head off the table.

"That was Chris," said Kim, "who lives down the street from Joan Handley. She heard something juicy about Jack Lawrence and she knew I'd want to know. He and his wife got in a big fight last night. Obviously after you left. Apparently, he was getting ready for another round of fireworks, and she came outside and started yelling at him to stop bothering everybody, and they got louder and louder, and somebody called the cops."

Karma sat up in her chair. Only the high quality of this gossip could have pushed aside the impulse to kill Kim and dismember her body.

"Chris swears it wasn't her who called the cops," said Kim, "so I bet it was Joan Handley. Anyway, they showed up and he got off with a warning, but he told the cops—and I'm quoting here—he doesn't care what his damn wife or the damn neighbors think. He said he's gonna light his damn fireworks any damn time he damn well wants to."

Bianca got up to fill coffee cups. "What a *damn* asshole," she said. "Why didn't they just arrest him? Or shoot him?"

Kim shrugged, holding out her cup. "I guess they couldn't, since they stopped him before he broke any laws."

"Sounds like a domestic disturbance to me," said Jeanette. "Or disturbing the peace."

"I can't believe he keeps getting away with shit like that," said Kim. "We should get Karma drunk again and send her to his house to steal his fireworks."

Karma made a rude gesture. "You should do standup comedy. My entire life just flashed before my eyes, and you're making jokes. Pass the caramel sauce." Karma dipped an apple wedge and shoved it into her mouth. "God, Kim, you're such an old bag," she said, although it came out more like, "Gaaa Kih you sush a ol' baaag."

"Oh, come on," said Kim. "We make a great team. You commit the crimes and the rest of us watch. Besides, you just said you did the neighborhood a favor, so do another one."

Sue Ellen giggled.

Kim wasn't finished. "No, really. I think the chick in the red car learned a lesson when she found her tires slashed all to hell, I really do. It's not a coincidence that she's driving slower. So maybe Jack Lawrence needs a lesson in manners, too."

Jeanette smiled. "Wouldn't that be something."

Karma looked into her coffee cup. It was odd to hear her own thoughts coming out of Kim's mouth, but even so, the idea was ridiculous. "I think you need a hobby."

A chorus of high-pitched screams erupted from the basement. It was impossible to tell which kids were screaming, so everybody jumped up from the table and headed toward the commotion. Except Karma. She started to get up, but then sat back down; it was almost certainly an issue with Little Jeffrey, and she didn't feel like dealing with him today. She didn't feel like dealing with *anybody*. Molly was good at staying clear of him, and if not, somebody would let her know. She wanted to be alone for a few minutes.

She sat quietly, hands wrapped around her coffee cup, breathing in the sweet steam. She could hear the muffled sound of Jeanette whining at Little Jeffrey, but she didn't care enough to really listen—probably the same reaction he was having. Her eyes were drawn to the valance over her kitchen sink, cream and beige with green leaves. She still liked the pattern and the colors, although it probably should be washed someday. She'd had it made by a neighbor who did alterations and sewing, back when this house and homeownership itself were new and exciting. Back then, Bedford Commons had seemed like paradise, and the house a mansion compared to their tiny downtown rental apartment with its thin walls and sketchy neighbors.

71

So what was happening in paradise? The jerks and the crazies were taking over, that's what was happening, and sarcastic emails from the HOA president weren't going to stop it. The streets weren't safe, pregnant women were being attacked with fireworks, and nobody was doing anything about it, not even the cops. Kim was making her usual stupid jokes, but Karma wasn't finding any of it funny.

She rose and started cleaning up the food, plates, cups, and napkins the kids had left. The worst part about hosting playgroup was the mess left behind when it was over, after you'd worked so hard to impress your friends. Why couldn't clean things stay clean? Of course, she knew the answer. She had barely passed high school chemistry and she didn't know her emulsions from her elbows, but one concept had stuck with her: the Second Law of Thermodynamics. Even in high school, she had related to the idea that order inevitably deteriorates into disorder. Ice cubes melt, metal rusts, bodies age and decay, tidy closets devolve into disarray, and clean kitchens turn to crap.

And so, it seemed, do neighborhoods.

Karma scooped the uneaten food from the kids' table into the trash can. But couldn't you stop the steady slide into chaos, at least for a while, by *doing something*, by adding energy into the system? Couldn't you defeat the encroaching entropy of life by fighting back? That's what she was doing here at the kids' table, expending energy to reduce chaos and restore order. That's what Dave did when he enforced the homeowners' association rules; he was preventing entropy from ruining the neighborhood. Life was a science experiment.

And then Truth (with a capital T) lit up Karma's consciousness. *Kim's joke wasn't a joke.* If people in the system—the Bedford Commons system—sat by and let bad things happen, the bad things would just keep happening until utter chaos took over. People had seen that red car screaming around the neighborhood for weeks, but nobody had called the cops until Molly was hit. A millimeter difference, and she could have died. She could have hit her head and suffered brain damage. Karma had put a stop to it through mental and physical action, by expending energy and using a rudimentary tool (with a nicely decorated handle, thanks to Tupperware). She had administered a big dose of entropy to the tires of the red car, but the system as a whole had been improved.

Life is a science experiment, part physical science and part social science. I blew my chance to have the woman who almost killed my child arrested, but I solved the problem and that is what matters. I did that.

Karma washed the crumbs off her hands and dried them on a kitchen towel. The kids' table was clean now, another small battle won in the never-ending war on domestic decay.

Her thoughts turned to Jack Lawrence. *Maybe I can do something about him, too; I don't have to let him ruin this neighborhood. It's just a matter of the right strategy and appropriate action.*

Strategy and action. Action and strategy.

And in that moment, leaning against the simulated granite top of her suburban kitchen island, Karma felt the exhilaration that Marie Curie must have felt when she discovered radioactivity or radio waves, or whatever it was. Or Jane Goodall, when she revealed the secrets of gorilla society. A high-pitched scream rose from the basement. It occurred to Karma that Ms. Goodall could have saved herself a trip to Africa and helped a lot of mothers if she'd studied the secrets of preschool society.

She cut herself another slab of cinnamon roll, and thought about her next move, waiting for the sound of footsteps on the wooden basement steps. She didn't have to wait long.

73

Jeanette was the first one to poke her head around the door. "Sorry about your DVD player," she said. "Little Jeffrey says it was an accident."

Kim was at Jeanette's heels. "If you want, I'll have Dave take a look at the drywall. He's patched bigger holes than that."

Sue Ellen looked pale and chewed nervously on her lower lip, but said nothing.

Bianca was the last mom to return to the kitchen. "You might want to have a little wine before you go down there. Maybe a lot of wine. On the bright side, the kids are all still alive and no blood got on the carpet."

Karma nodded. Whatever had to be done, it could wait until Sam got home. She had more important matters on her mind than her basement. She waited until everyone was seated at the kitchen table, cups and plates replenished. She wanted to explain this in just the right way, her new Theory of Neighborhood Entropy, but decided to skip the theoretical and get straight to the point. "I've been thinking. Jack Lawrence is going to assume that Joan Handley called the cops on him last night. He's going to go after her."

"Probably," said Kim.

"Somebody else could have called," said Jeanette. "The whole street heard him fighting with his wife."

Karma shook her head dismissively. "It doesn't matter who called. He'll *think* it was Joan and he'll try to get back at her. The problem with the police is that they can't do anything until he commits a crime, and then it's too late."

Kim's deep brown eyes were dark twinkling slits. "Are you suggesting a preemptive strike? Get Jack before Jack gets Joan?"

"I am," said Karma. "The key is prevention—stop him before he has a chance to do something worse than he's already done. The police can't do anything, but we can."

There was a long silence. Jeanette looked wary. Sue Ellen looked horrified. Bianca's expression was unreadable.

Kim looked downright gleeful. As a child in Wisconsin, her adoptive Tiger Mom wannabe had sent her to chess camp every summer, and Kim was already three moves ahead of the rest of the group. "We can," she said. "Definitely."

Sue Ellen put down her orange slice and looked around the table in utter astonishment. "*We* can do something? *We?*"

"Of course," said Karma. "Who better than us?"

Sue Ellen tugged on the collar of her pale yellow polo shirt and looked around the kitchen table again, studying the faces of her new friends. Nobody was laughing. They were acting like this conversation was perfectly normal, which was, of course, completely crazy. "Are y'all serious?" she asked. "Karma, are you kidding about this? I think you're kidding. I hope you're kidding."

"I'm not kidding," said Karma. "My daughter was almost killed because people ignored a chronic speeder, and I'm not going to stand around and wait for the next kid or pregnant woman to get hurt." All eyes were on her. "Look at us. We're smart, we're strong, and we're home all day. We know everything that goes on around here. We're just the right people to handle things like this. We'll be doing the neighborhood a favor, and nobody has to know."

Bianca tapped a long, manicured nail on the edge of the table. "If it's such a favor, why keep it a secret?"

"Yeah," said Sue Ellen. "Why would you do something else that could get you in trouble?"

"Because she's nuts," said Bianca.

"We're not going to break any laws, exactly," said Karma. "We're going to prevent a crime. That's a good deed—my people call it a *mitzvah*."

"Thanks for the Jewish lesson," drawled Bianca, "but *Jesus Christ*, I don't even know Joan that well. I'm not sure I'm ready to get arrested for her or get her crazy dumbass neighbor mad at *me*, instead of her. Why doesn't she just call the cops like a normal person?"

"She probably did that," said Karma, "but it didn't do any good. Jack Lawrence aimed an explosive device at her, for God's sake. He could have killed her, but this isn't just about him, it's about deciding what kind of neighborhood we want to live in, and what kind of world we're going to leave to our children."

Karma's juices were flowing, and she jumped aboard the Overblown Hyperbole Express, heading toward parts unknown. "The purpose of society is to protect women and children. If we don't protect the weakest and most vulnerable members of society, we're just animals. No, we're worse than animals, because animals *do* band together to protect mothers and babies. Calling the police hasn't worked because he's not afraid of them. And he's right because they can't stop him until he actually hurts a pregnant woman. What if she loses that baby because we didn't do anything to help her?"

"We got no business getting involved in this," said Bianca. "No business." She crossed her arms to give her words the finality they deserved, but if she were honest, she saw Karma's point. She knew her father and brothers and her uncles back in Pennsylvania would have known how to handle a *scemo* like Jack Lawrence. The sonofabitch wouldn't have walked straight for a month, if he could walk at all. She also knew that she wouldn't have needed any of them to take him on. *One good-sized sauté pan and let the guy turn his back for just a second.* The problem with most women was that they lacked her common-sense approach to problem-solving. It was their loss.

On the other hand, she had left Pennsylvania to get away from that kind of thinking. The last thing Bianca needed was

Pennsylvania trouble in her new Indiana neighborhood. So she turned to Kim. "You gonna jump in here, or wait till Karma breaks out the torches and pitchforks."

Kim shrugged. "Hey, I think she has a point. It's like a neighborhood watch, only we don't just get to watch, we get to participate. Sounds like fun to me."

Bianca made a rude noise, thought it might have been an Italian curse.

Jeanette cleared her throat dramatically, and the women turned to look at her. "I'm in, too," she said. "Like the Bible says, 'All that's required for bad people to prosper is for good people to do nothing.'" Jeanette was misquoting Edmund Burke, rather than the Bible, but it didn't matter; this was a matter of principle, and Jeanette had firm principles. She didn't know Joan Handley very well, but Joan was good friends with Betsy Shaw, who had been the room mother at Little Jeffrey's third preschool. Betsy had refused to sign the petition demanding that Little Jeffrey be expelled after the incident with the Lincoln Logs and the mustard packets. As far as Jeanette was concerned, Betsy was nice, and if Betsy liked Joan, then Joan must also be nice, and Jeanette believed that nice people should be treated nice. This was her personal Golden Rule.

Sue Ellen couldn't believe the direction this conversation was going. "C'mon," she said. "We could get in lots of trouble. If we get caught or arrested it would be completely embarrassing." She looked at Bianca, who was nodding her agreement. She was gratified to have at least one ally in the room. What in the world was wrong with the rest of them?

As for Karma, she wasn't surprised by any of their reactions, but she was ready to close the deal. She looked into Sue Ellen's pale blue contact lenses and used the soft voice that, back in her radio station days, had forced many a reluctant client to lean in just to hear her. "Sue Ellen," said Karma, "if somebody was after *you,* wouldn't you want us to do something about it, especially if the police couldn't help you? How would you feel if nobody cared enough about you to take a tiny little risk to save you?"

Sue Ellen opened her mouth, then closed it. She tried to hold Karma's gaze, tried to think of how to challenge the argument. "Of course I'd want someone to help me, but that isn't the same...it isn't a fair...you can't just expect..."

Karma smiled a warm, understanding, reassuring, completely insincere smile. "You don't have to get involved if you don't want to. You just have to keep quiet about it if we decide to do something. You, too, Bianca. And we haven't decided, so there's really nothing to worry about."

"That's right," said Kim, picking up on Karma's tactic. "We're just considering our options. We'll take a little time and think it over." She leaned back in her chair, looking casually uninterested in all the fuss. Kim had already done all the thinking she intended to do. *Jack Lawrence is f'ing toast.* The guy was nothing but a schoolyard bully. Jack Lawrence was every jerk back in high school who had laughed when Kim passed in the halls. They made fun of her because she was the only Asian in the school, and because her thighs rubbed together when she walked. They made fun of her straight dark hair, her short stature, her clothes, and her makeup. Guys like Jack Lawrence used to call her *Fat Chink* in front of the teachers, and nobody had stopped them. Kim had never told her adoptive parents, who were tall, slim, blond Norwegians. She knew they were already disappointed in her, no matter what they said, and knowing she was being taunted in school would just make it worse. She was supposed to be the exotic Asian Barbie doll of their dreams, but it hadn't turned out that way. Had there ever been a child who looked less like a Barbie doll than she had?

And now, all these years and all these diet programs later, Kim could feel the old rage again. Her inner fat girl was crying out for revenge against all the Jack Lawrences of the world. It was too late to stick it to the high school boys, but it would be a total pleasure to take down Jack Lawrence. Of course, if something went wrong, her husband, president of the Homeowners Association and all-around good guy, would be supremely pissed. That gave Kim the tiniest hesitation, but she would simply make sure they didn't get caught. Dave never had to know. *Yes, Jack Lawrence was definitely toast.*

Jeanette took her empty cinnamon roll pan off the table and set it in Karma's sink, then filled it with hot water to soak off the sugary goo. "There's just one thing," she said, over her shoulder. "Now that we've discussed this as a group, if we *do* get caught doing something, even if somebody doesn't participate, it's a conspiracy."

Conspiracy. The word hung in the air, as hot, sweet, and sticky as her Grandma Bibi's famous cinnamon rolls.

CHAPTER 8:   SECRETS

The following day was the second Saturday of the month, the Saturday that Karma Kranski missed neighborhood yard sales, school fundraisers, and parties. The Saturday when Sam stayed home with Molly and told people that Karma was out shopping. He always gassed up the minivan the night before so Karma wouldn't have to worry about it. She never asked him to do this; he just quietly took care of it after dinner the night before, every month, and when Karma thanked him, as she always did, he just smiled. Someday she would have to explain these monthly absences to Molly, but she wasn't old enough yet, and knew nothing about where her mother was going.

As she drove north, Karma kept the car radio off. For the next two hours she would be alone with the hum of the van and the buzz of her thoughts. She ought to use the time to think about Jack Lawrence and what might be done about him, but her mind kept wandering back to where she was going and what she would do when she got there.

Karma set her cruise control to nine miles an hour over the speed limit, counting on Sam's theory that the police wouldn't bother her for a lousy nine miles an hour. Sure enough, she saw several police cars along the way, but none stopped her. They were usually busy ticketing other speeders anyway. As always, at the Prescott exit, she drove through a McDonald's for a Coke Zero. At the Charleston exit she peed and bought another one. The interstate was straight and flat and boring, but it was fast.

Finally, she took the exit at State Road 42, and headed west, watching for the stone marker that indicated the right turn onto the tree-lined gravel lane that led to Good Shepherd. The sight of it filled her with nervous dread, but she fought it down and kept on driving. As always.

Karma parked her van under a large oak tree, and, as always, watched the residents out on the manicured lawns for a few minutes. Some didn't notice her, some stared blankly, others waved at her with great enthusiasm. A few came running. Visitors were a big deal here. Karma was sometimes the only one, but today there were a few other cars in the guest parking lot. She turned off the engine and took a few deep breaths, calming her nervous heart. A loud thump on the window inches from her head almost made her wet herself.

"Hi, Lady," said a young man. His voice was muffled by the closed window. He had wispy blond hair, wide-set eyes, and a broad, bland smile.

"Hi, Lenny," said Karma, opening the car door. "How are you today?"

"I like your car."

"I know you do, Lenny." Karma climbed out, careful not to let the door hit Lenny. Then she shut the door and hit the door lock on her key fob. Last year she had forgotten to do so, and Lenny had climbed into her back seat, curled up and fallen asleep. Half-way down the gravel lane, his smiling face had popped up in the rear view mirror and Karma *had* peed herself.

Lenny was quickly joined by Marvin and Alice, and together, they walked Karma up to the entrance. It wasn't easy to hold hands with three people, but Karma did her best. The three residents tried to accompany her into the building, but were shooed back to the lawns by Glenda, in her crisp light-blue uniform with a white smock and orthopedic shoes.

"C'mon, y'all know it's fresh air time, so go get you some." She turned to Karma. "Hi, Mrs. Kranski. Don't you look nice today? She'll be glad to see you. She is always so happy when you come."

"Thanks, Glenda. Is she having a good day?"

"Oh, yes, a pretty good day I think."

Karma signed in at the front desk and pinned on a visitor's badge. There was the usual acrid smell of bleach in the air, which got stronger the closer she got to the Chronic Care wing. Fortunately, the weather was pleasant and windows were open today, so the odor didn't assault her nose as it did in the winter when the building was closed up. As a kid, Karma had associated the smell of bleach with the panic she felt before every visit to Kathleen. Her mother had learned to clean her floors only when Karma was at school, and even in winter, opened the windows to get the smell out before Karma came home. Grown-up Karma didn't own a bottle of bleach.

The door to room C218 was open. Karma stopped at the threshold, assumed a pleasant expression, and stepped inside.

"Hi, Kathleen," she said. Kathleen might have twitched a little, maybe at the sound of her name, or maybe not. If so, it was only a twitch.

A young woman Karma had never met came out of the bathroom, drying her hands on a paper towel. Judging by her polo shirt, loose scrub pants, and athletic build, Karma judged her to be a physical therapist. Her ID badge said *Denise*.

"Are you a relative of Miss Kathleen?" the girl asked. "You two kinda look alike. You mind if I work? I have a full schedule today. I'll be quick."

Karma didn't mind. Denise began to gently stretch Kathleen's tight leg muscles. Kathleen whimpered in protest.

"C'mon, Miss Kathleen," urged the young woman, "we don't want our legs to get stiff, do we? We need to keep our muscles strong, don't we?" This was the way they all worked, asking questions Kathleen would never answer, and referring to her as *we*. It was part of *engaging the patient* and *making life-affirming connections*, at least according to the website. Karma sat down in the padded leather recliner in the corner and watched Denise work.

"I'm Karma, Kathleen's sister."

"I figured," said Denise. "That's a pretty name. Sounds like candy. It's good to meet you. You sure you don't mind?"

"No," said Karma. "Take your time. I don't want to mess up your schedule." The longer the therapist stayed, the easier this visit would be. Karma had no illusions that Kathleen looked forward to her visits, nor missed her when she wasn't around, nor even recognized her. Visits to Kathleen were not about sisterly chats and catching up, or talking about old times. There were no old times, no childhood memories to share. This was about doing the right thing and making sure Kathleen was receiving good care. You heard horror stories about people in nursing homes being abused and neglected, and their mother was determined that wasn't going to happen to Kathleen.

Denise moved to her arms and fingers, massaging and stretching tight muscles. Kathleen grimaced and made unhappy grunting noises. She could obviously feel pain, but she didn't really fight the therapy. She never did. Karma would have given anything to see Kathleen sit up and grouse, the way Karma herself would have. *Hey, if I'm going to get pummeled like this, at least have the decency to be tall and Scandinavian and named Lars.*

But this wasn't about wish fulfillment; it was about promise fulfillment. Specifically, Karma's promise to her mother, made years earlier. Only Charlotte could have made Karma agree to such a dramatic, deathbed promise. Except she hadn't been dying; she wanted to move to Boca. *You only live two hours away. Promise me you'll visit your sister at least once a month. Someday you'll be the only family she has.* Karma wasn't crazy about having this particular torch passed to her, and she could have claimed Sam and Molly as an excuse for not visiting Kathleen so often, but she hadn't.

When her twin daughters, Karmella and Kathleen, had been born, one healthy, the other not, Charlotte had tried to care for Kathleen at home, changing diapers, cleaning feeding tubes, calling ambulances when a crisis would arise. But the older Kathleen got, the harder it had become to care for her. After Charlotte had thrown Ed out of the house for cheating on her again, she'd said she couldn't handle Kathleen by herself, and she'd moved her to Good Shepherd. From that day to the day Karma went off to college, she and her mother had spent virtually every Sunday here. It was what they did, like other families spend weekends at the lake, or at the beach. Karma and her mother and, occasionally, her father, spent Sundays *at Kathleen's.* Karma had wanted to complain, but she hadn't, or at least not often. She understood what was never said aloud: that by the grace of God, the umbilical cord had not wrapped around *her* neck, and this was the least she could do to atone for the sin of being born healthy.

When Denise finished and excused herself, Karma was left alone with Kathleen. It didn't really matter what she talked about, but it was her habit to talk. She described Molly's plans for the summer: swimming lessons, nature camp, and taking the training wheels off her Barbie bike. She told Kathleen about Molly's broken arm, and how she had been determined to find the red car, but for some reason, she stopped short of telling Kathleen what she had done when she found it.

Kathleen seemed to make eye contact a few times, and her mouth contracted into a smile at the sound of her sister's voice.

Karma thought she probably did that at the sound of any voice, but she wasn't sure. Of course, Kathleen said nothing in return.

Was the person Kathleen *should have become* trapped in that shell, or had that soul flown away before her birth? Was Kathleen just a set of autonomic brain-stem functions? Nobody could be sure. And what if Kathleen was trapped in that body, aware of herself and her terribly limited life? That was too horrible to even imagine.

Since childhood, Karma had experienced a recurring dream in which Kathleen showed up at their parents' front door on a bright summer day, to announce that she was cured and ready to join the family. She had Karma's thick curly hair pulled back in a matching ponytail, Karma's dimply smile, and identical pink plastic-framed glasses. In some versions of the dream, Kathleen sat at a school desk next to Karma's, wearing identical clothes, and in others, they danced together at Karma's after-school dance class.

"I love you," said Kathleen in every dream. "Now we can be real twins forever."

The drive home from the extended care facility was like all the others. Karma blinked back tears for the first thirty minutes, and spent the remaining ninety minutes drinking Diet Coke and getting her game face back on. It was the second Saturday of the month, the Saturday when Karma did the right thing, engaged the patient, made life-affirming connections, and felt her heart break into a million pieces.

CHAPTER 9: THE PLOT THICKENS

The week got no better. On Monday, Karma was late leaving the house for preschool pickup, which caused every traffic light to turn red, every highway worker to turn his "Slow" sign to "Stop" just in front of her, and every elderly driver to simultaneously occupy all available lanes. When she finally arrived at Temple Beth Israel to pick up Molly, Karma thought she was only ten minutes late, but the principal informed her that she was actually *twenty-five* minutes late, as today was an early dismissal day, due to a Jewish holiday that Karma had never heard of. Karma had to endure the disapproving looks of Ms. Goldberg, the assistant principal, who was waiting in the lobby with the last sad-faced, pathetic, obviously neglected child (hers) and a yellow slip which said she would be charged an extra twenty bucks for the late pickup. It was Karma's fourth offense for the year.

None of this was her fault. At least once a month, Molly's Jewish preschool found an obscure Jewish holiday to honor, which required that they send home their charges fifteen minutes before the usual closing time. Those fifteen lousy minutes were the difference between being a respected member of the religious preschool community and an over-assimilated disgrace to The Chosen People. Apparently, the Almighty had chiseled an Eleventh Commandment about early preschool dismissal on the back of one of the tablets he gave to Moses, and Karma had missed it. In fact, she would have testified in front of the Lord Himself that these holidays were the invention of preschool teachers who wanted to go home early. Her transgressions were made worse by Jewish law, which commanded that every Jewish holiday must start at sundown on the night *before* the holiday. So every one of these dubious holidays was preceded by *Erev*-What-the-Heck-Are-We-Celebrating, which meant that there were *two* days when she was supposed to remember to show up early. And, of course, today was one of those days.

With a tight-lipped smile and an insincere apology, Karma took the late slip and Molly's backpack from the assistant principal, and led Molly out to the van.

"You're *late*," scolded Molly.

"There was traffic," said Karma. She buckled Molly into her car seat and headed for home. Two blocks down the road she looked in the rear-view mirror, and smiled. Molly, always a gifted car napper, was asleep.

Pulling into the driveway, Karma took care not to let her keys jingle as she turned the car off. She carefully unbuckled Molly, eased her over one shoulder, and carried her into the house. She maneuvered the little body gingerly through the doorway into the mudroom, around the floor lamp, then across the room to the living room couch. Although Molly was a sound sleeper, it was essential to avoid letting her head or feet bump into walls, tables, and door frames. It was the home version of *Operation*, but in this game, the penalty for failure would be a miserable four-year-old who would be crabby until bedtime.

Karma gently deposited Molly on the family room sofa and watched with held breath until Molly rolled onto her side and, still asleep, curled into fetal position. *Thank you, God, I promise to read the preschool calendar more carefully, amen.* Then Karma covered Molly with a blanket and stepped carefully and quietly away. Just as she was congratulating herself, her cell phone sang out. Jumping over Molly's discarded backpack and the toys that always seemed to be where her feet landed, Karma wrestled the phone out of her jeans pocket and ran into the living room, where she could talk without whispering.

"Hey, Karma," chirped Jeanette. "I saw your van drive in. Did Sam tell you I called Saturday? You didn't call me back."

"No," said Karma. "He forgot to tell me." Karma felt a rush of heartburn. Here came the questions: *What did you buy? Where did you go? Why didn't you ask me to go with you?* Jeanette didn't know Karma had a sister; none of her Bedford Commons friends did. Karma didn't want to talk about it, didn't want to answer questions, didn't want their sympathy. It wasn't a big lie; it was a lie of omission. Barely a lie, if you really thought about it, as nobody had ever *asked* her if she had a brain-damaged twin sister in a nursing home. *God, I am a bitch.*

"Anyway," continued Jeanette, "I've been thinking about Jack Lawrence. Let's send him a message that he can't aim his fireworks at pregnant women."

Karma peeked around the corner at Molly, who had rolled over and kicked off the blanket, but was still asleep. "A message? You mean like a note?"

"Not like a note," said Jeanette, sounding a bit exasperated. "We *do* something that *sends* a message. Like what Kim said; we sneak into his garage and take his fireworks. That kind of message."

Karma had already thought about that. "He'll think some kid stole them, and he'll just go out and buy more. If we're going to send a message, it has to be clear. He has to know somebody is taking action against him, that he can't just do whatever he wants around here. Just like the woman with the red car."

"Then let's put a flaming poop bag on his front porch."

"Oh my God," said Karma.

There was a heavy sigh on Jeanette's end of the phone. "I'm out of ideas," she said. "Let's you and me and Kim meet on the playground after she gets home with Lindsey, and we can work on it together."

Karma agreed, and Jeanette said she'd send a text to Kim. Karma ended the call and assessed the situation. Their meeting wouldn't be earlier than 3:15, Molly was still asleep, there was plenty of time to work on dinner, and the kitchen was no messier than usual. Karma set the baby monitor on the coffee table next to Molly, and tossed the receiver in a three-day-old basket of clean laundry. She carried the basket upstairs.

Karma hung up Sam's shirts, folded Molly's little shorts and tops, and tried to imagine an appropriate "message" to send to Jack Lawrence. An anonymous note threatening to call the police might work, although it wasn't very creative. Karma stretched across her bed to think. She stared up at the gently rotating ceiling fan, yawned and waited for inspiration.

"Mommy."

The voice was coming from far away. Karma looked through the thick smoke and tried to find the source, but fireworks were going off in her face, and she couldn't see anything.

"Mommy come."

Molly? Why was Molly dressed like a clown? Why was she throwing matches into Kathleen's big box of fireworks? Kathleen was encouraging Molly, which was not something a good aunt would do.

"Mommy COME."

Karma opened her eyes. She was lying on her own bed, and there were no fireworks. *What time was it?* The light coming

89

through the bedroom window said *mid-afternoon*. Karma swung her leg carefully over Spike, the big gray cat, who had found a comfy spot between Karma's stiff knees. He blinked at her, but true to the Cat Code of Conduct, didn't move so much as a whisker to get out of her way.

"MOMMY COME." Molly's urgent voice was coming from Karma's left hand, which still held the baby monitor receiver. She stumbled stiffly down the stairs to find Molly sitting up on the family room sofa, her eyes round with fear. "Where were you?"

"Sorry, sweetie," said Karma. "I fell asleep upstairs, and I didn't hear you right away."

"I'm hungry."

Still drowsy, Karma went into the kitchen to make Molly a peanut butter and jelly sandwich. She was reaching for the jelly when the doorbell rang, which reminded her of the "sometime after 3:00" meeting at the playground. *Jeez.* It was almost 3:30 and Karma hadn't even thought about what she'd cook for dinner, much less how they'd deal with Jack Lawrence. The doorbell rang again, and Karma headed for the front door. *Oh well*, she thought, *this is why God invented pizza delivery.* She opened the door and saw Kim and Jeanette and their kids standing on the front porch.

Kim noted the half-completed sandwich Karma waved in greeting. "Yummy. Come to the playground when you're ready."

Karma returned to the family room to tell Molly to find her shoes, only to see that she was once again asleep, curled up on the couch like a little comma. The baby monitor transmitter was still on, so Karma turned on the television and lowered the volume to a soft murmur, then hooked the receiver to the waistband of her shorts. She ate the sandwich—wasting crunchy peanut butter being a sin—and walked quickly to catch up with her friends, who were still on the walking path that led to the playground.

"How far can you go with that thing?" asked Jeanette, pointing to the baby monitor receiver.

"I have to stay at the closest bench on the playground," said Karma. "That's why I turn on the TV. As long as I can hear it, I know I'm still in range and I'll be able to hear Molly, too."

"Genius," said Kim.

When they arrived at the playground, the kids ran off to play. The absence of Bianca and Sue Ellen felt odd to Karma, but they had made it clear that they wanted to stay uninvolved. Besides, whoever had designed the playground hadn't given much thought to the comfort of grown women. The benches were barely wide enough to accommodate the three of them, and were made of unpadded, unforgiving, indestructible steel. But it was that or sit in the mulch, so there they sat, three suburban musketeers, ready to plot revenge. As Karma expected, Kim already had a plan.

"He thinks he's Mr. Powerful with his stupid fireworks. We'll show him what a big dumbass he is, and embarrass the hell out of him at the same time. I've got it all figured out."

Kim always had things figured out. She outlined the rest of her plan while Karma and Jeanette listened and stole doubtful glances at their feet and at each other. They were having the same thought: maybe a bag of burning dog poop wasn't such a bad idea after all. Kim's plan was complicated. Jack Lawrence would certainly know he was being targeted, but there were so many details to work out, and at least a dozen things could go badly wrong. But Kim was so proud of herself that Karma hated to argue with her. And she knew that if she did argue, Kim would challenge her to come up with a better idea. The flaming poop bag wouldn't impress Kim.

91

"Sue Ellen was right about one thing. We'll look like idiots if we're caught," Karma said. "Absolute idiots."

"We can't get caught," squeaked Jeanette. "Oh my God."

"We won't get caught," said Kim. "We just have to plan it out and be careful. I've thought of everything."

Karma kicked at the mulch beneath her feet. "It's going to take more than being careful," she said. "We have to know when he's gonna shoot off the fireworks, and be ready *before* he does it. How are we supposed to do that?"

Kim crossed her arms and set her lips in a childish pout. "So come up with something better."

No one spoke. Karma fiddled with the volume control on the baby monitor and held it up to her ear, just for something to do. She recognized the dulcet tones of a TV pitchman, in the middle of the *"but wait, there's more"* part of his pitch. Her butt was getting sore. *Stupid bench.*

"It's too bad we can't put your baby monitor in his house," said Jeanette. "Maybe we'd hear him talk about the fireworks."

Karma wasn't listening. Where did Kim get the right to get mad, just because Karma pointed out the obvious flaw in her plan? *Sometimes she's too damn bossy.*

"I bet he'll shoot them off on Friday night," said Kim. "We'll be ready on Friday, and if he doesn't do anything, we'll do it again on Saturday."

"Or maybe instead of fighting with him," said Jeanette, "we could send him an email explaining how Joan is pregnant and she didn't call the cops and he should just leave her alone? Dave has his email address, right?"

Kim huffed, "He's not going to stop being an asshole just because we send him an email." Her dismissive tone was not lost on Jeanette. She looked hurt.

Karma opened her mouth to tell Kim that Jeanette's ideas were no worse than hers. But then Jeanette's words whacked her on the head. *An email. An email to Jack Lawrence. And a baby monitor.* Karma smiled.

I'm a genius.

She reached across Kim and gave Jeanette's knee a friendly pat. "You *are* the smart one. In fact, you are brilliant. We can make Jack light his fireworks exactly when we want him to. And I know just how we'll do it."

CHAPTER 10: DIVERSIONARY TACTICS

Karma and Kim huddled over Dave's computer while Molly and Lindsey made a mess of Kim's clean basement. Dave was at work, of course, and had no idea what they were up to. He would never read his latest presidential email, which was good because not only had he not written it, neither had he asked his wife and her best friend to write it.

Karma and Kim composed and revised, wrote and rewrote, deleting and un-deleting until the message struck just the right balance of pomposity and menace. They would erase it from his Sent folder of course, but if Dave found out about it, they could legitimately claim that they were just protecting their pregnant friend and that they hadn't *lied* about anything. The worst they'd done was imply that Dave had more power to rule over his neighbors than he actually had, and again, only to protect an innocent pregnant woman.

Kim closed her eyes in concentration, as Karma read the message aloud once more.

To: Jack Lawrence
From: Dave Wallace
Date: Wednesday, July 23
Re: Your Fireworks

It has come to my attention that you've been lighting fireworks and deliberately violating the rights of your neighbors to peacefully enjoy their property. While there is no specific ban on such activities in the Neighborhood Covenants, as the elected President of the HOA, I insist that all residents conform to rules of common courtesy. Beginning this Friday night at 10 p.m., I will authorize the board to levy a fine of $100 per incident on residents who violate the unwritten, yet obvious, rules that govern such conduct. If you choose to continue your outrageous behavior after 10 p.m. this Friday night, I will take it as a personal challenge to my authority.

Kim opened her eyes. "It's totally obnoxious. I love it."

"We are brilliant," said Karma.

"We are," said Kim.

Karma held her cursor over the Send button and her trigger finger over the mouse. Common Sense and Maturity had one more chance to intercede, but they were out today, enjoying a three-Appletini lunch. Karma hit Send, launching Step One of their brilliant plan to take down Jack Lawrence and defend pregnant women everywhere.

"Okay," said Kim. "He's going to light his fireworks at 10 p.m. on Friday, just to piss off Dave. And we'll be ready, thanks to your brilliance."

"Sometimes I scare myself," said Karma. "Let's call Jeanette and let her know the plan."

Kim made a face. She had argued against involving Jeanette, whom she considered rather dim, but Karma reminded her that Jeanette had provided the original inspiration for the plan, and was there when it was hatched. And Jeanette had promised on her mother's grave not to tell anybody what they were doing. Her mother was alive, Jeanette had admitted, but she owned a cemetery plot, so it still counted. Secrecy was essential. Gossip in Bedford Commons was like oxygen: essential to life, but highly flammable. Besides, this was a three-woman job, and Jeanette had a critical role to play.

Karma's contribution to the plan was just this side of dazzling, if Karma did say so herself. The battery life on her baby monitor transmitter was eight hours. Just in case Jack didn't start right at 10 p.m., the transmitter couldn't be turned on before 3 p.m. If the battery died before the fireworks began, everything could fall apart.

The biggest problem in Kim's opinion was that the transmitter had to be hidden as close as possible to the back door of Jack's garage. "How do we put it back there without anybody seeing us?"

Karma had already considered this. "We don't have to worry about Jack and Luann, because they both work until at least five, and their kids are in after-school care."

"Yeah, but this neighborhood is full of nosey people with too much time on their hands," said Kim. "Besides us, I mean."

The answer had come from Jeanette. "If Little Jeffrey throws a tantrum in front of the Lawrence house," she said, "nobody will be paying attention to what's going on behind it."

Karma hadn't understood. "How are you going to get him to throw a tantrum at just the right time?"

Jeanette's laugh was bitter. "Where have you been? He pitches his little hissy fits twelve times a day." She looked down at her feet and spoke more quietly. "I know everybody thinks I don't know what kind of kid I've got, but I'm not stupid. I know what people say."

Guilty heat rose in Karma's cheeks, but Jeanette looked at her and smiled, like she knew what Karma had said about Little Jeffrey behind her back, and had already forgiven her. "I'll take my kids for a walk in front of Jack's house, and when you give me a sign that you're ready, I'll give you a big commotion."

At 3:45 on Friday afternoon, they got into position. Jeanette took Little Jeffrey and Allie and the baby around to Brentwood so they could walk past the Lawrence house. Kim and Karma walked Kim's little mutt, Totsy, around Applewood Circle, which was Joan and Greg Handley's cul-de-sac. The Handley's backyard met the Lawrence's backyard, with just a four-foot fence between them. Totsy was always happy to pee in new territory, and it was easy to let the retractable leash get a little long, and let Totsy lead Kim and Karma between the houses and around to the Lawrence's side yard.

They were pleased to see an incredible mess of toys, tools, and backyard lawn equipment around the side and back yards, including hoses and sprinklers. Plenty of camouflage here. Karma noticed a Y-connector that sent two lengths of hose off in different directions from a single hose connected to the outdoor faucet. "That's genius," said Karma. "I'm going to have to tell Sam about that. He could water our lawn in half the time."

"Just don't tell him where you saw it," said Kim. "Hey, there's Jeanette."

Right on time. Karma gave her a little nod. She hadn't asked how Jeanette was going to pull off her part of the plan, and morbid curiosity made her linger behind, as Kim continued to let Totsy pull her along behind the Lawrence house.

"Jeffrey," said Jeanette in a firm voice, loud enough for the neighbors, and Karma, to hear, "when we're finished with our walk, we're going to the grocery store."

"I don't want to go," said Little Jeffrey. "My show is coming on."

"I'm sorry," said Jeanette, "but we're almost out of milk, so we have to go to the store. You can watch your show later."

"But it's on NOW," he cried. "I'm not going to the store. I'm going to stay home and WATCH MY SHOW." His voice was rising to a dangerous pitch.

"Young man," said Jeanette, "you're coming with me to the store, and that's final."

"Do I get a treat at the store? I want a treat," he wailed.

"No treats and no candy," said Jeanette, her voice cracking a bit. "You're coming to the store and that's it, so let's go. And just for being so uncooperative, you are grounded from TV for a week."

It was the kind of thing Jeanette had heard other people say to their kids nearly every day, but it was odd hearing it from her own mouth; it was a script written for a better mother, and she wondered if Little Jeffrey would just laugh, hearing it from her.

Not a chance. Little Jeffrey's ear-splitting shrieks rent the air. Though barely five, he achieved volume and intensity that would have made an Iowa pig caller proud. Windows rattled and frightened flocks of birds took wing.

As his screaming reached frequencies undetectable by human ears, Totsy cowered and dogs in distant yards howled.

People began coming out of their houses to see whose rhinoceros was being dismembered, but all they saw was Little Jeffrey on his back, screaming and pounding the sidewalk with his fists and heels as his mother looked on, red-faced with embarrassment, and his younger sister quietly sucked her thumb.

Thank God he's not mine, the neighbors thought in telepathic unison. As Jeanette had predicted, they were mesmerized by the commotion. Nobody was paying attention to the activity behind the Lawrence house. Karma turned on the transmitter and placed it in a thatch of untrimmed grass next to the back door. Then she ran to help Kim, who was pulling a hose and sprinkler assembly to the edge of the patio. Karma grabbed the other hose, still connected to the Y-contraption, and ran it a few feet to the right, and up into a small tree. She hung the sprinkler over a leafy branch behind a birdhouse, which hid it pretty well. Unless you were really looking—and this yard didn't look like anybody paid attention to it—you wouldn't notice it. Kim found the hose spigot and pointed it out to Karma.

Their work was done, and in plenty of time; Little Jeffrey's lung power rivaled that of an Olympic swimmer. Kim grabbed Totsy's leash and she and Karma ran back to the street, then walked quickly toward Jeanette, who was still standing over her screaming son. A small gaggle of neighbors had gathered to watch him as well.

Poor Jeanette, thought Karma. Poor Little Jeffrey, too. He was finally wearing out; his volume had decreased a bit, and he was reduced to repeating earlier threats and epithets, having run out of new bad words and bad-sounding combinations of words to throw at his mother.

Jeanette flinched when she felt Karma's hand on her shoulder. "Okay," she said. "If you get up right now, you can watch your show. I'll go shopping when Daddy gets home and I'll bring you back a treat. Two treats." As though a switch had been thrown to the *off* position, Little Jeffrey stopped screaming. He looked warily at his mother to make sure she wasn't going to change her mind, then got to his feet and began to walk silently and sullenly toward home, his world having returned to what passed for normal. Allie, mute observer of so many of her brother's outbursts, silently followed him, still sucking her thumb. Jeanette brought up the rear with Karma and Kim.

"Great job," said Karma quietly. "Wow."

"Yeah. Wow," said Jeanette with an uncharacteristic edge of bitterness. "I give him what he wants and he stops until the next time. I've never let him go on so long before, especially in front of people."

Suddenly Jeanette looked like she might cry, which made Karma feel like dirt. Using Little Jeffrey like this had been Jeanette's idea, not hers, but suddenly, she didn't feel so good about it.

"I'm sorry," said Karma. "We should have figured out something else."

Jeanette kept walking. She couldn't look at Karma or Kim. The entire neighborhood had seen just how bad a parent she was. She knew that everybody assumed he acted like he did because she was raising him wrong, but the truth was so much worse. Jeanette squared her shoulders and walked a little quicker.

Karma and Kim exchanged guilty looks. They hadn't meant to embarrass Jeanette, but this was a conversation they'd had *about* her at least a dozen times. *Never negotiate with terrorists, even when they're five years old.* The women walked in silence, pausing to let Totsy sniff mailboxes and bushes, but keeping Little Jeffrey and Allie in sight.

"Do you think God punishes us for things we do wrong?" asked Jeanette. "I think He does."

The question caught Karma by surprise. She threw a look to Kim, but Kim could only pantomime her own confusion. Did Jeanette really think that Little Jeffrey was a punishment from God? What could she have done to deserve *him*?

"Anyway," said Jeanette, too cheerfully, "are we all set?"

"Yeah," said Kim, with one more puzzled look at Karma. "Everything's in place. As long as Jack Lawrence doesn't decide to water his lawn or clean up his trashy backyard, we're in good shape."

"Then we're safe," said Karma, "He obviously doesn't give a rip what his yard looks like. I'll see you guys tonight at eight, and we'll hang out 'til dark."

Kim nodded. "Just in case the guys compare notes, remember, we're going to a Pampered Chef party."

Jeanette frowned. "Could we make it a candle party? I haven't been to a candle party in ages."

After dinner was served, the dishwasher was filled, and the kitchen restored to a pre-meal level of messiness, Karma told Sam about the candle party. She accepted his good-natured eye-rolling, and Molly's disappointment that Mommy was leaving, and kissed them both goodbye. "Don't wait up." She was meeting Kim and Jeanette at the playground. She grabbed her cell phone, dashed out the door, and nearly knocked Kim and Jeanette off her front porch.

"I know we're early. I just couldn't sit around my house another second," said Jeanette. "Don't we look sexy?" She was wearing black stretch slacks, a black turtleneck sweater and a black rain slicker. Kim was wearing a slimming pair of black boot-cut Levis and a tight black hoodie. They looked like Charlie's Angel's older sisters. Karma suddenly felt frumpier than usual in her baggy mom jeans and PTO volunteer tee shirt. "What's the matter?" she asked. "Run out of camo face paint?"

Jeanette giggled, but Kim was all business. "Do we all have our phones? Did you bring the baby monitor?"

Karma opened her purse and pulled out the receiver. They headed for Brentwood to make sure the transmitter hidden in Jack's shrubbery was still working. A block or so away, they began to detect sounds of activity. It sounded like the Lawrence kids were playing. Sure enough, when Karma, Kim and Jeanette casually walked past the house, the three Lawrence kids were alternately biking, skating, pushing, and shoving their way up and down the driveway and around their cul-de-sac. They had the unruly air of the marginally supervised, and didn't acknowledge the women as they passed.

"So now what?" asked Jeanette, consulting her phone. "It's early."

"We need to check the hoses," said Kim. "If somebody moved them or they fell down, we have a problem." They walked around the block, and made their way toward Joan Handley's house.

"You guys walk up and down the block so you're not standing here looking obvious," said Karma. "I'll go in the backyard and peek over Joan's fence." Karma entered through Joan's side gate, and tiptoed around the house toward the back. Nobody was on Joan's deck, so Karma kept moving. Just to make it look good, in case she'd been spotted, she stopped at the mulch bed and bent down to examine the plantings in the corner. Joan's variegated hostas were blooming with long-stemmed purple blossoms, which gave Karma something to pretend to give a crap about as she sneaked a peek over the fence. Her heart was hammering in her chest. In the dimming light, she could just make out the hoses she and Kim had laid out. The sprinkler on the right was fine, but what was on the ground by the tree? It was the hanging sprinkler, only it wasn't hanging anymore. *Damn it.*

"Hey, Karma," called a voice, startling Karma so badly she nearly screamed. Joan Handley was standing on her deck, one hand on her pregnant belly, the other holding a bottle of water. "Whatcha doin'?"

"Umm, well, I didn't want to bother you. I know how tired I was when I was pregnant. Kim was telling me about your hostas, and how big they're getting, and I'm having trouble with mine, I mean I don't have any, but I want to get some, so I just...I was just..."

"It's late to be out spying on the neighbor's plants, isn't it?" said Joan with a smile. "But honestly, I'm glad you came over. I'd love to help you with your hostas, when you get some. Come sit and we can talk. Greg's out of town until tomorrow, and I'm supposed to be resting, but I'm bored out of my mind. My ankles are swelling, my blood pressure is up, and if this baby doesn't come soon, I'm going to lose my mind."

There was no choice. Mind racing and heart still thumping, Karma followed Joan across the lawn. Joan's backyard deck was a good place to keep an eye on Jack Lawrence, but what about Kim and Jeanette? What would they do when she didn't come back? She stuck her hands in her pockets and felt the baby monitor receiver *she'd forgotten to give to Kim.*

"Hang on, Joan," she said, "I'm going to close your gate." She turned and ran back around the side of the house, out of

Joan's sight, where she caught sight of Kim and Jeanette, who were clutching each other's arms and making faces of mock horror at her predicament of getting caught by Joan, which apparently struck them as quite funny.

Karma made a rude gesture with her middle finger, and tossed the receiver over the fence. Kim caught it and crept away with Jeanette into the growing darkness. Karma hustled back to Joan's deck and sat down on a wicker chair.

"So how are you feeling?"

Joan gave her a quizzical look. "Like I just said, my ankles are swelling and my blood pressure is up. Also, the baby keeps kicking me in the bladder. The worst part is that Greg's away, and I'm worried that my stupid neighbor is going to shoot fireworks at me again."

"Your neighbor?"

Joan was looking oddly at Karma again. "Don't tell me you didn't hear about it," she said. "I figured everybody knew about that by now." She pointed at the Lawrence house. "He lives right over there and—"

Karma followed her gesture and looked toward the Lawrence house. *Oh crap. I didn't tell Kim and Jeanette about the fallen sprinkler. I suck at this. Please, Lord, let them see it.*

Joan was going on and on about Jack Lawrence, his personal grooming habits, his unruly children, his messy backyard. Karma shook her head and made concerned noises. *I can see the faucet on the corner of the house, which means Joan can see it, too. What if Joan sees Jeanette turn it on? And what if Jack Lawrence comes out and Joan starts yelling at him before he starts the fireworks? I need to get her off this patio.*

"Hey," said Karma. "I thought you wanted to talk about hostas. Where did you buy yours?" She jumped up out of her seat. "Let's go inside before the mosquitoes come out. You don't want to be itchy on top of everything else, right?"

Joan looked startled, but followed Karma inside. Karma grabbed a spot on the family room couch that faced the picture window, so that Joan would have her back to it. Karma could still see part of the Lawrence house, but Joan's fence blocked much of her view of the yard. Not only that, but the sun was almost down, and the security lights on the nearby houses were barely adequate. *C'mon, Kim, Karma thought, check the sprinkler.* Karma focused every bit of the psychic powers she desperately wished she had on her best friend. *Check the sprinkler... check the sprinkler... check the sprinkler...*

Kim and Jeanette should be strolling around the cul-de-sac by now, listening to Karma's baby monitor, which was turned on and in place near the Lawrence's back door. When Kim and Jeanette heard Jack come outside to light fireworks, they knew what to do. *Assuming he took the bait, of course, and came out at all.* If the phony email from Dave wasn't enough to provoke him, they were screwed.

"It's getting dark," said Karma. "Do you think that guy will be out again tonight?"

"Who knows," said Joan. "He's such an awful jerk. I hate being alone at night anyway, and I'm scared that he might know Greg is out of town." She sagged into the cushions of the couch and rubbed her pregnant belly. "I know that sounds crazy."

"No, it doesn't," said Karma. "Not to me." *Don't worry, Joan, we're gonna kick Jack Lawrence's ass for you.* Karma looked out the window. The back door of the Lawrence house opened, and there he was. Bathed in light from inside the house, Jack Lawrence stopped in his doorway, then turned back, apparently talking to someone still inside. Judging by his flapping arms, he was angry. He stomped out to his backyard shed and came back holding a large cardboard box. He dropped it onto the patio and slammed the back door, but without the light from the house, it was too dark, and Karma couldn't quite tell what he was doing.

Meanwhile, Joan was struggling to get her bulky body up from the overstuffed sofa. "Do you want something to drink?" she asked. "I have bottled water or juice, and there's diet soda in the garage; I don't keep it in here because I'm not supposed to drink it. Too much sodium, you know."

"Diet sounds great," said Karma. *Perfect.* She stood up, pretending she had to stretch, and saw exactly what she was hoping for: Jack setting up fireworks. *Where were Kim and Jeanette? Had they put the sprinkler back in the tree?*

Karma felt panic rising into her stomach. If they missed their chance, that was it. She would never get up the nerve to try this again. Karma ran for the front door, yelling back over her shoulder to Joan. "Hey, Joan, I just remembered I left my stove on. I'll be back in a minute."

She sprinted out the front door and down Joan's front steps, down the sidewalk and around the block toward Brentwood. Up ahead she saw Kim and Jeanette huddled together next to tall bushes two houses away from the Lawrence's. Kim had the baby monitor plastered to her ear. *Why were they still sitting there?* Karma slowed to a trot, afraid someone would see her running. She felt more like Maxwell Smart than one of Charlie's Angels as she ducked into the hydrangeas.

"Jesus Christ," squeaked Kim. "You want me to wet my pants?"

"Why are you just sitting here?" hissed Karma. "He's out there."

"We're listening for Jack to come out, and he hasn't," said Kim. "The sprinkler fell out of the tree and we had to put it back, then we came back here to hide."

"But he *is* outside," said Karma. "He's about to light the fireworks. I *saw* him."

105

Kim held the monitor tight to her ear. "All I hear is a whining baby."

"What baby? The Lawrences don't have a baby," said Karma. She looked around, trying to make sense of what was happening. There, in the second-floor window of the house next door to the Lawrences, were lacy curtains backlit by the glow of a nightlight.

"There's a baby in *that* house," said Karma, pointing. "Their monitor must be on the same frequency as mine."

Kim snapped at Jeanette. "Why didn't you tell me they didn't have a baby?"

"I didn't know you thought that was a baby. I thought it was one of their kids," said Jeanette. "It sounded like Allie."

There was no time to waste. The three women dodged and weaved from bush to tree to hedge, trying to stay quiet and out of sight. When they got to the Lawrence house, they crouched behind a clump of peonies that ran from the back corner to just under the dining room window, and peeked around the corner.

Jack was fumbling in his box of fireworks and talking to himself. "Goddamn bitch telling me what to do... give a shit about Dave Wallace and his fucking emails... hundred dollars... take his fine and shove it up his... screw that... do what I want... Luann better shut the fuck up... hit her again... stupid bitch."

Jeanette gave a horrified squeak. Her face was drained of color. "Did you hear what he just said? He hits her," she whispered. "He hits her. What are we gonna do?"

"We are going to do what we came here for, and teach him a lesson," said Karma. "I'm going back to Joan's and make sure she sees this."

"He hits her," said Jeanette.

"Focus," hissed Karma, brushing an ant off her shoulder. *Jeanette has the attention of a flea. Damn, these peonies are full of ants. Who plants peonies right next to their house? It's like*

106

inviting ants into your kitchen. I wonder if Jack really beats his wife. I wonder if Luann gets ants in her kitchen. I can't believe guys are beating their wives in my neighborhood. God, I hate ants.

"Keep your shit together, Jeanette, okay?" said Karma. "Get back to business. When Jack starts lighting the fireworks, people will hear the noise and come out to see what's going on. Don't do anything until I get Joan outside. Wait until you see me on the back patio. Got it?"

Jeanette nodded. Her eyes were filling with tears.

"You can cry later," said Karma, scratching at an ant bite. "He'll hear you and catch you, and if he hits his wife, God knows what he'll do to you." She backed out of the peonies and ran back to Joan's house, staying on the grass to cut down on the noise from her feet. She charged up Joan's front steps and knocked hard on the front door. *I can't take this crap. I've got to get in shape. Joan, get your pregnant ass out here and let me in.*

The door opened, and Karma pushed past Joan, heading toward the kitchen.

"Where were you?" Joan was holding a can of Diet Coke. "I came back in and you were gone."

"Sorry about that," panted Karma, smiling stupidly and holding the stitch in her side. "I do that all the time—forget to turn off the stove, I mean. Do you ever do that, or is it just me? Hey, let's sit outside."

Ignoring Joan's question about mosquitos, Karma opened the sliding glass door and stepped out onto the deck. From here she and Joan had a terrific view of Jack Lawrence's backyard. He'd been busy while she'd been running her ass off. Six wooden boards were now lined up in rows, and he was arranging the fireworks on the boards. Considering his yard looked like a junkyard, he was fussy about his fireworks. There had to be thirty or forty of them set out already, and he wasn't finished.

For a drunk, the guy was ambitious. Apparently he was gonna show the HOA president and Joan Handley and the rest of his neighbors who was boss.

The flare of his lighter made the breath catch in Karma's throat. *This is what it feels like at NASA when a shuttle is about to launch.* Karma turned to speak to Joan, but Joan wasn't there. *What the hell?*

"Hey, Joan," called Karma through the open sliding door. "Hurry up. Something's going on across the backyard."

Joan stepped onto her deck just in time. Jack was fast with that lighter. He was igniting the line of fuses like a real pro, and the glowing line of spitting fuses got longer and longer. Karma wondered if he was setting off everything he had, so nobody would be able to stop him. There was a pause, as the fuses burned down. Karma was holding her breath without even realizing it.

BOOM
BOOM
BOOM

Fireworks shot into the sky. Joan shrieked and turned to run back inside her house, but Karma grabbed her arm. "Don't go, you're gonna miss it."

"I need to call the cops," said Joan, trying in vain to pull away from Karma's tight grip. "I need my cell phone. You stay out here and be a witness. Oh my goodness."

BANG
BANG
BANG

It was glorious. Fountains of sparkling lights came streaming up from the ground, and bottle rockets lit up Jack's backyard like it was daylight. From homes on either side of Joan's, sliding glass doors opened and people burst out onto their patios and decks to see what was happening. All eyes were on Jack and his pyrotechnic extravaganza. He lit the last row and stepped back, hands on hips, back straight, proud as shit that everybody was watching him show up Big-Shot-Dave-Wallace-Who-Thought-He-Owned-The-Whole-Damn-Neighborhood.

When the first drops of water hit Jack's face, he looked up stupidly. He had just enough time to think *am I seeing rain?* and register the incongruity of precipitation coming from the cloudless night sky.

The next moment, sprays of water shot up from the ground and down from the trees, all aimed right at him. Hoots of laughter rang out from one patio after another. Jack stood transfixed, trying to understand what was happening, then hollered, hopped and danced in circles, trying to escape the downpour and save his precious fireworks. They were still shooting off in spite of the rain, as Jack had been careful to place them away from the low-hanging branches of his untrimmed trees.

By the time his beer-addled brain could register that his own sprinklers were somehow attacking him, and that one had climbed into a tree to do it, Jack Lawrence was soaked to the bone. He tried to grab the hanging sprinkler, but it was whipping back and forth, propelled by the force of the water pulsing from it. A crazed instrument of watery vengeance, the sprinkler evaded his grasp and whacked him twice on the head, once on the upswing and again on the way down. Jack fell backwards, knocking into a sputtering sparkler cannon.

The cannon, now aimed into the yard instead of up toward the sky, shot straight into Jack's open garden shed. Jack, cursing and slipping on the wet grass, was struggling to stand upright when the shed burst into flame, lighting up the tiny wooden building like a small sun. Apparently, Jack had left some of his fireworks in the shed after all.

Sparks shot out the open shed door in every color of the rainbow. Then the windows blew out, sending showers of glass in all direction. Whistles and bangs rent the air. Some neighbors held their ears against the noise; others held their phones aloft to catch the spectacular destruction.

What happened next became the stuff of neighborhood legend, as well as a lesson in storing petroleum-based fuel. Jack's rusty old lawnmower, also in the shed, was nearly empty of gas. Nearly. The less safety-conscious might have assumed that little gas meant little risk, but they would have been wrong.

The fumes that filled the nearly-empty tank were ignited by the heat from the exploding fireworks, and the lawnmower exploded like an IED. Hunks of lawnmower shot through the roof and walls. Jack had just managed to stand up when the blast knocked him off his feet again. As the neighbors watched open-mouthed, a nasty chunk of mangled lawnmower fell to the earth, missing Jack's head by inches, steaming and sizzling in the wet grass. The smell of hot metal reminded Jack of outdoor barbecues. And summer. He smiled.

He never told a soul what happened after that, because they would have said he was crazy. And maybe he was, because he saw something that couldn't have been real, something definitely impossible. He saw an enormous yellow *snake* sliding out of the remains of his shed. As it slithered past his head, it hissed at him in obvious disgust. *I need a beer,* thought Jack, just before he passed out.

CHAPTER 11:   WHAT WOULD OPRAH DO?

By the next morning, Jack Lawrence was the epicenter of neighborhood conversation. The only people not laughing about him with their friends were those who were laughing, but hadn't called their friends yet. The only exception were the three people thinking *most* about Jack Lawrence. They were *not* laughing. Well, two were laughing a little.

"He's done with fireworks for a while," smirked Kim.

"Thanks to us," said Karma.

"Thanks to us," agreed Kim.

Jeanette said nothing.

The co-conspirators were back at the neighborhood playground, sitting on the landscape timbers that separated the grass from the mulched area that held the swings, slides, and other kid-friendly equipment. The low, hard timbers were even less comfortable than the benches, but they were farther away from other parents. This conversation had to stay private. Kim smiled and waved at Lindsey, who was on a swing, frantically pumping her skinny legs to get it to move. As soon as Molly's cast came off so she could hold the swing properly, Karma would teach her to pump, too. It would be so nice to sit and relax, and never again hear the dreaded *Mommy, push me on the swing. Mommy, do an under-duck. Mommy, higher!*

"Dave talked to the fire marshal this morning," said Kim. "He's meeting with the county prosecutor. They're not sure what charges to file, since Jack only damaged his own property."

Karma turned to Jeanette, who could usually be counted on to have an opinion on such matters, but Jeanette said nothing.

Karma didn't mind if no charges were filed. An asshole had been put in his place. It would be years before anybody in Bedford Commons looked at Jack Lawrence and didn't picture him lying in the mud, watching his shed explode. Maybe he'd have the good taste to move away. *Neighborhood improved; mission accomplished.* "It was perfect," Karma said. "A perfect plan."

"Our work here is done," said Kim.

Jeanette spoke quietly. "No, it is not. What about Luann? What about what Jack said? What if he beats her because of us?"

Karma was confused for a moment. In all the excitement of the explosion and the fire trucks and the ambulance, she'd forgotten about Jack's threat against Luann.

"It's our fault for sending that email and making him so mad that he hit her," said Jeanette.

Kim arched an eyebrow. "*You* didn't send the email."

Jeanette looked right back at her, not backing down. "I'm not blaming you and Karma. I'm just saying that we provoked him, and now he's going to beat his wife, or he already has, and we have to do something about that." She looked close to tears.

A few heads turned in their direction, and Kim gave Jeanette a warning look.

"Do what?" said Karma. "Maybe he was just talking. Maybe he didn't really mean it. Even if he did, we didn't *make* him do anything. If he even did it. It's not our fault."

Kim elbowed her in the ribs. "Keep your voice down."

"You don't believe that. We are responsible," hissed Jeanette. "We have to do something about it."

Karma couldn't remember ever seeing Jeanette like this, so assertive. She didn't like it. "Okay, let's say you're right. Let's assume he hit her *one time*. What can we do about it? We can't call the police and report something we shouldn't know about in the first place."

Jeanette kicked at a clump of grass poking up through the mulch. "We can make an anonymous phone call to the cops and say we overheard Jack threaten Luann. Or maybe we can talk Luann into calling the police herself."

"We are *not* calling the cops," said Karma. "We'll get arrested for arson. Don't forget about caller ID; you can't make anonymous calls anymore."

"We can buy a burner phone," said Jeanette. "Like drug dealers use."

"Jesus H. Christ," said Kim. "We are *not* calling the cops and we are *not* talking to Luann." Kim mimicked Jeanette's high-pitched voice. "Hey, Luann, we were sneaking around your bushes getting ready to hose down your husband and we heard him say he hits you. Wanna talk?"

Jeanette's eyes filled with tears. "All I know is we have to make this right. It's our fault."

"For God's sake, Jeanette, calm down," said Karma, unnerved by Jeanette's loss of control in the middle of the playground. "We'll figure this out, but if you start crying, people are going to come over here to see what's wrong."

"Here," said Kim, reaching into her jacket pocket for a tissue. She felt guilty for imitating Jeanette, if that's what had made her cry. But as always, Jeanette was useless in a crisis and Karma was only a little better. As always, Kim knew, it would be up to her to take charge.

"Oh, shit." Karma waved an arm, smiling enthusiastically and snarling under her breath, "Here comes Bianca. Get it together, Jeanette."

"Yeah," reminded Kim, also giving a friendly wave. "We're *not* talking about this in front of Bianca or Sue Ellen, you got that?"

Bianca was just leaving the walking path, about fifty yards away. She was pushing two-year-old Ginny in her stroller, and considering a little domestic violence of her own. Caitlin had insisted on riding her Barbie scooter down the walking path, but she kept running it off into the grass because she couldn't steer the stupid thing. She'd fallen off six times. *How the hell do you fall off something that's three inches off the ground and still manage to tear a hole in your new pink stretch pants that you were told not to wear in the first place?* When she and the girls finally reached the corner of the big slide, Bianca pulled Ginny from the stroller to let her walk the rest of the way, then told Caitlin to leave the flippin' scooter in the grass before Mommy threw it in the trash.

Karma watched the drama unfold, glad that Molly didn't own a scooter; she'd break her neck. When Bianca finally reached them, she eased herself down onto the landscape timbers next to Karma and stretched her long, tan legs into the mulch. Her aquamarine toenails were freshly manicured and polished, and matched her fingernails.

"Hey," said Karma, "how's your day going?"

"My day?" Bianca gave a dismissive wave of her slender, perfectly-manicured hand. "Besides trying to get out here without killing my kids, pretty dull. I made breakfast, filled the dishwasher, started some laundry, watched a little news. The usual. Actually, I think you three bitches are leading much more interesting lives than I am."

Karma met Bianca's hard gaze with bland innocence. Then she picked up a particularly fascinating piece of redwood stained mulch and examined it closely. "Well, I ordered one of those detergent balls on TV. I'm pretty excited about that. You every try one of those?"

Bianca raised one perfect eyebrow. "No, never. I've never blown up a garden shed either."

114

"We haven't either," said Jeanette. "We were at a candle party."

"Without me?" said Bianca. "What did you buy?"

"Nothing," said Jeanette. "I mean besides candles. We just bought candles."

Bianca slapped her hand down on her smooth bare thigh. "I knew it. I knew it had to be you guys. Holy crap." Several moms look over at them.

"Keep it down," said Kim. "We don't know what you're talking about."

"Me neither," said Jeanette, "but you want to hear something terrible? Jack Lawrence beats his wife."

Kim groaned and Karma dropped her face into her hands, as details of last night's escapade poured out of Jeanette. To her credit, Jeanette was keeping her voice low, but Bianca's bilingual cursing got louder and louder as the story spun on. The other parents on the playground couldn't understand the Italian, but they kept turning around to see what the fuss was about.

"*Mizzica*," said Bianca when Jeanette was finished. "When you three stick your noses in other people's business, you don't screw around. But you're damn lucky; I've heard at least four versions of what happened, all different, but nobody mentioned any of you. Nobody can figure out how the sprinklers came on, but people figure it was one of Jack's kids."

"I can live with that," said Kim.

"Are you sure?" There was a chilliness in Bianca's voice that made Karma shiver.

Bianca looked around to make sure no one else was listening. "That's why I came out here to find you three. Jack thinks his kids were playing with the hoses, and the neighbors say they're all being punished until one of them admits they did it."

Karma felt her heart sink into her shoes. "Shit."

"You know that for sure?" asked Kim.

Bianca nodded. "Kathy Fitzgerald heard it from Jody Martin, and she's pretty reliable."

Kim swallowed hard, but said nothing.

"There's more," said Bianca. Her cold voice had turned to ice. "Kathy said that Jody said that the Lawrence's next-door neighbors heard him yelling at Luann that it's her fault their kids are brats who can't keep their hands off his stuff. He was really pissed. Jody says he spanked them with a belt. All three of them. Can you live with *that*?"

Jeanette started to cry again, but Kim still looked doubtful. "Somebody would know if that was going on."

"Don't you watch *Oprah*?" Jeanette dabbed at her eyes. "Nobody knows about this stuff until it's too late. We have to do something; this is all our fault."

"It was almost way worse," said Bianca. "When you blew up his lawnmower it coulda landed on his head and killed him. It almost did, right? Then you'd have blood on your hands. This isn't a joke. You coulda killed the sonofabitch. Like murder."

Neither Kim nor Karma had really considered this. Jeanette looked like she might scream.

"Stay calm, Jeanette," said Karma. Her nerves were crackling. "If you get hysterical, I swear to God I'm gonna slap you. He didn't die. We don't know what's going on with Jack *or* Luann *or* their kids, and we're not going to do something stupid until we're sure." She paused. "You know what I mean."

"But how do we find out?" asked Kim. "It's not something you can just walk up and ask somebody. 'Hey, I love what you're doing with your hair. By the way, does your husband beat you and the kids?'"

"Well, maybe that's exactly what we *should* do," said Jeanette. "She needs to know that people care about her."

"I'm trying *not* to care," said Kim. "Certain people are going to have a cow if they find out we had something to do with the fireworks last night." She looked sharply at Karma, who realized she was talking about Dave. He wouldn't appreciate being the presumptive author of the email that had set the whole affair in motion. Jeanette had left out that part of the story, maybe because she hadn't been there, but it was just a matter of time before it all came out.

Thoughts bounded and rebounded inside Karma's head. *We were protecting a pregnant woman. Now we've provoked a wife-beating child abuser. Why can't these things stay simple?* But then she had a new thought, a more hopeful one.

"Jack Lawrence being a jerk is not exactly a state secret," said Karma. "Lots of people know he yells at Luann, so somebody could talk to her about what *everybody* knows, that Jack yells a lot, and see if she'll admit the rest and get some help. That way, we've done the right thing, and we don't have to tell her how we found out about it."

Jeanette's eyes were wide as tea cups. "That's exactly what Oprah does. She confronts people with little stuff like that, and then they break down and tell her the whole mess, and everybody cries, and she pays for therapy and gives them a car." Her eyes sparkled. "Don't you just love Oprah?"

Karma had always appreciated Jeanette for her warmth and her innocent, childlike spirit, but right at that moment she wanted to shove her into the mulch. Even though talking to Luann had been Karma's idea, moments ago, now it sounded stupid. It wasn't going to end with hugs and free cars. Who in hell would sit down with Luann, whom they barely knew, and get her to open up about her twisted marriage and her sick-ass husband?

It was too bad there were no Intervention Home Party Consultants to provide handy check-lists, tips on how to invite the guest of honor, ideas for break-the-ice confessional games, and discount therapy coupons if you signed up tonight and booked your own intervention. "So who's going to talk to her?" she asked. "Not me."

"It was your idea," reminded Kim.

"You'd be better at it than I would," said Karma.

"Nice try. Forget it."

"Can I do it?" asked Jeanette. "Please? Let me."

"*Il mio Dio*," breathed Bianca.

"You *want* to talk to her?" asked Karma.

Pink splotches appeared on Jeanette's cheeks and her eyes were shining. "In high school I was voted *Most Likely to Have My Own Talk Show.* People tell me things, even personal things, even strangers. I can do it. I know I can."

Kim looked at Jeanette. "Your high school voted on who would have their own talk show?"

"Well, my daddy got transferred," said Jeanette, "and I did my senior year in Los Angeles."

CHAPTER 12:   INNOCENT BABY COWS

So it was agreed that Jeanette would handle the Luann Situation, which left Karma free to attend to a more personal and immediate crisis. Sunday was her mother-in-law's birthday, and Karma had invited the family to come for dinner and a small celebration. Sylvia was turning seventy-five, which she had announced was a "milestone" birthday. Her well-developed sense of entitlement had kicked into high gear, and she had declared to Sam and Karma that she wanted a special party with the entire family. *Special party* was a euphemism for *expensive nightmare*.

When Sunday arrived, Karma was up with the sun. She showered, dressed, hauled Grandma Minnie's good dishes down from the attic, washed each piece by hand, prepared a shopping list, and made a run to the grocery store, all before Sam and Molly woke up. When she walked back into the house, the familiar sounds of *Scooby Doo* were blasting from the family room, and Molly, still in her jammies, was cuddled up with Sam, sharing a bowl of sugar frosted somethings, sans milk. Molly and Sam were transfixed by the riveting action on the screen, and barely acknowledged Karma's presence. In other words, it was a typical Sunday morning.

"Don't tell me," said Karma, setting down her grocery bags. "There's a mysterious monster on the loose, but it's not really a monster, it's a diabolical mad scientist or a greedy real estate mogul pretending to be a monster to scare everybody away."

"Don't ruin it," said Sam.

"It's not a monster, it's a ghost," said Molly.

Sam extricated himself from under his daughter, and helped carry in the groceries from Karma's mommy van.

"Veal?" he asked, unpacking the first bag and examining a package wrapped in white butcher paper.

"I'm going to impress your mother," said Karma. "Veal scaloppini, French bread with olive oil for dipping, Brussels sprouts, ginger carrots, Caesar salad, and a chocolate cake with raspberry filling."

"Holy crap," said Sam, looking closer at the package of meat. "Thirteen dollars a pound?"

"Don't worry about the money," said Karma. "A few more episodes of *Scooby Doo* and we can stop saving for college. She'll never get in."

"I think you underestimate the real genius behind that show," said Sam, putting the carrots and romaine lettuce in the refrigerator. "It's not easy to do the same plot week after week and still keep it so fresh and believable."

"Hey, would you mind vacuuming?" asked Karma. "I don't need any cracks from your mother about my housekeeping skills."

Sam put his arm around Karma's shoulder, brushed her hair aside and kissed the back of her neck. "You don't have any housekeeping skills, so she probably won't say anything."

"You're a very funny guy," said Karma. She reached into a drawer and pulled out a cast aluminum meat mallet. "It's so sad about the tragic accident you're about to have."

Veal scaloppini turned out to be a daunting culinary challenge, made more nerve-wracking by the distinct possibility of destroying thirteen-dollar-a-pound veal. Karma pounded the veal steaks, accidentally rendering the first one so thin you could read the recipe through it. She'd eat that one, if necessary. She sprinkled the rest with salt and pepper, dredged them in flour, dipped them in beaten egg, and browned them in a mixture of butter and oil. It was a messy, time-consuming business, but Sam was just as busy as she was, straightening and vacuuming and cajoling Molly to put away her toys.

Karma tried to remember if her own father had ever pitched in like this. He and Charlotte had divorced when Karma was nine. He had remarried twice, while Charlotte put Kathleen in a nursing home, went back to work and devoted her free time to driving her remaining daughter insane. Karma couldn't remember her mother playing games with her or coloring or doing crafts; she was always cleaning or cooking or shopping. Karma's dad (or more likely his current wife) always sent a present on Karma's birthday and he usually remembered to at least call Molly on hers. He was an acceptable father and a decent grandfather, if you kept your standards low. Sam was far, far better, in Karma's opinion, and she was a far superior mother. Molly knew that she was more important to her parents than a freshly swept floor. In fact, Molly had rarely seen a freshly swept floor.

There was nothing like a burst of smug superiority to motivate Karma. She arranged the veal in a sparkling glass dish, then sliced and sautéed the fresh mushrooms. The earthy, sweet smell of butter and fungi filled the kitchen. After spooning the mushrooms over the veal, Karma unwrapped the Gruyere cheese, sliced it thin, and laid the pieces carefully over the mushroom-topped veal.

Stepping back to admire her work, Karma silently defied anybody to criticize this gastronomic tour de force. She covered the pan with foil and put it in the refrigerator for last-minute baking, shoving aside unidentifiable leftovers to make room. *I really should clean out this refrigerator*, she thought, but today's priorities were messes that *showed*, and anyway, if God cared about the insides of refrigerators, they'd have glass doors.

The rest of the afternoon was a whirlwind of activity. Karma made piles of Sam's stuff and Molly's stuff, and they dutifully put their stuff away. Karma stuffed *her* stuff into paper bags and stuffed them in the closet. Of course, there was still a stack of magazines on the coffee table, and a lot of shoes in front of the bookcase off the kitchen, but Molly dove happily into the task of arranging the foot ware in complex patterns of color and size, if not by actual pairs.

At the appointed hour, the birthday girl was the first to arrive. Sylvia walked into the family room, greeted her son and granddaughter with warm hugs and kisses, then turned and surveyed the room. She greeted her daughter-in-law with an understanding smile. "Karma," she said. "You're so lucky that Sam doesn't mind living in a messy house."

That turned out to be the high point of the evening. Karma learned from Sylvia that an *experienced* chef would never have refrigerated the veal scaloppini before baking, and that this was the cause of its chewy texture. The experience wasn't all bad—Karma learned new respect for her own powers of self-control, as she successfully fought off the impulse to sink a serving fork into Sylvia as she picked at her food.

But when it came to Most Dramatic Performance by a Crazy Relative, Sam's sister, Sharon, was a tough contender. Newly divorced, twenty pounds heavier than she'd been at Christmas, and traveling on her mother's credit card, she had sniffed theatrically as she entered the kitchen.

"What is that smell?"

"Veal scaloppini," said Karma. She had waited, smiling in anticipation of the coming ooohhs and aaahhhs.

Sharon's smile then froze, before morphing into a tight-lipped frown. "Veal? Seriously? Didn't Mom tell you?"

"Tell me what?"

"I'm a Vegan." Sharon had glared at her mother, who was sniffing the unused mushrooms on the cutting board and making a face. Sylvia glared right back.

"Vegan?" she said. "That's about food? I thought it was that 'Men are from Mars, Women are from Venus' thing. Honestly, Sharon, I didn't think Karma would care about that. I know *I* don't."

"Mother," began Sharon.

"Sharon," said Sylvia, interrupting and drawing herself up to her full five-foot-nothing. "Do not lecture me. I may not keep up with my children's hobbies, but I have always supported your interests. Didn't I buy a $600 vacuum cleaner from you? And $75 vitamins? And those minerals from the prehistoric rain forest? And the skin cream that gave me the rash? So when you tell me you're from Venus, I nod my head and say, 'That's nice, dear.'"

"I'm not from Venus, Mother," roared Sharon. "I'm a vegan. A VEEEE-GAN. And you would be too, if you knew what I know about veal. Innocent baby cows, Mother."

"Sharon," said Karma, with a nod toward Molly, who, at four years old, didn't need to hear about the fate of baby cows. "I'll scrape the cheese off the veal and you can eat that. In fact, I'll give you the cheese off *my* veal if you'll drop the subject *now*."

"I'm lactose intolerant," sniffed Sharon, "and anyway, I'm opposed to the cruelty of the dairy industry."

Karma sighed. "I've made two vegetables and a salad."

"Are there animal products in it?"

There was a long pause. Molly looked up at her aunt. "No dessert if you don't eat," she scolded.

Karma tapped Molly's shoulder to quiet her, but she should have reached for the duct tape.

"But my mommy says you don't need cake," said Molly, "and we can't have candles, because Grandma so damn old we'll burn down the house."

When the guests had gone home and Molly had been put to bed, Karma and Sam sat on the couch in the family room to finish off the wine. Sam slugged down the last of the red, straight from the bottle, and Karma did likewise with the white.

"That was great," said Sam. "I thought my colonoscopy was fun, but that was way better."

"I love your mom and your sister," said Karma. "I used to wish I'd been born into the Manson Family, but now I find I envy you instead."

Sam took another swig. "Everybody does," he said. "Hey, let's take a walk around the neighborhood before we go upstairs and hang ourselves in the bedroom closet? We don't even have to walk fast, just a nice slow pace."

Karma swung her feet off the coffee table, set down her empty wine bottle, and stood up. "That's a great idea. Maybe we'll get lucky and a bit of space debris will fall and kill us."

"That would be a fitting end to my mother's birthday," said Sam. "You get the baby monitor and I'll find our shoes in Molly's collection."

Karma climbed the stairs and crept into Molly's room to turn on the baby monitor transmitter. It wasn't there.

Where did I leave...

...oh my God.

CHAPTER 13:   GUESS WHO'S COMING TO DINNER

Karma wasn't the only one having a tough night. For the third time in minutes, Jeanette reached for the phone, then drew her hand back. Her mother's sarcastic sneer echoed in the empty kitchen. *Who do you think you are?*

Her own inner voice was no more comforting. *I'll mess this up. I mess everything up.*

But Oprah Winfrey had the last word: *You can be somebody's angel.*

Jeanette took the deep, cleansing breaths she had learned in yoga class, before Little Jeffrey bit the teacher and she had to quit, and dialed Luann Lawrence's number. *She'll say no. She'll be busy with her kids and sports and school programs and doctor's appointments. I can say I tried, but, oh well, what could I do?*

Minutes later, blinking in confusion, Jeanette hung up the phone. She wasn't sure what had just happened. Was it good or bad? It was good because Luann had accepted her invitation. But she was coming *tomorrow night*. And not to an easy, low-key lunch. Luann had said dinner was more convenient than lunch, and how about tomorrow night? And then she said, "We'd love to come." We? We *who*?

This was supposed to be a friendly lunch for Luann and Jeanette, so they could get to know each other and then Jeanette could talk Luann into leaving her abusive, wife-beating, jackass of a husband. Jeanette would be Oprah and Luann would be the Battered Wife in Denial Who Has an Emotional Breakthrough on the Road to Recovery.

But that's not what was going to happen. For heaven's sake, Oprah doesn't have the husband and kids on the set. *Everybody knows that.* They're supposed to wait in the Green Room, although Jeanette had read that this room wasn't really green. It seemed to her that it wouldn't be that difficult to paint it green; there were some really trendy greens out there. Jeanette had thought about painting her own family room green, but that would mean new furniture and Jeff had said no new furniture until Little Jeffrey left for college or juvenile detention, which Jeanette didn't find very funny, if you want to know the truth. But this lunch had somehow become dinner, and *I* had turned into *we*.

Sure enough, when the doorbell rang the next night, there they all were: Jack and Luann and the three Lawrence children. They'd even spruced up for the occasion. Luann had on a black print top with tiny red roses and silky black pants that were quite flattering. Jack's blue Polo shirt was stretched tight across his belly, but still, it looked like he'd gone to some trouble. His Sans-a-belt slacks were clean and creased. Did Luann do that for him, or maybe they came that way? Jeff liked natural fibers, but you had to iron them to get them to look right, unless you took them out of the dryer right away, which was hard to do when you were chasing three kids around all day. Also the buzzer on the dryer made Baby Jacob cry, so you had to listen for the sound of the dryer not making a sound, which wasn't really a sound, it was the *lack* of a sound and it's hard to hear a sound that's not there.

"Jeanette? Honey?"

Jeanette suddenly realized that she was staring at Jack's crotch. "I'm so glad y'all could come," she said stupidly. She had to relax. This night was about opening the door of friendship to Luann, just wide enough to kick Jack's big fat butt out of it, but now she had to figure out how to do it with Jack *here*. And without getting punched in the nose.

Starting the conversation turned out to be easy. Little Jeffrey looked up at Jack with his sweet little darling face and asked, "Did you really almost burn down your house?"

"Well, I guess you could say so," said Jack, "but I had help."

Jeanette stopped breathing. *OH MY GOD, HE KNOWS.*

Jack smiled down at Little Jeffrey. "Do you play with your Daddy's garden hoses? My kids can't seem to keep their hands off mine, although they won't admit it."

With no expression on her face, and not a word, Luann hustled her three young scapegoats past their father.

"Kids will be kids," said Jeff, with a half-hearted chuckle.

"Whatever the hell that means," said Jack.

"Good one," said Jeff stupidly, giving him a supportive pat on the shoulder and leading him into the family room. Jeff wasn't altogether sure why his wife had invited these odd people over for dinner, but Jack Lawrence didn't seem like a bad guy, in spite of what people were saying. Jeff could easily believe that children could hang garden hoses in trees and douse you with water when they should have been in bed. He was Little Jeffrey's father.

As the evening wore on, Jeff was more and more impressed with the Lawrence kids, who were remarkably well-behaved during dinner. Their quiet good manners provided quite a contrast to his own kids.

Jeanette saw the differences, too. She watched the three Lawrence children, ages six to nine, eating with utensils, wiping their mouths with their napkins, and drinking milk without protest and without spilling. She noted how they asked politely for more food, stopped kicking their feet when asked, and spoke to their parents and each other without arguing, spitting, screaming, cursing, swearing, shrieking, or whining. *It broke her heart.*

Those poor little children were so obviously abused, it was all she could do not to cry. As she wiped Little Jeffrey's spaghetti off the wall, reminded Allie again to stop eating the other kids' food with her fingers, and picked the pasta out of Baby Jacob's ears, Jeanette prayed that Jesus would help Luann, and remove the fear of their cruel father from these poor Lawrence children, so they could be normal kids like her own.

After dinner, the children went down to the basement to play, and the adults sat in the family room with the rest of the wine and a plate of Jeanette's homemade cookies. It was now or never, Jeanette told herself. She had to talk about the elephant in the room: Jack's abuse. She hoped that Jeff would jump in and help her, though he had no idea what this evening was really about.

Jeff had his own ideas about what the evening was about. The Bears were facing the Packers in ten minutes, and he'd established over dinner that Jack was a fellow Bears fan. He reached for the TV remote, but at the look Jeanette shot him, stopped, and rested his twitching hand in his lap. Jeanette, having simmered along with the spaghetti sauce all afternoon without thinking of a better strategy, took a big swig of her third glass of pink Chablis and fired the first shot.

"Luann, did you see the Oprah show about women who were abused by their husbands? They were so brave, I just cried and cried. Oprah's gonna pay for college for all their kids. Don't you just love Oprah?"

"I work during the day." Luann picked up her wine glass and took a little sip. "Where did you get these coasters? They're pretty."

Denial, denial, denial. Jeanette's juices were pumping now, fueled by desperation and pink Chablis. *If the mountain won't come to Mohammed, then Mohammed would go... no, that*

129

couldn't be right. A mountain couldn't go to somebody. What was that other mountain thing? About molehills? A molehill wouldn't look like a mountain unless you were very small, like a mole. How big is a mole?

"Honey," said Jeff, "Jack and I really want to watch the game. Do you mind? We can go downstairs."

"Jack," said Jeanette, "Do you think battered women should leave their husbands?" Even as she heard herself ask the question, Jeanette couldn't quite believe she'd just blurted it out like that. Jeff's mouth dropped open. Luann's expression was, as ever, blank.

Jack Lawrence, on the other hand, looked thoughtful. "I think it's hard to judge what's going on in other people's marriages."

Jeanette took another gulp of wine. It seemed to be helping. "But you don't think a woman should stay with a man who's beating her, do you?"

Jeff patted his wife's arm. "Honey," he said, "maybe we could talk about this after the game?"

"Don't you think people with problems like that should get help?" asked Jeanette.

Jack seemed to be searching for the right words.

C'mon, just say it, begged Jeanette from inside her head, or perhaps her wine glass. *Ask for help. Just ask.*

"We don't know each other well," he began, "and this is awkward, but there's something I want to tell you."

Jeanette held her breath. *Praise Jesus. Praise Oprah.*

"If Jeff here ever lays a hand on you, you call me. He's in better shape than me, but I think I can take him." Jack grinned broadly, and Jeff laughed and said, "I'll bet you could."

Still smiling, Jack stood up and stretched. "Well, I hate to break this up, but it's getting late. We'd better get our kids home. Thanks for dinner. It was delicious. Next time you'll have to come over to our place."

The men went downstairs to retrieve the kids, and Luann gathered up their coats. Jeanette sat on the sofa, dazed, trying to recall the license number of the truck that had just flattened her.

A few goodbyes, come agains, and thank yous, and the Lawrence family was gone.

Jeff took the kids up to bed, and Jeanette picked up dishes and serving platters and began to fill the dishwasher. She felt more than a little drunk, and more than a little discouraged. *How did I make such a fool of myself? Will Luann ever open up to me? Will Jack ever let her come back?*

Where did I buy those coasters?

CHAPTER 14:   GUILT & PLEASURE

Friday playgroup (at Kim's house) couldn't come soon enough. Karma was anxious to see Jeanette. She had left voice mails and texts for Jeanette asking when would be a good time to retrieve the baby monitor. She'd asked Kim, but she didn't have it, so Jeanette must have put it in her purse or her pocket or somewhere. It wasn't like Jeanette not to answer, especially a text. It was also worrisome that she hadn't called to report on her lunch with Luann. There had been no recent police calls to the neighborhood, so it couldn't have gone *too* badly, but still, it almost seemed like Jeanette was avoiding Karma.

So on Friday morning, Karma coaxed and cajoled Molly through selecting an outfit, combing her hair, and brushing her teeth, and hustled her out the door nearly on time. When they walked into Kim's house, just as Karma had hoped, it was clear that Jeanette was there. Karma floated in on the sticky sweet, soul-warming smell of cinnamon and nutmeg, with just a touch of cardamom. *God bless you, Grandma Bibi.*

Karma followed her nose into Kim's kitchen, which was sunlit and sparkling clean. The walls and curtains were a combination of muted greens, coffee browns, and rose pink. The effect was dramatic, and always made Karma wish she and Sam had been bolder in their color choices. Karma poured herself a cup of coffee and sat at her usual spot under the Green Bay Packer clock. Kim handed her the creamer pitcher shaped like a dairy cow, and Jeanette passed her a plate heavy with two big, warm, gooey cinnamon rolls. Sue Ellen was still scraping the

132

icing from her micro-sliver, and Bianca was nearly finished with healthy slab.

Only Kim was ignoring the smorgasbord she'd set up in her own kitchen, being too busy grilling Jeanette about her lunch with Luann to remember to eat. "C'mon, Jeanette, you didn't return two phone calls."

Jeanette was desperate to change the subject. "Bianca, you want another?" she asked, reaching for her plate. "Do you think they're overdone? I think they're a little dry today. Maybe I should go home and make another batch. It wouldn't take a minute."

She tried to stand, but Karma grabbed her by her sleeve. "Just stop. How did lunch go with Luann? I left you messages, too, and texts, and you didn't call me back either."

Jeanette sank back in her chair, pulled the end of her ash-blond ponytail around to the tip of her nose and stared at it, poking around for split ends. It was a habit from childhood that made her look cross-eyed, which had driven her mother crazy. She had only stopped nagging when young Jeanette had taken to biting her nails instead.

Jeanette took a deep breath. "I'm not really sure. I think I made a big fool of myself. Luann changed it to dinner, and all of a sudden it wasn't just Luann, it was her whole family, and she just wouldn't talk about anything important."

"Wait," said Karma. "She brought her family? For dinner?"

Jeanette nodded miserably and started picking at her cinnamon roll. "Jack was making fun of me, and her kids were there, so I couldn't say what I really wanted to say, and maybe she couldn't either, or maybe she didn't want to because I'm so stupid. I just don't know." Jeanette sniffed, like she might start to cry yet again.

Karma reached across the kitchen table and patted her arm. "That's not so bad. We knew it wasn't going to be easy. At least she knows she can talk to you about it. You did your best."

Jeanette pulled away from Karma's touch and attacked her ponytail again. "Well, that's not quite all. I should have made a fancier dessert." She paused, and her voice dropped just above a whisper. "And I may have drunk a little too much wine."

The table went silent.

"Jack was makin' fun of me, and I got so nervous."

Kim gave Karma a scathing look that screamed *I told you so*. She had told Karma a dozen times that Jeanette would screw this up. "How drunk were you?"

"Not drunk. Just a little… I don't know," said Jeanette, rising to full-on whine. "First Jack was bein' so nice, but then he ended up making a big joke outta me."

"The guy that beats his wife and kids and shoots fireworks at pregnant women?" asked Karma. "How nice could he be?"

"Well, he and my husband sure hit it off," said Jeanette bitterly. "Jeff thinks he's great. He thinks their kids are great, too. Of course Jeff doesn't understand children at all. I felt so sorry for those poor kids."

From the far corner of the kitchen, where she had retreated, ostensibly to arrange her daughters at the kids' table, Bianca gave a derisive snort. She had left the table in an effort to stay out of this ridiculous conversation, but she just couldn't. "Damn it to *fuck*, you guys. Leave it alone. Leave *them* alone. This is none of your business." She stalked back to the grown-up table and stood over the rest of the group, arms crossed and foot tapping. "Seriously, you guys, you don't know that Luann or her kids are being abused. I think you should just be glad you didn't get caught and nobody got killed. So just stop this whole thing. *Dio li fa, poi li accoppia*. 'God makes them, then he mates

134

them.' You got no business in their marriage. Besides, if they divorce they'll just find two other people to screw up."

"You weren't there," said Jeanette. "We heard him say it. He said he was going to hit Luann *again*."

Bianca shook her head. "It's not your business. This chick isn't some innocent little teenager. She's a grown woman who can look out for herself. If Tony ever hit *me*, he'd wake up in the morning dead."

"Not every woman is as strong as you," said Jeanette.

"They should be. My mom used to say to my dad, 'Go ahead and hit me, *bastardo*, but remember, you gonna fall asleep sometime.' You think he laid a hand on her? No ma'am. So let this Luann chick call the cops, and you guys stay outta her shit."

Nobody said a word. Bianca sat back down, glaring around the table. The silence went on for a bit too long. The friends ate, avoiding each other's eyes.

Finally, Karma couldn't take another second of the grim silence. "Hey, Jeanette, before I forget again," she said, "can I stop at your house after playgroup? I need the baby monitor."

Jeanette looked confused. "I gave it to you that night."

"You gave me the *receiver*," said Karma. "I need the transmitter we put in Jack's backyard."

Sue Ellen's perfect bow mouth dropped open. "You bugged his house? Is that legal?"

Karma rolled her eyes. "We didn't bug his house. We just put a baby monitor outside so we could hear when he started lighting his fireworks. That's totally different." She turned to look at Jeanette, and then Kim. "You did go back and get it, right? Kim said you had it."

Jeanette looked at Kim. Kim looked at Jeanette. Jeanette looked down at her plate. "I don't remember us talking about that," she said softly. "I don't think anybody told me to do that."

135

Kim's olive skin went several shades paler. "Oh shit," she whispered. "I figured she had to have it because I don't have it."

"You guys hid it by the door, not me," said Jeanette. "I never know exactly where."

Karma felt sick. She had been the one to place it in the thick weeds near Jack Lawrence's back door. But Kim had been right there, too. "How could you forget to pick it up," she barked.

"How could *you* forget?" said Kim.

"Me? I was with Joan," said Karma. "You were right there."

Sue Ellen and Bianca trade looks that said, *Thank God we weren't involved.* "Maybe y'all should go over and look for it," said Sue Ellen. "Maybe nobody noticed it."

"Yeah, you said his yard was a mess," said Bianca. "You better get over there and see if you can find it before somebody else does."

"Like Jack Lawrence," said Karma, glaring at Kim.

"Or the cops," said Kim, not meeting her eyes.

Karma, Kim, and Jeanette did look for the transmitter, though not until the sun was going down and they were less likely to be seen. The Lawrence house seemed empty, thank God. They looked in the weeds near the back door, they crawled in the nearby bushes, even picked through the rubble of the shed. They took turns, one standing guard while the other two searched. No luck. Nothing.

Maybe the Lawrence children had it, or somebody saw it lying around and took it. Even if a police officer or firefighter had found it, and even if, somehow, they figured out why it was there, could they trace it back to Karma? As they walked home, empty-handed, Karma and Kim tried to convince each other that there was no reason to panic.

"If you get rid of the receiver, they can't match it to the transmitter," said Kim.

"You're right. I'll throw the receiver away and tell Sam the whole thing broke. It was old anyway."

"Good," said Kim. "Problem solved."

"Problem solved," agreed Karma.

"Except that if they found the transmitter, it has both of your fingerprints all over it," said Jeanette.

There were times when Karma found herself hating Jeanette. This was one of those times.

CHAPTER 15:   TEENAGE MUTANTS, NINJA MOTHERS

Part One: Crime

Although Molly and her playgroup friends weren't old enough to attend kindergarten, the abundance of kids in their neighborhood had already made its mark on the local school system. Bedford Commons, which seemed to have sprouted overnight, had already forced bus routes to change and a new grade school to be built. You couldn't throw a stuffed animal without hitting a preschooler. On the other hand, teenagers were in short supply among these young families. This was bad if you needed babysitters, but it was good if you wanted to be free from teenage mischief.

But nothing lasts forever. The trouble started with a tree house on Maple Terrace, built in the branches of a dead oak on the edge of the community. When it was found deliberately demolished, cigarette butts were discovered at the scene of the crime. Then three bicycles were stolen from the playground and found at the bottom of a retention pond. A few days later, someone crawled under a partly open garage door and stole money and electronics from an unlocked car. Professionals would have robbed the house or stolen the car, according to the police, so this, too, was presumed to be the work of teenagers. The victims lived just a few houses away from Karma and Sam.

Residents began locking their doors even when they were home, and keeping their security lights on at night. Dave Wallace, Homeowners Association president, sent out a neighborhood email suggesting continued vigilance and warning of the consequences should the miscreants be caught. The local police agreed to increase their nighttime drive-bys, as well.

Mrs. Dave Wallace and her playgroup friends shook their heads and clucked their tongues, and thanked God their children weren't nasty teenagers. Jeanette was particularly thankful. One fine day their fresh-faced, pink-cheeked darlings would be driving cars, tattooing their butts, piercing their tongues, and shaving their heads, but thankfully, that day was not today.

"I'll tell you what scares me," said Kim. "Someday Lindsey is gonna come home all excited because some pimply-faced bag of hormones has asked her to the prom, and I'm going to spend two hundred bucks on some hooker dress and take pictures of her on our staircase."

"Not me," said Karma. "I remember prom and after-prom. Molly is going to a convent school. I just have to find one that takes Jews."

Kim smiled and zipped up her jacket against the breeze. Considering that Indiana is almost always too damn hot or too damn cold, it was a nice day, if a bit windy, and she and Karma were on the neighborhood walking trail with Molly and Lindsey. Their final destination was the playground. They were taking the long way around because a few days earlier, Karma had asked Kim to encourage her to get more exercise. She was not to take GO TO HELL NO for an answer. Molly and Lindsey were on their scooters, so they were covering ground faster than their mothers. In fact, they had disappeared around a bend and were probably at the playground by now.

Kim would have lied if Karma had asked about *her* prom. Between being short, dumpy, and not Caucasian, Kim had never thought of even *hoping* to be asked to high school dances and proms. That was for the popular, pretty White girls. But Karma hadn't asked, and Kim had certainly not volunteered the truth, certainly not today, when she could barely zip her jacket. She was back to weighing herself before bed, before lunch, and first thing in the morning. The news wasn't good, nor did she like what she was seeing in the bathroom mirror.

The irony of Karma asking her for encouragement to lose weight wasn't lost on Kim. She was in constant battle with her Inner Fat Girl, who was struggling to break out of the size six, now eight, prison she found herself in. But thanks to the internet, Kim's secret weapon was on its way. She hadn't worked this hard before the move to Indiana to give up now. Dave's transfer to Indiana had been a gift from heaven, a fresh start and a chance to meet new friends who didn't know her back when she used to spend her Saturday nights with two-liters of Coke and boxes of Ding Dongs and Ho Hos.

A shriek split the air. Kim and Karma looked at each other, then took off at a run. Kim, in spite of her short legs, was paces ahead in seconds. *Damn scooter. Lindsey's fallen off again. Why didn't I make her wear a helmet and kneepads?*

But before Kim even made it around the bend, the two little girls came racing back toward their mothers. They were running, no longer riding their scooters.

"Mommy," cried Molly, burying her head in Karma's thigh, "some boys scared us."

Lindsey was more revved up than scared, babbling about big boys, and something about the tunnel slide and a penis.

Did she say penis?

Kim's blood turned to ice. She guided Lindsey into Kim's arms, then raced to the playground. No one was there.

It took time to get the story out, due to Molly's wailing and Lindsey's over-amped excitement. When they had arrived at the playground, ahead of their mothers, the girls had seen a few older boys standing at the top of the slide, climbing on top of the cylindrical tunnel at the top. All the kids did this, no matter how many times they were warned that they'd fall and break their necks. The boys beckoned the girls to come over, and when they hesitated, two of the boys slid down and walked toward them. They didn't look mean, said Lindsey, in fact they were smiling as they approached. Then a different boy slid down the slide and pulled down his pants. His underwear, too. Molly screamed and both girls dropped their scooters and ran.

The scooters were laying where the girls had dropped them. The sight of the abandoned scooters gave Karma a chill. What if they had found the scooters, but not Molly and Lindsey? She almost wished the scooters were gone. Then you could call this theft, or maybe a stupid prank. What did you call *this*? "I'm going to take Molly home," she said. "Let's talk later."

Kim nodded, locking eyes with Karma for a long, grim moment. "Call me."

Once home, Karma parked Molly in front of the television with a sippy cup of juice, and slammed around in her kitchen. She wanted to call Sam, but he was at work, and he'd just get upset and want to come home early.

Karma also wanted to call the police, but what would she say? Molly didn't know the boys, they hadn't touched her, and there were no other witnesses. Would the cops see the threat the way she did? Her mind raced ahead. The little perverts hadn't even stolen their scooters. What was the worst the cops could do, even if they could catch them? Put one little piece of crap kid on probation for indecent exposure? Would she really make Molly tell her story again and again for *that* miserable payoff?

Karma grabbed a handful of clean knives and forks from the dishwasher, intending to sort them into the silverware drawer, but instead, slammed the entire fistful on the counter. Molly jumped and looked at her with large, terrified eyes.

"Sorry, baby," said Karma. "Mommy dropped the forks." She had to stay calm. Molly was an emotion amplifier, and if

Karma showed her rage, Molly would fall apart. She closed her eyes and took deep breaths.

So who were these boys? All Molly and Lindsey could say is that they were "big." There weren't many older kids in Bedford Commons, assuming they were local. If this gang hung out together, somebody had to know them. When Karma and Kim found them, they'd wish they'd never been born. Their parents would wish *they* had never been born. What she and Kim would do to them would make slashing the tires on the red car look like... like... well, never mind. *It would be BAD.*

Part Two: Investigation

Karma waited until Molly was eating a snack to call Kim on her cell phone. "Did Lindsey tell you anything else?"

"Nothing new, she's sticking to her story. Nobody touched them, the two boys were smiling as they walked toward them, and the third boy pulled down his pants and exposed himself. What do you think it means? Were those boys going to hurt them? What I mean is, when we catch them, do we get to *kill* them, or just beat them senseless?"

"Both," said Karma.

"The part that bothers me most isn't the kid pulling down his pants. I mean it's disgusting, but maybe that's teenage boy stuff," said Kim. "It's the other two boys walking toward them. What were they going to do if the girls hadn't run away? I don't want to think about it, but I can't stop thinking about it."

"Did you call Dave?"

"He's in a weekly staff meeting. I'm going to talk to him when he gets home. Lindsey will tackle him before he gets through the door. She can't stop talking about it, and she keeps asking why that boy wanted her to see his penis. If I have to hear my four-year-old daughter say *penis* one more time, I'm going to scream."

"What did you tell her?" asked Karma.

"I told her he thought he was being funny, and we're going to find him and tell his mommy."

"So you left out the part where you and I rip his penis off and leave it on the front porch for his mommy to find?"

"Yeah," said Kim. "I left that out."

Karma's suddenly realized her phone ear was throbbing, she was holding it so tightly against her head. She switched the phone to her other ear. "So how do we find them?"

"I've been thinking about that. I already searched Dave's neighborhood database for the ages of local kids, and I've printed out a list of all the kids thirteen and older. The database isn't up to date, but it's a place to start."

"That's smart," said Karma.

"Not to sound like Jeanette, but I didn't watch *America's Most Wanted* all those years for nothing," said Kim.

"Bianca's got an older kid," said Karma. Maybe he knows these boys, or knows *of* them. Should I call her? She's all pissy about the Lawrences, but this is different."

"Yeah, call her," said Kim. "If she doesn't want to get involved, remind her not to talk about it. Then call me back."

So Karma called, and Bianca did not disappoint. She was almost as angry as Karma and Kim. As the mother of two young daughters, she expressed no qualms about murdering any *pedofilo* who came near one of them.

"I'll talk to Andy," she said, referring to her seventh-grade son. "If it turns out that *other steps* are necessary, count me in, okay? I don't mix in other people's business," she said, "but shit like this doesn't count."

Karma sat down at her kitchen table with chips and cheese dip to calm her nerves, then called Kim back. Of the twenty-two

143

names that Kim had come up with, twelve were girls, but Kim noted that homeowners with older kids seemed less likely to fill out the new neighbor form, so there could be more. "So we can't rely only on the database," she said. "We have to outsmart these little bastards. I'm still thinking about it. Sorry, but I'd better go; I've got to start working on dinner."

"Whatcha cookin'?"

"Something with chicken thighs. They were on sale," said Kim. "And you know Dave. If there's no cheese on it, it's not a meal."

"That's what you get for marrying a Wisconsin boy," said Karma.

"He was a Packer fan," said Kim. "And we liked the same beer. In Wisconsin that's considered a love match."

Karma was glad for the reason to smile. "It's a good thing I have leftover meatloaf to serve," she said, "because I'd probably poison everybody if I had cook. I still have to tell Sam what happened." She wasn't looking forward to that. *How was your day? Molly was almost molested. How was your day?*

As it turned out, bringing up the subject to Sam turned out to be easy. When he walked in from the garage, Molly ran to him with a mournful expression and a clingy hug. "Daddy, a boy scared me, and he was naked and I saw his penis and Mommy's gonna kill him."

Holding his daughter, Sam looked over at his wife for some kind of explanation. Karma came over, gently disengaged Molly from her death grip around Sam's neck, and carried her back to the couch. "You finish your show while I talk to Daddy."

"Mommy, tell Daddy how you gonna kill that boy," said Molly.

"I will, honey."

Back in the kitchen, Karma retold the story quickly and quietly. She didn't want Sam to scare Molly by getting angry and

144

yelling about what *he'd* like to do to the boys. But Sam didn't get angry, and he didn't yell.

He said, "You shouldn't have left Molly alone."

Karma stared at him. "Molly was riding her scooter with Lindsey, and they got ahead of us. You think I let her ride around the neighborhood on her own?"

"No," said Sam, wishing he could suck back in what he'd just said. "I didn't mean it like that. I'm sorry. I'm really angry. *Not at you.* It's not your fault." He tried to put his arms around Karma, but it was like hugging a bundle of rubber bands. That was his own fault, he knew. He, not his wife, had let his family down. He had said what he said to deflect his own guilt. This was his fault, not hers.

Even before he'd held newborn Molly in his arms, Sam Kranski had feared this day, when he would fail the child he had come to love and something horrible would happen. What did he know about babies? What if he dropped it or fed it the wrong stuff or forgot to feed it at all? What if he crashed their car and his baby died? He'd never said so while they were undergoing all that infertility crap, but Sam had almost hoped that he and Karma wouldn't have a child, so that he'd never have to lose one. And now, in the space of weeks, his daughter had been hit by a car and flashed by a rapist, and he had not been there to stop any of it. And he'd made it worse by saying something stupid to Karma.

He apologized about twelve more times and said nice things about the leftover meatloaf, but dinner was a quiet affair. Sam decided to take a walk after dinner and talk to Dave Walters, since Lindsey had been part of this, too. Maybe Dave would have an idea about what to do. Meanwhile, Sam swore to himself that he would stay calm. Karma was an emotion megaphone; if Sam showed any signs of what he was feeling, or what he wanted to do to those boys, Karma would just get more upset. He had to stay outwardly calm for now, for her sake.

145

But it was too late for that; the megaphone was getting more upset by the minute. Sam was so damn calm she wanted to scream. First he called her a bad mother, and now he was acting like nothing had even happened. Karma felt a hardness coming over her. That was exactly what was wrong with marriage; it gives you the expectation that your spouse will be there when you need him, and it turns out you're just setting yourself up for disappointment.

Okay, Karma told herself. *So be it.* She and her friends would take care of this like they had taken care of the red car and Jack Lawrence. She would hide her resentment and her plan—when she came up with one—and keep all of it from Sam, for the sake of her marriage—pathetic though it was, and her daughter.

When her cell phone rang after dinner, Karma read the caller ID. *Finally.* Sam and Molly were playing checkers in the dining room, and didn't notice Karma creep upstairs to talk. She shoved aside the basket of unfolded clothes and sat on the edge of her unmade bed. "Hi, Bianca, what have you got?"

"I think I got something good. Andy says a couple of bigger boys stopped him on his bike last week on the walking path, and said they were going to take it and throw it in the pond. He says they've been picking on the little kids for quite a while. I bet it's the same bunch of little bastards; we don't have that many teenage boys around here."

"Did they take his bike?"

"Hell no, that's the best part," said Bianca proudly. "And it's why he said didn't tell me about it, because he took care of it himself. He told them his Uncle Mario was a cop, and if they messed with him, Uncle Mario would pop a cap up their asses. They called him a few names, but then they got out of his way."

"Smart boy," said Karma.

"Yeah," chuckled Bianca, "considering my brother lives in Pennsylvania, and believe me, he's no cop. Not even close.

146

Apparently, these boys have been doing other stuff the younger kids haven't talked about, too."

"Like what?"

"Oh, like blocking their way when they try to ride past on bikes, calling them names, threatening to beat them up, crap like that. Bedford Common's got a street gang of little punks, and we didn't even know about it."

Karma felt anger rising from the pit of her stomach to the pulsing vein in her forehead. "We are not going to stand by while a bunch of creeps ruin our neighborhood. Does Andy know their names?"

Bianca sighed into the phone, "He says he doesn't know, but I think he doesn't want to tell me. It's a boy thing. He figures I'll go after them, and everybody will know he's the one who narced. There's one thing he let slip—one of them mows lawns for money. I'll keep talking to him, but that's all I got for now."

"Hey, you got a lot. Give Andy a hug for me," said Karma. "I'll talk to Kim and get back with you."

"And I'll let you know if he says anything else."

Her next call was to Kim, who was appalled to hear about the bullying activities of the teenagers, but pleased that there was a way to find the little bastards. All they had to do was wait until the weekend and cruise the neighborhood. Surely they'd find a kid or two mowing someone else's lawn. "Lindsey can help," said Kim. "I think she'll recognize at least one of the boys. We'll take her with us."

Karma hesitated. "Is it a good idea to put her through that?"

"Why not?" said Kim. "She thinks bad boys should be punished. I happen to agree."

Part Three: Stakeout

147

Kim, Karma, and Lindsey met in the early morning to begin looking for the teenagers. They made an interesting surveillance team; Karma drove Kim's car, Kim rode shotgun, and Lindsey, 4, was crouched on the floor of the backseat. She refused to sit in her car seat, insisting on peeking out the window *so the bad boys won't see me*. Karma thought Kim was crazy, but Kim insisted that her kid was tough enough to handle it. Karma had no such confidence in Molly, so she was playing at Bianca's house. Molly had only just stopped talking about the *naked boy penis*, and Karma wanted to keep it that way. The plan was simple: drive around looking for boys mowing yards, and strike up a conversation about their availability for hire, to give Lindsey a good look at them.

They found their first suspect on Robinwood: a skinny dark-haired boy in baggy black athletic shorts, a white tee-shirt with the sleeves ripped off, and a backwards baseball cap. Kim parked the car and walked over to talk to him. She positioned herself so that he faced the car, to give Lindsey a view of his face. The kid happily gave up his name, address and phone number. *I am smooth*, thought Kim.

But when she came back to the car, she found her daughter head down and practically stuffed under the front seat. "Lindsey, honey," she said, "I'm here. It's okay. Nobody's going to hurt you. Was that one of the boys?"

"Help me, Mommy," cried Lindsey, "I dropped my marbles under the seat."

Karma sighed. "Do we have a Plan B?"

Despite the setback, they decided to keep trying. The next young man they found mowing looked too nerdy to threaten anybody, and Lindsey didn't recognize him. They found another boy to talk to, then a third, but Lindsey didn't recognize either one. She was losing interest in crime-fighting, and began asking for the Happy Meal her mom had promised her.

Karma turned left onto Cherry Tree Court and saw another kid mowing at the end of the block. If they struck out again, the women agreed to try to come up with a better idea. Kim ordered Lindsey to look carefully at this last boy, and left the car to speak to him. She was gone for what seemed like forever to Karma, whose own attention was flagging. A Happy Meal sounded good to her, too. *This was a stupid idea. Maybe Bianca's kid was wrong. Maybe instead of mowing, the little predators are making their money the old-fashioned way, producing kiddy porn. I'm tired. I'll just close my eyes for a second.*

The slamming car door jolted Karma awake, and Kim's breathless *STAY DOWN, LINDSEY* had her heart racing. She drove around the corner where the boy couldn't see them, swerved toward the curb, and slammed the car into park.

Lindsey flung herself into the space between Karma and Kim, eyes wide. "That's the naked boy. He came down the slide. The baddest boy."

Without a word, Kim slapped the notebook on her thigh, and Karma put the car into gear, and sped off, sending a giggling Lindsey flying backwards into the seat.

"Robert Gardiner," crowed Kim. Like all the others, this stupid kid had readily provided his contact information, hoping for another lawn mowing gig. "On Oak Terrace."

"I don't know the family," said Karma.

"I do," said Kim, "or at least I've heard of them. Dave's had a few calls from their neighbors. Loud music, parties on weekends, stuff like that. Nothing super serious, but I should have thought of the Gardiner kid."

"So what do we do?"

Kim didn't answer, and they drove on in silence. Karma could almost see the plot hatching in Kim's head. She pulled Kim's green Toyota sedan into the driveway, parked, and they headed for the front door. Kim was talking to herself. "We'll need more people. Four, maybe five. We need to outnumber the little bastards."

Karma sat down at Kim's kitchen table and watched Kim empty the dishwasher and wipe down the countertops, still muttering to herself. Then she left the room and came back with a broom and dustpan, with Totsy the dog at her heels. The dog trotted over to his empty food bowl and looked hopefully at his mistress, who was now sweeping the kitchen floor and muttering.

Karma leaned over and scratched Totsy behind her ears. "Don't worry, dog, she'll notice one of us eventually."

Kim looked up and seemed genuinely surprised to see Karma sitting in her kitchen. "Sorry. I'm thinking of a plan, a way to get all them together in one place. We have to catch them all, and we have to be sure we've got the right ones. Maybe we can scare the little pissers into confessing. Then we can call the cops."

"What do we need with a confession? And why would they confess? It's their word against two little girls. They'll just say they were trying to be funny."

Kim dropped into a kitchen chair. She ran her fingers through her glossy, stick-straight hair, letting it fall over her face like a dark curtain. "We have to try. They need to be punished."

"They're not going to confess, and even if they do, the best we can hope for is probation, and probably only for the one who dropped his pants. There's no law against smiling and walking up to two little girls."

"So what was the point of figuring out they are?" demanded Kim.

"It wasn't to waste time on the police," said Karma. "We can take care of this ourselves."

"I'm not sure what that means, but I wasn't totally serious about killing them," said Kim warily. "Were you?"

150

Karma shrugged. "No, not really. The point is to stop them from ever daring to do anything like this ever again. That solves the problem, which is the only thing that matters."

Part Four: Take Down

On Monday afternoon at 2:35, Kim's doorbell rang. The semicircle of women turned toward the sound, nervous, but ready. They knew their lines and the action had been blocked. This bit of theater would open and close on the same day, and, sadly, it would enjoy no reviews. In fact, if all went well, it would never be spoken of again, at least not in public.

Kim's formal living room was the stage for the drama, chosen for its rigid high-backed chairs and polished dark walnut end tables. The furniture had been a wedding gift from Kim's paternal grandparents, Norwegian immigrants she referred to as *The Stiffs*. There was no comfort to be found in this room, no squishy sofas to sink into and forget your troubles with a good book. There was nothing that inspired ease or warmth. In that respect, it was much like Kim's paternal grandparents.

Hand on the doorknob, Kim turned back and said, "Watch what you say. We don't want to get sued."

"Or arrested," said Sue Ellen.

Karma gave Molly's arm a gentle squeeze. "You and Lindsey remember what we talked about. There's nothing to be scared of, and lots of reasons to be brave. We're doing this for all the other little kids in the neighborhood, right?"

Lindsey put a protective arm around her best friend, Molly. "We not afraid of big dumb boys."

"That's right," said Karma.

"*Dumb* is a bad word," scolded Molly.

Kim ushering four young men into the room. Robert Gardiner was in the lead, but when he saw the stony-faced women and the two little girls, he stopped so suddenly he almost caused a pile-up behind him. He tried for a smile, but fear and confusion turned it into an awkward grimace.

Molly Kranski was pressed against Karma's leg, but Lindsey Wallace stared down the bad boy. Lindsey was her mother's daughter, from her narrow dark eyes and pouty lips to her tightly crossed arms and wide fighter's stance—a miniature Korean-American Mulan.

Kim sat down in one of the uncomfortable straight-backed Napoleon chairs and patted the empty one next to her. "Sit down, Robert," she said. "I invited a few friends over because we're all interested in *lawn care*." Robert Gardiner appeared to be unable to move. "SIT," she repeated. Kim's will was strong; Robert Gardiner sat. His friends stood behind him.

"So tell us what kind of yard work you boys do," asked Kim.

Robert looked over his shoulder to see who wanted to speak for the group. The answer seemed to be nobody. A tall boy with dirty blond hair gave Robert a sharp prod in the shoulder. "We mow and do the trimming and shi—stuff like that," said Robert. "I charge $35."

"Me, too," said the blond boy.

Another, with dark hair and bad skin, nodded.

Karma nodded. "That seems fair. By the way, Robert, I think you've met my daughter, Molly. And this is Kim's daughter, Lindsey. The girls met you boys on the playground a few days ago."

"Yeah," said Kim. "They saw a lot of one of you."

Robert Gardiner was pale, but defiant. "We didn't do anything."

"What an odd thing to say. What is it you didn't do?" asked Karma.

Karma nodded at Sue Ellen; it was time for the little girls to leave the room. "C'mon, girls, you can go downstairs and play."

Sue Ellen put gentle hands on the little girls' shoulders and guided them silently out of the room. Kim's icy smile was still fixed on Robert.

"We didn't do anything," he said again.

"I'd still like to know exactly what you didn't do," said Karma. "And if you didn't do anything, how do you know that anything was done?"

Robert Gardiner's mouth hung open. The blond boy gave him another poke in the shoulder.

"You seem like *really nice* boys," said Kim cheerfully. "I'm sure you would never do anything that would get you sent to *juvenile detention*."

"Actually," said Jeanette, "teenage sex offenders are often tried as adults in this state."

"Wait, what?" sputtered Robert Gardiner.

"Yeah," said Bianca, "so they might put you in adult prison. That's a fun place for good-looking teenage boys. You'll make lots of friends there."

"We didn't—" began Robert.

"I know, you didn't do *anything*," said Karma. "You especially didn't pull down your pants and tried to lure two little girls off the playground."

"We didn't do that," said Robert, standing up so fast he almost knocked his chair over backwards, and his friends with it.

"I'm sure you didn't," said Kim. "And you haven't been bullying little kids in the neighborhood, either."

"And taking their bikes," said Bianca.

"It's a good thing, too," said Kim, "because if you did anything in the future, we would know just where to find you."

"And that goes for breaking into cars and stealing shit," said Bianca.

"I'm outta here," said Robert. He stood, looked like he was prepared to fight his way out of Kim's house, or at least try. He didn't appear confident that he'd win.

"That's fine," said Bianca. "I'm sure you boys have homework or something. Just remember, if anybody bothers the little kids at the playground or on their bikes or anywhere else, we're going straight to the cops."

Karma took a step toward Robert, who backed up into his chair. "I won't call the cops," she said, fixing him with the smile Betty Crocker would have worn if she had taken another path in life and become a serial killer. "I'll find you and neuter you with a rusty butter knife. You and all your friends."

She stepped back to let Robert pass. He walked quickly and carefully around her and headed for the door, followed by the rest of his friends.

"Bye, boys," said Karma. "Have a nice weekend."

"We'll let you know about the mowing," said Kim. "We've got your numbers. And all your addresses."

CHAPTER 16: SAM GETS LUCKY

Sam Kranski was the unwitting beneficiary of Karma's confrontation with the neighborhood boys. When she ran her bare toes up his pant leg during dinner that night, he kicked her, thinking it was the cat looking for table scraps. But when she gave his left butt cheek a squeeze and made him spill Molly's apple juice, Sam suspected he'd miss the late-night talk shows.

Sure enough, Karma hustled Molly off to bed thirty minutes early and made her plans for the evening very clear to her husband. Forty-five minutes later, out of breath, sweating, but quite pleased with himself, Sam turned to his wife. Her eyes were closed, but she was not sleeping. "I haven't seen you like this since... well, I'm not sure I've *ever* seen you like this," he said. "Not that I'm complaining, but did we win the lottery or something?"

Or something. Who knew that threatening to castrate a bunch of juvenile delinquents would make her so horny? If this was how men felt after winning a fight, it was no wonder there was so much violence in the world. Karma felt like Superwoman. She wished she could talk about it, but that was out of the question. "I just feel good tonight," she said. "Maybe it's my new vitamins."

"Keep taking them," said Sam.

Weeks later, Karma began to suspect that Sam wasn't the only one who'd gotten lucky that night. Her periods had never been completely regular, but she was pretty sure she should have

155

had one by now. She took it as a good omen; not only had there been no further trouble with the local teens, but maybe, by some miracle, she had become pregnant with no medical help. Conceiving Molly had been a six-month ordeal, including shots in the belly, shots in the butt, daily temperature charting, sex on a schedule, and hormonal rages that would have made Mother Teresa strangle orphans and lepers. Now, here she was, maybe, just maybe, pregnant without any help at all. If it was a boy, she'd have to name him Rusty.

Karma scheduled an appointment with a fertility specialist to find out for sure. If she had conceived, she knew she wouldn't stay pregnant without medical assistance to correct her body's hormonal deficiencies. That meant lots of blood tests and drugs, but it was a small price to pay for (she hesitated to even think the word, lest she jinx it) a *baby*.

The hardest part was not telling her best friends what might be happening, but after so many disappointments and miscarriages, she decided not to talk to anybody about it except her husband and their fertility doctor.

"Don't forget, we have an appointment at 1:30," said Karma, as she measured water for morning coffee.

"Huh?" said Sam. "Oh, yeah, right."

Karma put down the coffee pot and turned to Sam. He was spreading cream cheese on a toasted bagel, covering the surface smoothly and evenly, taking care that no cream cheese found its way into the center hole. He couldn't change a roll of toilet paper, but *this* he was good at.

"You're going with me, right?"

He didn't look up. "Sure."

Karma drummed her fingers on the kitchen island. "Your enthusiasm is knocking me out."

Sam looked up from his bagel. "I'm a guy. We don't jump up and down about this stuff, but I'm very excited. Inside, I'm doing back flips."

"You are such a jerk," said Karma.

"No, I'm not," said Sam. "If you're pregnant, I'm excited, and if you're not, then I'm excited about having sex when the schedule says we have to, and jerking off into little plastic vials, and discussing my sperm count with total strangers. I'm even excited about wearing boxer shorts again so my sperm don't over-heat. Mostly, though, I'm excited about your hormones and mood swings."

"You're giving me a mood swing right now," said Karma. "I'd hit you with a frying pan, but the big one's in the dishwasher."

"You can't kill me," said Sam. "You need my sperm."

The Northside Family Fertility Clinic was new and modern and sterile, pardon the expression. Sam arrived five minutes early, a lifelong habit, and Karma burst into the reception area ten minutes late, another lifelong habit, although to be fair, she had Molly in tow.

"Hi, Daddy, guess what?" said Molly. "Lindsey threw up."

"Virus going around," panted Karma, still winded from running through the parking lot. "Fever and vomiting. I couldn't leave her there."

"Is this a good idea?" asked Sam. "Don't we have, um, delicate things to discuss?"

Karma ran her palm a few inches over her own head, in the universal sign for *the conversation will go right over her head.* "Molly has promised to be very quiet and let Mommy and Daddy talk to the doctor, right, Sweetie?"

"Right," said Molly. "Zip it, lock it, put it in your pocket." She turned her fist in front of her mouth in the universal sign of

I'll keep my mouth shut, and deposited the imaginary key in the pocket of her pink corduroy pants. "We learn that in school."

A few minutes later, the three Kranskis were ushered into Dr. Weimer's dimly lit mahogany and velvet office. Karma gave him the rundown on their previous experiences with fertility. Karma's progesterone levels were far too low to support a pregnancy, her periods were irregular, and her hardboiled eggs refused to hatch unless coaxed with just the right chemicals. Dr. Weimer explained his approach to each of these issues in enthusiastic detail. He was knowledgeable and professional, with a pleasant manner and an obvious passion for his work. He suggested they do more tests on Sam, too, to make sure there were no new issues on his side of the equation, and reminded him, apologetically, about the necessity of switching from briefs to boxers.

True to her promise, Molly stayed quiet, bouncing from her mom's lap to her dad's, back to her mom's, and then down onto the floor, where she rooted around in her Barbie backpack for things to play with.

"At your age, Karma, there is an elevated risk for certain genetic issues, like Down Syndrome," said Dr. Weimer, "but it's still fairly small. Later we can do an amniocentesis, of course, though there's a slight risk to the fetus. It's something you'd want to think about in advance—what you would do if the test turns out positive. You'll have options."

Karma spoke without hesitation. "I'd have the baby," she said. "I wouldn't have an abortion."

Sam nodded his agreement. "My cousin has a boy with Downs," he said.

"And I've experienced way more serious problems than that," said Karma. "*Way* more."

"Aunt Kathleen," chirped Molly from the floor near Karma's feet.

Karma froze for a long moment. "What did you say?"

158

"I heard Daddy talk to Grandma," said Molly. "It's a big secret, right, Daddy?"

Sam looked down at his young daughter. His face had turned bright red. "Maybe we need to talk more about what *secret* means." He looked sheepishly at Karma. "She hears everything. I didn't know she was in the room."

"You didn't check to see if she was there before you talked to your mother?"

"*Your* mother."

"*My* mother?"

"She called looking for you."

"Why didn't she call my cell phone?"

"How would I know?"

Dr. Weimer cleared his throat to remind them that he was still in the room.

"When I can go see Aunt Kathleen?" asked Molly.

"I don't think it's a good idea. It's a long drive," said Karma, "and she can't play with you. She can't even talk to you. It might be too scary. When you're *older*." She was glaring at Sam now.

"I didn't tell her on purpose."

Molly climbed up onto Karma's lap and stared into her eyes the way only a child or an FBI agent can do. "Does she look scary to you?"

"No," said Karma, "but she makes me feel sad."

Molly reached up and held her mother's face between her small, soft hands. "I come with you," she said. Her authoritative tone that made Karma think of Grandma Minnie. "That way you won't be sad."

After a blood draw, which confirmed Karma's pregnancy, Dr. Weimer wrote out a handful of prescriptions for pills and suppositories, and Karma made a handful of appointments to monitor her hormones over the coming weeks. She found herself wondering if Miss Big Ears had any idea what was going on. "So, Molly," she asked on the way out of the office, "Did you like Dr. Weimer? Were you listening?"

"Yup," said Molly, just loud enough for the room full of prospective parents and the nurses in the back of the building to hear. "He said penis *six times.*"

CHAPTER 17:   CAFFEINE-FREE COFFEE KLATCH

Friday playgroup was at Karma's house this week. Maybe it was her raging synthetic hormones or just the usual stress of having people see her messy house, but Karma flew around the first floor like a suburban white tornado, shoving mail and other debris into paper bags. The moms usually stayed on the first floor, so she stashed the bags in corners and closets on the second floor. Karma had discovered that the best way to deal with the mountains of papers that came by mail, preschool, and the retail universe was to bag them so that nothing important would be lost. If she waited long enough, everything in the bag became irrelevant, and then she could toss the entire bag into recycling without looking in it.

She glanced up at the clock. *Time to start cooking.* First, she prepared an egg casserole the kids would eat, as long as they didn't find out the little green bits were diced chilies. Then she cut up a bowl of fruit and brewed a big pot of coffee that she had no intention of drinking. Karma couldn't remember if this week's groundbreaking medical study proved that coffee was bad for you or good, but just in case, she vowed to avoid it.

The past week had been tough. She wanted to celebrate her pregnancy with her friends. She wanted to talk about names and how to decorate the nursery. She particularly wanted to ask if she could drink coffee. But it was too early and too many things could go wrong. Too many things *had* gone wrong in the past, three times, so she decided to get through the first trimester before announcing anything. Molly didn't appear to know anything, despite having been at the doctor's office with her parents. Her biggest concern was that Mommy had to lie down after she took her special medicine each night (progesterone suppositories) and couldn't come back in her room to read more bedtime stories.

Karma wished that was *her* biggest problem. Given her history, she had blood drawn every three days. Her hormone levels should double with each test if the baby was developing at a normal rate, but it took the better part of a day to get the results, resulting in nearly nonstop anxiety. Nevertheless, Karma resolved to set aside her worries for the morning and enjoy overeating with her playgroup friends and discussing the aftermath of their latest neighborhood activities.

Kim and Bianca and their daughters showed up together, just as the egg casserole was coming out of the oven.

"Any buzz around the neighborhood?" asked Karma. "Do you think the boys told their parents?"

Bianca walked over to the coffee pot on the counter, and made a rude noise. "I never told my parents when I got in trouble with the neighbors. Unless I knew they were going to call my house, and I had to get my bullshit story in before they found out what really happened."

Kim smiled. "Nobody's called Dave. Besides, I don't care if they *do* tell their parents. Lindsey recognized that Gardiner kid, and I trust her. If they want to get mad about what we said to their sweet, innocent little boys, I want an explanation about what they were trying to do to our little girls."

"No shit," said Bianca. "Andy says there's been no trouble since we had our little talk. Far as I'm concerned, that's proof we had the right little pieces of shit." She poured herself a cup of coffee, and walked back to the table with the pot as an offer to pour for the others.

"No, thanks," said Karma. She took another sip of orange juice.

Kim held out her cup out to Bianca. "So when are you due?"

Karma's jaw dropped open before she could stop it, but she quickly put on her best innocent face and tried to look bemused. "I'm just cutting back on caffeine. It's bad for you, you know."

Another rude noise escaped from Bianca's bright coral lips. "So you are pregnant, you sneaky bitch, and you weren't going to tell us?"

Karma threw up her hands. "All I did was not drink coffee."

"I'm very intuitive," said Kim.

"Me, too," said Bianca. "I could see it in your eyes."

"You have a sort of glow about you," said Kim.

Now it was Karma's turn to make a rude noise. "What did Molly tell you?"

Kim grinned. "She said she went to the doctor with you and her daddy, and the doctor said penis seven times."

"It was only six times."

"She and Lindsey were playing," said Kim, "and she said, 'You be the baby and I'll be the Mommy, and I'll be laying down because I took my medicine and I can't walk.' So I figured you were either on progesterone suppositories or vodka martinis."

"Damn," said Karma. "There's no point trying to keep secrets around here. Who else knows?"

"Just us," said Kim, "and Sue Ellen."

"And Jeanette," added Bianca, "and Joan Handley, because she was with Sue Ellen when Sue Ellen told Jeanette."

"And some of Joan's friends by now," said Bianca, "because you know what a gossip *she* is, and I bet her bridge club."

"Jesus," said Karma.

Kim held out her coffee cup, and Karma clinked it with her juice glass. "We're just happy for you."

Bianca leaned down and grabbed Karma in a bear hug. "Congratulations, Mommy. Are you excited? Is Sam excited?"

"Let's just say we're cautiously optimistic," said Karma. "I've had three miscarriages."

"Well, when you need somebody to watch Molly, like for doctor's appointments, just call." said Bianca.

Karma nodded her thanks. "I will. And if it all works out, I expect big baby gifts from all of you. Expensive things. And give me the receipts, so I can turn them in for cash."

"I was thinking Starbucks gift cards," said Kim.

"Make it liquor store cards," said Karma. "I'm going to miss that more than coffee."

They sipped and nibbled in silence for a few minutes, each thinking back on pregnancy and all that had come with it: morning sickness, high blood pressure, thinning hair, moodiness, swollen ankles, hope, pride, miraculous kicks, glowing skin, and wonderful babies.

The reverie was broken by the sound of the front door opening. Karma hoped it was Jeanette. At least she could still eat cinnamon rolls. Sure enough, Jeanette appeared in the kitchen, but she wasn't carrying the aluminum pan of bliss. In fact, she was barely holding onto Baby Jacob. She was wearing an old sweatshirt and mismatched sweatpants, and had a bad case of bed head. Baby Jacob was still wearing his pajamas, and judging by the swell and sag of his bottoms, he was in desperate need of a change. Allie sucked her thumb and clung to her mother's leg, and Little Jeffrey stood behind Allie, arms folded, staring grimly at his shoeless feet. They looked like Bosnian war refugees.

"Luann Lawrence is hiding at my house," whispered Jeanette. "Jack beat her up."

CHAPTER 18:   THE FUGITIVE

Jeanette was more addled than usual, so it took considerable time and effort to get the whole story out of her. At around 3 a.m. that morning, she had been awakened by pounding on her glass patio door. Jeff was out of town on a sales trip, so she'd grabbed her cell phone and Little Jeffrey's junior hockey stick for protection. It was an excellent weapon, as she had learned at Little Jeffrey's first and last hockey game, so Jeanette was prepared to call 911 *and* bash in the intruder's skull.

Some part of her realized that crazed killers don't usually knock on their victims' patio doors, but you can't be too careful. Hoping to scare the intruder away, she had snapped on the patio light and pulled back the vertical blinds, brandishing the hockey stick. She was shocked to see Luann Lawrence. When she slid open the door, Luann pushed past her.

"Turn out the light," she'd commanded. "I don't want him to know where I am."

"What?"

"We had a fight. I had to get out."

In the predawn darkness, with no lights on in the house, Jeanette had done her best to lead Luann into the family room, kicking toys, books and shoes out of their way as she went. She pulled the drapes closed, then turned on a small table lamp. It was just bright enough to give her a closer look at Luann, and she was horrified to see that Luann's eye was bruised and swollen, and there was a cut on her lower lip.

"Jack did this?"

"I told you," Luann had snapped. "We had a fight."

The playgroup moms silently soaked in the import of the story. "My God," said Karma, "We shouldn't be surprised, right? But I am."

"What were they fighting about?" Kim wanted to know.

"She didn't tell me," said Jeanette, "but it had to be something bad. You shoulda seen her eye." Bianca set a cup of coffee in front of Jeanette, who looked like she seriously needed one.

"Jerk," said Karma.

"*Stronzo*," said Bianca.

"Yeah," Jeanette nodded. "I'm just so sure he's done something awful and Luann found out about it and they had an argument and he beat her up. She waited until she was sure he was asleep, then she came to my house."

"Betcha he was drinking," said Bianca.

"Where is she now?" asked Kim.

"She's asleep in my guest room," said Jeanette. "She doesn't have anywhere else to go. Luckily I changed the sheets in there. Just the other day I was thinking, 'I should wash those sheets,' so I did. Isn't that weird?"

"It's weird that she came to your house," said Kim. "Doesn't she have any family around?"

"I guess not," said Jeanette. "I didn't ask her."

"What about her kids?" asked Kim. "Were they with her?"

"She had to get out quick," said Jeanette. "She didn't know where she was gonna go until she saw my house. She was scared."

Karma's mouth dropped open. "So she left them with Jack? Are you kidding?"

"She said he'd get them on the school bus when he realized she was gone."

166

"She left them?" Karma couldn't believe it.

"I think *you* should be scared," said Bianca. "What if Jack Lawrence shows up at your house? Jeff's out of town and you've got kids, too."

Jeanette's big cow eyes seemed even bigger than usual. "I am scared, but I couldn't say no, you guys. She needed help."

Karma put down her orange juice and squeezed Jeanette's hand. "You've got a big heart, Jeanette, and you did the right thing. We'll help. We just have to figure out what to do next. When does Jeff get home?"

"Day after tomorrow," sniffed Jeanette. "What am I going to tell him? He thinks Jack Lawrence is this great guy. What if he gets mad at me?"

Karma brought over a box of tissues and placed it in front of Jeanette. "Jeff's not going to be mad at you. He couldn't possibly take Jack's side in something like this."

"You don't think?" sniffled Jeanette.

"With her black eye? Of course not," said Karma. "You're tired, and you're not thinking straight."

"Yeah," said Kim, "I agree. You need some sleep."

"And a shower," said Bianca. "You look like shit."

"And do something with your hair," said Kim, the hint of a smile on her face. "Or put on a hat."

"Makeup, too," said Karma. "Lots of makeup. And burn those sweatpants. They make your butt look like the damn Hindenburg."

Startled, Jeanette looked down at her clothes and then started to laugh, which, because she was still crying, came out in chokes and a loud snort, which sent them all into welcome giggles.

"I love you guys," she snuffled. "You're my best friends. What's a hindenberg?"

167

After more discussion, it was decided that Karma would go home with Jeanette and stand guard while Luann slept and Jeanette showered and tried to nap. Kim would take Molly to her house. Bianca called a girlfriend who worked as a secretary at the elementary school. She gave Bianca the standard line about privacy rules, which prevented her from sharing information about students. Bianca gave her the standard line about cutting the bullshit, and her friend checked the computer, then reported that the older Lawrence children were in class like always, and would be cared for until 6:30 p.m., when the after-school program for working parents officially closed.

The next question was *Where is Jack?* Karma dialed *67 so that her name wouldn't appear on caller ID, then used her cell phone to call the Lawrence house. There was no answer, which didn't prove anything, but strongly suggested that Jack had gone to work. It figured an ass like him could beat his wife, then act like nothing had happened.

So after putting away the uneaten food from playgroup, Karma followed Jeanette and her kids back to Jeanette's house, avoiding Luann's street in case Jack was lurking nearby, and prepared to stand guard in the living room while Jeanette went upstairs.

Sitting in the relative quiet of the formal living room (Little Jeffrey and Allie were bickering in the basement and the baby was asleep), Karma thought about Jack and Luann. She wasn't sure why, but she had a nagging, uneasy feeling about them. What kind of man beats up his wife, then puts his kids on the school bus? What had he told them about why their mother was gone? Was he going to pick them up from their after-school program, or did he assume Luann would come home and handle it? Maybe it was asking too much to expect a dysfunctional couple like the Lawrences to think of these things, but mothers are supposed to consider all the angles.

Those thoughts led to the one that had been nagging her since she'd heard the story: What kind of woman leaves her children with a man who's just beaten her? Karma dialed their number again, just to be sure. If Jack answered, she'd ask for Harriet or Diane or somebody, then apologize for dialing the wrong number. If Jack showed up at Jeanette's house, Karma would call 911 and have the big jerk arrested. If he forced his way in, she'd hit him with Little Jeffrey's hockey stick.

She thought about the home security TV ads in which the evil bad guy bursts through the door, hears the alarm and the noise alone makes him flee in terror. *I want to see the one where the homeowner takes out her Glock and blows a nice hole in the criminal. I could write Glock commercials.*

She kicked off her sandals and put her feet up on Jeanette's coffee table. She hadn't spent much time in this room before today. Like Kim's living room and her own, it was fancier than the rest of the house, so typical of neighborhoods like hers. Every builder's model included a room with fancy furniture that nobody sat on, much like Grandma Minnie's parlor. The Formal Living Room was the one you decorated in case the Royal Family showed up and you needed a place to serve High Tea. Jeanette's featured heavy, dark furniture and fancy little dust catchers that looked like family heirlooms, but could just as easily have come from Target. The walls were decorated with family pictures in fancy scrolled metal frames, including Jeff and Jeanette's wedding photos. Karma rose from the couch and looked more closely. Jeanette looked deliriously happy in her fitted off-white suit. *Why a suit and not a long dress?* It was a smallish wedding, judging by the shot taken in the church, which showed maybe thirty guests.

Then she noticed a partly-open drawer in the coffee table she'd had her feet on. Karma pulled the knob and found a wedding album inside. She settled back on the couch and flipped through it. There were all the usual staged photos of the bride and groom holding hands, shoving cake into each other's faces, dancing. *Boring, boring, boring.* But tucked behind the last photo of Jeanette with her grandparents was a manila envelope. *If I'm gonna snoop...*

It was just another wedding photo featuring Jeanette and Jeff with her parents. In this one, though, Jeanette's mother was holding a baby in a blue blanket. *Probably one of the grandchildren.* Karma had met Jeanette's mother the previous year. In person, as in this picture, Della had the pinch-faced look of a woman disappointed by life and by everyone and everything around her. Or maybe she just needed more fiber in her diet. Jeanette's mother was one of those people who made you appreciate your own mother, at least for a few minutes.

Karma's own mother, Charlotte, was more pleasant to be around than Jeanette's but not by much. Karma would call her in Florida to talk about Molly's latest exploits, but inevitably, Charlotte would turn the conversation to Karma's father and all his shortcomings, as well as those of Roberta, his new wife. Karma wasn't president of the newest Mrs. Ed Moskowitz fan club either, but still, Charlotte's sniping was annoying. What was the statute of limitations on bitching about an ex-spouse?

"Hi." A voice behind Karma made her jump. "Are you Karma?"

"Yes," said Karma, trying to regain her composure. She slipped the album back in the drawer. "Hi. Yeah, that's me. We met at the pool last summer, I think. Good to see you. I mean, it's not *good* to see you. I mean, I'm sorry for what you're going through." *Please, God, shut me up.*

"Thanks," said Luann. "I just talked to Jeanette upstairs. She explained why you're here. I appreciate what you're doing, but I'm not going to talk about my problems. I'm not used to sharing my problems with strangers." She sat down on the loveseat and

170

crossed her slim legs. Her posture was straight as a stick and she had a cool, dignified not-quite-smile on her bruised face. It made for an incongruous picture. "Sorry. That didn't sound very nice."

Karma tried to look as unconcerned as Luann. She'd never been face to face with somebody who'd just been beaten. *Where were you supposed to look?* "It's okay," she said. "It's not easy to have your private business out there where everybody can see it. Well, not everybody, of course. Just a few of us. Just like three or four." Karma felt like a babbling idiot again. It was Luann. Whatever you called the quality that puts other people at ease, this broad had none of it.

The two women sat in silence. Karma had about a thousand questions she wanted to ask, though maybe there was really only *one* question: *How the hell does a smart professional woman with kids get into a mess like this with a jackass like your husband and what the hell attracted you to him in the first place when you should have just walked out the door the first time he dared to lay a finger on you, because this can't be the first time it's happened, and if you were being honest with yourself, you saw the signs when you were dating and what the hell were you thinking when you went ahead and married him anyway and had three babies with him?*

Instead she asked, "You want some coffee?"

"No, thanks," said Luann. "It's bad for you."

"Yeah, I've heard that," said Karma, "but I could put some brandy in it. I know where Jeanette hides it."

Luann gave a short, humorless laugh. "I suppose I look like I could use some."

Karma felt a blush rising into her cheeks. "I didn't mean it that way," she said. "You know, under the circumstances, you look pretty good." She rubbed her temples. "Sorry. I really am trying to shut up."

171

"You don't have to. It was nice to meet you." Luann rose from the loveseat and started toward the front door.

"You're leaving?" asked Karma. "Where are you going?"

Luann looked at her oddly, like she's asked a ridiculous question. "I'm going home." She walked toward the door, and Karma jumped off the couch to follow.

"Home?" asked Karma. "What about Jack?"

"He's at work."

"But he'll be home later. Don't you want to go to a shelter or something?"

"Why?" Again, she answered as though it were a bizarre notion. Luann headed for the door, and Karma jumped up to follow.

"Wait a minute," said Karma. "I'm confused. I thought you'd be looking for someplace else to live with your kids. Aren't you hiding from Jack?"

"We had an argument. It's over and I'm sure he's sorry. Couples fight, you know."

Karma felt like a character in a bad made-for-TV movie. "He hit you," she pressed. "He gave you a black eye and you came here in the middle of the night to hide."

"He's been under a lot of stress," said Luann. "We had a fire at our house a while back. I'm sure you know about that."

Karma felt hot blood rushing back into her face. *What the hell did that mean? What does she know?* A horrible thought occurred to her. She and Kim had sent in Jeanette to talk to this woman—Jeanette, who couldn't keep a secret in a paper bag. *What the hell were we thinking?*

"Yeah, I guess I did hear about it," Karma said, as casually as she could. "But that's no excuse for him hitting you. What about your kids?"

"It's actually none of your business," said Luann, an edge to her voice, "but Jack is a good father. He would never hit our kids."

Karma wanted to shout at her. *Everybody knows he hit them with a belt after the shed blew up.* But she didn't say it.

"Good fathers don't beat their kids' mother," said Karma, "and good mothers don't let them."

Luann's frosty expression turned to stone. "Tell Jeanette I'll talk to her later." She let herself out and didn't look back.

Karma's face was burning. She knew she shouldn't have been so blunt and tactless, but damn it, she had wanted to blacken Luann's *other* eye. She locked the door.

Lovely to see you, she thought. *Let's do this again real soon. Assuming your husband doesn't kill you.*

CHAPTER 19: EQUAL TIME FOR EQUAL CRIME

"Oh, Karma, isn't it awful?" Jeanette was on the phone and on the verge of tears yet again.

Karma set down the spoon she was using to stir spaghetti sauce, turned off the burner under the pot, and went into the family room. She leaned back on the couch and put her feet up on the coffee table. Judging by Jeanette's tone, this would take a while.

"What's going on, Jeanette?"

"I just keep thinking about poor Luann."

Karma understood. She didn't *like* Luann Lawrence, but still, she felt sorry for her. You didn't watch daytime television when you're supposed to be cleaning house without learning how hard it is to get out of an abusive relationship. And women weren't the only ones who stayed around for abuse. Karma's father had put up with her mother's crap for decades before finally leaving her and finding Louise, then Darleen, then finally, Roberta.

Karma listened with half her brain to Jeanette bemoaning poor Luann, and with the other half, wondered if she would have to testify against Jack in court, since she'd seen Luann's fresh bruises. Karma didn't know anybody who had actually testified in court. She'd never even been on a jury, though she'd always hoped for a juicy murder trial where you get interviewed on *Dr. Phil* or *Oprah* or *60 Minutes* after it's over, to talk about the verdict.

174

"I think she's going to be okay," said Jeanette. "Poor thing's embarrassed, mostly. I just can't believe what happened. It's unfair and maybe even illegal."

This was often the way conversations went with Jeanette. You started with the answer and worked your way back to the question. It was like a game of Jeopardy. *I'll take abused wives for fifty, Alex.* Karma's job was to work backwards and try to find out what had happened that prompted Jeanette to call. She considered what she knew so far: Luann is embarrassed because of something that's unfair and possibly illegal. Her marriage perhaps?

"Obviously she should have walked away years ago," said Karma, after some deliberation, "but it's Jack who should be embarrassed."

"Oh, he is, I'm sure," said Jeanette. "No guy wants to be seen in a situation like that."

Hmmm. What situation? It has to be a legal situation.

"So you think he'll plead 'not guilty?'" asked Karma. "I'll testify against his sorry butt."

"He'd be testifying, not you," said Jeanette, "but I'm sure it's not gonna come to that. At least I hope not."

Okay, maybe I missed something. Why would Jack be testifying? They can't make you testify against yourself.

Jeanette was still talking, and how she sounded like she might cry again. "Don't you think they'll drop the charges? Or at least plea bargain it down? I mean what about the kids?"

"Wait a minute, what?" Karma had obviously lost this round of *Guess What Jeanette is Talking About.*

"It only happened once," wailed Jeanette. "She just shouldn't have done it when the police were watching."

Karma felt a headache coming on. "I give up, Jeanette."

"Exactly. She did, too," said Jeanette. "That's why it's so unfair."

Like so many of Jeanette's stories, this one took time to straighten out. The previous night, neighbors in the cul-de-sac had heard the Lawrences arguing again and had called the police, and right in front of the cops, five-foot-nothing Luann had landed a perfect upper-cut right to six-foot-one Jack's nose, leaving the officer no choice but to arrest her for domestic battery. And if that weren't *News of the Weird* enough, Jeanette was now calling to see if Karma would contribute to a go-fund-me page she wanted to start to help pay Luann's legal fees.

"Why don't we raffle off tickets to their next fight?" said Karma.

There was a long silence. "You're being sarcastic."

"Yes," said Karma. "Put me down for sarcasm and a big fat NO. Why does she keep coming to you, anyway?"

"She knows I care about her. Anyway, she didn't actually come right out and say she needs money," said Jeanette, "she just wanted to tell me what happened. It's okay with me—I want to help her."

Karma was glad Jeanette couldn't see the face she was making, as it would have surely hurt her feelings. "It's not okay, Jeanette. The more contact you have with Luann, the more likely she'll find out what we did," said Karma. "If Jack Lawrence is willing to beat up the mother of his children, what the hell do you think he'd do to us? By the way, she hasn't said anything about finding a baby monitor in the yard, has she?"

"No," said Jeanette. Disappointment was heavy in her voice. "Maybe she can get money from one of her credit cards." There was another pause. "I have another favor to ask. It's kind of a big one, so you can say no if you want to."

"What is it?" *I'm not hiding that broad in my guest room.*

"I hate to ask, but I don't know who else to call."

"What do you need?" *I'm not baking a file into a cake for her either.*

176

"I really mean it; I won't be mad if you say no."

"JEANETTE."

"Would you watch Little Jeffrey tonight?"

Karma fought down the impulse to hang up, have her phone service disconnected, change her name, and apply for Witness Protection. *Why couldn't you ask for something easy, like one of my kidneys?* "You need a babysitter?" Karma's mind was racing, trying to think of a plausible way to refuse, like a Zika quarantine or smallpox. "Tonight?"

"Yes," pleaded Jeanette. "It's our anniversary, and Jeff and I want to go out, and I had somebody from church lined up, but she just called and said her therapist said this isn't a good time for her to be under stress. Could you just watch him for a few hours, say four or five, so we can go to a movie and dinner?"

Four or five HOURS? "You only need us to watch Jeffrey? Not the other kids?" *Can I interest you in a little bone marrow instead? My unborn child? Sex with my husband?*

"It'll be easier that way," said Jeanette, trying to sound like she actually believed this. "Allie has a sleepover at her cousin's, and Jacob is going to the Smith's."

The next question was too obvious not to ask. "Little Jeffrey can't stay with his cousins or the Smiths?"

"Well, you know he's high spirited, and my sister-in-law has a hard time with that," said Jeanette, "and the Smiths are still a little mad about their dog. Most of the hair grew back, but you know how they are."

"Yeah, of course," said Karma, trying to keep the abject horror out of her voice. "Well, I guess he could hang out with us. Would I need to feed him dinner?"

"Oh, that would be great," said Jeanette, practically giddy with happiness.

"What does he eat?" asked Karma. For a time, Little Jeffrey had eaten nothing but peanut butter and marshmallow fluff

177

sandwiches. Three times a day. Jeanette had brought them to playgroup, sent them to preschool, and took them to the few restaurants in town that would still let her family in. She was excited to find his favorite brands at Sam's Club, which she promptly bought by the case, after which he refused to touch the stuff. He was like a young Howard Hughes, but without the money, good looks, or charm.

"He likes processed American cheese slices and Ritz crackers now," said Jeanette. "I have the cheese, and I can buy the crackers before we go."

"I've got Ritz crackers," said Karma, as gamely as she could under the circumstances. "Just bring the cheese, and you and Jeff go out and have a great time and don't worry about anything. We'll get along just fine."

"He'll be on his best behavior," said Jeanette, "I promise."

Karma was pretty sure she'd experienced Little Jeffrey's *best behavior*, so this was small comfort.

"He's eating our curtains."

Sam Kranski was monitoring Little Jeffrey's activities from the kitchen, where he could see into both the dining and family rooms, as well as the front and patio exits, in case of an escape attempt. "I've asked him three times to get the drapes out of his mouth."

Sam turned to his wife, who had invited this demon spawn into their home, and who was now cooking dinner and pretending not to see or hear what was happening. "I never thought I'd hear myself say, GET THE DRAPES OUT OF YOUR MOUTH even once in my life," he said, "and now I've said it three times."

Karma looked up from the raw hamburger she was bounding a little too forcefully. "Welcome to my world," she snapped. "While you were in the bathroom hiding for twenty minutes, he

178

chewed the arm off Malibu Barbie." She wrenched her hand out of the raw meat and pointed to her left eye, accidentally flicking a chunk of ground round into the salad. "Look at my eye. It's twitching. My eye is *twitching*."

"When's dinner?" asked Sam. "Maybe he's just hungry."

"It won't help," said Karma. "I'm not serving Barbie limbs."

She probably should have. Karma set out burgers, rice pilaf, salad, and green beans for her own family, and two slices of plastic-wrapped, processed American cheese food and a stack of Ritz crackers for Little Jeffrey. "Dig in, everybody," she said, finger pressed to her convulsing eyelid. "Whoever eats their dinner gets chocolate cake for dessert."

Little Jeffrey kicked the legs of his kitchen chair and sniffed suspiciously at the cheese. He unwrapped the first slice, tore it into tiny pieces and placed them on the table in the general vicinity of his plate, though not on it. Then he picked up a cracker and examined it with suspicious eyes. "These aren't the crackers I like."

"Sure they are," said Karma. "They're Ritz crackers. Your mom said they're your favorite."

"They have lines on them," he said. "The crackers I like don't have lines on them."

"Oh, that's nothing," said Sam lightly. "They're just a special kind made to look like little baseballs. See, the lines are like the stitching on a baseball."

Scowling and scratching his mousy brown head, Little Jeffrey put the cracker back onto the stack. He folded his arms and glared down at his plate.

"If you don't eat dinner," said Karma, "you can't have dessert."

Sure, thought Sam, *threaten the little beast. That'll help.* Sam could smell the rising danger, like the stink of a rhino about to charge.

Little Jeffrey slowly raised his head and looked up at Karma, the smirk on his face just begging to be smacked off. "I'll just get some when you're not looking."

Karma met his smirk with tempered steel. "No, you won't," she said. "Nobody around here gets dessert if they don't eat their dinner." She turned to Molly. "And you eat your vegetables like always."

"That not fair." Molly's face was set in a miserable pout.

Sam gathered his composure and reached into his bag of Parental Clichés. "Molly, you're going to grow up big and strong because you eat vegetables. Jeffrey doesn't eat healthy food, so he's not going to grow big strong muscles like you."

Jeffrey reached into his bag of Obnoxious Comebacks. "I can beat *her* up," he said, indicating Molly. "Your food stinks. I'm gonna watch TV." He slid off the chair, slunk into the family room, turned on the television, and plopped his bony, vitamin-deprived butt on the couch. Sam's mouth dropped open in disbelief. *Does Jeff put up with this bullshit?*

"Remember," said Karma quietly, "don't leave any visible marks."

"They'll never even find the body," whispered Sam. "What the hell goes on in their house? I thought I knew Jeff; I can't believe he lets his kid get away with crap like this."

"*Crap* is a bad word," said Molly.

"They're thinking about counseling," whispered Karma.

"What is *cow sling*?" asked Molly.

"We'll talk about it later, sweetie," said Karma. "After Little Jeffrey leaves."

"When that's gonna be? He not being nice, and I never get to watch TV at dinner."

Karma regarded her young daughter. The stress of spending the evening with the spawn of Satan was playing hell with her grammar. Maybe it was time to level with her and hope she was

180

old enough to understand. Karma kept her voice low. "Look, sweetie, they have different rules at their house, and that's why he's so skinny and so hard to get along with, and why he doesn't have any friends. You just be glad that you're growing up to be a good girl, and you have lots of friends, and all the mommies like having you around. When Daddy and I want to go out on a date, we can always find somebody to let you play at their house."

Sam cleared his throat.

"Nobody wants him around," said Karma. "I wanted to say no to his mommy, but I just--"

Now Sam coughed, loudly. With a sinking feeling, Karma recognized it as one of those noises that means *the person you're talking about is right here.* She looked up and saw Little Jeffrey standing in the entryway to the kitchen, looking at her, no expression on his face. Time slowed down to a crawl. The demon child now looked like a sad, misunderstood little boy. Karma felt like a monster.

"Hey, buddy," she said, with unnatural brightness, "if you eat some of your dinner, we'll all have cake, and then maybe we can play a game or something."

"I don't like the crackers," he muttered.

"I don't blame you," said Karma. She knew she would be blamed when Little Jeffrey ended up in a bell tower later in life, picking off coeds with a rifle. "Crackers shouldn't look like baseballs. It's just *wrong.*"

"You can just eat some cheese," offered Sam.

Little Jeffrey slipped back onto his chair. He scraped up a big handful of cheese bits and stuffed them into his mouth. "Baseball is for sissies," he said, orange bits of artificial *fromage* spraying over the table. Karma turned away. He was eating like a farm animal, but at least he was eating. When dessert was served he practically inhaled two large pieces of cake. He seemed to enjoy it, although he let Karma know that it wasn't as good as his mother's cake, the frosting was the wrong kind, and she shouldn't have put sprinkles on it.

When Jeanette and Jeff arrived an hour later to take their son home, Karma could feel their nerves crackling in the humid night air. They were clearly waiting for Karma to explain a) What he'd done, b) the cost of repairs, and c) how many people and pets had been injured. Nobody invited Little Jeffrey over a second time.

Thus Karma was proud to report that Jeffrey had eaten some of his dinner, had earned dessert, and had played well with Molly. That last part was a stretch, but he hadn't physically injured her, and Malibu Barbie could be replaced. Little Jeffrey proceeded to put his shoes after only the second time Karma asked him to, and even let her zip up his jacket. Hopeful that Jeanette and Jeff would notice the effectiveness of firm discipline, Karma Kranski, soon-to-be-anointed Babysitter of the Year, watched them walk down the sidewalk into the quiet night. *I shall write a parenting book.* "Goodnight, Jeffrey," she called. "I'm glad you came over."

"Bye, poopy head," he yelled back. "I hate you."

CHAPTER 20:   RED CAR REDUX

The neighborhood playground was the gravitational center of Bedford Commons. If you wanted to be in on the latest news, weather or gossip, the playground was the place to go. The regulars gathered there on warm spring nights to relax and exhaust their children before bedtime. Occasionally a new face would show up, which gave the regulars something to wonder and whisper about, until someone was drafted to wander over to introduce herself. This would begin the obligatory ritual of asking which model you lived in, where you'd come from and why, and mutually compliment each other's children.

On this evening it was Kim who was nudged by Karma in the direction of a too-thin middle-aged woman sitting alone on the bench nearest the tiny trees that would, in seventy years or so, provide shade. She had jet-black (obviously dyed) teased hair and was wearing a slightly ratty dark blue sweatshirt and jeans. She was either stylishly sloppy or just sloppy.

"Do we know her?" asked Karma.

"I don't," said Kim.

"Is that little dark-headed kid hers? The little tiny thing by the slide? I don't recognize him, either."

"Come with me," said Kim, rising from her seat. "Let's be sociable."

"You mean nosy."

"Same thing."

As they approached her bench, the woman looked up and smiled at them.

"Hi," said Kim. "Is that little boy yours? He's a doll."

"He's my grandbaby," said the woman with appropriate pride. She spoke with a drawl that said southern Indiana or Kentucky. If you were from northern Indiana, as Karma was, those were close enough to the same thing.

"You don't look old enough to be a grandmother," said Karma. She wasn't being completely untruthful. The woman's face and hands had the weathered appearance of a long-time smoker or obsessive tanner, but even so, she didn't look much over fifty.

"Aren't you sweet. He's my daughter's little boy. He turned two in August."

"He's very cute," said Kim. She turned and pointed at the swing set on the opposite side of the playground. "My name's Kim Wallace. That's my daughter, Lindsey in the yellow, and Karma's daughter, Molly in the pink, on the swings. They're both four."

"Karma Kranski," said Karma, holding out her hand. "I live a couple doors down from Kim. What's your grandson's name?"

"James Patrick," said the woman, giving Karma's hand a fast, but firm, shake. She had the hands of a woman who had worked hard. "We live on Robinwood. I'm Dora Lee Fuller."

"It's nice to meet you," said Karma. "Does your daughter live in town?"

"You could say that," said the woman. "She and the baby live with me."

"Oh," said Karma, trying for a nonjudgmental, I-applaud-you-for-making-lemonade-from-those-lemons tone of voice. "It's nice that you can do that for her. And you get to see your grandson every day."

"Yeah," said the woman. She sounded less than overjoyed about this. "She ain't married, and they got no place else to go. But he's a sweet little thing." All heads turned to James Patrick, who was trying to climb up the rope ladder like the bigger kids, but couldn't swing his chubby leg high enough to make the first rung.

Dora Lee frowned and turned to Kim. "Did you say your name was Wallace?" she asked. "Is your husband in charge around here?"

"He thinks so," said Kim with a smile. "Is there something you need help with?"

"Sure is," said Dora Lee with a flare of anger. "It's about Brandi's car—James Patrick's momma's car, that is. The tires was slashed right in front of my fucking house, pardon my language, and I wanted to know if he could help me find out who done it."

The buzzing in Karma's ears drowned out much of what Dora Lee said next, but she caught the gist of it. Some f'ing jerk had slashed the f'ing tires on Brandi's f'ing car late one night. At first, Dora Lee and Brandi assumed it was Brandi's useless piece of crap ex-boyfriend and baby daddy, but he swore it wasn't him and two of his buddies swore he was with them that night. They was probably up to no good, but that's boys for you. Besides, the next-door neighbor said he heard *women's* voices on the street that night, although nobody cared enough about nobody but themself to even look out a f'ing window, which ain't how things *used* to be back when people weren't so busy gossiping about other people's business, like her Brandi, who made plenty of mistakes, that's for f'ing sure, but that's just girls for you.

Karma focused on not screaming and running away, instead waved at Molly, who had figured out how to wrap her cast around the chain of the swing, and was happily, if crookedly, swinging.

Meanwhile, Kim was in rare form, even for Kim. "So nobody saw anybody?" she asked, shaking her head in disbelief and indignation. "I can't believe nobody even looked outside. I swear

185

I'm going to have Dave send an email. Neighbors need to look out for one another."

"I think it was one of them girls from Brandi's school," said Dora Lee. "Probably jealous of Brandi or something. You know girls. But I thought maybe your husband could send out one of his emails or something and ask around."

"It happened a while ago, right?" asked Kim. "It might be too late to find out anything useful."

"Well, we tried to get the cops to look into it, and they said they would, and I kept waiting for them to get back to us, but they never did. They said it's almost impossible to find out about crap like this, but since hers was the only car damaged on the entire street, it was most likely somebody she knew."

"That makes sense," said Kim.

"Yeah, well, she used to be a cheerleader," said Dora Lee, "before the baby, a'course, and like I say, I think it might have been one of them girls. I just thought maybe somebody saw something or knew something."

Kim nodded sympathetically. "I'll talk to Dave. I sure hope he can help you."

"Probably nothing to be done," said Dora Lee, "but I'll tell you, I'll wring the neck of who did it if I catch 'em. Brandi works at Burger King nights, so she can be home with James Patrick, and she don't make much money at it. She's buyin' that baby his clothes and diapers and all that, and those four tires cost her a whole damn week of pay. I wanted to help her out, but my husband said she probably made somebody mad doing something stupid, and it was probably her own damn fault it happened."

Karma wondered if it was unrealistic to hope that the mulch beneath her feet would open up and swallow her.

"Your husband sounds like a good dad," said Kim.

"Yeah, he's not as tough as he'd like *her* to think he is," said Dora Lee. "He wouldn't give her money, but he found her a set of used tires and put 'em on for her. That saved her some."

Kim nodded her approval. "Well, let me talk to Dave, okay?" She looked at her watch and gave a little gasp, right out of The Big Book of Hasty Departures. "Hey, we'd better get going. It's getting late, and the girls have preschool tomorrow. It was good to meet you, Dora Lee. Please tell Brandi she's got a really cute little boy, and we're sorry about her car. And I'll get Dave on it right away."

Karma smiled, waved goodbye, and followed Kim across the playground to Molly and Lindsey. She didn't speak until they were far away from Dora Lee. "I can't believe what just happened. And I feel like crap."

"Why?" asked Kim.

Karma looked around to make sure no one else was close enough to hear. "Because I did it," she hissed. "You were there, remember?"

Kim looked at Karma as though she'd begun speaking Martian. "Are you seriously feeling guilty? Brandi almost ran over Molly, and then she gave you the finger." Kim said *Brandi* the way you might say *stinky cheese.*

"Yeah, but maybe she really didn't know she hit Molly. Dora Lee doesn't seem to know about it. And she's got a kid. What I did affected James Patrick." Karma said *James Patrick* the way you might say *innocent baby seal.*

Kim practically spat. "Stop being so dramatic. Nothing bad happened to James Patrick except he was born to a self-centered, irresponsible, bratty teenage idiot who drove too fast and had the nerve to give you *the finger*. I refuse to feel sorry for her. She's living off Dora Lee, so it's not like we made her homeless or something."

They walked the rest of the way home in silence. Karma tried to make sense of her jumbled thoughts. *Kim is right, of course. Doctor Laura on steroids, but right. Well, maybe not right, but not wrong. No, she was right. Definitely right.*

So why do I still feel like crap?

CHAPTER 21: GOT GUILT?

How was it already Friday again? Karma thought it would be a good idea to skip Friday playgroup. She didn't want to talk about Brandi and James Patrick in front of Bianca, she couldn't talk about Little Jeffrey in front of Jeanette, and she and Kim had spent so much time together in the past few days, there didn't seem to be anything left to talk about. She was also supposed to go in for yet another blood test, and if she went early in the morning, maybe they'd have the results by late afternoon. So far, her levels weren't rising as fast as Dr. Weimer wanted, but they were rising, and he said not to worry.

But that wasn't the real reason she didn't want to be with her best girlfriends. There was a dark and stormy cloud of guilt hanging over her. What had started out as a clean, surgical operation (tires slashed, speeder chastised, problem solved) had turned into an allegory of middle-class guilt. Dora Lee, whom Karma could swear she'd never even seen before that day on the playground, was popping up everywhere she went, at the grocery store, at the gas station, even at Goodwill. That was the worst. It was just yesterday, and Karma was donating unwanted clothing when Dora Lee drove into the parking lot.

"Hi, neighbor," called Dora Lee, as she drove past Karma, who was in the line of cars waiting in the drop-off donation lane, and entered the store. Dora Lee was obviously going in to shop, which made Karma feel even worse. *When did I become a member of the Oppressor Class? I was going to be a rebel. I was going to wear unbleached cotton and boycott grapes. I didn't know what was wrong with the grapes, but Geraldo was hot back then and he was complaining about them. I was going to grow my own vegetables and have a compost heap and raise money for the poor and everything. I voted for Jimmy Carter, for God's sake. Jimmy Carter. What the hell happened to me?*

Back at home, Karma slouched over her nearly empty glass of pineapple juice. *God, I miss coffee. I never even bought that coffee that's good for the rain forests or helps the natives or whatever. I suck.*

But Molly loved playgroup, and nobody would believe whatever lame-ass excuse she came up with. So Karma resolved to put aside her guilt and face the world, or at least a few of her friends. *But if Dora Lee shows up on the playground wearing one of my donated sweaters, I'll throw myself under a bus.*

"C'mon, Miss Molly," she called into the family room. "Let's get ready for playgroup."

True to her nature, while Karma was rationalizing her way through her guilt, Kim had avoided it altogether. When Karma let herself in Sue Ellen's front door, the first thing she heard was Kim telling Bianca all about Dora Lee's knocked-up tramp of a daughter. Bianca's explosive *"porca madonna!"* was followed by something less familiar, Bianca's daughter's triumphant, "Mommy, gimme money."

Karma shrugged off her jacket, aimed Molly in the direction of the other kids, and headed for the kitchen, where Kim, Sue Ellen, and Bianca were drinking coffee at Sue Ellen's three-hundred-pound, solid oak, made-to-look-like-an-antique kitchen table. Bianca's face was set in a scowl. Her daughter was standing next to her with one hand outstretched and the other perched saucily on her hip. Bianca dug into the front of her skinny black Levis and handed a coin to Caitlin, who dropped it into the front pocket of her pink and yellow jumper. Judging by the coin's metallic *clink*, it was joining several others.

Karma smiled. "So your daughter is a human swear jar?"

Bianca rolled her eyes. "Tony's idea. He's turning my own kid into a snitch. The money goes into our vacation fund; at this rate, we'll be going to Europe on the Concorde."

"They don't fly those anymore," said Karma.

"Well," said Bianca, "the way I'm going, Caitlin can buy one. Anyway, so whatshername, Brandi, works at Burger King? Which one?"

"I don't know," said Kim. "I didn't ask."

Bianca slid her chair over to make room for Karma. "I worked at Arby's in college. I smelled like roast beef. Dogs would follow me home."

"I used to love their Jamocha shakes," said Kim. "Gosh, I haven't had one in years." Actually, she'd bought one the previous day, but as always, she had stuffed the evidence into the bottom of the garage trash bin before going inside. She'd been sneaking her kids' snack food and driving through fast-food restaurants almost daily, but she was exercising more, too, and her clothes still fit, and that's what mattered. *You do what you gotta do.* That was Kim's motto, and she applied it equally to losing weight and punishing neighborhood jerks. She couldn't understand Karma's equivocating; right was right and wrong was wrong, whether the wrongdoer was a beer-drinking swine like Jack Lawrence or a little skank like Brandi. Excuse their behavior and you're asking for more of it.

Karma accepted a cup of orange juice from Sue Ellen. "Am I the only one who feels a little bad about this, now that we know who she is, and that she's trying to support a baby?"

"She almost hit *your* baby, remember?" said Kim. "And she's been driving slower ever since. Don't waste your time feeling guilty over a smart-ass teenager getting what she deserves. I still

191

say she knows it was somebody in the neighborhood, even if she *did* tell her mother all that crap about cheerleaders and ex-boyfriends." Kim squared her shoulders. "Nobody died. I can live with it."

Karma stared into her glass of juice. "Well, I feel guilty."

Kim gave a contemptuous grunt and helped herself to a scoop of fruit salad from Sue Ellen's Havilland china bowl. "Where the hell is Jeanette with the cinnamon rolls? You know what your problem is? You feel guilty because you're thinking about little whatshisname—James Patrick—when you should be thinking about your own kid and Brandi. Punish the guilty, I say. Tell her, you guys," she said, popping a hunk of cantaloupe into her mouth.

Bianca, stone-faced, said nothing. Sue Ellen, rinsing dishes at the sink, glanced over her shoulder at Kim, but also said nothing.

Karma would have preferred some actual support, rather than this chicken-shit silence. It was easy for the rest of them; they hadn't slashed Brandi's tires. She was the one who felt like crap. She'd been so angry at the woman in the red car, but now the woman was an unwed teenager with a name and a cute little toddler she could barely feed.

Jeanette showed up a few minutes later, juggling baby Jacob, the obligatory pan of cinnamon rolls, and her gigantic diaper bag. Sue Ellen took the first and last from her, dropping the bag by the table and maneuvering the baby into Daniel's old highchair, as Jeanette slid the cinnamon rolls in the already preheated oven.

"Hey," said Jeanette, as she snapped Jacob's bib and pulled a jar of baby mashed peaches from the bag. "What are we talking about today?" She didn't wait for an answer. "I heard something interesting. Guess what's really wrong with Jack Lawrence."

Distracted from her resentful reverie, and frankly grateful for it, Karma spoke first. "His parents were brother and sister?"

"His mother was a crack-head," said Kim.

"I know," said Bianca. "He was dropped on his head as a baby."

"He's a woman trapped in a man's body," giggled Sue Ellen.

Jeanette wrinkled her nose at all of them. "I'm serious. I found out what's wrong with their marriage. He's cheating on her and she knows about it and that's why they fight all the time."

Sue Ellen was still drying her hands on a dish towel, but she slipped back into her seat at the table, looking skeptical. "You know this for sure?"

"For positive," said Jeanette. "I met somebody at the grocery store who knows somebody who works with Jack, and she says there's a rumor that he's doin' it with somebody in the office."

"Not exactly something you could take to the district attorney," said Bianca.

"It makes sense," said Karma. "I bet it's true. Doesn't he seem like the type?" She poured herself more juice. "And just when I didn't think my opinion of him could get any lower."

"No kidding," said Kim. "Bastard's got three kids."

"You don't even know it's really true," said Bianca, "but if it *is* true, he's a freakin' scumbag."

Nobody spoke, but the entire table of moms was staring at Bianca.

"What?" she said. "*Freakin'* isn't swearing; it's *instead* of swearing." But still, she gave a quick peek around the corner to see if Caitlin had heard.

"I'd like to drop another lawnmower on his head," said Karma. "He's got kids to think about. Nice kids, right?"

"Very nice," said Jeanette. "Too nice. Like they're scared of him."

"What a pig," said Kim. "I miss the good ol' days when you could get a bunch of menfolk together to teach a guy like that a lesson."

Sue Ellen nodded enthusiastically, her blond bob swinging. "John Wayne would have taken him out and horsewhipped him. Don't you love movies like that; men protecting their women's honor? It's so romantic."

Karma agreed. *Where is Clint Eastwood when you need him? Or Zorro? Or Luann's brothers, if she has any? Society is just too civilized for its own good. Men are too sensitive, and everybody just looks the other way, instead of dealing with bad behavior and putting a stop to it. Well, not us, of course, but everybody else.*

And then she had another thought. *I sound like Kim. The world is black and white. Punish the guilty and don't look back.*

And then she had another thought. *This isn't just about punishing anybody. This is about making Jack Lawrence see the error of his stupid ways and be a better man.*

Karma leaned back in her chair. "I wonder if maybe this is something we could work on, now that we know about it. I mean we're already involved, God knows, so why not consider it part of the on-going project."

Sue Ellen wrinkled her perky pointed nose. "We have *projects*?"

"*They* have projects," said Bianca. "You and I have brains. We're staying the fu— the *heck* out of it."

"You helped with the teenage child-molester project," Karma reminded her.

Bianca shrugged. "That was different."

"Jack Lawrence is a *science* project," said Kim. "But what happened to your compassion, Miss Karma? I thought you were goin' all soft and squishy?"

Karma ignored her. "Maybe all he needs is a little talking to. A female perspective on what he's doing to his kids and his wife."

Kim sniffed at a stick of peanut butter-filled celery. "You sure you won't end up feeling sorry for the guy? You've gone all hearts and flowers over poor little Brandi. What if it turns out Jack's an orphan?"

Now Karma was getting angry. Kim was always so sure of herself, which was part of what Karma liked about her, but not at the moment. "This is not the same thing. I didn't know anything about Brandi at the time, and now that I do, I feel a little weird about it, but we know Jack Lawrence, and he needs to stop being an asshole."

Sue Ellen looked a bit queasy. "I don't know, you guys. He scares me. I wish we had a man we could get to talk to him." She looked at Jeanette. "Your husband and he got to be friends, right? Maybe he could talk to Jack, man to man."

Jeanette shook her head. "They're men; they don't talk to each other like we do."

Bianca nibbled on a chocolate chip cookie, looking thoughtful. "I don't know. Where I'm from, guys might do something like that. Like take a guy outside and beat the shit out of him if he got fresh with the wrong girl. My brothers would beat the shit out of Tony if he cheated on me. If I didn't kill him first."

Jeanette looked doubtful. "That's not communicating, that's fighting."

Bianca shrugged. "Where I come from, fighting is communication."

Karma smiled. "I think I'd like your brothers."

"They're jerks, but they're my jerks," said Bianca. "You got any brothers?"

"No," said Karma.

"Sisters?"

Karma didn't answer.

"You're an only child?"

"Yes," said Karma.

Playgroup was over and Karma was home. Molly was down for a nap, and Karma was alone with her thoughts. She wasn't thinking about Jack Lawrence or Brandi. She actually had just one thought: *How could I do that?* In all the time she'd known her playgroup friends, she'd never actually lied about her twin sister. If nobody asked if she had a brain-damaged twin sister living in a nursing home, it wasn't lying to keep that information to herself. Everybody did that. It was like Bianca talking about her family like they were mafia, but not quite saying whether they were or not. But Karma had crossed that line today. She had denied even having a sister. It made her sick to her stomach.

Her childhood had been hijacked by two intertwined events. The first was the disastrous birth of her twin. The second was her parents' bitter divorce, which resulted in Kathleen's move to Good Shepherd. Karma had spent every birthday after that, until college, in Kathleen's hospital room, because after all, it was Kathleen's birthday, too. Never mind that Kathleen was fed through a tube and couldn't eat the cake that her crazy mother always brought. Never mind that Charlotte insisted on lighting candles and singing. Never mind that Karma still associated her own birthday with the smell of bleach and the sad moaning that was the only sound Kathleen made.

Years later, pregnant with Molly and unable to sleep, she'd been paralyzed by the pounding fear that something horrible was happening inside her body. She had demanded extra ultrasounds to check on Molly's progress in the womb. And when Molly was born pink and perfect and breathing, Karma had made Sam and both their families promise not to talk about Kathleen until Karma decided that Molly was ready to hear about her. Molly would be a happy and innocent child, not burdened with something she couldn't do anything about. Molly's life would not revolve around Kathleen's sad, shadowy existence.

So when they moved to Bedford Commons, Karma simply didn't talk about Kathleen. What if Molly overheard something? Karma had told many stories about her past to these new friends, as they had to her, but she had left out the part about having a twin deprived of oxygen at birth, about making the drive to Good Shepherd every week after her dad walked out, and about continuing to drive there every month since her mother had moved to Florida. *I don't want sympathy, and I don't want to answer a hundred questions from every new neighbor I meet. That doesn't make me a bad person.* At worst, it was a lie of omission. Of course, thanks to Sam and his big mouth, Molly knew about Kathleen, but she'd stopped asking to meet her, after Karma had told put her off several times. She'd forget about it if Karma avoid the topic. Everything was back to normal.

But all that had just changed. Karma had denied having a sister, something she had never done before. She had said it in front of her friends and in front of God. She was despicable.

There was only one way to redeem herself.

CHAPTER 22:   ROAD TRIP

Sometime after the second trip through a McDonald's drive-thru and the third potty stop, Karma began asking herself what stupid, sentimental, guilty impulse had persuaded her to take her daughter to meet Kathleen. Add to this Molly's passion for Radio Disney, and Karma's nerves were jangling. Her patience for singing hamsters died before they made it to the interstate.

Molly, usually asleep before Karma left their neighborhood, was too excited to relax on this journey. Karma made up stories about heroic four-year-olds who put out forest fires and captured bank robbers, listened to the same knock-knock joke sixty-two times, and answered a thousand questions about Kathleen. Finally, Karma made the familiar turn onto the gravel drive that lead to the grounds.

"Hey, sweetie, we're here," said Karma, smiling at Molly in the rear view mirror. She was asleep.

After parking the car, Karma unbuckled Molly from her car seat, hoisted her limp body over her shoulder, and lugged her across the gravel parking lot to the front steps of Good Shepherd. Along the way, she gathered the usual phalanx of excited residents. Some wanted to pat the sleeping child, others scolded the wannabe-patters.

"You wake her, dummy," cried Lenny, as Alice touched Molly's back.

"You hurt my feelings," sniffed Alice.

"It's okay, Lenny," said Karma. "Alice was being gentle."

"Yeah, Lenny," said Alice, "you dummy."

It was remarkably like Friday playgroup.

Her entourage was shooed back onto the grounds by one of the attendants when they tried to follow Karma into the building. Signing the visitor's log with a child slung over her shoulder was awkward, but Karma managed. She was accompanied to Kathleen's room by a nursing assistant whom Karma hadn't met before. Betsy, who looked all of twenty, explained that she'd only started at Good Shepherd two weeks ago.

"Do you like working here?" asked Karma.

"Sure," said Betsy. "The people are okay, the staff, I mean, and I like working with the residents. It's a lot better than the place I worked at before, I'll tell you that. Way cleaner."

"It doesn't depress you that nobody gets better?"

She looked at Karma curiously. "Well, some of them do get *some* better. They learn to do things for themselves, that kind of thing."

Not my sister.

By the time they reached Kathleen's room, Karma's legs and shoulder felt like she'd lugged a hundred-pound sack of cement up Mount Fuji, and she'd stopped talking to Betsy because she was breathing too hard to speak.

"Why don't you just lay her on the bed? Miss Kathleen won't mind, and the baby will be more comfortable. You, too, I'm thinking."

Karma hesitated, but there was a safety rail on the bed, and she would be just inches away if Molly woke up. So she flipped Molly carefully off her shoulder, and with the nursing assistant's help, laid her gently along Kathleen's left side. The room was quite warm, as Kathleen's body couldn't regulate its own temperature, so there was no need for a blanket for Molly. Karma slipped off her little pink tennis shoes, and the two women regarded her peacefully sleeping form.

"She's a baby doll," said Betsy. "Isn't it amazing how they can sleep through anything? I've got a two-year-old; I play my music loud at night, and he never wakes up. I'll be back in a bit, if you don't mind. I've got to do afternoon meds."

Karma sat back in the reclining chair, alone with her thoughts. *What will Molly think of Kathleen? Will Kathleen even know she's there?*

She played a few games on her phone, but soon her thoughts drifted back to Jack Lawrence. There seemed to be no end to his worthlessness. First shooting fireworks at a pregnant woman and now hitting and cheating on his wife. Karma's father had left her mother, but he'd never been violent. In fact, he'd been a saint to put up with Charlotte all those years. Who could blame him when he finally couldn't take it anymore?

Dear God, I'm bored. Somebody wake up.

Was it possible that Luann was a complete raving bitch, like her mother, Charlotte, had been? Luann was a cold fish, but nobody deserved to be hit. And Joan Handley had done nothing to deserve being shot at with a bottle rocket, or whatever he'd used. No, Jack Lawrence was a jerk, and he had to be dealt with.

Karma reached for her phone again and punched in a number.

"Hey, babe."

"Hi, it's me," said Karma. "It's good to hear your voice."

"You just left this morning, but me, too," said Sam. "How did Molly do on the trip?"

"She fell asleep just as we pulled into the parking lot. I had to carry her in; she weighs a ton."

"Oh," said Sam. "I put her stroller in your trunk. I guess I forgot to tell you."

"I didn't even look. Oh well, I'll counting it as my exercise for the week. How's it going there? Are you getting much done in the kitchen?"

200

"I'm almost done priming. I'm going to watch the game, then start painting."

"There's a game?" asked Karma, smiling through a mild case of annoyance. *There is always a game.* "Don't forget, any painting you don't get done today, your four-year-old daughter will help you with tomorrow."

"Don't worry, I'll be done," said Sam. Karma could hear the smile in his voice, and it filled her with cheer. "Oh, she said, turning toward a noise from the bed. "I'd better go; Molly is waking up."

Molly Kranski was used to falling asleep in one place and waking up in another; it happened nearly every day, but this time there was a cold metal railing on one side, and a large sleeping stranger on the other. Eyes wide with panic, but without making a sound, she held out her arms to Karma and let herself be lifted from the bed. Yawning, she settled into her mother's arms and studied her surroundings.

"Aunt Kathleen?" asked Molly, looking at the bed.

"Yes, but she's asleep."

"She will wake up?"

"I don't know," said Karma. "I hope so. We can wait a while for her to wake up if you want."

"Can I wake her up?" asked Molly.

As if on cue, the door opened and Denise, the physical therapist, walked into the room. She was startled to see visitors. "Oh my goodness," she said. "I didn't expect anyone to be here. I can come back later."

"No," said Karma. "That's okay. Are you going to wake her up?"

"I should," said Denise, "if you don't mind." She spoke with the brisk confidence of a professional, but with the undertone of kindness that Karma remembered from her last visit. "We don't want her sleeping all day." She flipped on the television. "This usually does the trick." Denise was an old hand. She pulled back Kathleen's white cotton blanket and sheet, and started manipulating her right arm. Kathleen's eyes fluttered open and Denise began speaking to her. "You have visitors, Kathleen," she said. She spoke clearly and loudly, the way people speak to foreigners. Kathleen moaned in protest, then began her usual drifting gaze, turning her head from side to side. "Your sister is here, and I bet this is your niece."

"Yeah," said Karma. "This is Molly. Can you say hi, Molly? This is Miss Denise. She helps Aunt Kathleen do her exercises."

Molly murmured a cautious greeting, then slipped off Karma's lap and walked to the side of the bed.

"She can see me?"

"Sure, she can," said Denise. "Here, let's get up here where she can see you better." Before Karma could react, Denise lifted Molly and set her on the foot of the bed. Molly, who wasn't used to complete strangers picking her up, looked at Karma with wide eyes, but didn't protest. Karma smiled her approval and let Denise handle things. "If you want to talk to your aunt, you speak loudly and very clearly," Denise said, loudly and very clearly.

"HI, AUNT KATHLEEN," shouted Molly.

"Maybe not quite that loud," said Denise.

Amazingly, though, Kathleen's eyes stopped their ceaseless wandering and stayed on Molly for several seconds.

"Hey," said Denise, sounding surprised. "She's happy to see you. Keep talking."

"I'm MOLLY," yelled Molly. "I came to see you with my MOMMY."

Kathleen let out a long, sustained groan.

"I think she's trying to say hello." said Denise.

"I'm four-and-a-half years OLD," shouted Molly.

Kathleen groaned again. Karma felt a chill moving down her back. It did seem like Kathleen was trying to talk to Molly. And Molly, as timid as she was at times, was not freaked out in the slightest. *I underestimated both of them.*

"My teacher is Miss LaDonna. You want me to SING?" Molly took a deep breath, and burst into the Alphabet Song. "A, B, C, D, E, F, GEEE," she bellowed. "H, I, J, K, L-M-N-O-PEEE!"

It was astonishing. Kathleen was making long, sustained groaning sounds along with Molly as she finished with a dramatic, "Next time won't you sing… with… MEEE."

Molly turned to look at her mother, eyes bright with pride. "I teach her the song, Mommy."

"Yes, I think you did."

"She likes my singing."

"Of course she does," said Karma, trying not to ruin the moment with outright weeping. "You're a great singer."

"What I should sing next?"

An hour and many songs later, Karma and Molly walked hand-in-hand out the front doors of Good Shepherd Residential Center. Kathleen had drifted away again, sometime between *I've Been Workin' on the Railroad* and *Frosty the Snowman*, but something had kept her present in a way that Karma had thought impossible. Was it the high frequency of Molly's voice, her sheer volume, or something else?

"When can we come back?" asked Molly. "I had fun."

"We'll come back soon," said Karma. "It was fun for me, too." That was an understatement a lifetime. The day had been nothing short of a miracle.

The ride home was unlike any other. Laughter and songs for the first thirty minutes, and another ninety minutes to drink Diet Coke, eat chicken nuggets, and think about the possibilities.

What if being around Molly could actually help Kathleen? What if she could get better? What would it mean to finally bring Kathleen into the family? To truly have a sister and introduce her to the rest of the world?

On this day, nothing seemed impossible.

CHAPTER 23:   JACK'S HOT WHEELS

"Wanna hear something totally weird?" asked Jeanette.

"Always," said Karma.

"Pass me the salt."

Karma was in such a good mood after her visit with Kathleen that she was treating Jeanette to lunch at a local bistro. She owed Jeanette lunch because Jeanette had given her a grocery bag full of bologna and American cheese Lunchables and wild cherry juice boxes. She'd bought them for Little Jeffrey, after he'd taken a liking to them, and refused to eat or drink anything else for an entire week. But after she had stocked up on them, he lost his taste for them completely. Rather than feed them to Allie, with her weak tooth enamel and tendency to get thick around the middle, Jeanette had offered the entire stockpile to Karma at no charge.

To Karma's mild horror, bologna and cheese Lunchables and wild cherry juice boxes had quickly become Sam's go-to between-meal snack. But fair was fair, so Karma had asked Jeanette to lunch. They'd picked this restaurant because it was new and cute, and the owners were two retired local teachers who deserved the patronage. Over low-carb Chinese Chicken Salads and tall glasses of Diet Coke with slices of lemon perched saucily on the rims, Karma and Jeanette enjoyed the partly-sunny afternoon. They had chosen one of the tiny wrought iron tables in the back courtyard of what had once been a private home.

The courtyard was barely twenty feet square, and theirs was the only table in use. Thus it was purely for dramatic effect when

Jeanette peered over the frames of her sunglasses and looked from side to side to make sure nobody was eavesdropping, then leaned in close to whisper to Karma, "Guess who's going bike riding with my husband tomorrow morning?"

Karma sighed. It would be wonderful if, just once, Jeanette simply passed along her gossip, instead of making people work so hard for it. "Lance Armstrong," she said. "Caitlyn Jenner. Jimmy Hoffa. How can I possibly guess?"

"Jimmy *who*?" asked Jeanette. "C'mon, just guess."

Karma glared at her. "Do you want dessert?"

"Okay, it's Jack Lawrence."

"Well, you were right. I should have guessed," said Karma. "When did they get to be such good buddies?"

"You got me," said Jeanette. "One spaghetti dinner and suddenly my husband is best friends with him. See, I told you it was totally weird."

Weird, thought Karma, ran in Jeanette's family. After that same dinner, Jeanette had become Luann Lawrence's private marriage counselor and personal bodyguard. Jeff going riding with Jack Lawrence wasn't any weirder than Jeanette's budding friendship with Luann, but she kept that thought to herself; she didn't want to spoil their lunch.

"So Jeff rides," said Karma. "I didn't know that."

"Oh, yeah," said Jeanette. "He gets up early at least four mornings a week when it's nice like this. I guess they talked about it that night at dinner. Jeff's been wanting somebody to ride with him. They're going tomorrow morning at, like, six. Weird, weird, weird." Jeanette took another mouthful of her salad and made happy yummy noises.

Karma looked down at her own plate. She'd ordered the salad, but she'd wanted a big, greasy hamburger. Karma nibbled on a crispy won ton strip, wishing it were a French fry *Stop thinking about food. This could be our chance to talk to Jack.*

Where will they ride? Maybe Jeff would meet us somewhere, and we could all talk.

The door that led onto the patio opened, and a young Asian woman walked out, carrying a baby. She sat down at a table and the waitress brought out a highchair and steadied it while the mom maneuvered the wiggly baby into the seat.

Karma watched silently. Every three days she was having blood drawn, but her hormone levels were still just creeping up, not doubling, the way they were supposed to. Dr. Weiner had prescribed higher doses of medication and told Karma not to worry. *Yeah, right.* She'd taken to talking to the tiny little creature in her body. *C'mon, Peanut, be a strong boy and keep growing. Make those cells divide.* A girl peanut would also be fine, of course, but Karma found herself thinking of this baby as a boy.

When the waitress brought their locally-grown peach parfaits, Karma forced herself, again, to think about Jack Lawrence, and on what Jeanette was saying about Jeff. He did his early-morning biking at a rock quarry on the east side of town, which connected to a dirt bike path that wound around the banks of the White River. Years earlier, the county had set aside several dozen acres and created a hilly, winding hiking and biking trail. Few people used it during the week, which is why Jeff favored it. Mounds of discarded quarry stone marked the borders of the winding trail, which was partially hidden under wildflowers and brush. It was the closest a flatlander from central Indiana could come to an actual mountain bike trail. *If you wanted to have a private conversation with a cyclist, what better place to meet?*

"It's absolutely brilliant," cried Kim that afternoon, when Karma dropped in to talk. Karma had hoped Kim would like her idea, but she found herself alarmed by Kim's over-the-top enthusiasm. The news that there might be a time and a place to approach Jack Lawrence had sent Kim into a frenzy. She'd been working on laundry when Karma got there, and in her manic exhilaration, she had dropped Dave's boxer shorts in mid-fold and stood up so excitedly that she tipped the laundry basket off the living room couch. Clean, shirts and shorts were in a heap on the floor. Karma, who hated folding clothes once, much less twice, kept her seat on the couch and stared down at the tragic mess. *Hmmm, Dave wears tighty whities.*

"All we have to do is get Jack there alone, without Jeff," said Kim. She was walking in tight circles around her coffee table and barely missed stepping on the clean clothes she'd dumped. "What time are they supposed to ride? We have to make sure we've got the right place, too. How? Oh, wait, that's easy; we just have to talk to Jeff. But we have to be careful; we can't tell him why we want to know where and when he rides. Is it crowded in the mornings? What did Jeanette say? We don't want other people around. We have to make sure nobody sees us. Does Jeanette understand not to tell Jeff anything?"

Something strange was going on. Karma wasn't sure whether to shake Kim or make her breathe into a paper bag. She was tempted to stick her foot out and trip her on her next circuit around the table, just to get her to stop talking. "What's with you?" she finally said when Kim took a breath. "We're going to *talk* to Jack, not mug him and steal his bike."

Kim stopped pacing and looked down at her with undisguised contempt. "We can't just walk up to him and start a conversation. If we're seen with Jack or if we ask too many questions about him, it makes a *connection* between him and us. It's the *connections* between people that tip off the cops. If Jeff finds out we want to talk to Jack, or sees us hanging out at the dirt bike trail after his wife invited Jack to dinner, that makes a *connection* between Jack and us, and next thing you know, he starts wondering if we had anything to do with blowing up his shed. The cops arrest us or Jack comes and kills us. Either way, it's bad." Kim rolled her eyes. "How do you not get this?"

"Okay," said Karma. "I get it. But you need to switch to decaf, and if you say *connection* like that again, I will slap you."

They needed more input from Jeanette, so the details of the plan took shape over coffee, juice, and cinnamon rolls at Karma's house on Friday. Playgroup was short a few members, as Sue Ellen and Daniel were at the pediatric dentist, and Bianca, Tony, and their girls were on their way to a cousin's wedding in Pennsylvania. It was helpful, since Bianca and Sue Ellen were so negative about helping Jack Lawrence become a better man.

Truthfully, though, Karma was having second thoughts herself. She had a nagging sense that things were getting out of hand, and that something could go wrong. Okay, a few things had already gone wrong, like nearly blowing up Jack's house and crushing his skull, but his skull was fine, the house was barely scorched, and he'd probably get a nicer shed with the insurance money.

Nevertheless, after that weird scene with Jeanette, Karma had decided that, at least for her, this meeting with Jack Lawrence would be the last official intrusion into Other People's Business. She didn't want to get into a big discussion with everybody about it, but her mind was made up. She particularly didn't want to hear Bianca's *I told you so* when Karma admitted that they might be getting in a bit too deep with the Lawrence family.

But this final project, talking sense into Jack, was well underway, and it had to be handled properly. Jeanette, as usual, wasn't grasping the complexities of Kim's plan, nor the secrecy Kim was so intent on maintaining. "I don't see the harm in telling Luann," she said. "I think she'd appreciate knowing we've figured a way to help her."

"No," barked Kim. "This stays between the three of us. Luann might tell her stupid husband we're on her side or something, and ruin the whole thing." Kim pushed away from the kitchen table and walked over to Karma's cookbook shelf. "How can you find anything in this mess? Why don't you alphabetize these? I'll do it."

"Leave the books alone," said Karma. "I have a system and you'll ruin it. If you're having an OCD attack, mop my floors or go clean the bathrooms."

Kim sat down again, but her eyes kept drifting back to the bookshelf. Karma made a note to herself to have a talk with Kim about how jumpy and distracted she'd been lately. It would have to wait, though, because a thought that had been nagging at Karma was demanding attention. "Jeanette," she said, trying to sound casual, "Did you tell Luann about the whole blowing-up-the-shed thing?"

Jeanette's face took on a look of cow-eyed horror. "No, I wouldn't do that. I don't want her to be mad at me."

"*Her* being mad at you isn't the point," snapped Kim. "The point is for *me* not to be mad at you, and for her goddamn husband not to come and kill us or sue us or have us arrested." With a bark of frustration, Kim jumped up again and heading back to the cookbooks. "Do you want these arranged by author or title? Never mind, it should be title. No, subject."

Jeanette turned to Karma. "Really, you guys, I swear, I haven't told her anything."

But Karma was again focused on Kim, who was scanning the disordered shelf, back and forth, back and forth. She hadn't touched the books yet, but clearly, she was itching to get started. Her hands were practically shaking, and her voice was unnecessarily harsh. "You're not going to tell her about *this*, either. If we can talk to her idiot husband and get him to straighten up, we'll do it, but she's not going to know about it,

210

and we're not doing anything to let either one of them know we had anything to do with the fireworks or the shed."

"I agree," said Karma. "I just hope he's willing to listen. He doesn't even know me and Kim."

"Well, at least he doesn't think you're fools, like he does me," said Jeanette, sagging in her kitchen chair. "He won't care what I think."

"Maybe having Jeff help us might not be a bad idea?" said Karma. "Guys listen to each other."

"Maybe," mused Jeanette.

"What are you talking about?" Kim turned away from the cookbooks and stared at them. "You don't think we're going to let him *see* us?"

Karma and Jeanette looked at each other, confused. "How are we supposed to talk to him without him seeing us?" asked Karma. "We're meeting him in person, we're not writing an anonymous note."

Kim stared at Karma as though she'd just sprouted a really hideous second head. "Oh. My. God. He can't know who we are. What are you, fucking nuts? We have to wear disguises. Don't you listen?"

"Disguises?"

"What have we been talking about?" said Kim. "If he knows who we are, he's gonna put two and two together and figure out we're the ones who blew up his shed."

"Technically, he blew up his own shed," said Jeanette.

"Don't be stupid," said Kim. "You know what I mean."

"Jesus, Kim," said Karma. "Back it down about ten notches." She leaned back and peered into the dining room, where the girls were eating snacks and pretending to feed their dolls and stuffed animals. For once, Little Jeffrey was ignoring them and quietly playing on his mother's IPad. None of the kids seemed to be listening to their conversation.

Kim started taking the cookbooks off the shelf. "Topic. They should be arranged by topic. I thought you understood. We're going to wear masks. We're going to tell him that we know where he works, and if he doesn't stop screwing around on his wife, we'll rat him out to his boss and his wife, but we won't say her name so he'll think we don't know her personally. He'll think we work for his company, which is why we say we're going to tell his boss, who probably wouldn't give a crap, but it will throw him off the track."

"I am so relieved," said Karma. She downed the rest of her juice. "I thought you were going to come up with something ridiculous."

Kim either ignored the sarcasm or hadn't noticed it. "I've got Powerpuff Girl masks from Halloween. The whole set. I'm going to be Blossom because she's the leader, and it was my idea. You can be Buttercup. She's the tough one."

"Nope," said Karma, resting her chin in her palm and her elbow on the table. "There's nothing weird about this at all."

"What about me?" asked Jeanette. "Can I be Bubbles? She was always my favorite."

"Don't be stupid. Didn't I already say you can't go," said Kim. "He might still recognize you, and anyway, you won't remember to disguise your voice."

"I will so," said Jeanette. "No matter what you think, I'm not stupid."

"Then why do you say so many stupid things?"

Karma threw up her hands. "Oh my God, stop it, Kim. You're being a bitch. Say you're sorry for calling Jeanette stupid."

"I didn't call her stupid. I said, *don't be stupid*."

Jeanette looked plaintively at Karma.

"Apologize," said Karma. "You're being a raving bitch."

Kim sneered and rolled her eyes. "I'm sorry you thought I said you were stupid," she said. "But I didn't. You can come with us, and be Bubbles, but you can't speak."

"Is that supposed to be an apology?" Jeanette put her elbows on the table and rested her chin in her hands.

Karma gave her an understanding pat on the arm, and a shrug that said *let it go.* "I'm not sure we're doing you a big favor by having you with us," said Karma. "We don't know what Jack will do when we confront him, even wearing Halloween masks. Remember, he beats his wife."

"He won't dare touch us," said Kim. She had emptied the shelf and was starting to put books back up. "We're not his wife and we'll have him outnumbered. The only thing is, he does know Jeanette's voice and what she looks like, like how tall she is. If he recognizes her, we are screwed."

The oven timer dinged, and Jeanette got up to take out the cinnamon rolls. "I suppose you're right," she said sadly. "I'd better not go. Who wants a cinnamon roll?"

"Not me," said Kim. "I'm not hungry. You two eat; I'll start cleaning up." She abandoned the piles of cookbooks, grabbed a dish towel and strode toward the dining room where the girls were feeding their dolls. She grabbed Lindsey's plate and cup, and head for the trash can.

"Mom," yelled Lindsey. "You're doing it again. I'm not done eating."

Kim stopped, took a deep breath, and returned her daughter's food and drink. She looked embarrassed, and there was something about her furtive glance at the women at the table reminded Karma of someone, but she couldn't think of *who.*

Kim returned to the books. She moved more slowly and deliberately, trying to regain her composure. "It goes without saying that we have to keep Jeff from riding," she said, "because no masks will fool him. But we can't give him time to cancel far

213

enough in advance to stop Jack. So how about this? Just as he's about to leave, Jeanette wakes up with a migraine so he'll have to stay home and help with the kids."

"I don't get migraines."

"It would be a *pretend* migraine."

"Why would I wake up with a migraine when I've never had a migraine?"

Kim kept some of the aggravation out of her voice. "I think you're missing the point of the *pretend* migraine."

"I think *I'm* getting a migraine," muttered Karma.

Jeanette served herself a cinnamon roll, and licked the icing from her fingers. "Think of something else."

"We could take his bike and roll it into a retention pond," said Kim. "We could say the teenagers were up to their crap again."

Jeanette looked horrified. "It's a $900 bike."

"We'll clean it after," said Kim.

"Are you gonna jump into the pond to get it?" asked Jeanette.

Kim and Jeanette argued back and forth like children. Karma stayed out of it. Kim was right; they had to leave Jeff out of this, so they could get Jack alone. Something that didn't involve projectile vomiting or pretending to have a brain tumor or setting a small house fire. The key was simplicity. The way to keep Jeff out of the way was to make sure he couldn't ride his bike. How do you make sure someone can't ride their bike? Bikes and cars had something in common, didn't they? Karma had stopped a car. It would be easier to stop a bike. She smiled and clapped her hands three times, sharply, to get the others' attention. When they stopped yapping and looked at her, she made them wait a few seconds before she spoke.

"We don't have to steal Jeff's bike," she said. "We just have to make sure he can't ride it."

CHAPTER 24:   THE BEST-LAID PLANS

Like many men, Jeff Jorganson was a creature of habit. Before an early-morning ride, he opened the garage door, moved his bike onto the driveway, and then went back into the house to assemble his water bottle, helmet and zippered belt pack, in which he placed his house keys, cell phone and wallet. He didn't bring out his gear *first* because he knew he'd need two hands to extricate his very expensive bike from the tangle of strollers, tricycles, kids' bikes, scooters, roller blades and skateboards that inevitably surrounded it whenever he wanted to go for a ride, no matter how many times he pleaded for consideration from his wife and kids.

Karma thought about this as she shivered in the dewy grass behind Jeff's garage. The plan was simple. Once they heard the garage door open, she and Kim were to listen for the scraping, banging and cursing that meant he was disentangling his bike and bringing it to the driveway. The sound of the closing door, followed by silence, meant he was back in the house for his stuff, which would give them approximately one minute to disable the bike and get into position.

Clad in running clothes, with the masks hidden in a backpack under a shrub, they would then run down to the corner, then turn around and jog past Jeanette's house in time to see Jeff discover the problem. They would stop, commiserate with him, and offer to help him solve it, but he wouldn't be able to do so, because Jeanette would have already hidden what he needed in the basement. They would waste enough of his time to make sure

Jack had left his house before Jeff could stop him, and they would confirm that he was going to wait for Jack Lawrence to show up and encourage him to bike alone.

They would have to hope Jeff did his part, because they had to be gone before Jack arrived. To that end, they would resume jogging around the corner to where Kim's car was parked, and drive over to the bike trail. This would put them at the bike trail before Jack, which would give them time to pick a secluded spot to wait for him.

There was only one problem with this simple plan. No Kim. She hadn't shown up, and Karma didn't dare ring her cell phone at this ridiculous hour, lest Dave hear it, see the caller ID, and wonder why Karma was calling.

So Karma was crouched alone behind the damn garage, freezing and planning how she would kill Kim the next damn time she saw her. *Damn it.* They had run through the plan just last night. Karma could handle Jeff's bike without Kim, she could talk to Jeff without Kim, and she could get to the bike trail without Kim, but there was no way on this earth she was going to face Jack Lawrence alone. *Kim, you better have died in your sleep, because if you didn't, I'm going to make you wish you had.*

There was nothing else to be done. This opportunity might not come again. At least she had the masks, but no way in hell was she doing this alone.

Karma heard Jeff's and Jeanette's garage door open. Her heart was pounding. She ran along the back of the house, grabbed a handful of the small white stones that channeled water from Jeff's gutter downspout, and flung them up at Jeanette's bedroom window. If that didn't wake her, Karma was prepared to use her cell phone, but only as a last resort. It might wake the kids, or worse yet, Jeff might answer it. The stones made a fair amount of noise as they hit the window, but with luck, Jeff was too busy swearing at the crap in the garage to notice.

No response. Karma was focused on the master bedroom window, about to throw a second handful of gravel, when the sliding glass door opened just a foot from her, and Jeanette's head popped out. Karma nearly screamed. "Are you trying to break my window?" asked Jeanette. She pulled her fluffy pink bathrobe tightly around her against the morning chill.

"I had to get your attention," said Karma. "Kim didn't show up. You have to help me."

Jeanette's mouth fell open and the color drained from her face. A noise inside the house made her turn. She gave a squeak of alarm, and banged the sliding door closed.

What the hell, thought Karma. She looked left and right, begging Kim to come around the corner, but, of course, that didn't happen. She had to assume that Jeanette was going to help her. *Keep moving*, she told herself. *Jeanette understood. She's dim, but not stupid. Not completely stupid.* She crept back around the house to the driveway. There was the bike, leaning precariously against the house. *For nine hundred bucks, you ought to get a kickstand.*

After looking around to make sure no real joggers were coming, Karma pulled out her secret weapon—a turkey lacing pin—from her running suit pocket. She'd bought them the year she and Sam got married, in preparation for their first Thanksgiving as a married couple, but she'd never quite figured out what they were for. There had been a picture of a beautiful cooked turkey on the package, so clearly they had something to do with turkeys, but what? There had been no Google back then to consult, and Karma would be damned before she'd call her mother and ask.

Today, though, they would finally be put to use. Holding one in her fist, not unlike the pie server that had come before, Karma jabbed several neat little holes in the rear tire, far enough apart that a single patch kit would be insufficient. Ruining tires seemed

217

to becoming a *thing*, she mused. Then she jogged casually down the sidewalk toward her own house. She stopped at the corner and turned around, ready to trot back to the Jorganson house, as though for the first time that morning. Any moment now, Jeff should come out of the house, all set to ride. She slowed... even slower…barely moved… *Any moment now. Now. Okay, now. Right... now...*

No Jeff. Karma stopped two houses from Jeanette's and pretended to tie her shoes. Still no Jeff. First no Kim, now no Jeff. Bedford Commons had turned into the Bermuda Triangle.

Finally, Jeff emerged from the house, belt pack on, helmet and water bottle in hand. Karma straightened from her simulated shoe-tying, and jogged up to him. "Hey, Jeff, great morning for a ride."

"Hi," he said, startled. "I didn't know you ran."

"I used to, back in college. Thought I'd start again," Karma panted, running in place as though trying to keep her heart rate up while they talked. In reality, her heart was thumping like a bunny's, and threatened to shut down at any moment. Karma had never run for exercise, and couldn't relate to those who did.

"Well, good for you," said Jeff. "I ride. You have a good day. I'd better get ready; I'm meeting somebody."

Still running in place, Karma pointed to his back tire. "Your tire looks low."

He turned and looked. "Oh crap. I didn't notice that a minute ago." Bending down, he squeezed the tire and examined it more closely. "Man, those kids of mine. I'll never get that fixed in time."

"That's too bad," said Karma, still jogging and panting. "Can you call your friend?"

Jeff consulted his sports watch. "No, he's already on his way, I'm sure. He'll be here any minute."

218

Karma felt a stab of horror. *Oh shit! Jack coming here. He'll see my outfit, and when he sees me again HE'LL KNOW IT'S ME. Why did this sound like such a good idea last night?* "Well, I'd better get going, too," she said.

But just as she turned to jog away and forget the whole impossibly stupid plan, Jeanette flew out the front door. "Hey, Karma," she called, "Don't leave without me!" Jeanette was fully dressed in shorts, a tee shirt, and running shoes. It would have been hard to say who looked more surprised, Jeff or Karma.

"You want to go running?" they asked in unison.

"Sure," said Jeanette. "I told you at Friday playgroup that I wanted to go with you. Did you forget?"

"But I told you I was going biking," said Jeff. "We can't leave the kids alone."

"I heard you two talking just now, and you said your tire was flat, so I figured I could go, right?"

"But how did you... you heard me?" Jeff struggled to piece together what was happening. "Oh well, never mind. Sure, you might as well go," he said, shrugging in resignation. "I'll work on my tire, I guess."

"C'mon," chirped Jeanette. She yanked Karma's sleeve as she passed, forcing her to turn and follow, before stopping to wave at Jeff. "Bye, honey, we won't be long. If you have to leave, just go ahead; the kids won't be up for at least an hour."

Karma and Jeanette jogged away in silence until they'd rounded a corner and could no longer be seen by Jeff. Karma picked up the backpack she'd hidden under the bushes and slipped her arms into the straps. "Damn it," she said. "Kim's car was supposed to be here."

"That's why we're going to get your car," said Jeanette, heading toward Cardinal Drive. Karma followed, feeling rather stupid. *Most days Jeanette seems a bit simple, but when things go completely to hell, she turns into James Bond.*

219

"But what if Sam's up?" panted Karma. "How do I explain why I need the van to go running?"

"Tell him you're finished with the run and decided to go grocery shopping," said Jeanette. "This is the best time to go, you know; no lines at the checkout and you can get a parking place right next to the cart corral."

They continued jogging. *Only a block to go,* thought Karma. *I may live through this.* "I wish (*pant pant*) I knew (*pant pant wheeze*) happened to Kim? I don't know whether to be mad or worried."

"She's been acting funny lately," said Jeanette. "Kinda mean. Are she and Dave having problems?"

"She hasn't (*wheeze wheeze cough*) said anything to me about it."

"You're her best friend," said Jeanette. "I'm sure she'd tell you."

Karma wasn't so sure about that, but her lungs had collapsed, so she was just as happy not to speak.

By the time they reached her house, Karma was an inch from cardiac arrest. Jeanette waited outside while Karma went in to get her keys. Sam was up, but she kept calm. She had told him the night before that she was going to start running to keep from gaining too much baby weight. Knowing her as he did, he wasn't surprised to see her back within minutes looking like she'd run the Boston marathon, but he did seem surprised that she was now going grocery shopping. He reminded her that he had to leave for work in an hour, and Karma assured him she'd be back long before that, and promised to add toothpaste and shaving cream to her list.

She and Jeanette climbed into Karma's minivan. It felt good to sit. "Thanks for coming with me," said Karma, starting the engine.

"I didn't want you to go by yourself. If something goes wrong, you'll need backup."

Karma smiled and shook her head in amazement. "I am going to stop underestimating you. You're cool in a crisis."

"I grew up in a crisis," said Jeanette. "My dad was a drinker, and my momma was a crabby old bat who thinks I couldn't do anything right my whole life. Still is."

"Oh," said Karma.

"You met her," said Jeanette. "Didn't you notice?"

Karma focused on the road ahead. "I guess I did notice a little. She reminds me of my mom."

Jeanette gave a mirthless laugh. "That's why I get so upset about Jack and Luann. It just sends me right back to my childhood. That's why it means so much to me to help them and their kids. There's the turn." Jeanette pointed up ahead.

"I see it," said Karma.

They turned into the parking area. "I'll park behind the maintenance trucks and we can find a good spot to wait," said Karma. "He's probably only a few minutes behind us."

"What if he decided to go home and go back to bed?" said Jeanette. "I guess we'll know soon enough."

They left the minivan in the small parking lot, half of which was used to store county maintenance trucks, and walked up the hilly trail. This area was not meant for inexperienced bikers. The trail was littered with ruts and rocks, it narrowed in spots to just a few feet, and there were little side trails that banked sharply for the more adventurous riders.

"Does Jeff really ride here? It's pretty rough," said Karma.

"He loves it," said Jeanette. "Jack, too. They said it's like being in the mountains. We should take the kids here for a walk sometime."

Karma and Jeanette kept going until they found a secluded spot. Thanks to the hilly nature of the winding trail, they couldn't see the highway or Karma's van, but they had a decent view of other parts of the trail. They would see Jack coming in brief snatches, as tall rocks and dirt formations hid most of the path. To get the maximum effect on a small piece of land, the bike path wound tightly, back and forth, like Disney rope lines. They sat down behind a stand of scruffy bushes and exposed rocks, right at a sharp turn in the path, and tried to get comfortable. The rocks that marked their hiding place were big, and had obviously come from a quarry; they had flat sides and straight edges not usually found in nature.

Jeanette shifted her weight around. "He better hurry. I hate sitting on the ground. My butt's falling asleep."

It occurred to Karma that she should have brought some kind of weapon. What if Jack got mad and attacked them? Kim had been sure he wouldn't dare, but Kim wasn't here, was she? Karma selected a nice solid-looking stick and broke off the twigs and leaves sticking out of the sides. It wasn't much, but it might help.

Nobody came by for several minutes, and Karma felt creeping doubts begin to pile up. What if Jack decided not to ride without Jeff? What if he decided to ride somewhere else? What if somebody saw them sitting here, hiding behind rocks with these stupid plastic Halloween masks?

And then Jeanette grabbed Karma's arm and pointed. *There he is.* Her heart started pounding again. She and Jeanette donned their plastic masks as Jack made several passes at the base of the trail, coming closer and closer as the trail zigzagged back and forth. Karma had forgotten how hot and sweaty and smelly these masks were; no wonder Molly always wore hers on top of her head. It was also hard to see through the ridiculously tiny eye holes. She had to keep moving her head, and she could only catch brief glimpses of Jack. He was wearing one of those Spandex bike outfits with bright red stripes on the sleeves, clear yellow goggles which looked vaguely fly-like, and one of those goofy pointed helmets. His chin strap was undone and flapping around his head.

Finally he came around the corner and entered the stretch of dirt path that Karma and Jeanette had staked out. With one last look at each other, holding their collective breaths, the two Powerpuff Girls jumped out from behind the rocks, waving and calling Jack's name. His mouth opened in shocked surprise. This impossible image—two figures in horrifying children's masks, screaming at him and flapping their arms like mad crows, one waving a tree branch, would be the last thing he saw in this life.

Later, when Karma replayed the event in her mind, it occurred to her that she and Jeanette could have simply waited for Jack in the parking lot and talked to him *before* he entered the bike trail, instead of jumping out from behind a big rock wearing Halloween masks and scaring the shit out of him.

But hindsight is easy.

At the sight of the two weird creatures jumping out from behind rocks right in front of him, Jack gave a choked scream, jerked his bike to the left and hit a deep rut on the path. The bike swerved into the rut, but its rider continued straight ahead, flying over the handlebars. His helmet flew off, and with a sickening crack, his unprotected head hit the rock that Karma and Jeanette had been hiding behind. Jack's body landed and lay motionless as the bike crashed into the underbrush.

Frozen, mouth open behind the mask, arm still in mid-wave, Karma watched the scene unfold in bizarre slow-motion. A few seconds of sound and fury, and then silence. Too stunned to speak, she stared at the body and at the blood pooling around its head. One minute it had been sailing through the air like a clumsy bird, the next it was on the ground, as lifeless as a crash test dummy. *This is bad. This is really bad.*

"Jack, are you okay? Jack?" Karma bent down and gave his shoulder a tiny nudge.

"Don't," said Jeanette firmly. "Let me see if he has a pulse."

Karma stepped aside. *This is really really bad.*

Jeanette flipped her mask onto the top of her head, crouched down over the body for a minute, then looked up at Karma and shook her head. "Who thought he'd fall like that?" she said, getting to her feet. "He should have strapped on his helmet."

"Shouldn't we do CPR or something?" asked Karma.

"CPR? Look at his head," said Jeanette.

Karma's voice rose in panic. "I think I'm going to throw up."

"Don't you DARE" Jeanette turned on Karma like a fury and ripped off her plastic mask, taking more than a few hairs with it. "Take deep breaths. Do *not* throw up." She grabbed Karma's arm and shook it, looking at her with an intensity Karma had never seen before. "We cannot leave any DNA here. Do you want to be charged with murder?"

Karma felt the blood rush away from her brain. *Murder?*

Jeanette grabbed the branch Karma was still clutching and threw it into the bushes. She found another one with leaves still attached, and started brushing away their footprints, careful to leave the bicycle tracks intact.

Karma watched her like you watch a movie about somebody who knows what they're doing, though you yourself know that you would have no idea what you were doing. She felt surprisingly detached from the scene. Her primitive reptilian brain was calmed by Jeanette's cool demeanor and wily criminal ways, while from somewhere far away, her intellect was screaming, "RUN, YOU IDIOT, RUN."

When she finished wiping away the footprints, Jeanette picked up the masks and Karma's backpack, took hold of Karma's arm, and led her carefully off the path. Walking backward, Jeanette swiped the ground with the tree branch to hide their last few footprints, then pointed toward the distant parking lot. No one else had driven into the lot, thank goodness, and there were no other runners or bikers visible. It took forever to climb over the rocks and brush, and Karma kept looking back, which made her trip and stumble.

"He's not following us," said Jeanette. "Trust me. Watch where you're going."

When they finally reached the parking area, which was visible from the street, and therefore, potential witnesses, Jeanette tightened her grip on Karma's arm and set a casual pace across the lot. She also slipped the car keys out of Karma's pocket. Karma didn't protest. Even her reptilian brain knew she shouldn't get behind the wheel. So Jeanette drove the getaway minivan away from the scene of the crime. A student of decades of police dramas on television, Jeanette used proper turn signals, maintained a safe distance from the cars ahead of her, and stayed well-within the posted speed limit. No routine traffic stop would tie her to this location at this time on this day.

Karma Kranski, wife, mother, and murderer, sat mutely in the passenger seat of her Chrysler minivan, staring out the window. It was barely daylight, and she already had a dead body to her credit. What else would this day bring? Arson? A shoot-out with the cops?

Whatever else happened, Karma knew one thing for sure. From this day on, every event in her life would be shaped by what she had just done—the simple act of jumping out from behind a big rock and yelling, "Hey!"

CHAPTER 25: KARMA GETS SKEWERED

A short time later, Karma, still in the passenger seat of her minivan, waited for Jeanette to come back with the groceries she had promised Sam. Her chest felt tight. She couldn't seem to take a deep breath. She could still see Jack Lawrence's bloody head and his lifeless, paunchy body stuffed into that ridiculous biking suit. *We didn't touch him. We just wanted to talk to him. He fell off his bike. It's not our fault.* But images of a terrifying future swelled in front of her, like an enormous poisonous toad.

"Your Honor, they hated this man and plotted to kill him."

"First they tried to burn down his house."

"His innocent wife and children were inside."

"They wanted Jack Lawrence dead."

"They are guilty."

"They are stone cold murderers."

Karma shuddered, trying to shake this vision out of her head. She looked around the grocery store parking lot. Jeanette was right about one thing, shopping this early, you could get a primo parking space. If she got up this early, she could get her shopping done in half the time. *Jack Lawrence is dead, why am I thinking about shopping? It's too much. I'll think about Jack tomorrow. I sound like Scarlet O'Hara. I love that movie. This whole thing is like a really bad movie. Do you get to watch movies in prison? Probably not violent movies. The Civil War was violent. Lots of people died in that one. One dead guy more or less wouldn't even matter. I'm so screwed. My little peanut will be born in prison. Peanut in prison. Sounds like a reality show.*

The side door slid open with a bang like a gunshot, and Karma jumped a foot. Jeanette strapped a sack of groceries into Molly's car seat and slid into the driver's seat. "Guess what? Peanut butter was on sale, so I got you two jars."

"What?"

"I didn't know if you like creamy or crunchy, so I got you one of each." Jeanette dug the car keys out of her purse and was reaching for the ignition, but Karma grabbed her arm. "You were supposed to get chocolate milk and toothpaste."

"And shaving cream," said Jeanette, "I did, but Skippy was 'buy one, get one free,' plus I had a coupon. It was practically free; I couldn't pass it up."

Karma raised her eyes and silently beseeched God to make Jeanette shut up about the peanut butter before it made her scream. She would be spending the rest of her life in prison. *Will they serve peanut butter? Probably the generic kind that comes in gallon drums. Do prisons shop at Costco to save money? FOCUS, YOU IDIOT.*

Karma squared her shoulders and sat up straighter in her seat. This was no time to fall apart. Everything she and Jeanette did today—well, starting now—had to look completely innocent and normal.

Jeanette slid into the driver's seat.

"No, I'll drive," said Karma. "If somebody who knows us sees you driving my car, they'll think it's weird." She unbuckled her seatbelt and walked around the car to trade seats with Jeanette. As she reached the driver's side door, she felt an odd stitch in her abdomen. *Did I eat this morning?*

Jeanette shrugged and switched seats, and Karma drove back to the neighborhood in silence. She dropped Jeanette off at her house, then went home. Amazing herself, she calmly walked into

227

her house with the sack of groceries, kissed her husband goodbye as he left for work, and hugged her daughter hello as she settled in for her morning cartoons. Karma, ever the cool criminal, behaved as though she hadn't a care in the world, as though there was no dead body on that bike trail, no Powerpuff Girl masks in her backpack, and no turkey lacing pin in her jacket pocket.

Oh, yes, turkey lacing pin. She would wipe it clean and put it back in the kitchen junk drawer before she forgot about it again. Then she would eat something to settle her stomach.

Karma reached into her pocket. There was no lacing pin in her jacket pocket. Karma checked her pants pockets. No pin. She checked the backpack. No pin. She went back into the garage and searched the van. *No pin.*

NO PIN.

Stay calm. Stay calm. STAY CALM.

Feeling like there was a lead weight in her gut, Karma walked back inside, refilled Molly's sippy cup, programmed the satellite to provide another half-hour of cartoons, then retreated to the kitchen to call Jeanette and tell her they were both going to prison for the rest of their lives. "We have to go back and look for the turkey lacing pin," she hissed. "My fingerprints are all over it."

"No way. Absolutely not." Jeanette's voice was tempered steel. "Only stupid criminals return to the scene of the crime."

"Well, I certainly don't want to be known as a *stupid* criminal," said Karma. But Jeanette was right. When the next biker or jogger came to the bike trail and discovered Jack's body, which could have already happened, the place would be crawling with cops. *Crawling with cops? Who talks like that? Anyway, could they get a good print off a thin metal pin? Maybe they won't even find it. Maybe I dropped it somewhere in the neighborhood. Maybe it won't become the central piece of evidence at my MURDER TRIAL.*

"Was it part of a set?" asked Jeanette.

"Yeah, I think I have three left," said Karma.

"Get rid of them. No, wait, don't do that. Find uses for at least one more of them and put it in a different place, like holding up a tomato plant or something. Or use one to poke a hole in a belt, and then put it in a dresser drawer, like you keep it there for that reason. If they search your house and find a set with just one missing, that's suspicious. If there's two missing, it's not so obvious."

There was a beep on the line that muted Jeanette's next words. "Hang on," she said. "Somebody's trying to call me." She clicked off. Karma waited. Call waiting had to be the rudest invention of modern times, right after erectile dysfunction ads.

When Jeanette clicked back on the line, her voice sounded odd and shaky. "That was Luann. Jack didn't come home from his bike ride with Jeff and she wants to know if I've seen him. I'll call you back." She disconnected the call.

Head suddenly thick and dizzy, Karma sat down in a dining room chair. The toxic truth of the situation flooded her brain. *Jack Lawrence is dead. His wife is a widow. His kids don't have a father. He's dead and it's our fault. It's my fault.* It was too much to handle, and suddenly all Karma wanted to do was sleep. *Maybe when I wake up this will turn out to be a really crappy dream.* Then something touched Karma's arm. She nearly screamed.

"Mommy," said Molly. "I'm hungry."

Karma looked into her daughter and tried to smile. *Mommy just killed somebody, sweetie, so she's a little busy right now. How about peanut butter and jelly?*

"Sure, baby," she said. "What would you like?

"Peanut butter jelly."

"Perfect."

229

CHAPTER 26:   BIG FAT SECRET

Karma eating the crusts of Molly's PB&J when the buzz of the doorbell sent her stomach up into her throat. She approached the door carefully, hugging the walls to avoid being seen through the side glass. The doorbell rang a second time. She dropped down on her knees and crawled the rest of the way. They'd be expecting a face to appear at eye level. She peered through the glass at shoe level and sighed. No lace-up SWAT team jackboots, no shiny black FBI wingtips. It wasn't even Luann Lawrence in casual flats with an assault rifle. It was Barbara Kim Wallace's shiny white Keds.

Karma hauled herself up off the floor and looked squarely into Kim's eyes, albeit through the beveled side glass of the door. Kim looked like last week's unrefrigerated leftovers. Her red, watery eyes were ringed with smudged mascara, her unwashed hair was sticking up on the left side, and her sloppy tee shirt was untucked on the right side. She had brought Lindsey with her, probably figuring Karma wouldn't beat her to death in front of her child.

Karma opened the door and stepped aside to let them in. She offered no greeting, and certainly no smile. Kim stared down at her feet. Karma sent Lindsey and Molly outside to play, then walked into her kitchen and sat down at the table. Kim followed her as far as the doorway, but then stopped, apparently unsure of what to do.

"Sit," said Karma.

Kim came in and sat, twisting a strand of her unwashed hair. "I'm sorry," she said. "I overslept. I haven't been sleeping very well. I meant to be there, I really did, I swear. I just overslept."

Karma's nodded. "You overslept? Well, that can happen to anybody. I wouldn't worry about it."

"I *was* worried. I *am* worried," said Kim plaintively. "What did you end up doing?"

"What did I *do*? I handled it without you. Jeanette came with me."

"Oh no," said Kim. "But it went okay? Did he realize who you were?"

"I'm fairly sure he didn't," said Karma. Funny, she thought, how watching someone die puts your life in perspective. A day ago, Karma would have been bursting with excitement to share every detail of such a bizarre story with her best friend. Now, she just wanted to hit her best friend with a sauté pan. "Do you know that old joke about the guy who's taking care of his brother's cat?"

Kim's eyes darted around the room in confusion. Cautiously, she said, "No, I don't think I do."

"Well, this guy asks his brother to watch his cat while he's on vacation," said Karma. "When he calls to check on the cat, his brother says, *Hey, man, your cat is dead.* And the guy says, *What's wrong with you? You don't just blurt out bad news like that. Couldn't you break it to me gently? Like tell me my cat's on the roof, and then later tell me that it fell off the roof. And then you could tell me the vet's trying to save it. Oh never mind, he says. So how's Mom?* And his brother says, *Mom's on the roof.*"

Karma sat back and folded her arms. Kim looked even more confused and maybe a bit fearful. "I don't think I get it," she said. "Did Jack talk to you? Did he listen? Did he get mad?"

"No, I wouldn't say that."

231

Understanding dawned on Kim's face. "Jeanette screwed things up, didn't she? I knew she would. Did she talk? Crap, he recognized her. Damn it, I feel so bad about not being there."

Karma raised a hand to cut her off. "Jack is on the roof."

"Jack is where? What?" Then Kim's eyes grew as big as Korean dumplings, and she slapped both hands over her mouth. "No. Oh. No. Damn."

Yeah, thought Karma. Now you get it. "When we jumped out, Jack freaked and fell off his bike and hit his head on a rock. We left him on the bike path. He's dead."

Kim's voice was still muffled by the hands covering her mouth. "Holy shit. Holy shit, holy shit, holy shit."

"He's dead and we killed him," said Karma.

Karma's cell phone silently vibrated on the fake granite of the kitchen island. Both women turned and stared at it. Karma slowly rose from her chair. It was going to be horrible news. Horrible, terrible news.

"Hi, Mrs. Kranski," said an officious voice. "This is Dr. Weimer's office. Did you forget you had an appointment this morning for a blood draw?"

Karma cringed. She had forgotten. She hadn't even thought about her blood draws. She hadn't thought about anything except Jack Lawrence. "I forgot," she said. "I've been... I've been... I'm really sorry."

"It is very important that you come in as soon as possible, so the doctor can check your levels. Can you get here before three o'clock today? That's the deadline for lab work."

Karma heard the telltale beep of another call coming in and peeked at the display. She said a quick *I'll be in for sure* to the nurse, and switched over. "Jeanette," she said, and listened for a bit. "Okay. Yeah. What'd you tell Luann?"

As she heard Karma speak the name, a look of shock came over Kim's face. Karma could relate. *Yeah, he had a wife and kids. I forgot for a while, too.*

Jeanette, God bless her, had pulled herself back together. She had told Luann no complicated lies that could trip them up later. She'd told only the simple truth, that Jeff had begged off at the last minute due to a punctured tire, that she had left to jog with Karma, and that Jeff was now at work. No, she hadn't seen Jack arrive at her house, but yes, she would call Jeff at work and talk to him, then she'd call Luann back.

Jeanette had proceeded to do exactly that, and had passed along the completely truthful information that Jack had decided to ride by himself and had left on his bike quite a while ago. The facts and nothing but the facts, but not *all* the facts.

"It's gonna hit the fan soon," said Jeanette. "So now we wait. Don't do anything out of the ordinary."

Karma ended the call. Kim looked at her with obvious sympathy. "You should have called 911 right away," she said. "After all, you guys didn't actually kill him; it was an accident."

Karma noted the "*you guys*," which conveniently, didn't include Kim herself. "Well, excuse me for not thinking as clearly as you would have," she said. "We got scared and took off. It's too late now. The masks were *your* idea, and that's what scared him, you know. Maybe if you'd been there, you could have shared this great wisdom about calling 911, but since you weren't there because *you overslept*, I don't want to hear your great ideas now."

Kim drew back in her chair, stung. "I said I was sorry. It's not my fault."

"You're sorry but it's not your fault? What does that mean?"

Kim stared down at her shoes, but Karma wasn't finished.

"Did you oversleep when you lost my baby monitor, which has my fingerprints all over it? Did you oversleep when you went

233

nuts over how my cookbooks were arranged? You are full of crap." Karma flung herself out of her kitchen chair and stalked over to the window above the sink, which looked out onto her backyard. Molly and Lindsey were outside on Molly's play set, swinging and laughing together without a care. So sweet. Karma wanted to shout at both of them to *knock it the hell off.*

She gathered herself and then turned to look at Kim, who was slumped in her chair, not daring to look back at her. Karma walked over and stood over Kim, hands on hips. "Tell me the rest of it right now," she said. "Tell me the rest of it or I swear I'll kill you, too."

"The rest of what?" Kim spoke without looking up.

"The rest of why you're not sleeping, and why you're not eating, why you acted like a maniac on Friday, and why you've been so bitchy. And don't lie to me. Don't bother."

Kim, barely five-feet-two as it was, seemed to get even smaller. She ran a shaky hand through her thick dark hair, then rubbed her puffy eyes. "Maybe it's the pills I've been taking," she said softly. "I gained weight, six pounds. I just wanted to lose a little weight."

"I knew it. I KNEW it." Karma's triumphant howl made Kim jump, and outside, the girls stopped swinging and stared up at the kitchen window. "*Maybe* it's the pills? *Maybe* it's sunspots, or *maybe* space aliens are doing experiments on your brain. How stupid are you? What the hell are you taking?"

"I'm not taking them anymore," said Kim, practically whining. "It's not worth it. I can't sleep, and now you're mad at me."

"Mad at you?" Karma stared at her. "Thanks to your stupid plan, there's a dead guy out there and Jeanette and I are probably going to prison, and you're worried about me being *mad at you*? Are you kidding? So what are you taking, not that it matters."

234

"It's just ephedrine and some kind of herbs," said Kim. "Lots of people use it."

"Isn't that stuff illegal?" asked Karma. "How'd you get it?"

"Internet. It used to be legal, you know. Every gas station sold it."

"It gave people heart attacks," said Karma, "and it turned you into an asshole. 'You guys?' What kind of bullshit is that? The whole thing was your idea, especially the stupid masks. 'You guys?' You have the nerve to say 'you guys' to me, like it's got nothing to do with you?" Karma paced around her messy kitchen, waving her arms and yelling. The stored up minutia from the last several years of their friendship came pouring out. She railed about the baby monitor again, and the ten bucks Kim had borrowed two months earlier and forgot to pay back, and the time she yelled at Molly when it was actually *Lindsey's* idea to give Totsy a bath with Kim's scented bath beads, and the fact that Kim never seemed to have tip money when they went out to lunch.

Kim listened, head bowed, without interrupting, and without arguing back. She didn't speak until Karma was completely finished, having ended with the current predicament. "You won't go to jail," Kim said in a quiet voice. "It was an accident."

"Tell it to the judge," said Karma, "assuming you don't go to jail with us for planning the whole thing. Which you practically did, you know."

Kim smiled a tiny, wry smile. "I bet I could lose some serious weight in jail."

"Maybe we'll get to share a cell. But since you brought it up," said Karma, "why did six pounds mean so much to you? I didn't even notice it."

Kim's smile was replaced by a cynical scowl and a tug at the front of her shirt. Karma recognized the move: *If I make the shirt look loose, you won't realize my big belly is under it.* But that didn't make sense. Compared to Karma, Kim was an anorexic supermodel, and she had those exotic Asian looks that guys find so fascinating. So why the shirt pull?

"Six pounds on me is like sixty pounds on anybody else," said Kim, now hugging her arms tightly around her middle. "Every ounce is a pound. Every pound is ten pounds." She looked at Karma, but seeing her lack of comprehension, shook her head angrily. "I'm a fat pig. I can't explain it to you, because you just won't get it."

"I won't get it? Are you kidding?"

Kim couldn't hear her. She had been fat all her life: a fat baby, a fat toddler, a fat teenager, and now a fat adult. Always picked last in gym, no invitation to the prom, first date at twenty-four with a fat guy from work who couldn't get anybody else to go out with him. It wasn't something she had ever talked about with her Bedford Commons friends.

"The only way I've ever lost weight is starving myself and taking pills," she said. "I've done it lots of times. I lost seventy-three and a half pounds the year before we moved here."

"You're kidding," said Karma. "That's amazing. I can't even picture it." And she couldn't. It was stunning, like finding out Kim had once been a man. Or a democrat. But she couldn't stop herself from *trying* to picture it. Her eyes, the little bastards, had minds of their own, and kept stealing glances at Kim's thighs, tummy, and hips for signs of their former girth. Judging by her scowl, Kim could read their nosy little thoughts, too. "You never mentioned any of this," said Karma.

"I lost the weight before we moved here," said Kim. "I worked my ass off to fit in with all the skinny women in this neighborhood, and you all acted like I was one of you, and not some fat freak. That's never happened to me before." She slumped down in her chair. "It felt good."

236

Karma shook her head, not sure whether to laugh or cry. "You're nuts. You're out of your mind."

"I knew you wouldn't understand," said Kim. "I'm a troll. Everybody in my family is six feet tall and blond and thin. I'm the fat little Asian midget."

"I think you're supposed to say *Little Person* now," said Karma. She was hoping to get a smile out of Kim, whose face was a dark mask of aching, unhealed wounds. *How can you know somebody so well, and yet not know them at all? Kim, who's always so sure of herself, so in charge of everything and everybody, is more insecure than me. I didn't think anybody on the planet was more insecure than me.* "So let me make sure I understand," she said. "You're embarrassed about being Asian, you think you're fat, and you never noticed that you're very pretty and that I have ten times more weight to lose than you do? You're a whole *Dr. Phil* show all by yourself, you know. No, you're an entire week."

Kim didn't appear to appreciate Karma's attempt to lighten the mood. If anything, she seemed angrier. "Thin pretty women have thin pretty friends," she said, "or haven't you noticed? If they do have a fat friend, it's so everybody will see them together and think the thin, pretty one is thin and pretty. You and Jeanette and Bianca and especially Sue Ellen, would you have given me a second thought if I were seventy-three and a half pounds heavier? If you and I went shopping together and you wanted to go to The Gap, and I had to go to Lane Bryant, do you think we'd actually *go* shopping together? Do you have any fat friends right now? No, you don't, except for me."

Karma threw up her hands. "Holy crap, Kim, I'm the fat friend, not you. But now my whole life makes sense. All my really good friends *are* thin and pretty." She smacked herself on the head in mock revelation. "Oh, wait, my *best* friend has a fat *head*. Does that count? I am the fat friend, not you, you idiot. If you think you look fat, I must look like the Goodyear blimp to you."

Kim shook her head emphatically. "You look great—I'm the one who's getting fat. Oh, and by the way, ab out all that other bullshit? I tip better than you do, you forgot about the baby monitor, too, and I didn't pay back that ten bucks because I picked up Lunchables for Sam a week later when they were on sale, and *you* never paid *me* back. So I don't owe you ten bucks, you owe me $4.50. Plus tax."

Karma stared up at the ceiling, trying to remember what she was... "Oh, shit. I forgot about that. Sorry. Anyway, you're still nuts, thinking you look fat, but since you think I look great, I guess it's okay." She reached over and gave Kim's shoulder a squeeze. "Can you stop taking those pills? Will you swear to me that you're not going to take any more? They're really messing you up. You've been really bitchy, especially to Jeanette."

Kim sighed. "Jeanette's a dolt." She shook her head, angry with herself for the outburst. "Sorry. It's just a habit. I'll stop ragging on Jeanette. I've just been scared about gaining the weight back."

"I can top that," said Karma. "I'm scared about going to prison and being somebody's bitch."

"I know. It's my fault. I'm sorry."

"Worst case," sighed Karma, "we'll do laps in our cells for the next twenty years or so, and we'll both get skinny." She sat down at the kitchen table again and picked at a spot of dried peanut butter. "Jack Lawrence is dead. How the hell did this happen?"

"What exactly *did* happen?" asked Kim. "Give me the details."

Karma recounted the story as best she could. When she got to the part about the unstrapped bike helmet, Kim's face lit up.

"That's it!" she said, jumping up from the table. "It really wasn't your fault. Why didn't you tell me that part right away? This is all gonna be okay, don't you see? He should have been wearing his helmet properly. It's his own fault that he died, not yours." She looked so happy and relieved that Karma could hardly bring herself to burst her bubble. But she did.

"Think about it," said Karma. "If it was Dave lying there dead, and you knew somebody had jumped out from behind a rock and scared him into falling off his bike, would you want to hear that it was his fault for not strapping on his helmet? Do you think the cops would just forget about the whole thing, forget about the masks and the planning it took to be there at just the right time, and leaving the scene of the crime? Do you really think the strap on his helmet is going to change everything?"

Kim closed her eyes. You could almost hear her mood deflate. "You're right," she said. "You're screwed. I mean we're screwed. We're screwed. We. We are screwed."

Kim's cell phone rang and she looked at it, but then set the phone down without answering. "It's Dave. I'm not in the mood to chat right now."

"What if he knows something," said Karma. "Don't forget, there's a dead body out there, and somebody's probably found it by now. What if the cops called him?"

As president of the Bedford Commons Homeowners Association, Dave maintained a good relationship with the local police, and though it wasn't strictly by the book, the police often called him when there was a problem that concerned the neighborhood. Reluctantly, Kim answered the fourth ring. "Oh my God," Kim said into the phone, eyes blazing into Karma's. "How did *that* happen? (pause) Oh no, oh, my God. Really. That's strange. (pause) Well, that's good. (pause) How awful. (pause) Of course we'll help. I'll call everybody. (pause) See you tonight. Love you." Kim ended the call.

Another bike rider had found Jack's body and called the cops. They'd identified him from the driver's license in Jack's wrist pouch, and from the recent visits they'd made to his house. The cop who tipped off Dave was pretty sure it was just a terrible accident, but there was something suspicious about it, so they were starting an investigation.

They found the turkey lacing pin. They're starting an investigation. Icy fingers squeezed Karma's heart. *An investigation.* Only Kim's firm grip on her arm kept Karma anchored to her kitchen chair.

"We are not going to panic," said Kim. "What could they have found? Please tell me you didn't leave a mask behind."

Karma took a deep breath. She'd left out that part of the story. "No, it's not a mask. I can't find the turkey lacing pin I used to puncture Jeff's tire. I must have dropped it, maybe when I was bending over Jack."

"Oh, shit," said Kim. "Well, that's not good, but it could be worse. I don't suppose they can get a good fingerprint off a skinny little thing like that."

"That's what Jeanette said," said Karma.

They sat silently for a minute or so. Karma turned toward the patio door and watched Molly and Lindsey climbing on the wooden swing set. How would Karma explain all this to Molly? *How will I tell her I'm going to jail, and that everybody is going to be talking about the horrible thing I did? And how will I explain to Little Peanut why he was born in the slammer?*

"Was it very gross?" asked Kim.

"Huh?"

"Jack," said Kim. "What was it like, you know, seeing somebody die?"

Karma slumped in her chair. God, she wanted a cup of coffee. "It was like a horrible movie," she said. "There was a smell like copper, and blood and brains coming out of his head. I can still smell that smell. And I keep seeing it in my head."

"How did Jeanette handle it? Hysterics, I suppose." Kim had that caustic look she always got when discussing Jeanette.

"Actually, she was great," said Karma. "Way better than me. She kept me calm, she stopped me from throwing up and leaving DNA all over the place, and she brushed away all our footprints with a branch. She was like an old pro." Karma was as proud as if she were discussing some new accomplishment of Molly's. And she was sick of Kim's unrelenting mockery.

Kim still looked like she was smelling curdled milk. "I'd never count on Jeanette in a crisis."

"Well, you're just wrong. She was fantastic," said Karma. "You'd think she killed people every day."

CHAPTER 27:   THE LUANN WATCH

The death of a notorious neighbor under unusual circumstances shook Bedford Commons to its very core. As news of Jack's demise spread, the neighborhood playground took on the aura of a newspaper city desk. Neighbors came and went, sharing various bits of information, calling in tips, and verifying sources. Gina Damico, who lived on the other side of the swimming pool, knew Jack's insurance agent's hairdresser, who reported that the cops had inquired about the beneficiaries of his life insurance policy. Stay-at-home-dad Mark bowled with a guy whose cubicle was just a few rows down from Jack's, and he heard that one of the women in Jack's department had suddenly asked for personal time off. Two moms whose kids attended the same daycare as the youngest Lawrence child reported that the poor little boy started crying when his mother tried to leave him there a few days after his father's death. The director suggested that Luann keep him home for a while, and agreed not to charge her for the days he missed, in spite of her contractual obligation.

But Jack's death inspired little actual sorrow in the neighborhood. Joan Handley was trying to feel bad, but she couldn't muster up any genuine emotion, except for guilty relief. The Baileys, who lived next door to the Lawrences, didn't really know Jack, but hadn't appreciated having their baby awakened by his fireworks night after night. They felt sad for his wife and kids, of course, but...

In fact, Jack's death devastated only one neighbor: Jeff Jorganson. According to Jeanette, he came home early on the day

242

of the accident, unable to focus on computer network administration or anything else. He had liked the guy, in spite of his wife's objections. Jack had a great sense of humor and even though he wasn't in the best shape, he liked being outside and active. Worst of all, Jeff felt responsible for letting Jack ride alone, even though he himself had been riding alone for months. Maybe if he'd been there, Jack wouldn't have fallen. Maybe he'd still be alive.

Jeff stayed home from work for the next two days and sat around in the family room in his pajama pants and tee shirt, unshaven and unshowered, ignoring his kids and barely moving as Jeanette cleaned around him.

"You couldn't know what would happen," she said for the fifth time. She pulled up the flowery couch cushion next to the one his butt was still parked on, and scooped up toys, coins, cracker crumbs, and candies. "He should have had his helmet strapped on."

Jeff picked up a stray M&M, lifted it toward his mouth, but then thought better of it and added it to Jeanette's trash pile. "His helmet? I didn't hear about a helmet."

Jeanette fought to keep the horror off her face. *Mama was right about me. I'm stupid. STUPID.* "Well, that's what I assume," she said, "because he hit his head and died." *THINK. THINK.* She replaced the cushion and moved to the other side of the room, so Jeff wouldn't see the fear on her face. "I figured he had it on when he got to our house because you would have told him to put it on if he wasn't wearing it because you're always telling our kids to put on their helmets, but probably he didn't actually strap it on, so it fell off. I mean, if he hit his head on a rock and died, it must have fallen off, and how could it fall off if it was strapped on?"

Jeff stared at Jeanette for a long moment, trying to follow what she'd just said. Nobody's mind worked quite like his wife's. "Yeah, I guess so. I didn't think it all the way through like that."

"Well, that's the difference between you and me," said Jeanette. "I think of these things."

The next day, Bianca and Sue Ellen showed up at Karma's door together, holding a pan of lasagna and a meatloaf, respectively. "For me?" asked Karma.

"For Luann Lawrence," said Bianca. "We were walking over to deliver these, and thought we'd drop in. You've been hard to reach lately." Her mouth was a tight Revlon Chinaberry smudge across her pale skin. She wasn't smiling.

Sue Ellen always smiled; she couldn't seem to help it. "Mind if we come in?"

Karma would have preferred the Spanish Inquisition, but, of course, she couldn't say so. Standing in the doorway, she tried to think of a reason to keep them out. *Swine flu? Cholera? Black Plague?* She stepped aside and let them into the foyer.

"So let's cut the bull crap," said Bianca. "Did you guys kill Jack Lawrence?"

"What?" Karma shut the door quickly and moved into the kitchen. But Bianca was right behind her. She set her lasagna on top of a stack of papers on the table, and stared at Karma with the don't-bother-lying-to-me look she usually saved for her husband and kids. Sue Ellen had finally stopped smiling. Her pinched expression suggested she'd rather be watching her house burn down than be in Karma's kitchen.

"You and Kim and Jeanette," repeated Bianca, "did you have something to do with it?"

"How can you ask me that?" Karma pulled the school papers and bills out from under the lasagna pan and started neatening up her messy kitchen table.

"Nice try," said Bianca. "Let's just get this over with. I want the truth. All of it."

"Me, too," said Sue Ellen.

Okay, here's the entire truth," said Karma. "Jack was our monthly human sacrifice, we keep the meth lab in the guest room, and the pot's growing in the basement. You want decaf?"

Bianca shook a shiny red fingernail at Karma. "You see me laughin'? We want to know what happened to Jack Lawrence. If you know something, you'd better spill your guts right now."

"Let's sit down," sighed Karma, heading for the family room, "but don't trip over the cable guy. I killed him this morning for not giving me free HBO."

Kim launched the Luann Watch a few days after Jack's death. Masquerading as the fulfillment of her promise to Dave to help the Lawrence family cope with their tragedy, the Luann Watch wasn't even slightly altruistic. Kim said that the best way to keep an eye on the police investigation was to stick as close to Luann as possible. Jeanette took the first shift, since she was the only one who knew Luann well enough to make the offer, and at Kim's urging, brought Karma with her in order to smooth her way into the Widow Lawrence's inner circle.

It wasn't much of a circle. Luann seemed to have few friends and no family in town, and only one of her brothers flew in for the funeral. Either they weren't people who drop everything and run to the scene of family tragedy, or they considered Jack's death something other than a tragedy. Jeanette started by organizing meals to be brought in, and she and Karma showed up on Luann's doorstep the first afternoon with a chicken noodle casserole, a crock-pot of chili, and a bucket full of sympathy and understanding.

Karma marveled at Jeanette's calm efficiency, and wished it were contagious. Death was one of those things Karma had managed to avoid for most of her life. Then again, so was murder. Standing at the Lawrence's front door with Jeanette, waiting for someone to answer the doorbell, Karma prayed that nobody would be home. No such luck, of course.

Luann answered the door herself and welcomed them inside with their offerings. She was solemn and dry-eyed, dressed in jeans and a sweater, no make-up. Her hair looked clean, but not fussed-over. The Lawrence children were sitting quietly in the family room, watching a movie.

Even under these difficult circumstances, Luann was a tidier housekeeper than Karma, but then, so was everybody. Karma carried the casserole into the kitchen. She didn't know if they'd eat it that night, so she decided to find room in the refrigerator for it.

It was not a problem; Luann's refrigerator was as neat and tidy as the rest of the house. The few leftovers were labeled and dated, in matching glass containers for easy visibility. The glass shelves were spotless, nothing spilled, no sticky residue. It was unnatural.

What was it like to be Luann right now, facing life without a husband, nasty as he'd been, and the prospect of raising three kids alone? When Molly was an infant, Sam had worked for a consulting firm which required lots of travel. There had been bad nights when he was out of town and Karma's morbid imagination had pictured him in a car accident, dead by the side of the road. Or in a hotel bathroom, dead from a heart attack. Alone in bed on those nights, she'd listen to herself breathe and contemplate her options. Move in with Charlotte? *No way in hell.* Rent an efficiency and work in the cafeteria at Molly's school? *Better.*

Eventually the phone would ring and it would be Sam, alive and completely unaware that his wife had, once again, planned her widowhood. Luann Lawrence had to have mixed feelings, losing the husband she'd been arrested for punching just weeks before. *How bad did she really feel? Do you forget all that anger and resentment when your husband is suddenly dead? Do you regret the fights and only remember the good times? Were there good times?*

Karma's heart nearly stopped when she saw the young black man seated at Luann's dining room table. Though he was wearing street clothes, his military haircut, stick-straight posture, and tiny spiral notebook tagged him as a cop. She realized she'd seen his unmarked tan car parked on the street. She was slipping; back in college, Karma could spot an unmarked police car from a hundred yards while going sixty in the opposite direction.

"Hello, ma'am…ma'am," said the cop, nodding politely to Karma and Jeanette.

"These are my neighbors," said Luann. "This is Detective Hunter. Jeanette's husband was the one who was supposed to go bike riding with Jack."

Jeanette's face flushed. "Jeff feels terrible about what happened. He's very upset about it. *Very upset.*"

Luann's voice was flat. "It wasn't his fault."

"Why didn't your husband go riding with Mr. Lawrence?" asked the detective, looking up from his notebook.

"His bike tire was flat," said Jeanette. "He didn't have time to fix it, so he told Jack to go on without him. He can't forgive himself for giving Jack directions; he can't even go to work."

"Hmm," said Detective Hunter. He wrote in his steno book, in silence, for a few moments. "Mrs. Lawrence," he said, "I'd like to ask you a few more questions about your husband. Maybe we could speak privately?" He looked pointedly at Jeanette and Karma.

Karma took a reflexive step back, but Jeanette didn't move. She didn't seem to have understood the hint, and looked at the detective with the bland innocence of an imbecile.

247

"I don't mind if they stay," said Luann.

Having no choice, Detective Hunter plunged on. "Well, ma'am," he said, "several times in the past year you reported your husband for domestic violence, including just a few weeks ago, is that right?"

"Yes, I did," said Luann. "We had problems. My husband drank too much and sometimes he'd get angry. He hit me several times over the years. It was difficult."

Karma tried to keep her face from revealing her astonishment. She and Kim and Jeanette had spent hours trying to figure out how to get Luann to open up about her problems, and now she was just blurting it out to a cop?

"We were working on our marriage," Luann continued. "I know he loved me. We were planning a marriage retreat."

Karma's stomach did a back flip. *They'd been trying to work on the marriage? A retreat?* This was exactly what she and the others had been hoping for when this whole mess started a lifetime ago. They had cooked up the whole stupid scheme, Powerpuff Girl masks and all, to motivate Jack to work things out with his wife. And now, to find out they had already been trying? Thanks to her meddling, Jack and Luann would never have a chance to solve their problems. Karma felt sick.

She was shaken from her guilty thoughts by a turn in the conversation. Detective Hunter was talking to Jeanette. "Ma'am," he asked, apparently for at least the second time, "would this be a good time?"

"For what?"

The detective now spoke slowly and enunciated very clearly, as though he suspected English might not be Jeanette's first language. "Since your husband is home, ma'am, would this be a good time to talk to him about the accident? H was supposed to ride with the victim, so I need to speak to him."

"Oh, sure," said Jeanette. "I'll come with you."

"That's not necessary," said Hunter. "I'd prefer it if you'd just give me your address."

"But I—," began Jeanette.

"Would you mind staying here, Jeanette?" asked Luann. "I want to lie down for a while, and maybe you could keep an eye on the kids?" She turned to Karma. "No offense, but they don't really know you. You're welcome to stay, of course."

Karma, born and raised on Hoosier basketball, knew double teaming when she saw it. Jeanette had just been boxed out of supervising the interview with Jeff, and had no choice but to give Hunter her address. *What would the cop ask Jeff? Did he suspect anything? What would Jeff say?*

Detective Hunter excused himself, and Luann went up to her bedroom, taking her youngest child with her to see if he would nap. Karma stood with Jeanette at the living room window and watched the detective pull away from the curb, do a sharp U-turn, and head toward Jeanette's house. There was nothing they could do about it.

Karma and Jeanette filled the dishwasher and began tidying up the kitchen and dining room. There wasn't much to clean up, but they needed to do *something*. Karma wanted to talk to Jeanette about the cop, about Jeff, about what they would do if Jeff said something suspicious to the cop, but the older Lawrence kids were in the next room. Then, barely making a sound, Jeanette covered her face with a dish towel and slid down the side of the kitchen island. Karma thought she was fainting, but then realized she was crying. Jeanette's shoulders shook with silent, violent sobs; the effort to stay quiet and not scare Luann's children was making her entire body convulse. Karma knelt down beside her and patted her back, feeling more than a little scared. Jeanette had been so strong lately, so cunning, so... Kim-ish. What if one of the kids walked in on this? Jeanette finally calmed down to a hiccupping sniffle, pulled the towel away, and looked up at Karma. "What have we done? What have we done?"

"Quiet," ordered Karma, her eye on the door. "It was an accident. We didn't do anything."

"Yes, we did," whispered Jeanette. We have to tell Luann. We have to."

Karma grabbed Jeanette's arm and shook it. She wanted to smack her silly face off. Had Jeanette completely lost her mind?

"What about *your* kids?" Karma hissed, "and mine? What's the point of going to jail? It won't bring back Jack, but our kids will grow up without *us*."

Jeanette stopped sniffing and pulled her arm out of Karma's grip. "Maybe we won't go to jail," she whined. "It was an accident."

"Exactly," said Karma. "So why tell anybody?"

Jeanette froze, struggling with the logic of the argument. She opened her mouth to speak, then closed it again. In fact, she opened and closed her mouth several times. Thoughts flew in, but seemed to die before they could quite reach her brain.

Still on her knees, hiding from view behind the kitchen island, Karma put her hands firmly on Jeanette's shoulders and looked into her teary, mascara-smudged cow eyes.

"Don't you get it?" said Karma. "We have to get away with this, not because we did something wrong, but because admitting it would be wronger. More wrong. We have to protect our families by doing the right thing, which seems like the wrong thing, but it's *not*. We have to keep our mouths shut and not admit to anything because that's the right thing to do for our families. They come first. The only reason we could possibly have for turning ourselves in would be to stop ourselves from killing anybody else, and we're certainly never going to do that, so there's absolutely no reason to turn ourselves in. Do you get that?"

It was amazing. Karma was aware that she was trying to convince herself as much as Jeanette, but the more she talked, the more sense she was making, at least her in personal opinion. Honestly, she found herself rather convincing, but now she had to stop talking and let Jeanette process the argument. She'd learned in radio sales that you can lose a sale by not shutting up in time. Talk them into the deal and talk them out again, and you lose. An amateur's mistake. And if that didn't work, she was still prepared to smack Jeanette.

Jeanette frowned and tried to think. How could there be justification for what they were doing, and what they had already done? Yet Karma's reasoning began to make sense to her, too. It was like being lost in a dark cave and suddenly seeing a chink of light that showed the way out. Could there be a way out of this that didn't involve going to prison? Or hell? Jeanette felt a sudden rush of understanding, hope, and joy; everything was going to be okay.

She felt like Jennifer Jones in *The Song of Bernadette*. They showed that movie on TV every Christmas when she was a girl, and it had been her favorite in junior high school, during her I-want-to-become-a-Catholic-nun phase. That stage in her life had been particularly hard on Jeanette's Southern Baptist parents.

"I get it," she said as tears gleamed in her moist brown eyes. "I get it."

CHAPTER 28:   BOYS' NIGHT OUT

"I don't get it," said Kim. It was the fourth time she'd said it, but Karma didn't criticize. She was lounging in a kitchen chair, legs crossed, sipping her decaf, and watching her kitchen being cleaned as it had never been cleaned before. Kim had already swept the floor, wiped down the baseboards, dusted the overhead light, and climbed on a stool to pull down a few cobwebs from the corners of the ceiling. Then she'd organized Karma's eating utensils and cooking tools, and sorted the mess on the kitchen island. Unpaid bills were now in one pile, credit card offers in another, and coupons sorted by expiration date in a third.

There was a time when Karma might have objected to this intrusion into her privacy, but what the hell. She thought briefly of moving the conversation to the messy family room, but instead, she grabbed Kim's sleeve as she passed and tugged her down into a kitchen chair. "Is there anything you want to tell me? Anything about little pills? Or possibly cocaine?"

"What? No," said Kim. She looked confused, but then she held up her hands in a gesture of surrender, and took several deep breaths. "Sorry," she said. "No. Really. No. It's because I'm *not* taking the pills. I'm either too sleepy to get out of bed or too hyper to sleep. I've been through it before; it'll pass. I'm done with pills, for sure."

It was a partial truth. Kim *had* been through this before, but that morning she had found a prescription she'd been given for jittery nerves. They were a couple of years past expiration, so she'd allowed herself only two—also because she had so few—

but they wasn't working as well as she had hoped. Her eyes were drawn to crumbs on the kitchen table. They screamed for her attention, but they were Karma's crumbs on Karma's table, and Kim knew she should ignore them. She focused her attention back on Karma and the conversation they'd been having. "I'm fine. But still, I just don't get it; they've never done this before, so why do they want to do it now? And why tonight?"

"We do it all the time," said Karma, "so we couldn't say no. It wouldn't be fair."

"Life isn't fair," said Kim. "And anyway, who ever heard of *Boys* Night Out? It's stupid."

"Sam says they just want their turn."

"I don't like the timing. It's too suspicious," said Kim. "Right after Jeff talked to that damned detective and we don't even know what he said? We don't even know what's going on with the investigation."

Karma waved her hand in front of her face, trying to shoo away that terrible word. *Investigation*. "We're talking about *the guys*," she said. "They'll play poker, drink beer, and eat pizza. What do you think, they're getting together to talk about what we've been doing? No way. If they knew anything important, we'd know about it."

Kim was up again, re-organizing the dirty dishes in Karma's dishwasher. Karma had to admit that she did an impressive job. She'd found room for everything Karma had left in the sink, and there was barely a square inch of wasted space, yet it wasn't overcrowded. She was tempted to take a picture.

"You're right," said Kim. "We've never gone wrong underestimating our husbands. Why stop now?" Kim filled the soap dispenser and shook the nearly empty box of detergent. "You're almost out of this. Want me to make a shopping list?"

Karma looked around; her kitchen hadn't been this tidy since the last time her mother visited and cleaned it. "That's okay," she said, "Let's go sit in the family room."

As Karma had pointed out, the women had no grounds to fuss about Boys' Night Out—at least none they could talk about—and tonight was the night. Despite her assertion that there was nothing to worry about, Karma found waiting for Sam to come home nerve-wracking. It was partly that she was also worried about what they would talk about, but also, it was a weird reversal of roles, since she was typically the one running off to the jewelry party or the stamping demonstration or out with the girls celebrating somebody's birthday or half-birthday or whatever else they could come up with. Sam occasionally worked late, but as Molly had observed crossly, he almost never missed her bedtime routine. "Bath is a daddy job, not a mommy job," she groused as Karma dried her off. Karma heartily agreed.

The worst part of the evening came after Molly finally fell asleep. Karma sat alone in her unusually tidy family room. She turned off the television and sat quietly, feeling her belly for kicks (there were none, but it was too soon) and trying to enjoy the stick-straight vacuum trails Kim had left in the carpeting and the unobstructed expanse of the glass-covered coffee table. Her mind kept wandering into uncomfortable territory. *What's Luann doing right now? Will she have to give up her house? Are her kids crying for their dad? What does it feel like to lose someone like Jack? What if I lost Sam? What if he finds out what I've done and leaves me? What if I go to jail and he divorces me?*

Of course, this was silly. There was no comparison between her life and Luann's, especially in the selection of husbands. Sam was a great guy. Not a perfect guy, but a great guy and a great father. He wasn't the kind of guy who aimed firecrackers at pregnant women or hit his wife. He hardly even yelled at Karma, even when he was mad. Of course, up to know, he hadn't had that much to be mad about, as she had never killed anybody before. He might howl a bit if he found out that his wife had jumped out from behind a rock and scared one of the neighbors to death. What if that turkey lacing pin *did* have her fingerprints all over it and the police *did* tie her to Jack's death? What if she went to prison and Sam left her for some little tramp who kept the house clean and didn't screw with other people's lives?

The sound of the key in the lock woke Karma from the nap she wasn't aware she'd been taking. She sat up, yawning and stretching, and started to greet her husband, but Sam tossed his keys on the counter and his jacket on the couch and went straight to the kitchen without even acknowledging her. Maybe he didn't realize she was awake.

"Did you have a good time?" she asked.

"Yeah."

"Win anything?"

"No."

"Lose much?"

"No." He stood in the doorway, still not looking at her, then went to fill a large water glass.

"Too many salty chips?" she teased, "or avoiding a hangover?" When she and Sam were still young and childless, and had the freedom to go out with friends and drink too much, he had taught her the secret to avoiding headaches: one large glass of water for each drink, and two Tylenols before going to bed. It was something they still teased each other about, long after parenthood had largely ended their partying ways. But tonight, he was clearly not in a mood for teasing.

"I'm thirsty," he said. "Do you have a problem with that?" Karma's spider senses were definitely tingling now, but she was determined to keep the conversation friendly. He wasn't going to be able to blame her for the fight he seemed determined to start. She would be the innocent, injured party, friendly to a fault.

"So you had a good time. That's great. What else did you do besides play poker?"

"Nothing. I'm tired." Sam turned and left the room without waiting for Karma to join him. Did he even want her to sleep in the same room? She was stung and scared. Sam didn't act like this, he just didn't. The words of Miss Clavel from Molly's favorite bedtime book, rang in Karma's head:

Something is not right.

The trouble didn't end with poker and pizza. The next evening, as dusk settled over Bedford Commons and families gathered on the playground to wear out their kids before bedtime, playgroup husbands Jeff, Sam, Dave, Don, and Tony were still bonding in some weird and unnatural way. They were standing close together and talking in quiet voices, deliberately out of earshot of their wives.

Their wives were standing close together, deliberately out of earshot of everybody, trying to decide if this behavior was just odd, or actually suspicious. Sure, the men were lined up behind their children at the swing set, making a good show of pushing the kids on the swings, but the women wasn't fooled by this display of normalcy. Karma, Jeanette, Kim, Sue Ellen, and Bianca stayed at the other end of the playground, pretending not to watch. "What the hell are they talking about?"

"Probably what everybody else in the neighborhood is talking about," said Kim. "Jack Lawrence. Sam's looking. *Smile.*"

Karma smiled and waved at Sam, but he barely nodded in return. "I don't like this. Jeanette, did Jeff tell you what that detective asked him?"

Jeanette shrugged. "He wanted to know when they decided to ride together, why Jeff didn't go with him, and whether Jack was wearing his helmet when he got to our house."

"Did Jeff say anything about you and me?" asked Karma. "Did he tell him we went running?"

Jeanette hesitated, sucking in her lower lip and looking troubled. "I don't know. I didn't ask him."

"What about the turkey skewer?" asked Kim. "Did the cop say anything to Jeff about finding it?"

Jeanette faltered again. "I don't know," she said. "I didn't ask him." At Kim's disgusted sneer, she said, "I couldn't ask *that*. I'm not supposed to know about it. If I ask about the turkey skewer and nobody knows there even *was* a turkey skewer, that's practically confessing."

Jeanette was right, of course, but the scowl remained firmly on Kim's face. She was still convinced that Jeanette would be their eventual undoing. Karma had to admit she was getting worried, too. These days, Jeanette seemed to alternate between hysteria and denial. She was also having way too much contact with Luann, too often without Karma. Worst of all, she hadn't found out anything useful about Jeff's conversation with Detective Hunter. James Bond had turned back into Barney Fife.

Kim nudged Karma in the ribs. "Here comes Sam."

Karma plastered a *we-weren't-just-talking-about-you* smile on her face as he approached. But there was something about the way he was looking at her that filled Karma with fear. *What is he coming over here to say in front of everybody?*

"Since Jeff had the guys over for poker," said Sam. "I thought maybe we could do something and invite everybody."

Karma almost laughed with relief. *Was that all he wanted? What a relief.* "Yeah, that would be great," she said. "We could do burgers on the grill or maybe steaks."

Sam's face was impassive. He reminded her of Luann. "I was thinking more about something different," he said. "How about if we roast a turkey?"

CHAPTER 29:   JUST BECAUSE YOU'RE PARANOID DOESN'T MEAN THEY'RE NOT OUT TO GET YOU

Karma was stuck in a waking nightmare, trapped in an impossible situation with no way out. Things spiraled down and down, but as much as she wanted to, she couldn't end it by waking up screaming. Unfortunately, she was already awake. This was what *normal* would be like if *normal* had been invented by Alfred Hitchcock. She tiptoed on hot coals around her husband, waiting for the explosion, but it didn't come. She acted normal, Sam acted normal, and Molly *was* normal, yet *nothing* was normal. There was an eight-hundred-pound gorilla in the room, but Karma stepped carefully around it all week, just in case Sam was just being paranoid, and Sam hadn't noticed it.

It was *Attack of the Pod People* without the pods. Sam looked like himself—so did all the guys—but they were *different*. Maybe there was nothing wrong, and Sam really did want her to cook a damn turkey for their friends. That was possible, wasn't it? Sure. Just ask the Easter Bunny.

Karma had to keep her cell phone in her pocket at all times, and silenced, so Sam wouldn't see it or hear it, and wouldn't be able to read the text messages bouncing back and forth.

> **KARMA:** They know!!
> **KIM:** Y no Qs?
> **KARMA:** They already know As. We R screwed!!
> **KIM:** Stay calm
> **KARMA:** Can't!!!

259

KIM: Don't act guilty.
KARMA: I feel guilty.
KIM: Get over it.
JEANETTE: *Can I borrow cup brown sugar?*

The stew thickened the following week. Gina Damico went back to her hairdresser to have her roots done, and reported back that the cops were now asking so many questions about the circumstances of Jack's death that the insurance company was refusing to pay Luann. Nobody was sure how much insurance Jack carried on himself, but wild guesses by the completely uninformed ranged from $250,000 to $2,000,000, which, according to Gina's hairdresser, might pay double if he died by accident. Nobody knew and nobody had the nerve to ask Luann, but everybody had an opinion. More than one wagging tongue wondered if Luann herself had something to do with his accident, while others wondered wistfully what it would be like to lose a jerk like Jack and then get a big fat check from the insurance company as a bonus.

Of course, the irony was that there might not be a big fat check at all if the ambitious detective didn't curb his enthusiasm and close the case on Jack's accident. He had come back twice to ask Luann more questions about her rocky relationship with her late husband.

Poor Luann was suffering, according to Jeanette. "She's lost her husband, and now she has to worry about how she's gonna support her kids. Jack's company is going to send his last paycheck soon, but then that's it; she and the kids will have to live off her income and she's so distracted at work she's afraid she's gonna get fired." Jeanette shooed a fly away from her iced tea. "I wish there was something we could do."

This conversation took place on Jeanette's back patio. She and Jeff had paid extra to have it enclosed and screened, and it was perfect on a cool morning like this. Karma was still kicking herself for letting Sam talk her into saving money by settling for the plain concrete slab, which he'd promised to turn into an even better sunroom than the builder would have provided, but which was still not built. Between the first mortgage on the house, the second mortgage to pay off credit cards, and Molly's preschool (including late fees), they had no money for a fancy patio. This had left Karma suffering from Patio Envy, and Sam suffering from Sullen Wife.

Of course these days, that was the least of their problems. Karma stirred more sugar into her tea and looked out onto Jeanette's backyard. Little Jeffrey was next door, jumping on the neighbor's trampoline and screaming like a maniac. On each upward flight, his head and upper torso would be visible for a few moments as he cleared the fence, which Karma suspected the neighbors had put up in a desperate and futile effort to keep him off their trampoline. On each downward plunge he would shriek again, as though his life were ending.

"He certainly has a lot of energy," said Karma.

"Yeah, he does," Jeanette said fondly. "And he just loves that trampoline, but he's only allowed over there when they're not home."

Karma looked at her. "Don't you mean he's only allowed when they *are* home?"

"No. I thought it was kind of strange, too," said Jeanette. "Hey, I was looking at the calendar this morning—is this the end of your first trimester? Are you excited?"

"One more week," said Karma.

"You gonna find out if it's a boy or a girl? Hey, we could have a reveal party with pink and blue balloons."

Karma didn't answer. She'd never made it this far with a pregnancy since Molly was born. She'd had a couple of painful twinges of pain, and she was spotting, though not every day and not very much. Dr. Weimer wasn't happy that her hormone levels were rising so slowly, but he wasn't freaking out either.

"I don't give up on pregnancies, Karma," he had said on the phone. "I've seen too many happy outcomes, even when things don't seem to be going quite right. But make sure you're getting lots of rest and keeping your stress level down."

Now you tell me, thought Karma. She didn't want to talk about this. "Did Jeff ever say what the guys talked about on Friday night? I couldn't get anything out of Sam. Do you think they know anything?"

"I don't think so," said Jeanette. "If Jeff thought I did something wrong, he'd be asking me about it, and he's not." She slipped off her sandals and appraised the condition of her pink toenails. "Hang on," she said, standing up. "I'm gonna touch up my toes while we're sittin' here." She walked back into her house and returned with a bottle of Precious Pink and an ingenious foam device which held her toes apart. "I was thinking of talking to Dave," said Jeanette. "Do you think we could do some kind of benefit for Luann and the kids?" she asked. "Maybe a neighborhood fundraiser or something?"

"I suppose." Karma took another sip of iced tea. "The only thing is, hardly anybody around here knows her. She never comes out to the playground, and she's almost never at the pool. Most people are going to say, 'Luann who?'"

Jeanette shook her head sadly. "That's terrible. She's a widow with three kids."

"I'm not saying we shouldn't help her," said Karma. "It's just gonna be a little harder. I mean let's face it, people knew Jack, not her, and they didn't like him."

Jeanette dabbed polish on her big toenail. "I suppose you're right. I just hope the insurance company quits draggin' their feet. I told Luann to call that cute anchor guy on Channel Six and see if he can do anything. She needs that money."

It took a moment for these words to sink into Karma's brain, where they exploded, tiny lawnmowers of impending doom. "What? What did you say?"

"Hey," said Jeanette. "You bumped my arm." She grabbed a tissue to wipe Precious Pink off her knee. "I told her to find that 'Call 6 for Help' guy on TV. He's good at helping people fight big companies. And I thought maybe they'd put her on TV and people would send her money and stuff. I saw this one lady who... got... a... big..." Jeanette trailed off, having noticed that Karma's eyes were bugging out and her mouth was open in a silent scream. "Was that not a good idea?" she asked in a timid voice.

"It depends," said Karma. The menacing calm in her voice belied the deep red color of her face and the bulging vein in her forehead. "Do you think it's a good idea to have reporters looking into Jack's death? Do you think that will help us get away with this or make it harder?"

"Oh," said Jeanette. "I didn't think of it like that." She sucked in her lower lip and made grimacing faces down at her shiny wet toenails.

Karma tried to calm herself and see things from Jeanette's point of view; she was only trying to help Luann and her kids. But the roaring in her head and Little Jeffrey's screaming made it hard to think about anything other than throttling Jeanette with her bare hands and leaving her dead body on the screened-in porch. *Gotta calm down. Jeanette didn't mean to get us thrown in jail.*

Karma massaged her temples. "I'll bet Luann won't make the call," she said. "She's pretty quiet, right? She won't like the idea of going public with her personal problems."

Jeanette said nothing, but squirmed in her wicker chair and stared down at her pink toenails.

Karma sighed. "There's more, isn't there?"

263

Jeanette still wasn't meeting Karma's eyes. "A little more. It turns out you don't actually have to call them. They have a website. You can type your problem right on the computer."

"And you helped her, didn't you?"

"I might have helped a little," murmured Jeanette. "Just with the typing part. And the sending part."

Karma sat back and watched Little Jeffrey's head popping up and down behind the neighbor's fence. The squeak of the trampoline springs as he landed, alternated with his shrieks as he rose, were hypnotic. Squeak, shriek, squeak, shriek. Horrible, yet hypnotic.

"I suppose it could be worse," said Karma. "You could have rented a big neon sign that says PLEASE INVESTIGATE MY HUSBAND'S SUSPICIOUS DEATH, and put it up on Luann's front yard. Maybe you can order a sign like that. Maybe see if Groupon has a deal with a sign company."

Jeanette stuck out a pouty lower lip. "Now you're making fun of me," she said. "Why does everybody do that?"

"I'm not making fun of you," said Karma. "I'm trying to come up with a good reason not to strangle you."

As she walked home with Molly, Karma considered whether or not to call Kim and tell her this latest news. It would certainly confirm Kim's low opinion of Jeanette, whom she already called *Our Village Idiot*. But maybe it wasn't necessary. After all, what was the likelihood that the TV station would jump on this particular request? Surely dozens of emails and hard-luck stories were sent in every week. *There is no way they can handle all of them, right? How do they choose which requests to deal with, and which to ignore?*

Karma had worked with TV people in her past life in radio, but mostly with the advertising types, not the news types. However, it didn't take a genius to understand TV journalists;

they'd pick the problems with the most visual appeal, like the slim attractive widow with three solemn, good-looking young children who couldn't get the Big Bad Insurance Company to pay the claim on her late husband who'd died in a freak bicycle accident.

Or maybe they'd lead with the irony of the suspicious young widow who had assaulted her late husband in front of police, and had very likely planned to divorce him, but who got lucky when he died in a freak bicycle accident, and who was now trying to rip off the insurance company, which is why rates are so high.

Maybe they'd latch onto whatever bake sale or walk-a-thon or miniature-golf tournament Jeanette came up with to help Luann and her kids, and do one of those "Neighbors helping Neighbors" stories they loved so much. They could work in the bicycle safety angle, too, and who knows, if they dug deep enough, maybe a sidebar on the dangers of shooting off fireworks too close to gas-powered lawn mowers.

We are totally screwed.

Karma took out her frustration on a stone lying on the sidewalk and almost kicked it into Molly, who was riding her scooter a few yards ahead. *Stop being ridiculous. They get hundreds of calls and tweets and emails every year; what are the odds that this one will get any attention at all? And even if it does, the producer will make a phone call to the insurance company, they'll write the check, and it'll be over before they have time to do a story about it.*

It made sense, didn't it? *Sure, it did. There was nothing to worry about. Not. A. Thing.*

The Channel 6 News truck passed Karma and Molly just as they turned onto their street. They were heading straight for Luann's house.

265

CHAPTER 30:   FIFTEEN MINUTES OF FAME, BUT IT SEEMED LONGER

It was 6:18 p.m., and Jeanette was so nervous she could hardly eat the carryout mu shu pork and fried rice she'd brought to Luann's house. China Wok had the best egg rolls ever, but Jeanette was watching her weight in case she got the chance to be on TV like Luann, who had such a sweet little figure. She was sorry it was just herself and Luann tonight; it would have been so much more fun to throw a Premier Party for Luann's television debut. Jeanette would have made guacamole and mini tacos, or maybe desserts and chocolate fondue, and invited people from the neighborhood that Luann might like to meet. Karma and Kim probably wouldn't have come because they weren't happy about Luann being on TV, but plenty of other people would have shown up.

To Jeanette's disappointment, Luann had flat-out rejected the idea of a party and had insisted that Jeanette come alone. It was just as well. Five minutes after the handsome anchorman said the story was coming up next, the 90-second *Call for Help* segment was over, and Jeanette was kinda glad she hadn't planned a party around it. It had happened so fast.

Still, it was exciting. The story started with an introduction by the cute girl consumer reporter, and then Luann came on. She wore a black suit which was very slimming, but maybe a little severe. Jeanette would have chosen a softer, more feminine look if Luann had asked her, but she hadn't asked. Her part was kinda short, but then the cute girl consumer reporter said that

266

representatives the insurance company had declined to appear, but had sent a letter saying that until the police investigation of Jack's death was concluded, no payment could be made.

The police also refused to be interviewed for the story, but their written statement referred to *outside forces* which may have contributed to the accident and would have to be explained before the case could be closed. They said they were interviewing persons of interest, but would not reveal their identities. *They're talking about Jeff and me,* thought Jeanette. *Oh my.* The segment ended with a head shot of the consumer reporter, who gravely intoned the best close of her young career:

> **REPORTER:** This is an unusual case. What started out as the story of an insurance company abusing the trust of a widow and her fatherless young children may turn out to be something more sinister. Perhaps murder. Back to you, Steve.

Jeanette turned to look at Luann, only to find Luann looking back at her, sort of studying her, which felt kind of creepy. But before Jeanette even had a chance to think of something to say, phones began to ring—first Luann's home phone, then seconds later, her cell phone. Luann answered the landline and waved Jeanette over to the kitchen counter, where her cell phone was vibrating. Jeanette had no more answered it when another call beeped in. The same thing was apparently happening to Luann, judging by the way she kept pulling the receiver away from her ear in mid-sentence to check caller ID. Forty minutes and a dozen calls later, each, Jeanette and Luann put down their respective phones and looked at each other again, this time in quiet awe.

"I had no idea there were so many lawyers in this town," said Luann.

"And they all watch the news," marveled Jeanette.

Luann returned to the living room, turned off the television, and sat down on the couch. She slowly turned the pages of her phone pad, which was full of names and numbers, quietly studying what she'd written. "They want to help me sue the insurance company, and maybe even the police."

"Yeah, I know," said Jeanette. She handed Luann the pile of envelopes and junk mail she'd grabbed from the counter to write on. "They say they can get you lots of money. It's exciting, don't you think? You'll be able to send all the kids to college."

Luann set the stack of papers on the coffee table, leaned back into the sofa cushions, and looked off into space. She didn't speak for a long time, and her expression was, as usual, unreadable. "I know how this goes," she finally said. "They'll keep most of the money if I win, and I'll owe them thousands in expenses if I lose."

"But what if they can help?" asked Jeanette. "What about you and the kids? I wish I had money to give you, I really do. So does Jeff."

Luann turned to Jeanette, an odd smile on her face. "I know," she said. "But it won't be necessary. Everything will work out. I hate to rush you out of here, but I'm tired."

Jeanette wondered why it wouldn't be necessary, and what Luann was going to do for money if the insurance company didn't come through soon, and how she could be so calm at a time like this, and where she'd bought that suit she'd worn on TV, which was so slimming it practically made her look anorexic. But poor Luann was obviously tired after such a long day, although it wasn't even seven o'clock, so Jeanette helped her put away the leftover Chinese food and then walked home. Only then did she look at her own cell phone. She hadn't realized that all the while she had been talking to callers looking for Luann, her own phone had been quietly filling up with voice mail messages.

(BEEP) Hey, Jeanette, it's Karma. Did you hear him say *outside forces*? Call me *now*.

(BEEP) Kim here. I think the You-Know-Whos are bluffing about you-know-what, but stay away from the You-Know-Who until I say it's okay. Got it? I'm serious. I mean it.

(BEEP) Karma again. Where are you? Call me right away.

(BEEP) It's Kim. You'd better not be with you-know-who. I swear, you just better not.

Jeanette deleted the messages from her cell phone as she listened. *Boy, that Kim is bossy.* Jeanette already knew the cops were bluffing; she and Karma hadn't left any incriminating evidence behind, unless you counted the turkey lacing pin, and how could that little thing be tied to the crime when Jack had died of a head injury, not a puncture wound? *Sheesh.*

As for staying away from Luann, what a terrible thing to suggest at a time when Luann needed a friend. What kind of person abandons a widow with three children? As soon as the police admitted that Jack's death was a simple accident, Luann would get her money. In the meantime, Jeanette would do what was right, which meant supporting a friend in her hour of need. After all, killing Jack had been an accident, but avoiding Luann would be plain ol' *mean.*

Avoiding the news media turned out to be the more pressing problem. A local newspaper story followed the *Call 6 for Help* piece, which was picked up by the AP, UPI, and Reuters. The plight of a photogenic family faced with tragedy and then abused by a heartless insurance company was easy to relate to, and when you added the freakish nature of the husband's death, it was also

269

juicy. More stories followed, and more national attention. Within days, Luann had found messages from the producers of *Good Morning America, Montel, The View, Morning Joe,* and *Jerry Springer*. The 24-hour cable news people didn't bother calling; they just showed up, blocking traffic on Luann's street and attracting every nosy neighbor within a five-mile radius.

All you had to do to earn your fifteen-second sound bite of fame was to claim to know Luann or her late husband. There was always a producer anxious to fill some airtime, no matter how much or how little you had to say...

> **WOMAN:** I go to the church they used to go to before they switched to the church they go to now, and she always said hello to me, but Jack never did. I always thought that was weird.

> **MAN 1:** When his shed blew up it could have taken my house with it. We're just a block away. My kids have nightmares.

> **MAN 2:** I was gonna ask him to start riding with me, but I never got the chance. It just shows you how fragile life is. Especially your head. That part is really fragile.

Having said all she wanted to say, the Widow Lawrence declined all further interviews, which drove the media crazy. And the bits of video they managed to capture of her refusing to be interviewed didn't exactly warm the hearts of the viewing public. Her demeanor was icy, which did nothing to build public sympathy. Jeanette urged her to keep a hanky on hand so she could pretend to be tearful when a camera was pointed at her, but Luann refused to even try it.

Yet the media stayed focused on the story. News producers were determined to find an approach to either the freak accident angle, the recalcitrant insurance company angle, or the possible murder angle. They continued to drive the story forward, and as they moved through the neighborhood looking for people to interview, they began to hear the same two names: Karma Kranski and Jeanette Jorganson.

These women had been seen coming and going from the Lawrence house ever since the accident. One had the same last name as the guy who was supposed to ride with the victim (a two-minute Google search confirmed she was the wife), and the other had made many public statements to neighbors criticizing the victim, both before and after his death. But when producers called, texted, and knocked on their doors, neither woman would consent to be interviewed. It was highly suspicious.

Unfortunately, the energetic young cop, Detective Hunter, *did* agree to talk to CNN. He wouldn't reveal what evidence was found at the scene, but didn't deny that its discovery had led him to look for female witnesses. Geraldo took a crack at him later that day. ("So you're not saying that Ms. Kranski and Ms. Jorganson *aren't* persons of interest?") Hunter's silent non-response was about two seconds too long; the viewing public let out a collective "Aha!"

The next morning, Detective Hunter's shift supervisor appeared on *The O'Reilly Factor* and confirmed that Jeanette's husband was the neighbor who was supposed to ride with the victim the morning of his suspicious death. The media tried to wangle an interview with Jeff Jorganson, but he refused, claiming that he might have to testify if there were a trial. With nothing else to go on, and nothing more interesting to report on, the media redoubled its efforts to get to his wife and her friend. Failure was apparently *not* an option.

In the end, Nancy Grace persuaded a police dispatcher to admit, on camera, that she'd heard that Detective Hunter had questioned both women. Her interview was the confirmation that everybody was looking for. All hell broke loose, all privacy was lost, and all attention was focused on Karma and Jeanette. True, the death of Jack Lawrence wasn't exactly *breaking news*, but it was one of those small, personal stories that the average person could relate to, as opposed to tensions in the Middle East and deficit spending by Congress. The dispatcher was given a three-day unpaid suspension, and then fired. She decided to pursue a career in home-based skin care sales, but was careful not to book parties in Bedford Commons, lest she would run into Karma or Jeanette or any of their friends.

In live morning updates, reporters on every network groping for a new angle began to speculate on whether Karma and Jeanette might be charged with the murder of Jack Lawrence, and if so, when? Perhaps this was this a love triangle (or quadrangle) gone bad. Was the Widow Lawrence in on it in some way? Was it a conspiracy? Were the women planning to split the insurance money?

One ratings-starved cable news network even suggested a connection to modern witchcraft, given the secrecy of the group. Was this *Friday playgroup* a euphemism for *coven*? It boosted their cumulative ratings for that quarter hour, so other networks followed suit.

Next up was Robert Gardiner Sr., who had just discovered that Mrs. Kranski and her band of crazy homicidal females had traumatized his son, Robert Jr., with insane accusations of sexual misconduct. His son, a wonderful boy, was approaching B honor-roll status in high school and semi-regularly attended church. He was haunted by the threats Kranski and her minions had made against him, and might never be the same.

Robert Sr. wasn't willing to discuss the accusations the women had made against his son, but assured Anderson Cooper that the charges were baseless, the invention of sick minds you don't expect to find in the suburbs, especially in a nice

272

neighborhood like Bedford Commons.

> **ANDERSON COOPER:** Karma Kranski sounds like a dangerous lunatic at the center of a suburban reign of terror. Why is she allowed to roam freely?

> **GARDINER SR:** My point exactly. My son is lucky to be alive.

> **ANDERSON COOPER:** (*turning to the camera*) And for the record, we invited Karma Kranski and Jeanette Jorganson to appear tonight, but they refused.

They certainly did refuse. Emphatically. Not only did Kim insist on it, but Karma couldn't picture herself going on national television and trying to explain why she had threatened to use a rusty butter knife to neuter a group of teenage boys who hadn't even touched her daughter. It had made so much sense at the time, but it was difficult to explain now.

When phone calls, texts, tweets, Facebook posts, and televised pleas to Karma and Jeanette to tell their side of the story failed, news producers turned to bribery. Flower arrangements and potted plants from Fox News, fruit baskets, candy and frosted *Hardball* cookies from MSNBC, carrot cake muffins adorned with icing in the shape of the CBS eyeball... you name it, Karma and Jeanette found it on their doorsteps. Soon every flat surface in their kitchens, family rooms and dining rooms was loaded with brightly wrapped baskets, boxes and gift bags. Little Jeffrey snuck off to his bedroom with the entire box of colorful NBC peacock tea cakes and vomited rainbow colors all over the floor of his closet.

It was positively embarrassing when Kim came over to Karma's house to discuss strategy with her and Jeanette. She spent the first twenty minutes going from room to room, peeking in boxes and reading the enclosed cards. Barbara Walters' offer to come out of retirement for a one-hour special, tentatively titled *Real Desperate Housewives of Indiana,* gave Kim a fit of snorts and giggles, but the elegantly wrapped box the producers had sent, along with a round trip ticket to New York, reservations at the Ritz, and an invitation for a guest appearance on *Good Morning America,* stopped her cold.

When Kim peered inside the box, she sounded like she'd just seen the Virgin Mary reflected in the champagne sent by Jimmy Fallon. "Manolos," she breathed. "Manolo Blahniks. These are $750 shoes. And they sent a matching bag. Do they fit?"

"Who cares?" said Karma. "You want them? I can't wear them in front of Sam, he's ready to kill me."

"I might sell mine on eBay," said Jeanette. "They pinch my toes."

Kim rubbed the black leather against her cheek. "It's like butter. Why did I have to oversleep? Nobody is sending me anything."

Karma's grabbed the shoe from Kim and threw it back in the box, knocking the Swarovski crystal soccer ball (sent by Tyra Banks) off its pedestal and onto the floor. Spike the cat, who had been sleeping on a *Today Show* blanket, hissed and stalked off to find a quieter place to nap. "C'mon," said Karma. "Help us figure out how to get out of this mess. I don't want shoes; I want my life back."

But Kim was useless. For the first time in Karma's memory, Kim had no plan of attack, no clever approach to lead the media astray, no ideas whatsoever. All the cunning had been knocked out of her by a pair of expensive shoes. She left Karma's house promising, unconvincingly, to try to think of something, with a ceramic flower pot of lilies from Maury Povich in one hand and a Dolce and Gabbana scarf from Dr. Phil in the other.

The next evening, Greta Van Susteren did a live shot for *On the Record* from the sidewalk in front of Jeanette's house, speculating again on why the prime suspects refused to speak to her. Inside the house, Jeff paced, Allie sucked her fingers, Baby Jacob spit up, and Little Jeffrey jumped on the couch in front of the picture window, flipping off America and calling Greta a *poopy head*. You could read his lips when the camera zoomed in.

Karma, a devoted fan since Greta's *Court TV* days, watched the whole thing live from her family room. It was surreal. Was this rock bottom? Could things get worse? *What a stupid question.* Just as Karma was reaching for the remote, hoping to find something to calm her nerves, like a mixed martial arts tournament or a raging California brush fire, Greta introduced a forensic psychologist. He admitted that he had never met any of the people involved, but he was undeterred. He was certain that on an unconscious level, Jack Lawrence had failed to secure his helmet on purpose, and had thus committed suicide by bicycle, owing to his obvious self-esteem issues and marital problems.

> **GRETA:** That's interesting, since suicide would nullify the victim's life insurance policy. Next, in an *On the Record* exclusive, we'll talk to a very close friend of the two suspects who says she knows what mysterious evidence was found at the scene of the crime. Stay tuned, because this could blow the case wide open.

Karma sat up straighter, watching as the camera zoomed out. There, standing next to Greta Van Susteren, was Kim. Karma felt remarkably calm. Out-of-body calm. Just back from the dead calm. She watched the car insurance lizard and the disability insurance duck, followed by a pitch for a household stain fighter she'd actually tried once. It hadn't worked. Then Greta had come back on and introduced Mrs. Barbara Kim Wallace, long-time resident of Bedford Commons, wife of the HOA president, and best friend of the prime suspects. Kim looked nervous, yet fetching, in a tan sweater with red piping which was set off perfectly by her new Dolce and Gabbana scarf.

> **GRETA:** You claim to have information about the evidence the police found at the scene of the 'accident.' Can you tell us why you're revealing this information now?
>
> **KIM:** Well, I'm just trying to explain that my friends had nothing to do with what happened. After all, Jack Lawrence didn't die of a stab wound. He fell and hit his head.
>
> **GRETA:** A stab wound? We haven't heard about a stab wound. What did they stab him with, and where did the police find the weapon?
>
> **KIM:** No, no, that's not what I said. He *didn't* die from being stabbed.
>
> **GRETA:** So they stabbed him, but that's not what killed him?

Karma wondered if the heavy, tingly sensation in her arms and legs might be the first signs of shock, although she supposed that people in shock don't know they're in shock. Maybe this was a heart attack. Or, if she was really lucky, a fatal stroke.

> **KIM:** There's no knife. I mean they didn't stab him. It was just a turkey lacing pin.
>
> **GRETA:** What's a turkey lacing pin?
>
> **KIM:** It's just a skinny metal...

276

GRETA: Is this what they used to stab the victim? How badly was he injured? Did this happen before or after he fell off the bike?

KIM: No, they didn't stab him. The pin was for the... I mean, it wasn't for anything, it was just a pin. I mean I don't know anything about the pin.

GRETA: There was a hole in the tire of the bike that Jeff Jorganson was supposed to ride that morning. Were they trying to cause Mr. Jorganson to have an accident? Did they use the pin to disable the victim's bike as well? Is that what caused his death?

KIM: No. They stabbed... I mean they didn't *stab*... They just... the pin... it's just a thing... like at Thanksgiving...

Karma wished she still had the turkey lacing pin. She would have enjoyed meeting Greta in person, right after she killed Kim on live television with the pin through her disloyal, attention-seeking, rotten little heart.

GRETA: So your friends stabbed Jeff Jorganson's bike tire and then attacked Jack Lawrence with the same weapon? Why didn't you go to the police with this information, and what do you think their motivation was?

KIM: No, they didn't attack—they just wanted to talk to him.

GRETA: But you've just placed them at the scene of the crime. If they just wanted to talk, why did they take a weapon? Do you think *he* attacked *them*?

KIM: No, no, he didn't attack them.

GRETA: So it wasn't self-defense. So why did they attack him?

KIM: They were just out for a run.

GRETA: With a weapon?

KIM: Not a weapon, it was just a pin.

GRETA: A sharp metal object they used to puncture Jeff Jorganson's tire, deliberately preventing him from riding with the victim.

KIM: (*unintelligible sputtering*)

GRETA: It looks like your friends devised an elaborate plan to make sure that Jack Lawrence would be alone that day. That's premeditation. Were you part of the planning or just the cover-up after the crime?

KIM: (*unintelligible sputtering*)

GRETA: (*turning to the camera*) Well, this is certainly an interesting new development. If the County Prosecutor is watching, you might want to come in early tomorrow, Madam. This is beginning to look like a conspiracy.

Greta teased the next segment ("Why do stay-at-home mothers kill? A spokeswoman for the National Organization of Women will give us her controversial theory."), and as the show went to a commercial break, Kim, still standing next to Greta, looked like she, too, might be having a stroke.

Karma turned off the television. How peculiar it felt to watch her entire life destroyed on live television by her former best friend. Kim had just placed Karma and Jeanette at the crime scene, revealed the weapon they'd used on Jeff's bike, and made a strong case for premeditated murder. Greta had it a bit wrong, but it all made sense. Karma gleaned a tiny morsel of sick satisfaction from the fact that Kim had implicated herself, too, but Kim would get herself out of trouble. She always did. Only Karma and Jeanette would end up being given the death penalty by a jury of their peers. *After all that bitch's lectures and threats about keeping a low profile, what changed her mind? Expensive shoes? Luggage? Is she wearing a new sweater?*

"Very nice."

Karma looked up to see Sam standing in front of her. His face was dark with anger.

"When you screw up our lives," he said, "you don't mess around."

CHAPTER 31: IF *60 MINUTES* CALLS, TAKE A MESSAGE

Karma peeked out from behind the bushes at the line of satellite trucks parked nose to tail on Brentwood Circle, and wished that war would break out, or there would be a political scandal or a flood somewhere, so the goddamn reporters would leave her alone.

Maybe the head of ISIS will convert to Judaism. Or O.J. will find the real killer. Elvis and Bigfoot could be photographed shopping together at Walmart. Something, *anything*, to get the attention off Jack Lawrence and his "untimely, tragic death at the hands of vigilante Soccer Moms."

Karma and Jeanette had their own spectacular graphic opening on CNN and theme music on Fox News. It was an ironic, almost cartoonish melody, but what really irked Karma was this *Soccer Moms* business. Molly and Allie didn't even play soccer, and Little Jeffrey had been kicked off the peewee team after the unfortunate incident with the coach's son and the Gatorade. So what genius had started calling them *Soccer Moms*, and how had it caught on so damn fast?

Oh well, there wasn't much she could do about it now. Karma ducked down behind the bushes and started sneaking home. In spite of her pregnancy and thoroughly un-athletic nature, she might have made it if the engineer in charge of the Fox News Channel truck hadn't stepped out for a smoke just as she was making a run for the Crandall's evergreens.

"Hey," he yelled to the reporter inside the truck, "there's one of 'em!"

Karma had the advantage for several blocks, as the cameraman had to grab his gear and the on-air talent had to find his hairspray, but they jumped in their rental car and quickly caught up to her. Leading this band of vultures to her house would be a big mistake, as Molly was napping and Sam was already furious because he couldn't leave the house without running into reporters with microphones. Karma cut across several yards, then made her way past Brentwood, hoping to lose them at the playground. She thought she had it made until she saw a white Ford Escort with the rent-a-car license plate holder heading straight for her. *Crap.* She turned and raced down the sidewalk back to Brentwood, the car at her heels.

"Karma, we just want to tell your side of the story," cried the reporter driving the car. Karma resisted the reflex to turn her head toward the sound. The camera lens was sticking out the open car window. They wanted a shot for tonight's Soccer Mom Update, and Karma would be damned if she was going to cooperate.

"Go away!" she shouted, without looking at them.

"Do you run to keep fit?" he called. "You look great. Is it true that you just signed a book deal for *The Soccer Mom Diet*?"

Nice try, Pretty Boy.

Neighbors, hearing the commotion, were peeking out of doors and windows, of course, but no one came to Karma's rescue. She'd brought this plague of flaxen-haired, baritone locusts unto their houses, and Bedford Commons had gone from giddy excitement to righteous anger in hours, as their streets became blocked and their children were accosted by smiling strangers with microphones.

"Karma! Yoo hoo, Karma!"

Karma's ears perked; the voice was coming from one of the houses up ahead. A white house with beige trim. (what else?) The door opened and a woman with obviously dyed, jet-black hair stepped onto the front porch, beckoning. *Oh hell no.*

But Karma was out of options and the FNC reporter was still yelling out questions, so she sprinted toward the house. She was half-way up the driveway when the woman on the porch raised her arm and Karma saw that she was holding-- *A GUN POINTED RIGHT AT MY HEAD.* Trying to stop her own momentum, Karma opened her mouth to scream.

"Leave her alone, ya bastards!" shouted Dora Lee. She swung the weapon past Karma's horrified face, took aim, and fired at the white Ford, which screeched to a stop, slammed into reverse and sped away, tires screeching and gears grinding. Karma stumbled and grabbed the railing around Dora Lee's front porch to stop herself from falling, as a painful cramp gripped her left side. Dora Lee waited until the car was out of sight, then lowered the weapon.

"Assholes are gonna wreck the transmission," she said, shaking her head in disgust. "Oh, it's just a rental."

Dora Lee examined her weapon and flicked something out of the barrel with her thumb. Pale, dripping with sweat, and confused, Karma gaped at Dora Lee, who smirked back at her. "You never seen a tater gun before? Actually, you'd have to call this an eggplant gun, 'cuz I grew so damn many this year I give 'em to James Patrick to play with." Dora Lee picked up half a dried up, pock-marked eggplant from the front porch and poked the gun into the end of it to reload.

"You like ratatouille?" she asked. "I have a great recipe." She fired, and the eggplant bullet flew a good fifteen feet before hitting a tree trunk with a tiny wet *punk*. "Can't let James Patrick in the house with this baby," she said. "He keeps missin' the cat and hittin' my walls." She opened the front door. "Come on in, honey, you'll feel better after a beer."

Although she had to settle for a root beer because of her pregnancy, soon Karma was feeling better. In fact, she was genuinely happy to be hanging out in Dora Lee's kitchen. First of all, Dora Lee was the first person who had been nice to her in days. And her kitchen was warm and friendly and cluttered, with dozens of magnets on the refrigerator holding up a multitude of family snapshots, coupons, and James Robert's childish scribblings. The counters were overflowing with unread mail, half-eaten snacks, empty juice boxes, and Happy Meal toys. It felt like home.

"Did you see that blond guy in the front seat when I took a bead on him?" said Dora Lee with a mischievous grin. "I've seen him on the news. I bet he had to change his shorts."

Karma snorted with laughter. "I almost had to change mine," she said. "I thought you were gonna shoot *me*."

"Now why would I shoot you?"

Karma swallowed hard. She could think of at least four white-walled reasons for Dora Lee to shoot her, but Dora Lee didn't seem to know anything about that, thank God. "Oh, Dora Lee," she said, "this thing has gotten so far out of hand, I'm surprised the whole neighborhood doesn't want to shoot me. You're probably the only person still speaking to me."

Dora Lee pushed away from the kitchen table, walked over to the pantry and pulled out a bag of pretzels. "Yeah, you girls got yourselves in pretty deep."

Yeah, and the Grand Canyon is a pretty big hole in the ground.

Dora Lee sat down on the padded brown kitchen chair and looked at Karma appraisingly, pushing the bag of pretzels toward her. "Eat," she said. "You look kinda pale. Is it true what I heard on the news? You're expecting?"

Karma smiled and started to answer, but a noise in the hallway caught her attention. A pretty teenage girl in tight jean shorts and a halter top loped through the kitchen, grabbing a handful of pretzels as she passed, then flopped down on the family room sofa with the TV remote. Adrenaline pumped through Karma's veins.

"Hey, missy," scolded Dora Lee, "where's your damn manners? We got a guest."

The girl waved from the sofa. "Hey."

Dora Lee was still giving the teenager the stink eye. A dramatically long moment later, the girl rolled her eyes, and with what appeared to be great effort, hauled herself off the couch and sloped back into the kitchen. "Sorry. Hi. I'm Brandi."

"Karma Kranski."

Brandi nodded. "I know you," she said. "You're one of the Soccer Moms."

I swear to God, Molly will join the boy's wrestling team before I let her play soccer. And here I am, face to face with the girl who ran her over, the girl who gave me the finger, the girl I've wanted to slap the shit out of all this time, and I'm just sitting here smiling like an idiot.

"When's your shift start?" asked Dora Lee.

I should be screaming at her, or trying to strangle her.

"In an hour," said Brandi. She plopped back down on the sofa and flipped through the TV channels. "I'll feed James Patrick before I go." She gave a sudden shout of surprise. "Hey, look, it's you guys."

Karma's head jerked around. There on Fox News was Dora Lee, looking like Annie Oakley's grandmother in a halter top, and Karma, stumbling up the driveway, thinking she was about to be shot with a wad of zucchini.

"Holy cow," said Dora.

"Wow, Mom, you look hot," hooted Brandi.

284

It was beyond weird to see the scene play out again from the camera's point of view. Karma could feel her fear rising up again as the gun rose up in her face. Meanwhile, Shephard Smith, manning the anchor desk, was having fun at the expense of the on-scene reporter as the image shot from the side window of the vehicle wobbled and shook, then was lost completely.

> **SHEPARD SMITH:** Chase, it looks like your mother should have named you *Flee*.

> **REPORTER:** Very funny. All I can say is that the Indiana suburbs are more dangerous than they look. Back to you, Shep.

"Wow," said Dora Lee, fingers poking at her scalp. "I've never seen myself on TV before. I better do my roots."

"You're gonna get arrested," sang Brandi from the sofa.

"Nah," scoffed her mother. "You don't need a permit to carry a tater gun. And I didn't hurt that guy, now did I?"

Karma stood up. "I should get going. I don't want to get you in any more trouble." She stretched her wobbly legs and moved toward the door.

"You're always welcome, hon," said Dora Lee. "Any time. I think you're gettin' a raw deal."

"Thanks, Dora Lee," said Karma, "I really appreciate that. Maybe when all this is over, you guys could come over for dinner. I make a mean veal scaloppini."

"I'll bring my ratatouille," said Dora Lee.

"Hey, what the hell?" yelled Brandi. "Come listen to this. You, too, Soccer Mom." Brandi's tone had shifted, and Karma's heart lurched. She was tempted to make a run for the door, but Dora Lee might have tackled her before she got there.

285

The image on Dora Lee's flat-screen TV was now split between Shepard Smith and a female reporter who was standing outside the St. Vincent's Trauma Center. Karma's heart leapt up into her throat in a futile attempt to escape from her body, but it was just as trapped as she was, in the home of the girl whose car she had vandalized and who was going to beat the crap out of her very soon.

> **SHEPARD SMITH:** So in addition to being alleged killers, the Soccer Moms are also suspected vandals?
>
> **REPORTER:** That's right. Apparently the vandalism of the car took place soon after the daughter of one of the Soccer Moms was taken to this emergency room. We don't yet know if there's a connection.
>
> **SHEPARD SMITH:** And this may have been the first crime in the Soccer Mom crime spree? Vandalism of a car? Incredible.
>
> **REPORTER:** Yes, at least police think so. All four tires were slashed.

Brandi stood up and took an angry step toward Karma, who backed up, slipping on a bit of zucchini on the floor.

"You busted my tires? What the hell for?"

"You almost killed my daughter."

"Did not."

"Did so."

Dora Lee stepped between Brandi and Karma, her eyes on Karma. "What are you talking about?"

"She was speeding down my street and she hit my daughter and broke her arm."

"When?"

"A few months ago."

286

"A few months?" roared Dora Lee, turning to Brandi. "Why didn't I hear nothin' about this?"

"Cause it didn't happen."

"Yes, it did."

Dora Lee was now giving Karma the stink eye. "If you thought Brandi ran down your kid, why didn't you call the cops?"

"I did. They couldn't find her. She broke Molly's arm and then drove off like nothing happened."

"Nothing *did* happen," said Brandi. "I never hit no kid in my life."

"Yes, you did." Karma felt like she was six years old.

Dora Lee's face, so friendly a minute ago, was now rigid with anger. "I don't see the cops coming after *her*, just *you*. And you knew who she was 'cause I told you about her tires on the playground that day. So why didn't you call the cops then?"

There was no way Karma could explain without making herself like the bad guy in this story. She just looked at Dora Lee's reddening face, unable to speak. Karma could see very clearly that if she had to fight her way out of the house, she wouldn't stand a chance.

"You had the nerve to come into my home today when you knew what you'd done to my daughter," said Dora Lee. She stopped and looked down at Karma's midsection. "You're expecting a baby, so I'm gonna give you a break. Just get out of my house and never show your face here again."

"She was speeding. She broke my daughter's arm."

"If that was true, you woulda told the cops. You just leave. Right now. Before I do something I shouldn't."

Karma felt tears welling up in her eyes—angry, sad, shameful tears. *This is so unfair. What I did wrong was nothing compared to what she did wrong.* But there was nothing to do except leave. Thankfully, the news crew had given up, and the street was nearly empty.

Karma trudged home, head down, hands in pockets. No friends stepped outside to say hello or share a cute story about their kids. Nobody invited her in for a Diet Coke. The few people she passed looked away without speaking to her. All Karma wanted to do was get home where no one could see her, sit in a bathtub with hot water and bubbles and have a good cry.

But when she walked in her back door, the look on Sam's face made her want to turn around and leave again. They'd hardly spoken in days, and for the first time since they were married, Karma wondered if he was planning to leave her. He brushed past and murmured an "excuse me," but didn't look at her. It felt like a blow. Even Molly seemed angry. She was in the living room playing with her Barbies, and like her father, didn't even look up when Karma came in.

Karma walked into the kitchen. It was more a mess than usual, which wouldn't have seemed possible until recently. A mound of crusty dishes filled the sink, spilling out onto the counter. Puffs of cat fur skittered across the floor on every breeze, and trash was spilling from the overstuffed garbage can. With the press lurking outside, they couldn't go out to eat, but Karma couldn't grocery shop in peace either. The remnants of meals crusting on dishes were desperate combinations of soup, frozen entrees, scrambled eggs, crackers, cheese, and canned vegetables. The only upside to all the crap Karma was going through was that the refrigerator had never been cleaner. It was practically empty.

Bubble bath and therapeutic cry forgotten, Karma opened the dishwasher, which had been run days before, but never emptied, and stacked the clean dinner plates on the counter, after wiping off something sticky off the surface. If nobody was speaking to her, at least she would keep busy.

What would Dr. Laura say if I had the nerve to call and ask her how to save my marriage? Not that I can call her—she'd figure out who I am and remove my spleen on satellite radio. Karma put the dinner plates into the cabinet, then started on the small sandwich plates. *She'd say, "Apologize and eat dirt." She'd say I have it coming. She'd say everybody hates me because I'm a murderer and a vandal and a child predator and I deserve to rot in prison for the rest of my life.*

A few of the spoons had nested together and were still dirty, so Karma scrubbed them before putting them away. *She'd tell me to start behaving like a loving wife, and show Sam that I intend to be honest with him from now on and not repeat the same mistakes.* Karma fished out a sippy cup lid that had slipped through the top rack and was resting on the bottom of the dishwasher. Of course, that would mean actually being honest with Sam. Honest about Jack and the shed and the fireworks and the red car and the tires and the pie server and the teenage boys and the rusty butter knife and Dora Lee and Brandi. That was a lot of honesty. She would start on it tomorrow.

Karma pulled out the salad bowls, turned toward the cabinet, and jumped. Sam was suddenly at her elbow. His arms were crossed and his mouth was set in a tight, thin line. *I don't think he's here to help with the dishes.* Karma moved carefully past him, put away the bowls, and then the coffee mugs.

"Saw you on TV. Who was your friend with the gun?"

"It wasn't a real gun," said Karma. "It shoots zucchini. Her name is Dora Lee and I met her on the playground a while back. I told you about her. I think."

"No, you didn't, but there are a lot of things you never bothered to tell *me*," said Sam. His voice dripped with resentment.

"Well, I thought I did, but maybe I didn't. It doesn't matter now because she's not speaking to me anymore. Like everybody else." A fresh load of bile and bitterness pushed aside the good intentions of a moment ago. "Do you think I brought this mess into our lives on purpose? Do you think I like being chased down the street by camera crews?"

"Well, how would I know what you like?" Sam exploded. "You have this whole other life that you didn't choose to share with me."

"That is totally unfair," said Karma. "This is not my fault. We were trying to do something good, and it just went... it just went... kind of wrong."

Sam's eyes bugged out. It was not attractive. "Kind of wrong? You killed a guy."

"It was an accident. He hit his head."

"So I heard. On the news, of course, not from you."

"Well, maybe I didn't tell you because I knew you'd react like this." This was the most childish argument this side of *Kim made me do it* that Karma could have come up with, and she knew it, but it was all she had.

Perhaps it was the sheer stupidity of what she'd said that rendered Sam speechless for a moment, but before Karma could regroup, there came a plaintive wail from the next room, followed immediately by the ringing of the landline telephone. Karma felt a sick stab of pain. She had completely forgotten that Molly was in the next room. She pushed past Sam to get to Molly, and held her sobbing daughter in her arms, rocking and shushing her and apologizing for fighting with Daddy.

Sam answered the ringing phone. Karma couldn't hear a word he was saying over Molly's howling, but from the look on his face, something bad was happening. *The prosecutor's office? The police? They're filing charges. I'm going to prison. The last thing Molly is going to remember is me yelling at her dad and making her cry. I've turned into my mother.*

Sam finally hung up the phone and looked at Karma with a stricken expression. He looked more sad than angry. *It's over. I'm going to prison, but at least he's sorry about it.* Karma gently pulled away from Molly, who was still sniffling.

"I'm going to talk to Daddy," she said. "I promise, no more yelling. I really promise. You just sit here for a minute and I'll be right back." *Maybe if I plead guilty, I can make a deal. Maybe just a few years in jail. Maybe one of those ankle bracelets like Martha Stewart had. I wouldn't have to do the grocery shopping or carpool. That wouldn't be so bad. Why does Sam look so sad? It's good that he looks sad. Maybe he'll miss me, or maybe he's just pretending because he wants an excuse for divorcing me.*

"That was Good Shepherd," said Sam quietly. "It's Kathleen. Her heart stopped about a half-hour ago. Your mom had signed a Do Not Resuscitate order, so there was nothing they could do. She's gone."

\

CHAPTER 32:   KARMA CIRCLES THE DRAIN

The funeral service was held in Good Shepherd's tiny chapel. It was about the size of Karma's family room, with small stained glass windows and four rows of hard wooden pews. There was room for about twenty mourners, which was probably enough if your life ended in a place like this.

Karma sat between her divorced parents, Ed and Charlotte. Charlotte had flown in from Florida the night before. Ed and Roberta, his current wife, had flown in from Atlanta that morning. Sam's widowed mother, Sylvia, was sitting in the pew behind Ed and kept reaching forward to pat his shoulder. To the untrained eye, it would have appeared to be an act of kindness and sympathy, but like everything concerning Sam's mother, there was subtext.

Back in the late 90's, at the family Seder, Sylvia, tipsy from the requisite three glasses of Manischevitz, had made a pass at Ed. Charlotte had never forgiven her. Never mind that Charlotte and Ed had been divorced for decades when it happened. To Charlotte, it was a matter of principle; ex-husbands were off limits, in perpetuity, to any woman who had been friendly with the ex-wife prior to the divorce, unless expressly authorized by said ex-wife. The only thing Charlotte would have authorized for Ed, in perpetuity, was a bad case of boils.

The rabbi officiating at the funeral quoted the standard Biblical passage about greener pastures, but Karma was barely listening. *I was supposed to visit last week, and I forgot all about it. My sister died alone. I was the one person in the world she should have been able to count on, and I was too busy to think about her.*

Karma couldn't bring herself to tell her mother that she'd missed her last visit with Kathleen; Charlotte would never have forgiven her. Never mind that she herself had retired to Florida and only visited her other daughter a few times a year; she had passed that sad baton to Karma, and Karma had dropped it.

Actually, everything about Karma was disappointing to her mother, from her messy home to her sloppy clothing and mousy hair, to her decision to give up her career to raise Molly. Charlotte had managed to juggle divorce, motherhood, and a career in real estate, and couldn't see why Karma didn't do the same, if only to make enough money for decent clothing and a more stylish hairstyle.

Molly was Karma's only real success in life, as far as Charlotte was concerned, especially dressed up as she was today, in the white velvet dress, tights, and shiny white shoes that Charlotte had brought from Florida. She had assumed, correctly, that Karma wouldn't have a suitable outfit for Molly, since she rarely dressed herself appropriately. If Charlotte was aware that clothes shopping without an unwanted media entourage was nearly impossible for Karma these days, she hadn't said so. Nor had Karma thanked her for bringing the outfit, which looked adorable on Molly.

That was the only bright spot on this horrible day. Karma sat on the hard wooden pew between Sam, who surely hated her, and Molly, who would come to hate her when she was old enough to understand what Karma had done. Karma was responsible, not only for Kathleen's death, but for breaking her daughter's heart.

The irony of the situation was unbearable. She'd kept Kathleen a secret to spare Molly the cruel misery of knowing about her aunt, then she'd given in and let Molly meet Kathleen, and now, because of Karma's cruelty and neglect, Molly was in misery. She had been so excited about her next visit, and the chance to teach her aunt the new songs she'd learned in preschool. *If we'd come up here last week, like we were supposed to, Kathleen would have had a reason to stay alive. What if she let go of life because we didn't show up?*

It was too horrible to consider, so Karma forced herself to pay attention to the funeral service. It would be quick; nobody would be standing up to eulogize Kathleen and talk about all the great times they'd had together. There were no childhood memories to share, no funny stories about college pranks, no warm or touching moments to recount.

The rabbi cleared his throat. "Miss Denise Mobley would now like to say a few words about Kathleen."

From the back of the room, Kathleen's physical therapist walked up to the small oak podium, nodding to Karma and Molly as she passed. She expressed sympathy for the family, then began to talk about Kathleen: how her eyes followed Denise when she came in to do therapy, and how she often had a smile on her face, though not when her muscles were being stretched. There were smiles and chuckles at this. Some patients, said Denise, were truly absent from their bodies, but those like Kathleen seemed to still reside there, finding pleasure in the sound of a human voice and the touch of a human hand.

Karma felt the unspoken rebuke. *I only thought of her as a burden. Why couldn't I see her the way Denise did? Why didn't I visit more often?*

Karma wouldn't have believed she could feel any worse, but somehow she was managing it. She thought about getting up to speak, maybe even taking Molly up with her to tell the story of meeting Aunt Kathleen and singing songs with her. *But I didn't prepare Molly. She might be scared. And I didn't ask Sam. What if he gets mad? What if he think I'm only using Molly to look better to these people? What if that's the truth?*

294

In the end, Karma hesitated a little too long, and the rabbi ended the service with a final prayer. It was too late. Karma could have stood up and asked for more time, but she didn't. Another lost opportunity. Another failure.

Then there was the fact that she hadn't planned anything for *after* Kathleen's funeral service. Her house was hours away from Good Shepherd, and it was still the target of cable news crews and cameras. Besides, although Karma had seen it in movies, she had never sat *Shiva* for a deceased relative. How do you invite friends over to help you mourn the sister you never told them you have?

So the inauspicious conclusion of Kathleen's memorial service was a stop for lunch along the interstate on I65, on the way back toward Indianapolis. At least Karma had found a sit-down restaurant. There was probably some special hell for those who took their relatives to McDonald's for a post-funeral Quarter Pounder with cheese.

"Will this be on one ticket?" The cheerful young waitress fairly sparkled with enthusiasm, probably assuming that a table full of well-dressed adults would guarantee a good tip.

"What do you want?" Charlotte addressed Karma over the rims of her reading glasses as though Karma were a child, and she would be required to relay this information to the waitress.

"I haven't decided yet."

"The waitress is here. You need to decide."

Karma deliberately turned away from her mother and looked at Molly, the only person at the table who might actually need help ordering. "Do you want the chicken fingers or the spaghetti?"

Charlotte pursed her lips in the *You're Disappointing Me* expression Karma knew so well. "Do you think spaghetti is a good idea when she's wearing white?"

"Molly will be careful."

"Christ Almighty," said her ex-husband, Ed, from across the table. "Let the kid eat what she wants."

"I'm not telling her what to eat," said Charlotte. "I'm just suggesting that Karma not encourage her to ruin the outfit I bought."

"It's inappropriate anyway," said Sylvia. "I told you, she should have worn the black dress I bought."

"So you mentioned about ten times," said Charlotte.

"Drop it, Mom," said Sam. "She'll wear your dress to the next funeral."

"Samuel Allen Kranski," scolded his mother. "What kind of a way is that to talk?"

"Do you need a few more minutes?" asked the waitress.

"Do you see how my son talks to me?" asked Sylvia, looking up at the waitress. "Karma, I just hope your son—knock on wood you should be so lucky to have a son—doesn't talk to you like that. My book club says you're having a boy, by the way. I showed them your picture, and with all the weight you're gaining in your hips, they all agree it has to be a boy. A big boy."

"That's not the pregnancy," said Charlotte. "She inherited those hips from her father's side. You should have seen his mother. Like a pear, that woman."

"Better a pear than a dried-up old prune," said Ed.

"Ed," scolded his wife, Roberta, though she was smiling.

"Would you like to hear the specials again?" The waitress was not smiling.

"I'll have the sausage lasagna with extra cheese," said Karma, "and chocolate cake for dessert. A BIG PIECE."

"The baked chicken would be better." Charlotte looked her up and down. "You know Sylvia's got a point about your hips. She's wrong about that awful black dress for a little girl, but you never lost all the weight from your first baby, and now, well, you know me, I don't like to say anything."

Newest wife Roberta shook her head in sympathy. "I'm always on a diet. Ed likes me in a two-piece when we go to the beach."

"You should see her," said Ed with a broad wink at his son-in-law.

Charlotte and Sylvia rolled their eyes. Roberta was the only thing they agreed on. They hated her. Karma handed her menu back to the waitress. "Forget the lasagna. Just bring the cake. All of it."

"I'll have the fried chicken," said Sam.

"You're lucky," said Ed. "With my heart I'm not allowed to eat fried."

"If you'd eaten better like I told you years ago, you wouldn't have a bad heart," said Charlotte.

"Stop telling everybody what to eat," said Ed. "You did that the whole time we were married."

"And you're on heart pills because you didn't listen."

"Not listening to you was the only thing that kept me from killing myself."

Sylvia giggled. "You're such a card, Ed. And you don't look old enough to have a daughter Karma's age. By the way, when's your flight? We can ride to the airport together."

Now old wife Charlotte and new wife Roberta were united in eye-rolling disgust. Karma found it amusing, until she flashed forward to the alarming possibility of her father divorcing Roberta and marrying Sam's widowed mother. That would give Charlotte the fatal heart attack she'd been predicting for Ed since the Johnson administration.

"Sorry, Sylvia, but we had a team from NASA work out the schedule for the airport runs," said Karma, "so we're not changing anything. Let's finish ordering so the waitress can get on with her work."

"Is the chicken marsala fresh?" asked Sylvia. "If it's frozen I don't want it. The black dress would have been beautiful on Molly, by the way. It's appropriate to wear dark colors on these occasions. And what a lovely service, Charlotte. I'm so sorry for your loss."

"Thank you, that's so kind of you," said Charlotte. "Baked chicken and mixed vegetables, but not if there's a lot of butter on the vegetables. If there's a lot of butter then I'll just have a salad. I'm sorry, but black is not suitable for a child."

"If she's old enough to go to a funeral, she's old enough to wear the right dress," said Sylvia. "I'll also have the house salad. Thousand Island on the side. Which is something I tried to discuss with my son, but you see how much he cares about my opinion."

Charlotte nodded. "Children these days don't show respect. I'd also like a Caesar salad, very light on the dressing. Molly, sweetheart, do you want Grandma's croutons? I told my daughter that Molly was too young to go to the funeral, but do you think she listens?"

"It's a different world," agreed Sylvia. "Is the chicken marsala frozen? You didn't answer so I'm asking again, which makes me think it's frozen and you don't want to admit it. If it's frozen, I'll have the baked."

"I'll go check," said the waitress. She practically ran toward the kitchen, disappearing behind the swinging doors.

"Wouldn't you think she could answer a simple question about the menu?" asked Charlotte.

"Sam, don't over-tip that one," sniffed Sylvia.

After lunch, Sylvia tried to wangle a seat in Ed and Roberta's rented Cadillac, even suggesting that Roberta might be more comfortable in Sam and Karma's minivan so she could nap while Sylvia and Ed caught up on old times. But Roberta, while younger than Sylvia, was just as shrewd. She was afflicted with an instant case of car sickness that could only be cured by looking out from the front seat of her own car, thank you.

So Sam helped his disgruntled mother into the back of his minivan, next to Molly. Charlotte sat on the other side of Molly, who fell asleep in her car seat within minutes of leaving the parking lot. Charlotte dozed off soon after, which left Karma and Sam sort of alone, silent, but not *not* speaking to each other. Karma had to admit that Sam had been kind to her since Kathleen died; he hadn't thrown up to her that she'd forgotten what would have been her last visit to Good Shepherd, and, more importantly, he hadn't tattled to Charlotte.

Karma stared out the window, watching the bare trees fly past. She was fourteen weeks pregnant. The magic Second Trimester. With Molly, she and Sam had celebrated every milestone; this time they were barely communicating. Just months ago, Sam had assured Dr. Weimer that he'd love this baby no matter what, but a few days ago he had mentioned the possibility of having the amniocentesis when the time was right. Just to be sure, he had said.

Dark voices whispered inside Karma's head. Any day now she would start feeling the baby move—how could he even think of not going through with this pregnancy? Of course, he hadn't actually said that, but she knew that's what he was thinking.

"You okay?" Sam was looking at her. "Is anything wrong? I mean besides everything?" He sounded genuinely concerned.

Karma smiled in spite of herself. *He's being nice. How does he change my rotten mood with just one pleasant comment?* But she already knew the answer. Sam was a good man, probably better than she deserved. He could have missed this train wreck of a funeral by staying home with Molly—a perfect excuse—but he had chosen to be here when Karma needed him. *I will be pleasant, too.*

"I was thinking how nice Denise was to get up and talk about Kathleen," said Karma.

"Yeah," said Sam. "It was good to know that people there really cared about her."

Karma couldn't believe it. *Bastard. Here we go again, just when I'm going out of my way to be nice to you.* "People *there*? What's that supposed to mean?"

"Just what I said. The people at Good Shepherd really cared about Kathleen."

"Like *I* didn't?" said Karma. "She was my sister. *I* cared about her. I was going to stand up and talk about her, but I didn't have a chance."

Sam took his eyes off the road to stare at Karma. "Is that what you heard me say?"

"Well, you implied it, didn't you? That they really cared about her and I didn't?"

"I'm pretty sure you are losing your mind," said Sam.

"Watch the road."

"I can watch the road *and* talk to you. I'm formulating a theory about you. In fact, I'm close to a breakthrough. So help me out and tell me what Denise said at the funeral."

Karma huffed impatiently. *Jerk.* "She said that Kathleen was aware of it when people talked to her and touched her. There's a cop. Slow down."

"And how did that make you feel?" asked Sam.

Who the hell does Sam think he is, Dr. Phil? She glanced into the back seat to make sure Molly, Charlotte, and Sylvia were still asleep. "It made me feel like crap," she hissed. "Like I should have been there more often. Happy?"

Instead of answering, Sam checked his mirrors, flipped on the hazard lights, and pulled off the highway onto the gravelly shoulder. Karma held her breath. *What the hell is he doing? I am*

NOT getting out of this car. If he thinks he's leaving me by the side of the road he'd better think again.

The van wheels spit gravel and rolled to a stop, and Sam turned to face her, but to her surprise, he didn't look angry. He was smiling, his expression triumphant. "I just figured it out," he said. "I know what the hell is wrong with you."

\

CHAPTER 33: THE UGLY TRUTH

"Do tell," said Karma as the car was buffeted by the wind coming off the passing trucks. "But hurry up, before we get crushed by a semi."

"Your problem is that you have become completely self-absorbed. You see everything through your own self-interest; even your guilt is self-centered." Karma opened her mouth, but Sam held his hand up to silence her. "What Denise said had nothing to do with you. She saw Kathleen as a real person and cared about her. That's a good thing, especially in a nursing home, but you turned it into something bad about you. It wasn't about you; it was about Kathleen. Do you see that?"

The draft from a piggyback trailer shook the minivan like a Matchbox car. God's own exclamation point. Even He was ganging up on Karma. "Can we get back on the road?" she snapped. "You're gonna get us killed."

"We're fine," said Sam. "You need to think about what I said."

"I agree," said a prickly voice from the back seat. Karma flipped down the make-up mirror. Her mother was awake and scowling.

"I haven't said a word about all this," said Charlotte. "But I'm not stupid and I'm not blind. I've seen what's going on. You'd better straighten up, young lady, or you're going to lose your husband and your family."

"Yeah, well, you'd know about that," said Karma.

"Don't sass me," said her mother. "This is about you and the way you've been behaving."

"Stop talking to me like I'm a six-year-old," said Karma, sounding very much like a six-year-old.

"Notice that *I'm* not mixing in," called Sylvia from the rear of the van. "I'm not even listening."

"I know you're not six, Karmella," said Charlotte. "You're a grown woman who's been acting like a teenager, running around and getting into trouble with the police. It's ridiculous." She checked Molly's sleeping form. "Did you spend one minute thinking about what all this would do to your daughter, or were you too busy sticking your nose into your neighbors' business?"

Karma stared at her mother's reflection in the mirror. How did she have the nerve? She'd driven Karma's father out of the house and ruined Karma's life by being cold and demanding and critical, she'd abandoned Kathleen in a nursing home, and now she was going to tell Karma how to be a good wife and mother? *What a joke.*

"I was trying to help people," said Karma. "You're the one who never thought about anybody but yourself. You never thought about what ruining your marriage would do to me, you never thought about whether I needed a father, you never thought about anybody but yourself. You couldn't even be bothered to take care of Kathleen; you put her in a nursing home, then you left me to take care of her while you ran off to Florida."

The look on Charlotte's face was murderous, but she was silent for a long time before she finally began to speak. "I promised your father all those years ago that I wouldn't talk about our marriage or bad-mouth him in front of you," she said, "but I can see that I should have been honest, because you took my not talking as some kind of admission of guilt. I've always known you thought I was the one who wrecked my marriage, and

I accepted that, but I thought you'd figure things out eventually. Looks like I over-estimated you."

A chill ran through Karma. *What was she talking about?* "Figure what things out?" she said. "You made Dad miserable and he left. What's to figure out?"

Charlotte shook her head. "How can you be as smart as you are and yet be so stupid?" She turned her eyes to Sam. "It's no wonder she gets in so much trouble—she sees one side of a story and thinks she understands the whole thing."

Sam nodded. "It's easier to judge everything and everybody if you don't have to admit they might have a valid point of view."

"I do not do that," said Karma.

"You most certainly do," said Charlotte. "You've been judging me for thirty years, based on what? Did you ever talk to me? Did you ever ask me what happened? Did you ever ask me why I put Kathleen in Good Shepherd? Did you ever ask me how it felt to be left by your father?"

"*Left?* You weren't *left*, you kicked him out."

Charlotte took a deep breath and studied her daughter's reflection. Those eyes hadn't changed much since she was a little girl. Some wrinkles in the outer corners, and no more sparkly pink plastic eyeglasses, but still just as hurt and accusing as they had been when she was nine years old, when Charlotte had agreed to keep Ed's halo untarnished in exchange for a quick divorce, the deed to the house, and uncontested custody of Karma and Kathleen. "You saw everything, but you didn't understand any of it. You didn't understand what you were seeing," she said quietly.

Karma opened her mouth to retort, but there was something about the sadness and vulnerability in her mother's voice that stopped her. *What didn't I understand?* She had thought about

304

her parent's divorce a thousand times, a million times. *What did I miss?*

"Oh, shit," said Sam. He was looking in the rear view mirror. Karma turned around to see what the problem was. Coming up behind them on the shoulder, red and blue lights flashing, was a police car. Probably the one they'd passed a minute ago. *I told him to slow down. He never listens. That's what's wrong with him.* The cruiser stopped behind them and the officer came out, hand on his holster. He walked up to the minivan and looked suspiciously at Sam, hand still on his weapon.

"Is there a problem, folks?"

"No, Officer," said Sam, "no problem at all."

"It's not safe to pull off here, sir. You should wait for a rest area if at all possible." He peered into the backseat.

"Sorry, Officer," said Sam. "We'll get moving."

But the cop was staring at him. Then he looked at Karma again. He stared at her for a long moment. Then a huge smile broke across his face. "It's you. The Killer Soccer Mom."

"I didn't kill anybody," said Karma.

"They all say that," said the cop with a wink at Sam.

Molly yawned and rubbed her eyes. "We get a ticket?"

"Not yet," said Sam with an ingratiating smile for the cop.

The officer peered into the backseat and winked at Molly. "No, little lady, no ticket. I think your daddy has enough problems."

"You have no idea," said Sam.

"Are you married," asked Sylvia. "You're so good-looking."

"Somebody shoot me," grumbled Karma.

"I bet you have a few neighbors who would be happy to shoot you," said Charlotte.

"Notice I'm not saying a word about that," called Sylvia.

"Hey, did you get to meet anybody famous?" the cop asked Sam. "Like Oprah or Larry King or anybody?"

305

"Well, Geraldo chased me through the parking garage at work. Does that count?"

"Oh yeah," said the cop. "I think I saw that." He threw a stern look at Karma. "You sure have caused a lot of trouble."

"Could you go harass some speeders?" snapped Karma. "We were trying to have a discussion here."

The cop regarded Sam sympathetically. "The side of a busy highway isn't the place for it. But I'm not gonna give you a ticket. Just be careful getting back on the road." He reached and shook Sam's hand. "Good luck," he said, with a sympathetic nod toward Karma. "Looks like you need it."

Sam waited until the cop got back into his car, then turned on his turn signal and eased the minivan back onto the highway. The cop followed for a quarter-mile or so, then sped up and passed Sam on the left, smiling and waving as he flew by.

"Nice guy," said Sam.

"Big jerk," said Karma. "Why was he so worried about *you*? I'm the one who might go to jail."

"You're doing it again," said Sam. "Thinking about yourself." Karma huffed and sat back in her seat.

"Mommy going to jail?" squeaked Molly.

"No, sweetie," said Karma, "Mommy's not going to jail."

"But you said."

"Mommy was kidding." Karma twisted around so she could look directly at her daughter. Charlotte and Sylvia were stroking Molly's hair and patting her little hand, respectively, trying to comfort her. Charlotte looked up at Karma with deep parental disappointment. Nothing new there. "So what was it you were going to tell me?" asked Karma. "What didn't I figure out?"

Charlotte pursed her lips and glanced at Molly, then took a moment to choose her words carefully. "Let's just say that I had reasons to act the way you thought I was acting during my marriage. Your father wasn't the saint you thought he was.

In fact, he liked to make *new friends* while we were married," said Charlotte, left eyebrow up to add significance to her words. "I met one of them one afternoon in my own house. When I wasn't expecting company."

Karma turned around in her seat and gaped at her mother. "What? You're absolutely sure?"

One of Charlotte's eyebrows crawled so high up her forehead, it was completely hidden behind her wispy silver bangs. "I don't think she was there to read the gas meter. At least she wasn't dressed for it."

A cold shudder ran through Karma's body. *Was that really true? Would my dad do such a thing? I'd kill Sam if he did that to me. I'd kill him and the woman and bury them both in the backyard.* Karma turned back around in her seat, staring at the road ahead and trying to gather her thoughts. *She's probably just making the whole thing up as an excuse for being such an old bag all these years.*

Yet somehow she knew that it was true. It explained everything about Charlotte's attitude toward Ed. And she had seen funny, sociable, life-of-the-party Ed flirting with younger women. Why hadn't she put it together? Only one thing could make it worse. "Did I know her? Was it Louise? No, wait. Darleen?"

"Darleen came before Louise, but this wasn't one of the ones he married," said Charlotte. "But the same type. *Young.*" Charlotte aimed that last bit at Sylvia, who wasn't even pretending not to listen anymore.

"You never said anything," said Karma, her voice subdued.

Charlotte's voice was equally restrained. "I promised him I wouldn't. I always assumed you'd figure it out."

"I can't believe you never told me."

"It wasn't your problem. In my day we didn't drag our children into our personal problems."

307

That bit was aimed at Karma, and a plethora of retorts bubbled up, but she didn't say any of them. What do you say when you find out your angry, controlling, hyper-critical, angry, impossible-to-please, angry, controlling mom had reason to be so pissed off all your life? *You keep your mouth shut.*

Sam's mother reached across Molly's car seat and gave Charlotte a sympathetic pat on the arm. "You poor thing. What he put you through. Did you notice how he was flirting with me all through lunch? Disgraceful."

CHAPTER 34: TROPICAL DEPRESSION

In the privacy of her own head, Karma made one of those lists where you put all the positives about your life on one side of a sheet of paper, and all the negatives on the other:

POSITIVES
- I'm still pregnant
- I'm still married
- I'm not in prison

NEGATIVES
- My sister is dead
- My neighbors hate me
- The entire country hates me
- I'm about to be indicted for murder
- My husband is barely speaking to me
- My daughter is wetting her bed again
- My father is a lying, cheating sonofabitch bastard
- My mother was cheated on, so I have to be nice to her

It was not a reassuring list. But just when it looked like there was no hope left in the world, Brian entered the picture. He became a beacon of hope, a lifeline Karma could cling to, the promise of better days to come. When she heard his name mentioned on television, Karma's pulse would quicken and a thrill would race through her body. She prayed for Brian's strength and long life as she'd never prayed for anything before.

He was the first thing she thought about in the morning, and the last thing she thought about at night. Brian would save her. *He had to.*

And so he did. In a near-record three days, Karma's prayers were answered. Tropical Depression Three officially became Hurricane Brian, a legitimate news story that drew the media away from Bedford Commons as effectively as a big pile of poop attracts flies from a small pile of poop.

The news trucks and rental cars fled Bedford Commons for South Florida, and Karma rejoiced. She was off God's Top Ten Target List; He was going after the trailer parks again. Of course, she tried to think helpful and positive thoughts about the inhabitants of Cuba, Louisiana, and Florida, so as not to tempt The Almighty to stomp on her again, but that wasn't easy; it would take devastating hurricane damage to keep the reporters from returning to Indiana. She tried to pray for devastating hurricane damage that would not kill anyone, and would be fully covered by insurance.

"Want to go for a walk?"

Karma was startled to see Sam looking down at her, holding their new baby monitor receiver. Karma had finally told Sam why he couldn't find the old transmitter anywhere in the house and had purchased another system. How long had it been since they'd taken one of their evening walks? It felt like years.

"That sounds nice," said Karma, rising from the sofa. She felt a tingle, like a coed being asked on a first date by a cute guy. "Is Molly asleep?" *Maybe Sam isn't going to file for divorce. Maybe he'll at least visit me in prison.* "I just have to put on my shoes and use the bathroom. Give me a second."

Isn't this funny—I'm actually excited to get some exercise. Maybe Hurricane Brian really was the omen of good luck that Karma had been hoping for. She practically skipped to the bathroom. Sitting there, playing with her phone, she forgot herself for a moment and started to type a text to tell Kim that Sam was being really nice. She deleted it.

Karma was reaching for the toilet paper when she felt a sudden, painful sensation, like a stab to her belly. She froze, trying not to cry out. A second stabbing pain forced a moan out of her, but she had to stand up, had to yell for help, had to at least pull up her pants. She got herself to a standing position, then bent over with another spasm of pain, Karma looked behind her into the toilet bowl. It was full of blood.

Sam and Molly were downstairs in the hospital cafeteria eating ice cream. Karma was in her room on the fourth floor, lying in bed, eyes closed, but not asleep. She heard a faint whisper on the other side of the privacy curtain, so soft she couldn't quite make out the words.

"Is somebody there?"

"I asked if you were asleep," said a tiny voice. "Are you asleep?"

Karma smiled. "No, Jeanette. C'mon in."

Jeanette's head poked out from between the panels. "I didn't wake you, did I? You're sure? I came as soon as I heard."

Karma smiled. "I'm sure. You can come in."

Jeanette pulled the curtain carefully shut behind her. She stood for a moment and looked down at Karma, Her big soft eyes already blinking back tears. An enormous diaper bag was slung over her shoulder, but Karma was grateful to see that she hadn't brought her kids. "So it's over? For sure?"

Karma nodded. She'd lost count of the number of doctors and nurses and physician's assistants and techs who had poked and prodded and examined and checked vitals. None of it had made a damn bit of difference. "Yeah, it's done. There was nothing they could do." Karma's voice cracked.

Jeanette pulled out a few tissues from the box on the bedside table for herself, then handed Karma the tissue. "You're gonna try again, though, right? I mean, you're not gonna give up."

"JESUS CHRIST, JEANETTE."

The curtain flung back and Bianca strode up to the bed, stiletto heels clicking on the tile floor. "Can you give her twenty minutes to get over this before you tell her to get knocked up again? You're like Tony's mother; I was still dilated after Ginny, and she's askin' me when I'm gonna give her a grandson."

"Bianca," sniffed Jeanette, "I don't think it's nice to remind Karma that you've had two babies when she just lost one."

"I think she knows I had two babies. The little one's three freakin' years old, for Christ's sake. They've met."

"It's still not nice to remind poor Karma about it. She can't help it that she has (*Jeanette dropped her voice to a whisper*) fertility issues."

"Well, I'm not the one upsetting her. You're the one telling her to get pregnant again. That could take *years*."

The privacy curtain swung back again.

"Good gracious, you two, this is a hospital. I can hear you all the way down the hall." Sue Ellen was holding a large potted plant with a big white bow around it. "She's supposed to be gettin' some rest. And next time, one of you call me so we can drive together. I went to the wrong hospital."

Next time?

"Can I use that cup?" asked Sue Ellen. "This poor thing needs water." She did a quick survey of the room. "Y'all didn't even bring flowers?"

"I brought something better than flowers, thank you very much," said Bianca. "Shut the door." She opened her Gucci bag and pulled out a metal flask.

"Oh, my God, you're gonna kill her," said Sue Ellen. "She's on some kind of intravenous stuff."

"That's just morphine," said Bianca. "They give drunks morphine when they get hurt, don't they? So she'll get a little drunk and have a little morphine. It'll make her feel better. Hell, I wish I had some myself."

"And I brought the cinnamon rolls," said Jeanette, reaching into her diaper bag. She pulled out a Tupperware container. "They're barely warm, I'm afraid, but still, you can't get *these* in the hospital cafeteria."

Maybe it was the morphine, but Karma was suddenly overcome with happiness. Tears came as she listened and watched her friends bicker and arrange chairs around her bed and swipe paper towels from the bathroom to use as plates for the cinnamon rolls. After feeling so alone, this was better than any drug. Playgroup had all but fallen apart since camera crews had made it impossible to get together without ending up on the news, but her best friends were here now, when she needed them, and they still loved her. Except Kim.

Although Karma was planning on never speaking to Kim again, nothing was the same without her. Karma had reached for the phone a dozen times before remembering that they weren't friends anymore. She couldn't share her anger and frustration, and now her pain, with the one person who had always been able to make her laugh.

Bianca cursed herself for forgetting shot glasses, but she was not to be thwarted. She found a stack of plastic pill cups in a cabinet and poured a tiny round of peach brandy. Standing at the foot of Karma's bed, she cleared her throat. "I know this whole thing is awful, but I think we should drink a toast to Karma and the baby. I'm a good Catholic and all, but I think this baby will come back to you." Bianca swallowed hard and raised her cup. "He's just waiting in line again for *when you're ready* (she shot a hard glance at Jeanette) to try again. Like reincarnation. Holy crap, maybe I shoulda been a freakin' Buddhist."

They laughed and they drank. The pill cups didn't hold more than a tablespoon, but they were refillable. The brandy went down like sweet fire, and warmth spread through Karma's entire body. Sue Ellen sniffed and pulled a tissue from the box that Karma was still holding.

"I wasn't gonna cry, but I just can't help it," she said. "You didn't even drink coffee; it's just not fair. Do you know if it was a boy or a girl? Could they tell? Or maybe you don't want to talk about it. I'm sorry." She looked stricken.

"A boy," said Karma.

"Any word from the District Attorney?" asked Bianca, taking her seat again. "Maybe they'll hear about this and drop it."

Karma shrugged.

"They don't really have proof that you did anything, do they?" asked Bianca. "I mean just because Kim opened her big pie-hole doesn't mean they can prove anything. It's hearsay or some shit like that. I still can't believe the little snitch did that to you. *Dai nemici mi guardo io, dagli amici mi guardi iddio."* At Karma's questioning look, she translated. "I can protect myself from my enemies; may God protect me from my friends."

Jeanette passed around the cinnamon rolls and they ate in silence. Even Sue Ellen took a big bite, frosting and all. Karma had a feeling they were all thinking the same thing she was. There was a soccer mom missing, and her absence left a gap you could drive a minivan through. Bianca refilled everyone's plastic cup and drained the last few drops of brandy directly from the flask. "So, you two ever gonna make up?"

"I thought you just called her a snitch?" said Karma. "Anyway, it's not up to me."

"It sure as hell is," said Bianca. "Kim screwed up, but I happen to know she thinks it's her fault you lost the baby. She says you missed a doctor's appointment after Jack died, and if *she* had been there to help you, Jack maybe wouldn't have died and you wouldn't be going through all this, and having all the stress, and you'd still be pregnant. She feels like shit about it."

Jeanette gaped at her. "I'm the one who took her place that day. Does she thinks all this is *my* fault?"

"No," said Karma. "She thinks everything's about *her*. She's the most self-centered person I've ever met. Why do I have to worry about *her* feelings? I just lost my son."

Well, so much for self-control.

There was not enough brandy, morphine, nor tissues to stop the tears this time. It started with Karma and spread quickly, and soon all four women were so busy sniffing and dripping tears that they didn't even notice Sam walk in, take a horrified look at the scene, and steer a confused Molly back down to the cafeteria for cookies to go with her ice cream.

"It's nobody's fault," hiccupped Karma, "but mine. I was so busy with Jack Lawrence, I didn't think about my own baby. I was supposed to avoid stress and watch my diet, and take my pills and go in for blood tests. I forgot my last appointment. All I was thinking about was stopping Jack Lawrence from beating his stupid wife, who I didn't even like. I still don't. It was like I was bored or something. Like I needed something to keep me busy. Like being pregnant wasn't enough." She slumped back into her pillows. "Well, I sure took care of that."

Bianca and Sue Ellen looked at each other with pained expressions, but Jeanette let out a wail, leapt up and grabbed Karma in a hug. She almost knocked over the rolling stand that contained the morphine pump, but Bianca caught it in time.

"Don't say that," cried Jeanette. "This is not your fault. Like Sue Ellen said, you haven't even had a cup of coffee since you found out you were pregnant."

"*Il mio Dio*, so what if you missed a freakin' doctor's appointment?" said Bianca. "You didn't cause this; shit like this just happens. So you had a little stress; we all have stress."

"We don't all kill our neighbors," sniffed Karma.

"It was an accident," said Jeanette. "He hit his head."

"We don't all get chased around the neighborhood by camera crews."

"Exercise," said Sue Ellen. "I ran every morning when I was pregnant so I wouldn't gain weight."

"It's not like the doctor put you on bed rest," said Bianca.

"Sam thinks it's my fault. He'll never forgive me."

"Yes, he will," said Bianca. "He's a good man and he loves you. Your problem is you have to forgive yourself."

Karma disengaged herself from Jeanette. "It's not just about Jack Lawrence," she said. "There's more."

Bianca looked suspicious. "Oh my Jesus. Did you snuff somebody else?"

Karma gazed up at the ceiling and didn't answer. Could she go through with this? Just when her friends had come back to her, she was going to drive them away again.

Bianca crossed herself. "*Porca vacca,*" she said. "What the hell else did you do?"

"It's not that," said Karma. "It's something else I feel bad about. Something I never told you guys." She took a deep breath before speaking. "I have a sister. *Had* a sister. A twin."

"Another one, or the one in a nursing home since she was a baby because she was brain damaged at birth?" asked Sue Ellen. "The one that just died?"

Karma gaped at her.

"You shouldn't trust family secrets with your family," said Bianca.

"Molly." Karma shook her head. *I should've known.*

"You wouldn't tell us where you went every month, so I finally asked her," shrugged Bianca. "Little stoolie sang like a canary, but she didn't say you killed her. Holy shit, woman."

Karma scowled at her. "I didn't exactly. I was supposed to visit her, and I did, every month, but this month I was so wrapped up in my own problems that I forgot all about it. I didn't even think about her. She was my sister, my *twin sister*. I left her alone there and she thought I didn't care about her anymore." Karma was sobbing again. "I killed Jack Lawrence and I left my sister alone, and now she's dead. I'm being punished."

Bianca held up a blood red polished nail. "Okay, back up the truck. Do you think God killed your sister because you skipped a visit or because you accidentally killed Jack Lawrence? Which is it? Neither one makes any fucking sense, just so you know."

Karma didn't answer. She looked out the window at the parking lot below. An ambulance with flashing lights was pulling around the building. *Since when did things have to make sense? How had it make sense to Charlotte that her umbilical cord had strangled her own child? How did it made sense that her own husband would turn on her after that and bring another woman into their bed? And how did it made sense that after trying so hard to do something as simple as have a baby, something women do squatting in a damn field, my son is dead before he even had a chance to be born.*

"Maybe it doesn't make sense to you," she said, "but I feel like it's because of me. I spent my entire childhood visiting Kathleen and listening to my parents argue about her. I resented it. I resented her. Every birthday, every Hanukkah, every *everything* was about her."

Jeanette looked stricken. "So that's why you never told us about her?"

"Not exactly. I didn't want to talk about her."

There was a long silence, the kind that somebody usually ends by saying something shallow, or changing the subject, or making a joke, but this time, nobody cooperated.

317

"It sure has been a shitty week," said Karma. "But c'mon, Jeanette. You can't think I blame you."

"I'm just so sad about what Bianca said before, about forgiving yourself," hiccupped Jeanette. She sat up a little taller in her padded hospital chair. "I feel bad about something, too. Something I did a long time ago, that I've never told you guys, and I've never forgiven myself." Ignoring the wary looks exchanged among her friends, she took a long, deep breath. "I'm not thirty-one, like I told you all. I'm only twenty-three."

Mouths dropped open. Karma wondered if her morphine drip was set too high. "Who pretends to be *older* than they are?"

"At least until you're old enough to buy smokes and booze," clarified Bianca.

Jeanette's cheeks were blotchy and pink. "I didn't want you guys to do the math and figure out that I was sixteen when I got pregnant with Little Jeffrey." That raised several sets of eyebrows. Jeanette took a breath, gathering courage for the rest of the confession, which came out in one long run-on declaration of guilt. "I wasn't married, I never did finish high school, I used to drink a lot on the weekends and party and stuff, and I got pregnant and quit school, I got my GED, and I lied to you all about going to college. I never went." All this came out in a gush, a busted pipe of guilt and confession.

"Holy shit," said Bianca. "And here I've been so jealous of your skin this whole time. For thirty-one, you looked fabulous; for twenty-three, you're just okay. So maybe I actually like you better now."

"Wait," asked Sue Ellen. "How old is Little Jeffrey?"

"Five."

"If you got pregnant at sixteen, you can't be twenty-three."

"I'm almost twenty-three. Give me a break," said Jeanette.

318

Karma had a sudden flashback to the afternoon she'd spent at Jeanette's guarding Luann Lawrence, and the photo album she'd found. "So the baby in your wedding picture?"

"That's—wait a minute." Jeanette recoiled. How did you see that picture?"

"It was a drawer, not a locked safe," said Karma.

"It wasn't even mounted in the album," said Jeanette. "I keep that picture in an envelope. You were snooping."

"You were sleeping and I was trying to keep busy. It was that day we thought Jack might come over and try to kill Luann. He never showed up, so I got bored. Sorry."

Jeanette signed. "Oh, I suppose it doesn't matter now. That's why my momma has that look on her face like she's sucking on lemons. I thought she was gonna kill me when I asked the photographer to take that picture. I should have thrown it away, but I just couldn't. I don't have that many pictures of Little Jeffrey where he's not sticking his tongue out or screaming or trying to bite somebody."

"Why keep it such a secret?" asked Karma. "You're not the first woman to have a baby before she's married."

"First in *my* family," said Jeanette bitterly. "Well, my cousin Jimmy got his girlfriend pregnant, but they got married when she was seven months along, so, you know, that was *okay*." She slumped down in the hospital chair and stuffed the last bite of her cinnamon roll into her mouth. "Sometimes I think Little Jeffrey's the way he is because of how upset I was, and ashamed and all, the whole time I was pregnant with him. Like he absorbed all that negative emotion."

Karma wondered if it was the weekend beers he'd absorbed, but she didn't say so.

"Jesus Christ, Jeanette," said Bianca. "You just need to kick his ass once in a while," she said. "He'll straighten out. My brothers were all hell-raisers, but my mother didn't just *talk*; she

319

knew how to get their attention. *With the back of her hand.*" She pantomimed a sharp rap across the mouth. "Now they're good boys working in the family business."

Karma saw the opening. She couldn't help herself. "What *is* the family business?"

"Dry cleaning," said Bianca. "I've told you that."

"Yeah, you did," said Karma. "Dry cleaning?"

At the skeptical looks directed at her, Bianca scowled. "I know you all think my family's in the mob, but my father really is a dry cleaner."

"Seriously?" Karma couldn't hide her disappointment. "Doesn't your family have a lot of money?"

"He's a really good dry cleaner."

"Maybe he launders money."

"Funny," said Bianca, in a voice that made it clear she was not even slightly amused. "I freakin' *love* mafia humor. I'm tellin' you, he's just a dry cleaner."

"You are Italian, though, right?" asked Karma. "If you're secretly Norwegian or something, I'm going to be pissed."

"Italian," said Bianca. "Just not a Soprano. Sorry to disappoint."

Sue Ellen cleared her throat and stood up to address the group. "Well, I guess it's my turn," she said, giving her golden tresses a dramatic toss. "I'm really embarrassed about this, but everybody's being honest, so I'm going to be honest, too."

Karma exchanged a look with Bianca. *This better be more interesting than the brand of peroxide she's been using.*

Sue Ellen swallowed self-consciously and continued in her sweet southern drawl. "I've been hiding something, too. A big lie. But I'm just gonna confess now because I've been feeling guilty, too. I want us all to be friends, and I should have trusted y'all and not tried to fool you." She had everyone's attention now. The ones on chairs were on the edge of their seats; the one in the bed sat up straighter. Twisting her paper towel in her nervous hands, Sue Ellen couldn't seem to find the right words.

"You can tell us anything," said Jeanette. "Is it about Daniel? Is he not Don's son? Did you cheat on him?"

Sue Ellen's eyes grew wide. "Nothing like *that*. I'm talking about back at my first playgroup. I told you all that I hired a decorator to do my house. That was a lie. And I didn't have a homosexual man hang my pictures. There was a homosexual decorator that I *wanted* to hire, but Don wouldn't let me spend the money. So I did all the decorating myself. I just wanted to impress you all." She hung her head. "I'm sorry."

Karma, Bianca, and Jeanette looked at each other, and at Sue Ellen.

"My God, Sue Ellen," said Karma. "That has to be the stupidest confession I've ever heard in my life."

"No shit," said Bianca.

"You just confessed to having good taste," said Jeanette. "And people call *me* a dumb blonde."

CHAPTER 35:   CRIME AND PUNISHMENT

Unfortunately, when Hurricane Brian drew the spotlight of media coverage away from Bedford Commons, the Hamilton County prosecutor came out of hiding. She hadn't appreciated having a TV personality, even Greta Van Susteren, whom she admired, telling her whom to charge and with what crime, but she couldn't ignore the situation either. Barbara Kim Wallace's interview had placed two local women at the scene of the crime or accident or whatever-it-was. Madam Prosecutor had called the sheriff at home that night and asked him to re-question all three women and continue his investigation. The next morning she had told the reporters camped outside her office that 1) Jack Lawrence's suspicious death was still under investigation; 2) specific charges were still being considered; and 3) no further statements would be made at this time.

Then she had called her deputy prosecutor into her office, shut the door, and told him that before she went after a bunch of stay-at-home mothers of young children, the evidence against them had better be airtight, if not better. He understood what she meant. He also understood that his boss's motives weren't completely judicial. Not only was she up for reelection next year, but she had her eye on the governor's mansion. The party leadership had never taken her seriously, which she attributed to her gender, but this case could be her ticket to the Big Show. National media attention would either make her a contender or a punch line. She would tread carefully. That was fine with her assistant, because he was ready to run for her office if she got the nod to run for governor. A boost in his public profile—a positive boost—was the key.

But all that changed after Hurricane Brian drew off the hounds, and the Story of the Year was suddenly yesterday's news. While reporters stood on rain-pounded balconies and risked their lives and hair, a call came in on Madam Prosecutor's private cell phone. The caller was unknown to the general public, but infamous within the circles in which political insiders dwelled. "Button this up now," he said in his cartoonish gravelly voice. "If you lose this case and a bunch of killer housewives go free, you look stupid. If you win and the news is full of babies crying for their mommies who you put in jail because they killed a lousy, good-for-nothing wife beater, you look even worse. You were stupid to pursue this, but since you did, finish it. Now."

Sam was visiting Karma in the hospital when his lawyer called to warn him about a rumor he'd just heard at the courthouse.

"I know this looks bad, Sam, but as soon as they file, I'm going to move for a continuance, then file a motion with the court to have the whole thing dismissed."

"Will that work?" Sam had worded his question carefully. He wasn't alone with Karma in this damn hospital room, and he didn't want to provide information to the constant stream of nurses and aides and techs who kept coming in to catch a glimpse of Karma and, Sam suspected, listen to their conversations. They'd taken selfies with her and posted them on social media until Sam complained. Two guys were in the room right now, very slowly changing light bulbs. "Preventive maintenance," they'd claimed.

"No, it won't work," said the lawyer, "but we want to drag things out as much as possible. If they want to move fast, we slow 'em down. If they see that we're going to embarrass them in

323

public, they might deal. Damn hurricane won't last forever. Karma's miscarriage—sorry for your loss—works in our favor. Rumor has it the prosecutor wants to run for higher office, which probably means lieutenant governor, and sending a woman to jail who's just lost a baby—I'm really sorry, you know—doesn't look good to voters. I can get the continuance at least, due to Karma's condition. Push the docs to keep her in the hospital for another day or two, sit tight, and for God's sake, don't talk to any journalists. Don't talk to anybody."

Sam needed time to think. The prosecutor was preparing to file charges of involuntary manslaughter against Karma and Jeanette, and obstruction of justice charges against Karma, Jeanette, Sue Ellen, Bianca, and Kim. Their lawyer couldn't stop them, but he was going to try slowing them down at least, hoping they would plead down to something lesser. No guarantees. Not exactly news to celebrate. He tucked his cell phone back in his pocket and tried to think of the right way to relay this news to Karma, assuming the two guys with the lightbulbs ever left the room. But before he could think of a good opening sentence, a peppy shave-and-a-haircut knock sounded on the door and Karma's father poked his head in.

"Hey, Princess," said Ed. "Surprise!"

Karma was surprised. Her father wasn't the type to drop everything and rush to someone's bedside. She accepted his hug and kiss and watched him set his flowers on the bedside table, but her mind was racing. *Did you really cheat on my mother in our own house? Where was I? Did you think about Kathleen lying in the next room? I wish I still had my morphine pump.*

Karma had been angry with her father since that conversation with her mother, but now he was standing right here with that big grin on his face. He looked like the beloved father she'd never had enough time with and couldn't wait to see each week. It was a struggle to keep the mad on.

"Hi, Dad," she said. She looked up at the two techs, still conferring over the light bulb. "Sorry, guys, could you finish up? If anything exciting happens between me and my dad, I'll let you know. I'll take notes." They managed to actually change the bulb and leave with their tools and ladder fairly quickly. Sam took a seat as far from Ed and Karma as he could, considering the size of the room. They needed room to talk.

"I came as soon as I could. Your mother called and told me what happened. You know how sorry I am, right?"

"Mom called you?"

"Of course."

"I didn't think you two talked anymore."

"We talk about *you*," said Ed. "We're still your parents, you know. I said I'd come for both of us and see how you were doing."

Karma stared down at her hands.

"So? I came all this way and you're not happy to see me?"

"I'm happy. Sure. Of course. No, I'm not. I might as well get this over with. After the funeral, Mom and I talked about a few things. Like your divorce. Stuff I didn't know about. *Bad stuff*." Karma forced herself to look up at her father, who seemed to sag before her eyes. He sat down heavily in one of the chairs still ringing Karma's bed. Without his usual cocky smile, he looked his age.

"Okay, let me have it," he said. "I should have been a better father, I should have called more often, I should have handled the divorce better. Give it to me good. What do the kids say these days? Bring it?"

"Well, here's a place to start," said Karma, the anger in her voice surprising even her. "You shouldn't have cheated on my mother."

"That's what she told you? That I cheated on her?"

"You didn't?"

325

"No, I did, I did," said Ed with a shrug, "technically, but our marriage was already over. We were planning to split up as soon as we found the right place for Kathleen. Figures your mother would leave that part out."

Karma scowled. That wasn't the way Charlotte had told it, and it wasn't the way she remembered it. "Mom sent Kathleen away *because* you left. She couldn't handle taking care of her on her own after she had to go back to work. *Because you left.*"

Ed gave Karma a quizzical look. "That's not quite the way it happened, Princess. Kathleen was getting too big for your mother to lift and clean up after, and with my bad back, sure it was tough, but that's not why we took her to Good Shepherd. Don't you know that?"

The door opened and a smiling candy striper with an autograph book poked her head in. Seeing the look on Karma's face, she retreated without a word.

"Of course it was," said Karma. "Why else would you send her away like that? It was because you walked out on Mom and she had to go back to work."

"We sent your sister away because of you."

Karma's mouth fell open in disbelief. That's ridiculous. How was it my fault? Is there anything in the whole world that's not my fault?"

Ed turned to his son-in-law. "Fault? Did I say fault? Who said fault? I did not say fault."

Sam held up a hand. "I am Switzerland, Ed. I'm staying out of this one."

"You were angry all the time," said Ed, turning back to Karma. "You said nobody ever paid attention to you, and Kathleen was the only one we cared about. You don't remember any of this?"

Karma had a sudden shivering flash of recall, an image of herself, looking up at her mother and screaming about

326

something. Charlotte was crying. *I made my mother cry. Why can't I remember how I did that?*

Ed spoke gently, yet there was an edge in his voice. "You wouldn't invite your friends over because you didn't want them to see your sister. You got teased at school. You even got in a fight once and got hauled into the principal's office. You don't remember that either? He was a big guy, ex-army or something. Always reminded me of an SS colonel, but he swore he wasn't German. I asked him."

"Mr. O'Leary," said Karma softly. "He was Irish." *This is nuts. I remember that fight; I was hurt, but I wasn't in it. I didn't get into fights.* Karma could picture the two girls fighting, a shoe coming at her. "You've got that all messed up, Dad. I wasn't in that fight. Sarah, my best friend, told Mr. O'Leary it wasn't me. I remember that very clearly. I just got hit with somebody's shoe."

Ed shook his head, but he was smiling. "No, your little friend tried to lie for you to keep you out of trouble, but the janitor saw the whole thing. You were hitting the other girl with your shoe, but she got it away from you and gave you a whack on the head." Ed grinned. "Little *mouzik* got the worst of it, though. I was proud of you that day. You were sticking up for your sister."

Karma was dumbfounded. "I hit a girl with my shoe? Are you sure? That's not how I remember it."

"You wore corrective shoes—cost me a fortune—so of course I remember. Your mother was mad at you, but the other girl was making remarks about Kathleen, called her a retard or something, and you tried to beat her brains out. I didn't think you had it in you, but that day you were little Cassius Clay. The son I never had." Ed winked at her again, an enormous grin blooming on his face. "Your mother was mad at you for fighting, and with me for telling you how proud I was that you got in the fight and won. Ooowwweee, was she ever mad."

327

Karma gasped. It was all flooding back to her. "Michelle. Her name was Michelle. Oh my god."

"Coulda been," said Ed, "but we had to face facts. Kathleen wasn't gonna get better, and it was getting too hard on you, always having to put her needs ahead of yours. We had some big arguments about it, your mother and me, but she was right, your mother. We had to do something for you for a change."

"Sending Kathleen away was about me?"

"It was the right thing to do."

Karma lay back on the pillow. Her brain was a blender, spinning her thoughts so fast and mixing things so thoroughly she couldn't keep up. No, wrong metaphor. It was a centrifuge, spinning to separate out the confusion she'd lived with all her life without even realizing it. What do you do, she wondered, when you find out you weren't the person you thought you were, and nobody around you was who you thought *they* were. Like one of those talk shows where you think you're there for a makeover, but then you find out you were brought in to be told that you were adopted, or your sister is really your mother, or your father is really a woman.

"I think that's why your mother was so nutso about never missing a visit to Kathleen. Because it was her idea."

Karma rubbed her temples. "Why are there always two sides to everything? I spent thirty years being mad at Charlotte, a week being mad at you, and now I'm not supposed to be mad at anybody? Or maybe just myself. I can't believe you put Kathleen in an institution because of me. Shit."

"Since when do you curse so much? And don't call your mother 'Charlotte,'" said Ed. "It's disrespectful." He fingered the buttons on his brightly flowered Hawaiian shirt. "Like I said, it was the right thing to do. And maybe we should have done it sooner. All your mother's time was focused on your sister and you, but not so much on *you*, honest to God. Me, I wasn't even on the list." Ed looked over at Sam again. "I hope with all the *mishegas* going on at your house, this one's not doing the same thing to you."

Switzerland said nothing.

Ed stretched his hairy legs and rested his feet on the frame of Karma's hospital bed. He was glad he'd come to see his daughter, his grown-up Princess, and glad they'd actually talked about something more important than the weather. He could go home with a clear conscience. And maybe he and Roberta would come up more often now, and get to know Molly better. Maybe when the kid was a little older she'd come visit them. They had a good thing going down there, fruit trees in the yard, lots of sunshine. On Sundays he put on a tie and took Roberta—the sexiest wife in their group of friends—to the early bird buffet, but aside from that, it was casual all the way. They had fun. It was certainly a different life than he'd led with Karma's mother, who was always chasing after him with a lint brush and making him get his hair cut. The early bird diners would get such a kick out of Molly, too.

"Take some advice from an old man," he said to Sam. "Don't put up with too much crap; that was my mistake. I kept my mouth shut too long, and by the time I realized what was happening, we weren't even friends anymore. Strangers. Strangers who didn't like each other so much. So I found someone who *did* like me. Not a capital crime, I think."

"Mom made it sound like you found a lot of someones who liked you," said Karma.

Ed winked at Sam before turning back to his daughter. "I never said I wasn't likable. So, you can say what you want, but your mother was no picnic to live with. I thought you would have figured that out by now, a smart girl like you."

Karma looked sadly at her father. *That* part she *had* figured out. "If I were a smart girl, I would have stayed out of people's business and I wouldn't be about to be arrested. Maybe I'd still be pregnant."

Ed looked at his only living child for a long moment, then stood up, leaned in, and kissed her on the cheek. "If, if, if, Princess. *Az di bobe volt gehat beytsim volt zi geven mayn zeyde*," he said. "It's Yiddish. Know what it means?"

Karma shook her head.

"If Grandma had balls, she'd be Grandpa. Think about it. And now, if you'll excuse me, there's a pretty little nurse who I promised a nice lunch and a foot rub."

"WHAT?" Karma nearly levitated off the bed.

"Just kidding," said Ed with another wink. "Actually, I left Roberta in the gift shop. She's buying a little *tchotchke* for Molly. I'll send her up; I need a cigarette."

"It's a non-smoking hospital," said Karma.

"Not for long."

Karma watched Ed bounce out of the room. He sure knew how to make an exit. He always left her wanting more.

"Relationships aren't so simple," said Sam from his seat in the corner.

"*Nothing* is simple," said Karma. "Maybe prison will be simple. Three square meals a day, an hour of exercise, back in my cell by nine o'clock. It's starting to sound good to me."

"It gets better," said Sam. "Your mother says if you go to jail, she'll come live in the guest room and raise Molly until you get back, even if it takes *years*."

Karma raised her eyes to the ceiling, and the brand new florescent light bulb shining down at her. "Thanks. You just ruined prison for me."

\

CHAPTER 36:   UNLIKELY SAVIOR(S)

But prison would have to wait. Before her office had time to file charges, the county prosecutor was stymied by a force she had never expected: Luann Lawrence. The grieving widow, who had refused to talk to the media since her fateful appearance on *Call 6 for Help,* finally granted an interview. But instead of the nationals, who had sent everything from flowering calla lilies to sling back Ferragamo pumps, she chose to speak to the local guy, the handsome Channel 6 news anchor.

In an understated navy suit, she revealed that her late husband often refused to wear his bike helmet because he found it hot and uncomfortable. She somberly recalled urging him to be a better safety example to their children. She also said that he had mentioned helping plan an upcoming neighborhood block party. No, she didn't know where the meeting was going to take place, but yes, it could have been at the bike path in the early morning hours. He wouldn't have had time during the work day, and if there were women on the planning committee, he wouldn't have dared to invite them to the house, given his history of infidelity.

The county prosecutor was startled by this new development, though she tried to look smooth and gubernatorial when the local news crew showed up to get her reaction. "We want to get to the truth of this matter," she said, "no matter where it leads. We are proceeding with our investigation. We are *not* dropping our case against the so-called Soccer Moms at this point in time. We have a duty to the citizens of this county not to over-react, nor to underact. We are dedicated to the unvarnished truth."

Karma heard this along with the rest of central Indiana when it ran on the Eyewitness News at noon. Sam was due to check her out of the hospital at any minute, and a nurse had brought in her discharge paperwork.

"Sounds like good news for you," said the nurse, flipping off the television.

"I hope so," said Karma warily. Her mind was racing. *What the hell is Luann Lawrence up to? Why risk a perjury charge by telling that crazy nonsense to the prosecutor's office?*

But Luann stuck steadfastly to her crazy nonsense. She didn't have a motive to lie, after all, as she wasn't being charged with anything.

By the time Karma returned home from the hospital, word had spread about her miscarriage. To her great surprise, food began showing up at her door. Chicken and rice with Campbell's Cream of Chicken, pork chops with potatoes and Campbell's Cream of Mushroom, and tiny shrimp and vegetables with Campbell's Cream of God-Knows-What. Karma was grateful for the outpouring of sympathy, if not the actual food.

It seemed to mean that her neighbors had forgiven her for all the trouble she'd brought to Bedford Commons. Maybe they were afraid she really *was* innocent, and they didn't want to be the last to acknowledge it. Maybe they just felt guilty for all the hostility they'd shown her. And then there was her miscarriage. Nearly everybody who came to her door had her own depressing story of miscarriage, tubal pregnancy, infertility. and disappointment. How had the human race not died out long ago? *Maybe it was all that soup.*

Jeanette showed up at Karma's front door with a chicken and cheddar cheese soup casserole. She was practically in tears over Luann risking a perjury charge to get her dear friends out of trouble.

Something about it wasn't adding up for Karma, but it wasn't in her best interest to question Luann's story, nor her motivation to tell it. After all, it made Jack's death an accident caused by his own poor judgment. This was better than murder, especially if you're the alleged murderer.

Then it was the Soccer *Dads'* turn to come to the rescue of their wives. Jeff Jorganson confirmed that Jack had made a negative comment about his helmet that fateful morning, a detail which, in his grief and confusion, he had forgotten to mention to the police until Luann's interview reminded him. Likewise, when Detective Hunter went to Sam Kranski, he confirmed Luann's block party story, saying he'd suggested a neighborhood get-together to his wife before the tragedy, even suggesting the menu (roasted turkey), but had changed these plans and arranged a simpler "Boys' Night Out" after Jack's death. No, it wasn't a conspiratorial meeting to devise an alibi for their wives; it was a natural consequence of their grief.

"A neighborhood block party seemed like the wrong thing to do after Jack died," said Sam, "but we guys wanted to drink a beer in Jack's honor. It was probably stupid to call it 'Boys' Night Out,' but we wanted it to be all guys, you know? We weren't trying to be disrespectful, it was just a way of making sure it was just us guys."

The rest of the *guys* were interviewed separately, and they confirmed the date and location of Boys' Night Out. Sure enough, records from a pizza restaurant showed delivery of three large pizzas and five orders of breadsticks to Jeff's house on the night in question. A local supermarket confirmed the purchase of two cases of beer. Case closed?

It was a crisp fall Saturday, and Karma was slouching in a kitchen chair in a baggy pair of sweatpants and a tee shirt, hair unwashed, playing with her bowl of soggy cornflakes and thinking about the meaning of life. Well, not the meaning of *all* life, just *her* life. Sam had left the house early that morning, before Karma was even out of bed. She supposed he was buying hardware or something, maybe riding his bike with Jeff. Maybe he'd run off with a waitress from Denny's. Karma didn't give a damn.

Being hounded by the national media had been terrible, but it had kept Karma busy, and now that they were all gone, there was nothing to take her mind off the reality that she had lost her baby and her sister, who had been institutionalized because Karma had been a spoiled brat. She had also played a major role in the death of a husband and father of three, her own father had cheated on her mother because her mother was a raving bitch, and she herself was turning out to be just as crappy a wife as her mother had been. She was still be facing criminal charges, too, and her former best friend whom she never wanted to speak to again hadn't even called to see how she was doing. Not that she wanted to talk to Kim. Ever. She absolutely didn't.

I need a cigarette. I wish I smoked.

She couldn't talk about any of this with Sam; he would accuse her of being self-centered again, and then she'd have to kill him, too. Her mother *and* mother-in-law were pushing to come and stay for a month or two to take care of Molly, which meant that Sam, traitorous bastard that he was, must have told them that Karma had taken a nose dive into her own navel and was refusing to climb out and take care of her domestic duties.

"I'll have a frontal lobotomy before I'll let either of our mothers move in here," said Karma.

"It's not about you and what you want," said the traitorous bastard. "It's about making sure Molly is being taken care of while I'm at work and you're sitting around here feeling sorry for yourself." Sam had become so pious and sanctimonious again that Karma wanted to whack him with something. He was also being totally, utterly, and completely unfair.

Karma was *trying* to pull herself out of the death spiral she was in, but it wasn't easy. Her friends had gotten tired of having their phone messages ignored, so they'd stopped calling. *Quitters.* More than anything in the world, Karma wanted to call Kim and commiserate with her about the current state of affairs, and how her husband had turned into a self-righteous asshole. But she couldn't do it. Kim had chosen a new outfit and fifteen minutes of fame over their friendship, and Karma wasn't even close to being ready to consider thinking about forgiving her yet. Not even close.

How had it come to this, she wondered? Did it start at the Tupperware party? When we blew up the lawnmower? No, it was that damned red car. Why do parents let their idiot teenagers drive anyway?

The sound of the key in her front door barely made her turn her head; burglars and serial killers don't use keys. And if this one did, more power to him. But when she looked up, Karma was startled to see not just Sam, but Jeff and Jeanette, Bianca and Tony, Sue Ellen and Don, and, bringing up the rear, Kim's husband, Dave. Without Kim. They weren't carrying torches and pitchforks, but it didn't look like a social call, either.

The solemn parade filed into her kitchen, and Karma folded her arms across her chest, trying to look defiant, but mostly wishing she'd put on a bra that morning.

"You look like hammered dog shit," said Bianca.

"It's good to see you, too," said Karma. "So what is this, the neighborhood block party I've heard so much about? An intervention? Are the men in the white coats waiting for me outside?"

"We have to talk," said Sam. "Tom called again yesterday. I didn't tell you because I wanted to talk to the guys first." He nodded toward the other men in the room.

Karma's heart began to pound. Tom was their lawyer. "So what did he say? What's going on?"

"The prosecutor's office called him. They're offering a deal and we all need to talk about it."

"We *all* need to talk about it? Isn't this up to me? Or maybe me and Jeanette?"

"I freakin' wish," said Bianca, "but they've been doing their homework. They're threatening to charge all of us with vandalism, destruction of property, misuse of explosives within the city limits, criminal confinement of those piece-of-shit teenagers, four counts of making terrorist threats against a minor, and—oh crap, I can't even remember the rest."

"Aiding and abetting, lying to an officer of the court, and obstruction of justice," continued Sue Ellen. She was practically spitting with anger. "I could get two years in jail and I didn't even do anything."

"You were at the scene of the first crime," growled her husband, "which was the vandalism of the car, which you didn't report to the police."

Karma dropped her face into her hands. *This is so unfair. Everybody is turning on me just to keep themselves out of prison.* Fortunately, there was just enough sanity left in her serotonin-deprived brain to register what a stupid idea it would be to say *that out loud.* "So what am I—what are *we*—supposed to do about this?" She looked at Jeanette, who was showing all the spunk of a wilted bag of lettuce.

"They're offering a deal, and you are going to take it and end this thing," said Sam.

Jeff nodded. "And you, *all of you*, are going to apologize to us for acting like we're a bunch of idiots who couldn't figure out

336

what you were up to," he said. "Like my bike tire going flat right after you show up at my house?"

"And jogging for the first time since college," said Sam.

"And claiming to be at the fifteenth home party in one month on the night that Jack's shed blows up," said Dave.

"It wasn't the *fifteenth* home party," mumbled Jeanette.

"Close enough," said Dave. "And, Karma, did you and my wife really think I'd never find out about the email you sent to Jack? You deleted it off my computer, but the police found it on Jack's."

Karma closed her eyes. *Shit.* She hadn't thought of that. Neither had Kim. *Where is Kim, anyway? Why isn't Mrs. Criminal Mastermind here to tell me and Jeanette how we ought to accept a couple of years in the slammer to spare her the embarrassment of a trial? She can't even face me. This whole thing is at least half her fault, and she doesn't even have the guts to be here and give me a bunch of crap about how I'll be out of jail before I know it.* "So what are they offering? Is it years or months?"

"Oh my God," moaned Jeanette, falling into a kitchen chair. "Years or months. We're going to prison for years or months."

Sam and Jeff exchanged disgusted looks. "Listen to the whole thing before you decide," said Sam. "It's a better deal than you deserve. It's certainly a better deal than Jack Lawrence got. Luann and their kids, too."

CHAPTER 37:   DOMESTIC SERVITUDE

It was butt crack early. The sun was just peeking over the pole barns, there was frost on the ground and an icy chill in the air. Karma followed Jeanette up the creaky metal steps into the rusty blue school bus, and took the hard, cold seat next to her. They always sat directly behind the driver. Sitting in the front of the bus was a last feeble finger-hold on their former status as a *nice women*, but it had the added advantage of seating them farther away from Tonette (larceny and check fraud), Lucinda (repeat DUI and possession of narcotics), and Candi (prostitution). It was Candi who had griped that first morning, "Fuck, it's butt crack early."

It summed up the situation so succinctly and elegantly that Karma had smiled at Candi, but all she received for her friendliness was a lascivious lingering gaze, a pantomimed tongue kiss and an invitation to meet Candi behind the bus when the guards weren't looking. So Karma stayed in the front of the bus, as near the driver as possible, and kept Jeanette close by at all times. Each morning, the two huddled together and tried to be invisible, which wasn't easy in a bus with only six women on it.

The homeless shelter was the largest in Indianapolis, the busiest, and the oldest. It wasn't air conditioned, and the windows that weren't broken and boarded up had been painted shut at least a century ago. It was also a model of efficacy. The facility served three meals per day to hundreds of people, had room for dozens to sleep safely indoors, and offered job training programs and drug counseling. Karma would have felt noble to call herself a volunteer, but you couldn't feel noble about having been *volunteered* by the Hamilton County Adult Probation Department.

Then there was the embarrassment of being recognized by *way* too many homeless people. How did all these homeless people watched so damn much TV? Everybody wanted to take selfies with the Soccer Moms, which slowed the serving line to a crawl and pissed off the paid staff. So Karma and Jeanette were reassigned to the back, where they washed dirty dishes and scraped crusty pots and pans. The temperature and humidity in the back approximated that of the Amazon rainforest during monsoon season. And although the meals served to the homeless looked reasonably appetizing, the soiled dishes and utensils they had to clean were positively disgusting. The detergent smelled like lemon-scented battery acid, and the water was scalding hot. When Karma asked where the rubber gloves were kept, the director of food service laughed out loud.

The next day Karma brought in her own gloves, but Tonette wiggled her long, sharp, sparkly gel nails in Karma's face and suggested that she needed the gloves more than Karma did. Karma, grateful not to be knifed, handed them over. The pair she brought in the following day were likewise demanded by Candi, though to be fair, Candi did offer sexual favors as compensation. Karma politely declined, but handed over the gloves. After that, Karma left her gloves at home. "We're destroying our hands, and Bianca and Sue Ellen get to play with kitties and puppies at the Humane Society," Karma grumbled to Jeanette. "This sucks."

To be fair, Bianca and Sue Ellen were scooping poop and scrubbing animal cages, but Jeanette didn't want to argue with Karma. She didn't mind her indentured servitude as much as Karma did. Sure they had to scrub toilets and dirty dishes, make beds, and wash endless piles of laundry, but it was peaceful and satisfying compared to being home with her children.

"Hey, Killer," came a gruff voice from the doorway. "You got a visitor in the lobby."

Karma looked at Jeanette. "She's means you," said Jeanette. "She calls me *dumbass*."

Waiting in the lobby was Luann Lawrence, dressed in clingy raw silk pants and a low-cut blouse with tiny mother-of-pearl buttons. She said she'd heard that Karma was *working* nearby and thought she'd stop in to say hello, since she was in the area. She had come downtown to have lunch with the anchor of the *Channel 6 Evening News*.

"He's been a real comfort to me," said Luann. "I'm sure you can understand."

"I saw him interview you on TV," said Karma. "It was interesting." *The most interesting part was when you lied through your teeth and kept us out of jail. Did you come here so I could thank you in person? Maybe I should.*

"It gave me a chance to clarify things," said Luann. She slid her big leather purse off her shoulder and reached inside. Karma sucked in her breath, half-expected to see a gun. Instead, Luann held out a box wrapped in brown paper. "Don't open it here," she said with her unreadable half-smile. "It's something I found that I thought you might appreciate. Say hello to Jeanette."

She turned and walked away.

Karma went back to the dish room and recounted the strange conversation to Jeanette.

"Do you suppose he's as tall and good-looking in person as he is on TV?" said Jeanette. "I bet he is. It's so wonderful that Luann has met somebody nice, don't you think?"

"It's a fairy tale," said Karma. It amazed her how Jeanette, Queen of Silver Linings, always seemed to miss the point.

"Did she tell you about her new car?" asked Jeanette. "It's beautiful. It's a convertible and she said it's got all the extras. It was super expensive, and I bet she looks cute in it."

I bet she and the anchorman look cute in it together, thought Karma, t*he Merry Widow Lawrence and her baritone boyfriend.*

And with that snarky thought came another rush of clarity, like the one that she'd experienced after her miscarriage. It made Karma almost dizzy. Something about the Luann and Jack Lawrence situation had been nagging at her, and it suddenly made perfect sense.

Of course Luann gave that interview. She wasn't trying to help me and Jeanette, she was making sure Jack's death would be ruled an accident. Double-indemnity. She got twice the value of his life insurance because he died by accident. Death at the hands of another person is never considered an accident, even if the person who committed it wasn't a beneficiary. She had to get us out of trouble so she could collect all that money. She wasn't trying to save Jeanette or me; she was guaranteeing herself a comfortable widowhood.

"Aren't you gonna unwrap your present?" asked Jeanette, nodding toward the box sitting on the stainless steel counter.

"I'm not sure it's a present," said Karma. "She just said she thought I'd appreciate it."

They looked at the brown paper-wrapped box and at each other, then around the room to make sure nobody else was paying attention. Karma picked up the box and tore off the paper.

Luann was right. Inside the box was something Karma was definitely interested in.

The baby monitor transmitter.

341

CHAPTER 38:   AND SO IT GOES

Karma had no choice. This had to be done. Her life in Bedford Commons had become unbearable, and she was the only one who could do anything about it, now that Sam had rejected her suggestion that they sell their house, change their names, and move to Costa Rica. He wasn't sure about their public schools.

So Karma raised her arm for the third time, but this time, she did what she had come to do. She rang the doorbell. It took all her strength to fight the impulse to ding-dong-ditch before the bell was answered. Thanks to all the running she'd done to escape reporters, Karma was in pretty good shape, and she would have made it to the bushes in plenty of time.

But she made herself stay on the porch. There was no way in hell she'd ring a second time, and if nobody answered she might never come back, but for now, she stayed.

When the door finally opened, Karma's best hope and worst fear were realized simultaneously. Kim stood in the doorway, frozen for a long moment.

"Hi," she finally said.

"Hi," said Karma.

A thousand things had changed between Kim and Karma in the past few months, but not *everything*. They ended up where they always ended up, sitting at a kitchen table drinking coffee. It started with unbearable silence as Kim brought out the coffee, flavored creamer, two mugs, and two spoons. She set them on a hot pad in the center of the table. Karma watched her work in the most inefficient way possible, one item at a time, multiple trips to and from the refrigerator and cabinets, probably because she had no idea what else to do and couldn't think of anything to say. It didn't bother Karma because she was equally unsure of how to begin. Finally, all the necessary paraphernalia was on the table, and Kim had no choice but to sit down and face Karma, who filled her cup with coffee and doctored it with creamer.

"I heard about the baby," said Kim. "I'm really sorry."

Karma nodded. "Thanks."

"Do you think you'll try again?"

"Probably. Eventually. Or maybe adopt."

Kim nodded and prepared her own coffee. Karma noted that she was using artificial sweetener instead of the real thing. "So you're doing outpatient rehab?" There was no point pretending she didn't know. Everybody knew. If they were going to be friends again, they had to be able to talk about it.

Kim made a face. "I've gained three pounds."

"So have I," said Karma. "Well, more like six."

"I'm sorry about your sister, too."

"Thanks."

"Do you think there are any secrets left in the whole damn neighborhood?" asked Kim.

Karma shook her head. "No juicy ones."

Kim took a sip of coffee. "I heard about Bianca's story about the family business. I don't buy it. Dry cleaning, my ass."

Karma set down her cup and looked at Kim. "Is it possible that Luann Lawrence tricked us into killing her husband?"

Kim was obviously surprised by the question. "You didn't kill him, you just, you were just, he…" She stopped, and stared off into the middle distance. Then she spoke again. "She couldn't have known he would end up dead. It's just not possible."

"No," said Karma. "Maybe not dead, but maybe she hoped if we keep badgering him, he would attack one of us. He'd go to jail for a while, she'd have a good reason to leave him, and maybe she'd get a good divorce settlement?"

Kim nodded thoughtfully, considering the idea. "But he died. She got lucky."

"Yeah, instead of just getting arrested for battery, he falls off his bike and dies. Her problem is solved *and* she gets a ton of insurance money."

"Double insurance money, according to Gina Damico's stylist." said Kim. "So much better than she'd have done in a divorce. She won the lottery."

They sat quietly, drinking coffee. The only sound was the ticking Green Bay Packer clock and the laughter of the girls outside. Karma wondered if she was being ridiculous. Nobody, not even Luann Lawrence, could have engineered Jack's death on the bike trail, or even predicted it. On the other hand, Luann and her marital troubles had somehow gotten under their skins. How had that happened? It had a lot to do with Luann showing up on Jeanette's patio with bruises. Was this why she'd come to Jeanette? Had she subtly nudged Karma and the rest to get involved, to provoke Jack? Was it just a happy accident when he died? Not happy for Jack, but very happy for his widow.

Karma stared into her nearly-empty cup. It was pretty far-fetched. *Maybe I'm so desperate to absolve myself of guilt, that I'm imaging all of this so I can put the blame on Luann.* Was it better to be the stupid puppet of a conniving wife, or a thoughtless idiot who caused a man to fracture his skull and die? Karma wasn't sure.

"So what's it like at the homeless shelter?" asked Kim, wrinkling her nose. "I have to start putting in my hours as soon as I'm released from rehab."

"It's like housework on steroids," said Karma. "But nobody thanks you for working your ass off, so you feel right at home."

"Have you met any nice felons?"

Karma brought over the coffee pot and refilled their cups. "They're a fabulous bunch of girls," she said. "Just misunderstood. We're starting a book club when everybody gets off probation. Make sure you introduce yourself to Candi and Tonette, if they're still around," said Karma. "Candi is super friendly. And don't forget to bring rubber gloves. Maybe an extra pair or two."

THE END

40622036R00210

Made in the USA
Middletown, DE
17 February 2017